DRAGON TAMER

Elizabeth James

Thrall of Darkness

Dragon Tamer was published serially on thrallofdarkness.com between 2019-2020.

ISBN-13: 978-1-944969-18-9

Cover design by: Elizabeth James
Printed in the United States of America

CONTENTS

CHAPTER ONE

Tribal War

Luke shifted uncomfortably in the café seat and glanced again at the pet store across the street. No one had approached it. Yet. It seemed Daniel and the others were keeping the rival tribe far away from the nesting grounds. He knew he shouldn't be here but the dragonlings had only been born days ago and he couldn't bear to be too far away. Their mother was dying. All mother dragons were dying. No one knew why. And without a dragon tamer, any dragons that were born were doomed to die. He would not let these die, not when it was the mother's last litter.

She was taking care of their physical needs and would for a while longer, but he was supporting them psychically and they needed that connection as well. He could go up to two miles away, he knew, but he didn't like being further than he needed.

He got out his cell phone and traced his finger along the case. A waitress appeared at his side.

"Can I get you anything else, sweetie?"

"Another chai, please," he said.

He wasn't really taking up a table since the café hadn't been full the entire time he'd been here, but he had been here most of the day now and she was probably getting tired of him. But she just smiled. He'd been trying to order something every hour to make her life easier. When she left, he turned on his cell phone again. He wasn't supposed to contact Daniel. Ever. Daniel would always make the first contact. But it had been hours, nearly the whole day. He hadn't heard a word. He had been wanting to contact Daniel for quite some time now.

He turned his phone off and pushed it just out of reach, then looked across the street again. Again, nothing. He knew that in some ways he was the least valuable member of the tribe, since he had such a limited role. It was a vital role, and the role that kept the tribe going, but he couldn't help with anything besides raising and controlling the dragonlings. And the dragonlings were a secret that no one in the outside world could ever know. So for the most part, it was the other tribe members who were active while he stayed at the nesting grounds. They protected the territory, they fought other tribes, they negotiated deals, they did all the things that kept the tribe functioning. He was just a glorified babysitter.

He didn't know much about the society he lived in outside of the dragonlings. Daniel had once told him about a Dragon Master who had been the first to tame dragons and it was because of him that Luke had the ability to mentally connect with the dragonlings and nurture him. It was one of the few things Luke knew about the history of the tribe, though, since Daniel rarely talked about it. Whenever his dragonlings cuddled him, he was always grateful for that Dragon Master who had allowed him such a close connection to the wonderful creatures. He felt safe with them, and safe with Daniel and his tribe. Usually.

There had never been an invasion like this before. An unknown tribe had swooped into their city with unexpected fierceness. For the first time, dragon tamers like Luke were at a premium and it was rumored that several tribes had lost their dragon tamers. Daniel had warned Luke to stay hidden. Daniel had technically warned Luke to stay in one of the safe houses, but they were all at the edge of Luke's range, so Luke was here instead. Guarding the nest where he ought to be.

The waitress brought him his chai and as she set it down, his phone vibrated. He snatched it.

5 minutes.

A grin broke across his face. The waitress laughed.

"Guy you're waiting for finally showing?"

"Yes," Luke said, not even caring that she assumed he was gay, or that she really thought he would wait over six hours for a guy.

He wondered briefly how Daniel had found him and if Daniel would be mad. Probably. But he didn't care. He was mad, too, for not getting a single status update the entire day. Daniel never sent him long texts; in fact, he insisted on brevity in case anyone ever got hold of their phones. But he could have said something.

He drank his chai, paid his bill, and sat down again to wait with his phone on the table under his palm in case Daniel got delayed. He kept watching the pet store to see when everyone returned. He knew he wasn't allowed to return until Daniel gave him permission even though he had the keys and now that he knew Daniel was safe, there was no reason not to go back.

Several men came into the café and talked to his waitress, and then to his surprise, one of them came and sat across from him. He was extremely handsome, with thick ebony hair and eyes so dark they were nearly black. But he was also very unwelcome. Daniel had taught Luke how to deal with men like him.

"Back off," Luke warned. "I'm waiting for someone."

His phone vibrated and he flipped it to see the screen.

Me.

Luke was puzzled, then noticed a phone in the man's hand. Daniel's phone. His eyes went wide and he gasped, about to leap up when a heavy hand landed on his shoulder and kept him in place. He stared at the two men surrounding him, looking to the casual observer like they were having a chat but clearly preventing him from leaving or even getting up. Luke swallowed and licked his lips before looking at the man across from him again.

"Where is Daniel? Is he hurt?"

"He'll be occupied for some time, but isn't injured. I just took this when he wasn't paying attention," the man said, tapping the phone with his finger. "He's a fool to leave you here, but then again, you're not supposed to be here, are you?"

Luke blushed. He regretted more than ever not listening to Daniel.

His phone buzzed and he glanced down to see an emergency message from another tribe member when the man holding him snatched his phone and gave it to the man across from him. The man smiled.

"Looks like Daniel just figured out his phone is gone and wants to warn you. Will you unlock your phone for me?"

Luke crossed his arms and glared. The man laughed.

"Well, I don't need your help. Let's see what he has to say."

* * *

Eric watched the boy as he took the phone. It was a cute phone, just as he was a cute boy, and Eric never would have believed it. His tribe's dragon tamer had been an old woman, part of the tribe since before Eric's birth. He never would have believed that such a powerful tamer could be so young, or so incredibly attractive.

The boy – Luke, he knew – had dusty blond hair that brushed past his ears and halfway down his neck in an enticingly casual style. Thick bangs brushed against his forehead. He had pale skin with just a hint of a tan and probably spent most of his time indoors. A sprinkling of freckles covered his nose and cheeks. His lips were full and naturally formed a heart and Eric felt an instinctive compulsion to kiss them. His eyes were sparkling green with flecks of brown, wide and innocent. He was young, and Eric could tell he was also very sheltered.

Eric turned his attention to the phone. He knew his tribe would be keeping Daniel and his tribe busy for several hours.

He didn't plan on killing any of them, but he would, if that's what it took.

Where

That was the first message from Daniel. Eric had been amused at how short the communications between Daniel and Luke were, especially compared to the messages between Daniel and the rest of the tribe. He hadn't been able to figure out why, but now he suspected it was because Daniel didn't want Luke to realize he was attracted to him.

Respond

That was the second message. Clearly Daniel was used to obedience. Eric decided to jump in.

I have him.

There was a long pause.

What do you want?

Eric smiled. He could practically hear the desperation through the letters. Daniel knew how rare a commodity Luke was even if Luke seemed oblivious. Eric looked at Luke, who was watching him with a similar desperation. Luke had no idea how precious he was, as a tamer and as a person. Maybe he'd toy with Daniel a little.

He's quite beautiful.

Don't lay a hand on him, Daniel replied immediately.

My hands should be the least of your concerns.

There was another pause and he knew Daniel was trying to figure out an answer that wouldn't insult Eric to the point where it might put Luke's life in danger.

"Stop it," Luke said suddenly.

Eric looked up in surprise. "Stop what?"

"You're threatening him. Stop it."

Eric reached out and stroked Luke's cheek. Luke looked surprised but didn't pull away from the gesture.

"I'm not threatening him. I'm threatening you. There's a difference."

"You can't threaten me. You need me. You don't have a dragon tamer and if you don't have my cooperation, your dragons will die."

Eric reappraised him. More than just a pretty face, then.

"I do need you. And I would like your cooperation; it would make things easier. But if you see a dragon in pain, I have a feeling you're going to help even if you want to kill me."

Luke looked like he was going to protest but he didn't. He just blushed again, that delightful pinking of his cheeks, and looked down. Eric returned his attention to his phone. Luke's phone, where Daniel had left a surprisingly calm response.

Don't hurt him. What do you want?

I'll be in contact, Eric wrote.

He handed Daniel and Luke's phones to Sam, his guard. "Destroy these."

"What?" Luke nearly leapt up again. "You can't destroy that, it's mine!"

"And Daniel can track you through it. I'll get you a new one."

"I'm not going with you," Luke warned.

"You can't stop me, even if I have to take you by force."

Luke gripped the edge of the table and leaned forward. Fire danced in his eyes and Eric recognized the bond of a tamer speaking. Luke was using dragongaze on him, but not at full strength and Eric knew how to get around it if he were careful.

"I will not leave."

"I assume they're across the street," Eric said, knowing from the waitress that Luke had been watching across the street the entire time he'd been here.

"Yes," Luke said, still in that fiery voice that Eric knew meant business.

"How far is your range?"

"Two miles."

Eric was impressed. He'd never heard of anyone with a range that far. Most people could go half a mile at most. He had assumed that was why Luke was across the street.

"Do you have a key?"

"I'm not letting you in."

"We're taking you more than two miles away. You're

bringing them."

Pain flashed across Luke's face and the intensity of his dragongaze lessened. "Their mother is still feeding them. It's her last litter and she deserves to keep them."

"They'll survive just as well with you feeding them. You know that. Their mother would rather have them alive and you know that too."

The fire in his eyes vanished, replaced with fear. "Why are you doing this?" he whispered.

"Because there are other dragonlings who will die without you," Eric said.

Luke's hands loosened on the table and he looked on the brink of tears. Eric nodded to Denis, his other guard, who helped Luke to his feet. Luke seemed almost in a state of shock and Eric slid his arm around Luke's waist as they left. Luke stiffened at the intimate touch but just like when Eric had stroked his cheek, he didn't protest. This time, though, it seemed he actually needed the support as they walked across the street and Luke leaned into him. Eric could feel him trembling. He knew if he let Luke go, Luke would collapse. When they got to the door, Luke's hands shook as he unlocked it.

The front was an ordinary pet store, but as they walked through, every single animal turned to watch Luke's progress. Eric hadn't realized that other animals would be sensitive to a dragon tamer's psychic touch but clearly they were. They went through three back rooms before finally reaching the nesting grounds, where a large crimson dragon curled around five very small dragonlings. They looked to be no more than three days old. No wonder Luke had stayed so close.

The mother dragon was dying, just like all the tamed female dragons. That was clear. But the young ones were healthy and strong and they chirped at Luke as he entered. When they saw Eric, though, they hissed and spread their wings. Luke pushed him away roughly and entered the nest alone. Only dragon tamers were ever allowed to enter the nest but he had never seen dragonlings react violently towards someone before. Then again, he was taking their tamer prisoner and separating them from their mother. Perhaps it wasn't unreasonable.

Sam and Denis stayed well behind him. They rarely had anything to do with dragonlings and were here to help with Luke only. Luke didn't say a word but Eric knew he was communicating with the dragonlings. The young ones cuddled with him sweetly and the mother nuzzled him as he caressed her. He had probably known her all his life. Eric glanced at his watch. They needed to hurry, but he wanted to give Luke time to say goodbye.

After only a few minutes, Luke stood. Leaving the dragonlings in the nest, he went to the shelves along the wall and began gathering things and piling them next to Eric. Food, milk, and bedding for the dragonlings. All good things to have since Eric hadn't anticipated traveling with dragonlings. Eric gestured Sam and Denis to carry the items out to the waiting jet. Then it was time for Luke and the dragonlings.

Luke looked at him with pleading eyes.

"Please," he whispered.

"I'm sorry," Eric said gently. "You'll understand in time."

Luke closed his eyes, then entered the nest and helped the dragonlings climb onto him. It was a good thing they were so small because they were going to have to walk in public a short way and if they were much larger, they would be noticeable. Luke kissed the mother dragon and then climbed out of the nest.

"I hate you," he said softly.

Eric ignored it. He expected as much. He led Luke down a few side streets until they reached a large office building with a landing pad on top. He had bribed the owner generously to give him access. Luke climbed into the plane and requested to sit with the dragonlings where the supplies had been put rather than in the cabin. Eric had suspected he would so the supplies were in a pressurized area with a bench, but not much else in the way of luxuries and Eric hoped he could lure Luke out for at least part of the trip.

"It's a twelve-hour trip, Luke," Eric said as Luke settled down and the dragonlings explored the area. "I'll bring you food and you can leave whenever you want. The door isn't locked. Bathrooms are on the left."

"I'm not leaving and you're not welcome," Luke said, but without force. He seemed exhausted and was on the brink of tears again.

Eric nodded and left, closing the door gently.

CHAPTER TWO

Pinned

Luke awoke to a sharp metallic vibration in his mind and he opened his eyes in confusion. His dragonlings were flying in circles around him exuding anger and trying to protect him from something. Someone. Eric was at the door and Luke winced and shook his head, trying to think amidst the roaring vibration.

"Stop," he managed to say.

The dragonlings instantly became sweet and landed on him and cooed. He sat up and mentally scolded them for being so loud in his mind that he couldn't think. They needed to learn to control their volume. Protecting him was good, but not to the extent that it disabled him. They nuzzled him. They were confused and missed their mother. He reassured them. He had fed them immediately before drifting off to sleep so they weren't hungry, but they were scared and it took several minutes to calm them down. The entire time, he was aware of Eric watching him.

When the dragonlings were taken care of and he had even convinced them to sleep for a bit, he stood up and took two steps towards Eric, crossing his arms and scowling.

"What do you want?"

"You didn't eat all day at the café and it's been several hours since then. You have to be starving. Come eat with me."

Luke glared. It hadn't taken him long to figure out that the waitress had been spying on him. She had seen him with

Daniel before, after all. And he was starving. He had already left the room to use the bathroom, but leaving it for more than that seemed a betrayal.

"You can bring me food here if you don't want me to starve," he said, hoping Eric didn't want him to starve.

"I want to eat with you," Eric said. "And they won't let me in."

Luke stared at him. He couldn't figure out why Eric wanted to eat with him. Eric already had his cooperation, after all. That was all Eric needed from him. But Eric kept looking at him the way Daniel occasionally looked at him, and he couldn't figure it out. He remembered Eric stroking his cheek, and then saying that he was threatening Luke. It didn't make sense.

"Please," Eric said, reaching his hand out to bridge the space between them.

Luke's gaze went from his outstretched hand to his eyes, and he felt flustered. He wanted to remember that this man was not only kidnapping him but his dragonlings as well, but Eric seemed so sincere. And he was so handsome. Luke took a hesitant step forward and accepted his hand. Eric squeezed it and led him out, making sure to close the door behind them quietly so as not to disturb the sleeping dragonlings.

Eric's henchmen were nowhere to be seen as Eric helped him sit in a small booth at a table already set with food before sitting across from him. The food was Asian and Luke wasn't exactly sure what all of it was but it looked delicious.

"Have you had this before?"

"No," Luke said.

Eric showed him how to eat it without the slightest hint of condescension, and seemed genuinely happy when Luke got the hang of it. It was delicious and when Luke had finished, Eric was only partially done. Luke looked longingly at his food. Eric stopped, took Luke's plate and left. He returned with another plate for Luke. He had truly been starving, Luke realized. When he was finally finished, he realized Eric was watching him.

"There are going to be several new customs you'll have to learn, but you'll get used to them," Eric said. "And people won't judge you."

"You realize Daniel's going to come after me, don't you?"

"I would expect nothing less. But he's not going to get you."

Luke glanced down. "You didn't hurt him, right? Or anyone else?"

"No. We just needed them out of the way."

Luke felt heat rising in his cheeks. They had needed the others out of the way to grab him, and he had made himself completely vulnerable by being out in the open instead of in one of the safe houses. If he had just listened to Daniel, he wouldn't be here now. He would be safe with Daniel. The dragonlings would be with their mother instead of clinging to the metal airplane hull.

"Why do you need me? What happened to your dragon tamer?"

"How did you become a tamer?"

Luke was startled for a moment. "What does that have to do with anything?"

"Depending on how much you know about tamers, I don't have to explain as much. And there's potentially a lot to explain, so it's easier if you go first."

Luke was puzzled, but didn't mind. "I'd always heard dragons, but never known what they were. I was an outsider. When I was twelve, I first heard one clearly. It was when the sickness first fell. She was the first to die. She called me to her so I could raise her last litter. I ran away from home to find her and luckily her tribe took me in until her dragonlings were raised. After the dragonlings left, Daniel's tribe took me."

"So you've been kidnapped before?"

"No, it was a dragon swap," Luke said sharply, insulted that Eric would think Daniel and his tribe capable of kidnapping. "It was her last litter, as I said, and at the time Daniel had two dragons. Their tamer didn't have the range to care for both so I went to them and she went to another tribe."

"How old were you then?"

"Fifteen."

"How old are you now?"

Luke hesitated. There was something predatory in the way Eric asked that he didn't like.

"Nineteen."

"How many litters have you raised for Daniel?"

"This is my third."

"Have you lost any?"

"Of course not," Luke said, appalled. He knew he would be devastated if he lost a dragonling. In truth it had never occurred to him that he might lose one, since they were always so content in his care. But he supposed accidents and disease did happen.

Eric tapped his fingers against his lips.

"If you were fifteen when you joined Daniel, it would have been up to him to teach you about tamers. You would have been too young before and since you weren't raised in our society, you wouldn't have soaked up any knowledge that way. But you're still young. How much has he taught you?"

"He's the leader of the tribe," Luke said slowly, wondering if this was a trap of some sort. "He doesn't know about dragon taming."

Eric's eyes narrowed and he looked furious. "He kept you in the dark, then."

"The dragons teach me what I need to know," Luke said angrily. He didn't know why Eric was so mad but he knew it was because of some perceived imperfection on Daniel's part and Luke wasn't about to allow that. "That's how it's supposed to work. The dragons would have told me if it were otherwise."

"If all you're supposed to do is sit around and hatch dragonlings, yes, the dragons can tell you what to do just fine," Eric said. "But that's not what a dragon tamer does."

Luke knew his confusion was showing. "What else would a dragon tamer do?"

Eric closed his eyes and took a deep breath and when he

released it, he opened his eyes and seemed calm again.

"I apologize, Luke. You are not to blame for what you do and do not know. I can't tell you why we lost our dragon tamer, not yet. It would be too much to explain. I will, I promise you that. Now please, come with me."

He stood and extended his hand again. Luke took it, expecting to be taken back to his dragonlings. Instead, Eric took him to a small but lush room with a bed in it. Luke looked at Eric. A flutter of fear ran through him. Daniel had told him time and time again never to be alone with a man because men were dangerous and would take advantage of him. He already knew Eric was very dangerous. What else was Eric planning to do?

Eric pulled him forward but Luke dug his feet in and refused to enter the room. Eric sighed.

"You need rest before we get there. Real rest. You're not going to get it lying on a metal bench. As long as you're comfortable, your dragonlings won't care that you're not with them."

Luke eyed the bed. It looked comfortable and incredibly inviting. The sheets were crumpled as if someone else had been lying on them, however, which made him suspicious. It also looked big enough for two.

"If I go in," Luke said, "You aren't."

A hint of a smile played at Eric's lips. "Oh, I'm coming in with you."

Without warning, Eric grabbed his waist, picked him up, and threw him over his shoulder. Luke was too surprised to protest. Eric closed and locked the door, then threw Luke on the bed. Luke tried to leap up but Eric pinned him in place with his entire body. Luke gasped.

Eric's face was inches from his, eyes boring into him, noses practically touching. He could feel the heat from Eric's lips. Eric's hands were pressing down on his upper arms, keeping him in place. Their chests were nearly touching. One of Eric's legs crossed his right thigh to hold it down. The other leg lay between his and while it wasn't pinning him directly, it was such clearly sexual positioning that it was paralyzing in a different way.

Luke was terrified and could feel his body pulsing as it tried to figure out whether to fight or flee. Eric still had that soft smile and Luke blushed. It was oddly arousing being pinned like this. Eric was studying his reaction, he realized, and blushed further. Eric shifted his hands so they weren't pressing his arms but rather positioned on the outside of his arms. He didn't move anything else, though.

Luke wanted to tell him to get away but with Eric's lips so close to his, he couldn't. He knew he could turn his head and speak but he found he didn't want to. He trembled in confusion. His body was sending him so many mixed signals it was hard to think straight and with those beautiful dark eyes staring at him, all he could focus on was the fact that he had never been kissed and Eric's lips were so close to his.

Eric backed away from him a little and he gulped for air. But even though he could talk now, he found he had nothing to say. Eric was so beautiful framed over him, and even though he knew he was in danger, he didn't want this moment to end. Finally, Eric spoke.

"Do you want me to leave?"

"What?"

Luke stared at him in confusion. He was tired of being confused around Eric. The man was infuriating with how confusing he was. First he threw Luke into a bed and pinned him in place, now he was asking if Luke wanted him to go?

Eric patiently repeated the question and Luke bit his lip. He knew the answer he should give. The answer he had to give. It was the only answer he could give in these circumstances. Daniel would kill him otherwise.

"Daniel-"

"No," Eric said, to Luke's surprise. "I don't care what he thinks. Do *you* want me to leave, Luke?"

Those dark eyes were staring into his again and Luke

shivered. He knew his answer but he was afraid to give it. Ever since he was twelve he had been under someone's control. He hadn't been allowed to make decisions for himself. Aaron, his first leader, had been cautious with him, and Daniel had been strict. He knew both had been watching out for him. But neither had ever really taken into account what he wanted. It was frightening to have that kind of control.

"Should I leave, Luke?" Eric asked again, gently.

"No," Luke whispered.

Eric shifted his weight so that one of his hands was free to stroke Luke's face. He stroked Luke's cheek and brushed back some of his hair before cradling his jaw. Luke leaned into the caress. Sometimes Daniel touched him like this, but it was rare and Luke craved it. Whenever he did, Luke would dream about the touch for days afterward.

"Tell me what you want, Luke," Eric said softly, those dark eyes still gazing into his.

Luke blushed. Again, he instantly knew the answer but this time he knew it was completely inappropriate. He didn't need Daniel to tell him; it would be obvious to anyone. Eric grinned.

"Something naughty, I see. I won't judge you. Tell me."

Luke turned his head to the side but glanced back to see if Eric was still watching him. He was. Luke let his eyes lower to Eric's lips and linger there. He ached to feel them. He blushed again and shut his eyes. He knew from Eric's confident positioning that Eric was sexually experienced and might laugh at his request, or refuse it. He felt so insecure and inexperienced.

The hand on his jaw drew his head back until he was facing Eric again and he hesitantly opened his eyes. The grin had vanished from Eric's face.

"It's all right, Luke. Tell me."

He wanted it so badly. He gathered all of his courage. After all, the worst that could happen was that Eric would laugh and say no.

"I want my first kiss to be with you," he said, trying to sound confident but barely managing more than a whisper.

Surprise flickered across Eric's face, then the man became tender. He stroked his thumb across Luke's cheekbone and Luke was taken aback by how gentle he seemed.

"I would be honored," Eric said in a serious voice.

Luke let out a breath. He hadn't laughed, and he hadn't refused. Now Luke was nervous, because he felt totally unprepared and he had no idea what was about to happen. Would Eric just kiss him? Would Eric warn him? What would the kiss feel like? He had read about kisses in books and seen them in movies, but he had never seen real people kiss. He knew Daniel would have liked to shield him from the books and movies if he could, but while Daniel could outlaw straight out romances, he didn't prevent Luke from other genres and nearly every book and movie had some sort of romance in it. He suspected if Daniel knew that he would have banned books and movies completely, but luckily Daniel was too busy with the tribe to bother himself with popular culture. He did put heavy restrictions on Luke's internet use, though, and on his cell phone.

"Don't worry, Luke," Eric said. "I won't kiss you until you invite me."

"I don't know how," Luke said, scared. He wasn't talking about the invitation and Eric clearly knew it.

"It's okay," Eric said gently. "I'll guide you. Hold me."

Luke realized he could move his arms. He reached up and cautiously set his hands on Eric's shoulders. The fabric was silky and he could feel strong muscles underneath. He took a deep breath. He wanted it. He did. He was just so scared. But as he looked at Eric, at those eyes that were so unexpectedly warm, he realized he wasn't as scared as he thought he'd be. Those eyes wouldn't hurt him.

He slid his hands behind Eric's neck and shut his eyes, raising his lips towards those beautiful lips he wanted so badly. The hand on his jaw glided behind his head and supported him upward until he could feel the heat of those lips, then they locked onto his. Eric's lips were silky and smooth and caressed him deliciously for several long moments as he clung to the man. Then he felt something else caressing him and realized with a start that it was Eric's tongue. His tongue traced the outlines of Luke's lips and he relaxed against Eric, luxuriating in the pleasure, and then Eric's tongue dove between his lips. Luke opened his mouth without thinking and Eric's grip on his neck grew tighter as Eric began really kissing him.

At first Eric did all the work as Luke clung to him and nearly drowned in the sensations, but Luke didn't want to be the helpless victim in this kiss. He wanted to kiss back. As Eric touched places that made him moan, he attempted to do the same to Eric. At first he failed, he knew, but it seemed like Eric was guiding him, teaching him, and soon he could feel Eric pressing against his body, hand tightly clutching his hair as Eric moaned as well.

He felt empowered by the kiss, and extremely turned on. He was aroused and he knew that with Eric's leg between his legs, Eric knew exactly how aroused he was. Eric must have been monitoring that because just before Luke worried he would have to pull away or risk it being a problem, the kissing slowed in intensity. Finally, Eric broke away, pecked him on the lips, and Luke felt him lean back.

Luke opened his eyes. His lips felt swollen in the most pleasant way imaginable and his heart was pounding. Eric wore a gentle smile and there were crinkles at the corners of his eyes that Luke hadn't noticed before. He was young, though, probably only a few years older than Luke. He must smile a lot. Luke couldn't help but smile back, though he blushed when he did it.

"That's the first time I've seen you smile," Eric said. "Now I do want you to get rest. Sleep as long as you want. No one will disturb you and you can return to your dragonlings when you're ready."

Luke nodded, exhaustion already creeping over him. He knew the dragonlings were all right. They were awake and extremely curious about what he had just been doing, but they were fine. They would settle into sleep again as soon as he did. Eric kissed him gently on the lips one more time before standing. He lingered in the doorway for a moment and seemed about to say something, but then left and shut the door without a word. Luke closed his eyes and clutched the pillow to his lips, trying to relive every moment of his first kiss.

CHAPTER THREE

Introductions

Eric leaned against the closed door and shut his eyes. That was the most spectacular kiss of his life. Luke had been frightened at first, even during the kiss, but then seemed to get over his fear and simply melted into Eric. And then, to Eric's complete surprise, Luke had met Eric's passion with his own and returned the kiss with a fire that more than made up for his lack of experience. The kiss had been intended for Luke, but it was Eric feeling like he had never been kissed so thoroughly in all his life. In a slight daze, he went to the room with the dragonlings and peeked through the small window. They were awake and chirping. Good. That meant Luke wasn't distressed at all. Even though Luke had asked for the kiss and enjoyed it, Eric knew that Luke would still be feeling very vulnerable.

Eric headed to the cockpit where Sam and Denis were with the pilot. The pilot was focused, but the other two men turned to him when he entered and he gestured them to follow him into the eating area so they could talk in private. Luke would have to walk through when he woke, but that wouldn't be for a while and they would see him coming.

To Eric's surprise, Sam looked disapproving.

"Don't tell me you've already bedded the tamer," Sam said.

"Why would you say that?" Eric asked, a little offended.

"You're glowing," Sam said, gesturing to him. "He's gorgeous and clearly a virgin, and you just took him to your room and stayed in there quite a bit longer than necessary."

"No, I did not bed him," Eric snapped. He was quite offended now and didn't bother to hide it. "And even if I did, what concern is it of yours?"

"He might not survive. I don't want you to get attached to him and then lose him."

There was a silence. Eric looked down, not wanting to acknowledge the truth of those words. He already was attached to Luke, but while he would be upset if Luke died, he wouldn't be heart-broken. Not yet. Would he? He hated the fact that they were bringing Luke somewhere where his life would be in danger, but they didn't have any choice. The dragons had commanded it.

"I think he'll survive," Eric said slowly. "He's been directly summoned by a dragon before. And he's been the cause of a dragon swap. The Western dragons seem to know his abilities pretty well."

"The Eastern dragons don't know him at all. And besides, they're not summoning him because they think he can do it, they're summoning him because he's their last resort," Denis pointed out.

Eric sighed. He hated thinking about it.

"I have to report to the elders. If you'll excuse me," he said. Sam and Denis left and he got out his laptop and soon was looking at the faces of the three eldest dragon tamers. Not the strongest, since those were dead, but the eldest. He had already informed them of Luke's successful capture and they had been pleased that Luke had chosen to remain close to his dragonlings rather than obey his leader and go in a safehouse, even if Eric thought it showed questionable common sense. He had been able to fill them in on very little else at that point, but now that he and Luke had talked, he would be able to give them what they needed to know to prepare the site.

The primary elder began.

"Does he know where he's coming yet? Why he's been summoned?"

"I couldn't tell him," Eric said.

"You haven't spoken with him?"

"He doesn't know enough."

The elders looked at each other in confusion. Eric swallowed some of his anger at Daniel for deliberately keeping knowledge of how the dragons worked from Luke.

"I want his leader Daniel killed," Eric said in a low voice. "He's had Luke for four years and hasn't told Luke anything about dragon tamers."

"There are plenty of other sources-"

"None available to him. He's an outsider. He joined our society when he was twelve. His first leader probably thought he was too young or too new for the truth and he joined Daniel's tribe when he was fifteen. It was Daniel's responsibility to teach him and he didn't."

"And how much have you taught him?" the second elder asked him with a note of amusement in his voice.

"I don't even know where to begin," he admitted, knowing it was hypocritical to demand death for Daniel for not teaching Luke and then confessing that he also wasn't teaching him. "I was hoping you could guide me."

"Don't tell him anything until he arrives," the primary elder instructed. "We'll teach him what he needs."

"Thank you," Eric said, bowing his head.

"What are his details?"

"He's a very powerful natural tamer who's heard dragons his entire life. He's served three dragons, one of whom directly summoned him and the other two arranged for him through a dragon swap. He's currently raising his fourth litter, five dragonlings that he is bringing with him. He's never lost any and looked shocked that I would even ask. His range is two miles but I don't think he likes going that far. He's completely isolated from our culture, probably at first because he was an outsider but once he joined Daniel's tribe, I have no idea. He's never met any other tamers and I don't know how he'll react. He's pretty possessive of his dragonlings."

"That's common for tamers who haven't met others of our

kind. He's never met anyone who isn't a threat to them. Do you think he stands a chance?"

The elders looked at him calmly, but he knew how desperately they were waiting for his answer. Eric was young, but he had a gift that the dragon tamers had quickly discovered and had unfortunately been forced to rely on more than Eric liked. He could sense a dragon tamer's power and while he couldn't tell if Luke was strong enough, he did know that Luke was stronger than any of the others he had felt. The Western dragons seemed confident in Luke; he had the same confidence. But he didn't want to give false assurances.

"He's very strong," he said simply.

They nodded and seemed to relax. They knew what that answer implied.

"We'll get everything ready," the primary elder said.

The communication ended and he called Sam and Denis back in.

"So he's an outsider?" Denis asked.

Eric glared. "Were you listening the whole time?"

"We like to stay informed," Sam said.

"You could have stayed in the room then," Eric said. "Just moved out of sight."

He wasn't surprised they had listened, and there wasn't anything wrong with them listening. It wasn't secret information. He wouldn't have minded them staying in the room, either, except that the elders preferred to be in private when they spoke to him. Perhaps that was why they had left.

"I'm glad you had a chance to talk to him," Sam said. "But I'm sure you got all the talking out of the way when you were eating. What were you doing in the bedroom for so long and why were you so happy when you left?"

Eric smiled, thinking of Luke melting under his body and beneath his tongue before rising up and kissing back ferociously.

"You're glowing again," Sam said.

"I kissed him," Eric said, hoping it would end the

discussion.

"You don't look that way after a kiss," Sam pointed out.

"He kissed me back," Eric said with a satisfied smile.

Sam and Denis exchanged a look.

"Still," Sam said.

Eric remembered the beautiful, blushing smile Luke had given him after the kiss. Luke was more gorgeous than he had imagined possible when he smiled. Either Daniel had never seen Luke smile or Daniel had more self-control than ten men combined to be able to resist such a smile. Eric had barely been able to leave the room. He had nearly asked Luke if he could stay.

Sam and Denis were still waiting for a response, he realized.

"It was his first kiss," he said, and stood up.

At least Sam and Denis looked satisfied by his response. Denis looked amused by it, but Sam was clearly worried.

"Don't get attached to him yet, Eric," he warned.

Eric sighed and led the men back to the cockpit. He wanted to give Luke the rest of the plane in peace when he finally woke up. But as he sat and stared out the window, he couldn't help but stroke his lips and remember the fire he had sensed in Luke's body, the lightning that had sparked when they kissed. He wanted Luke as he had never wanted anyone else before, and he might lose Luke. He couldn't bear to think of it.

* * *

Luke stroked his dragonlings and felt the plane begin to land. He was frightened again. He hadn't seen Eric or anyone else when he woke up and made his way to the bathroom and then back into the room with the dragonlings. He was grateful. He wasn't sure how he would react when he saw Eric again. He kept thinking of the kiss and how much he enjoyed it, and how much he wanted to repeat it. But each time his thoughts took a pleasant turn, he would wonder about where they were going and fear would overwhelm him.

Eric was taking him somewhere and he didn't know where or why. He wanted to trust Eric because of the kiss, but he kept hesitating. Eric had kidnapped him, after all. Eric was the reason he wasn't with Daniel right now.

There was a knock at the door and Eric entered. Luke blushed and stared at the floor, unable to meet his gaze. The dragonlings chirped around him, continuing to burrow into his clothes as they had been doing before Eric came in. Last time Eric came in, they had moved into attack positions, Luke realized. The dragonlings no longer saw him as a threat, which meant that Luke no longer saw him as a threat. And as Luke finally looked up at Eric, he knew that Eric recognized it too. Eric flashed him a smile and Luke blushed again. Would he ever stop blushing in Eric's presence?

"We're about to land. Things are going to move very quickly once we do. May I sit next to you?"

"Yes," Luke said shyly, sending his dragonlings to the other side of the room so they wouldn't bother Eric.

Eric wrapped one arm around Luke's shoulder and placed his other hand under Luke's chin. Luke was surprised by the forward move, but didn't mind it. Gently, Luke placed his hand on Eric's chest and was rewarded by a smile. He hesitantly smiled back.

"We may not get another moment alone for a long time," Eric said.

"Why not? I thought I was going to be your tribe's dragon tamer," Luke said, the familiar wash of fear seeping into him.

"You'll be a dragon tamer," Eric said, "And I'll fight to stay at your side. But there are other leaders, older leaders, who may claim you now that you're in the East."

"I don't understand," Luke said. "You brought me here to replace your tamer. If they wanted me, they should have gotten me."

"It's very complicated, but it will make sense when we land," Eric said. He sounded weary, and sad. "Just know that you are very special to me."

His eyes were filled with such sorrow that Luke didn't think as he leaned forward to kiss him. Eric's hands tightened as if in surprise, then stroked Luke as he returned the kiss. It was a gentle kiss, not passionate like before, but it reached just as deep and Luke's toes were tingling when Eric finally pulled away. Luke leaned his head against Eric's chest and took several deep breaths to steady himself. The dragonlings were watching curiously.

Then there was a gentle bump as the plane hit the ground and Eric's hands tightened on him once more.

"Be brave, Luke. I have faith in you."

But his words, no doubt intended to inspire him, just made Luke worry. Why did he need to be brave, and why did Eric have faith in him? Eric helped him stand and Luke ordered his dragonlings to return to him. They draped themselves over his body again, snuggling inside his clothes until they were barely visible. Eric led the way out of the room, through the plane, and outside down a ramp.

It was hot, dry, and bright. Far too bright. That was what Luke noticed first, because he was blinded by the sun and had to shade his eyes. When everything came into focus, it looked like an oasis in a desert. He could clearly see a desert in the distance, but in the foreground there were palm trees and lush green grass and red buildings that looked like they were made out of clay. There were also a lot of people, all facing the plane. Watching him.

Most of them looked to be Asian or African, but a few had white skin like him and he wondered how they didn't burn in the sun, as he was probably going to do in minutes. They were dressed in a variety of clothes, from suits to robes to the sorts of styles he associated with hip teenagers. He had never paid much attention to fashion since his exposure to culture had been so limited. He relied entirely on movies. There was a road leading through town into the desert and several jeeps, but he didn't see any other roads.

Eric gestured for him to continue down the ramp and he took the rail cautiously, not wanting to jar the dragonlings and expose them. He hadn't expected so many people. Eric should have warned him he would be in public so he could have hidden them better. And why were they all staring at him?

A short distance from the bottom of the ramp was a half-circle of older women dressed in casual slacks and white shirts. At one end was an odd pole with five branches sticking out so it looked like a tree. A younger woman seemed to be guarding it. Beyond the older women there was a white chalk line drawn in the road. He puzzled over it, but his attention returned to the women as Eric bowed to them, clearly respectful. Luke didn't. He didn't know them, after all. Eric shot him an annoyed look, probably that he hadn't bowed, but Luke also didn't want to risk upsetting his dragonlings in public. He glared back.

"It's all right, Eric," the woman at the center said, gesturing for Eric to step back. He did, and Luke felt abandoned. "Everyone in this village is part of our society, child. You don't have to hide your dragonlings."

Luke stiffened in shock at hearing the word said aloud so casually. He had only ever heard Daniel, Aaron, and Eric say the word 'dragonling' aside from the dragons and never around any other tribe members. And to find out that every single person here was part of tribe society was shocking. Especially since she had said "our" society. Daniel had never included him in most things, always emphasizing that as the tamer, he was different and had a very different role. Even though Luke knew he wasn't an outsider anymore, he had never really felt the shift to that of an insider.

"Why don't you have your dragonlings sit over there so we can talk, Luke?" the woman said, gesturing to the tree.

Luke looked at it again. It did look ideal for dragonlings. They would love to swing on the branches and nestle up against the pole and if everyone here did know about them and knew to keep away from them, then they would be safe. His dragonlings poked their heads out and chirped to let him know their interest. He walked over to it, eyeing the young woman standing between him and the tree. She bowed to him and as she did, something brushed against his mind. It almost felt like a dragon, but it wasn't. And then he felt that same something start to brush against the minds of his dragonlings. He slammed a wall onto that something. The woman cried out in pain.

His dragonlings snapped into action. Three of them pulled him away from the woman and two of them threatened her until she retreated and they returned to Luke, where the five of them began circling protectively.

Luke shook his head and silenced his dragonlings, who returned to his shoulders but let out hisses and snarls of displeasure. He wasn't in a much better mood as he glared at the woman.

"What did you try to do to them?" he demanded.

The woman looked at the older women as if for help, then back at him. "I'm sorry. I was just introducing myself to you and your dragonlings. I didn't mean to threaten you."

"What do you mean, introduce yourself?"

"I'm also a dragon tamer," she said, looking confused as if he were at fault.

He stared at her. Another dragon tamer? He looked at the older woman, the one who had clearly ordered Eric to bring him here.

"If she's a tamer, why do you need me?"

"She's not powerful enough to do what we need," the older woman said.

Luke looked at the young woman, who shrugged. He knew he was more powerful than a lot of other tamers, since he had such a large range, but he never thought other people knew about it and might specifically kidnap him because of it.

"So what do you need?"

The older woman eyed his dragonlings as if she were going to ask him to part with them again, then seemed to think better of it.

"We have a dragonling. A special dragonling."

"Just one?"

"She needs special attention."

At first the significance of that sentence didn't sink in. He was still wondering why a single dragonling would require a powerful dragon tamer when he could handle twelve without a problem. Then he realized what pronoun she had used. He blinked.

"She?"

CHAPTER FOUR

Female Dragonling

Luke's eyes widened as the woman's words sunk in. There were no female dragonlings. Everyone knew that. It was why the dragons were dying. All the females were laying their last litters and the dragonlings were all male. If there were a female dragonling, the whole world would know about it. But if there wasn't a tamer for that dragonling and that dragonling died, then the dragons really would be doomed.

"Why doesn't she have a tamer?"

"The other tamers who have tried have died," the woman said.

"I don't understand," Luke said. "Why would she kill them?"

"We don't know what happened exactly."

But it must be what happened to Eric's tamer, Luke realized. And Eric had said he had dragonlings. Did he mean this dragonling or did he have his own litter? It didn't matter. Luke would be tamer for all of them.

"How long has she been without food and a tamer?"

"Her mother requested you before she died. It took twelve hours to travel to you, ten hours to secure you, and twelve hours to bring you back," the woman said. "Every minute here is another minute wasted."

"Where is she?"

"In the nest, in the desert. The chalk line marks the two-mile point, your range. We didn't want you walking across it by accident. But you won't be able to bring your dragonlings with you."

"I'm not leaving them here," he said sharply, looking at the young woman.

"Anna is fully qualified to take them," the old woman said. "Despite your initial impression, she is one of the strongest tamers in the East."

Luke looked at the chalk line and how close it was to the tree, then out at the desert. He looked at the young woman again, who smiled at him and seemed to be attempting to mend things between them. He had no interest.

"My dragonlings will wait here for me, but they will still be mine. I'm not going out of their range and if you try to steal them, they will attack you."

Anna's smile withered. "And if you're forced out of their range for more than a few seconds? Or you find you can't hold the female and them at the same time, or she won't let you?"

Luke glared. It was a possibility. But he wouldn't give up his dragonlings until the last possible second.

"I will give them permission to go to you if it becomes absolutely necessary. But it will be their choice, not yours. You do not get to take them from me just because you feel like it."

Anna looked at the dragonlings and laughed. "No dragonling is capable of making a decision like that at their age."

"Maybe yours aren't," Luke said, liking her less and less. "But I take care of mine."

"Enough," the old woman said just as Anna's eyes narrowed and it seemed she was about to spit back an insult of her own. "Anna, if the dragonlings decide to switch to you, so be it. If not, they will remain with Luke. I have faith that Luke will not let them suffer. Luke, please come with me."

The dragonlings nuzzled Luke and then flew to the tree, careful to avoid Anna. The older woman took Luke's arm and began leading him towards the white chalk line. About five feet away, he stopped. He could feel the vibrations in the air from the female dragonling. This was going to hurt, and he knew he was going to need help.

"What's wrong?" the woman asked.

"She's scared and in pain, and she's screaming," he said.

"We're already in your range?"

"Not for hearing, luckily. But I can feel her. Once I get in her range, I'm not going to be able to walk because she's screaming so loudly. I need someone to drive me. By the time we get there, I'll have calmed her down enough so I can get into the nest and talk to her. Hopefully she'll let me feed her. Is there food there?"

"A small amount. You'll have to bring her back for a real feeding."

He looked over at his dragonlings, now prancing on the tree. They were about due for a feeding too. He could feed them together when he returned. Then he looked back towards the plane where Eric and his men were unpacking crates.

"I want Eric to drive me," he said.

The woman looked surprised and shook her head.

"I'm sorry. He's too important to us."

"But I'm not?"

"You're a dragon tamer," she said. "He's not. The dragonling is far more likely to kill him and we can't afford to lose him just so he can drive you."

"I won't let her kill him. Either he drives me or I don't go."

She stared at him and he met her gaze evenly. She didn't have to think too hard, though, because after a few seconds she gestured for another woman to come to her side, talked to her in a different language, and less than a minute later, Eric came up driving a jeep. The woman helped Luke in and wished him luck, then gave Eric instructions, again in a different language.

Luke braced himself but still wasn't ready for it and it was a good thing he had buckled his seatbelt because his body lost control and did its best to curl into the fetal position the instant they crossed the threshold. Eric kept driving, though, and Luke was grateful.

Luke sent warming, calming thoughts to the dragonling. He was almost surprised Eric didn't hear them, they were so overpowering, and he was willing to bet his other dragonlings were sound asleep. But he had to be overpowering to be heard over the scream. He kept up his volume the entire time, though the sound of her screaming faded as they drew closer. By the time they stopped with the nest in view, Luke was sitting up again.

He kept his thoughts going as he unbuckled and got out, gesturing for Eric to stay. He was focused on the little red shape at the center of the nest. She was out of range for his other dragonlings. He stepped into the nest and she perked up. She knew he was the source of calm and she was curious. He invited her over to his side of the nest. He promised her pets and rubs and playtime and the all-important food if she came over. She was a little scared. Other humans had offered her these things but when she had gotten too close, they had screamed and fallen over and never moved again. Luke looked at the nest again and saw body parts under the thick sand. He swallowed hard.

He reassured he that he would not be like them, that he would always be here to care for her. He promised her brothers to play with and she hissed. She had killed all her brothers. He scolded her and told her she would like these brothers. She decided she would try to like them. She hopped over towards him a little. He encouraged her, praising her strength and her hopping ability and asking if she could fly. She was too weak to fly. His instinctive longing to protect and feed her must have persuaded her more than his words because with a little cry, she hopped all the way over to him and into his arms.

He gathered her up and held her tightly, inhaling the dusty, cinnamon scent of her hide as he stroked her. She was so thin, he could feel each of her ribs and he ached for her. She needed food, but she needed love more and he could feel it like a hole inside her as he cradled her and kissed her tiny snout and poured all of himself into her. He could feel little echoes from his other dragonlings as they welcomed their sister and he felt her surprise at their love and acceptance.

He held her for a long time, consoling her, loving her, bonding with her, until he knew no one would ever be able to part them. Then he knew she needed food. He placed her on his shoulder and returned to the jeep.

"Eric, can you get the food from over there?" he asked. "It's out of my range."

Eric was staring at the female in awe. He bowed deeply to Luke and then ran to obey. As soon as he returned, Luke took one of the bottles and cradled the dragonling again as he instructed her to suckle. It sometimes took dragonlings two or three tries to get used to a bottle but she took to it right away. There were only three bottles and Luke knew she wouldn't mind driving while feeding, so he asked Eric to drive them back while he fed. Eric kept stealing glances at them and there was a relieved smile on his face. He stopped with the village just out of view and faced Luke.

"You have no idea how happy I am, Luke."

"I wouldn't let her die," Luke said, but Eric shook his head.

"No, happy about you. Happy that you didn't die. What I told you before is true, and maybe you'll understand it now. Many tribes will want you, and many have leaders with more experience and seniority than me. But I will fight for you, Luke. If I had my way, you would never leave my side."

Luke's eyes filled with tears. "I don't want to leave your side."

The dragonling cooed around her bottle and a little milk dribbled out.

Eric sighed and turned back to the road. Luke stroked the female and she sent him an outpouring of love just as he had sent her. He kept his eyes fixed on her. He would figure out his future later. For now, he had his dragonlings.

* * *

There was a stunned silence as Eric drove back into the village.

Everyone knew what his arrival meant, especially when they saw Luke next to him, but the dragonling was hiding in his clothes as dragonlings loved to do so there was no concrete proof yet. Eric got out and helped Luke out, steadying him as his feet nearly gave out. Luke was exhausted, Eric could tell. The actual drive had been short, but Luke had spent nearly two hours at the edge of the nest staring at the dragonling before she hopped towards him. And then he had cradled her another three hours before getting up to feed her. While he hadn't been doing anything physically exhausting, Eric knew how draining the effects of taming could be. But the female still needed a proper meal and Eric knew Luke wouldn't even consider resting until she was fed, and from what he had said about his range, he knew that Luke had kept his other dragonlings and they were undoubtedly hungry as well.

Luke ignored everyone and everything and walked straight to the tree where his dragonlings were now chirping happily and rousing as if from sleep. Anna looked annoyed but was keeping her distance. The five silver dragonlings began circling and then there was a chirp from Luke's shirt. Everyone gasped, even though everyone must have known. The little red female crawled out of Luke's sleeve and onto his hand, and stretched her wings. Luke held his hand up high. Everyone was utterly silent.

She chirped again and the five silver dragonlings flew over to her. There was a gasp and Eric knew they were afraid of an attack, but each male simply nuzzled her in greeting and then landed on Luke in what Eric was beginning to recognize as their usual places. Luke turned to Anna and lowered his eyes.

"May I have some food for my six dragonlings?"

Anna pointed to the elders. "Ask them. They're the elder dragon tamers."

Luke looked surprised and confused as he turned to face the older women.

"You're not dragon tamers," he said hesitantly.

"We are," the primary elder said. "We chose not to introduce ourselves the way Anna did because we knew you had never met a tamer before and wouldn't understand the greeting. We warned Anna not to use that greeting as well, but habit is hard to break."

Anna ducked her head. Eric knew she was the strongest tamer left in the East, but she was still young and where Luke had always lived his life as an outsider, she had only lived in the deepest circles.

"We have a room set up for feeding," the elder continued. "Would you like another tamer to help you feed?"

"No," Luke snapped.

The elder smiled kindly. "Then we won't. In places where there are multiple tamers it is common to share duties even while one tamer holds the primary bond, but we don't expect that from you since you have always been alone."

She gestured for Luke to follow her into one of the buildings. He started to, then stopped, looking back at Eric. Their eyes caught and Eric knew that Luke was realizing this might be the last time they saw each other. He had to know Eric would do everything in his power to prevent that, but once Luke walked through that door into the hands of the dragon tamers, it was out of his control.

Luke said something to the elder; it was too far away to hear what. She looked at Eric briefly and then drew Luke into the building. The door closed.

"He'll be fine," Denis said, taking Eric's arm. "He did what we wanted."

CHAPTER FIVE

Collapse

Luke was nearly at the end of his energy as the female finished her last bottle and his last male started to cry for his last bottle. He liked to devote most of his attention to the dragonling he was feeding but all of his dragonlings were a little neglected so he had also been splitting attention between them. He knew he was going to collapse soon but he didn't care. As long as they were taken care of.

He had felt brushes against his mind a few times, always very polite, and had shut them out immediately and with force. They were from different people, he could tell. They were probably trying to find someone whose touch he would tolerate but he wouldn't tolerate anyone. At least they knew not to reach out to his dragonlings anymore.

The room they had given him was ideally set up. There were plenty of nooks and crannies near the ceiling for the dragonlings to hide and play in while he wasn't feeding them, and he knew they would be safe while he slept after the feeding. There was plenty of food even though he had used most of it. The floor was lushly carpeted, though it didn't need to be since there were so many pillows intended for sitting and leaning against the wall. It formed a perfect nest for him to curl up and feed.

There was a knock at the door and Anna entered. He braced himself for the touch of her mind but there was none. He relaxed again. She didn't say anything as he transferred the female to his chest to burp her and arranged the male in his lap for his final bottle. He began stroking the female on her back, tapping her every few strokes. His males were old enough that they didn't need to be burped, but she was still two days younger. His male eagerly suckled the bottle. The other males were happily playing so he devoted the last of his attention to the two dragonlings clinging to him.

"What are you doing?" Anna asked gently, as if she didn't want to disturb him too much.

"Feeding," he said, knowing that probably wasn't what she meant but not knowing what else she could be asking about.

"You're exhausting yourself. You're driving yourself into unconsciousness. If we didn't know you cared about them so much, we would worry you were trying to kill yourself."

"I wouldn't abandon them," he said, but without anger. He was projecting peace and nothing could anger him. "If I truly am safe here as you claim, then I'm in no danger if I sleep after this."

Anna watched him. She probably knew that she also couldn't project anger even though he could tell she wanted to from the way her eyes flashed. He returned his attention to his charges and coaxed the female to burp. She obliged and he rewarded her with a kiss, then sent her to play with her brothers. He turned his full attention to his male.

"You're scared," Anna observed. "You're trying to hide in your duties but you're terrified."

"Shouldn't I be?" Luke snapped, then calmed himself. "You stole me from my home. You forced me to take these dragonlings from their mother before they were ready. You brought me to this place and tried to make me give them up. You keep intruding on my mind. You made Eric leave."

Her brow furrowed. "And it's that last one that bothers you the most, isn't it? Why? He's the one who stole you and brought you here."

"He was kind to me," Luke said. "That's more than any of you have been."

"We've been trying," Anna said, sounding exasperated. "We gave you our best feeding room. We've only been reaching out to you to monitor your health since you seem determined to exhaust yourself. You've snubbed all of our attempts. How else are we supposed to be kind to you?"

Luke considered. In truth, they probably couldn't have tried harder. He had been on the defensive since he arrived and they threatened his dragonlings. Ever since then, he hadn't given them a chance. They had been kind. He just didn't want to see it.

One of his males landed on his shoulder and nuzzled him in an attempt to cheer him up and he instantly changed his thinking to love and calm again. He could not project anything else after neglecting his dragonlings for so many hours. The male chirped and returned to the ceiling and the male in his arms nestled more comfortably as he enjoyed his bottle.

"They love you. You're good at this," Anna said.

He puzzled over her comment but refused to project it. Was she really not good at it? She was supposed to be a good tamer, after all. Did the East just have bad tamers?

"It's been my life since I was twelve," he said. "How could I be bad at it?"

It was her turn to look puzzled, though he noticed she didn't project it either. She wasn't bad, then. She could control her emotions. There was a dawning understanding on her face and she seemed to look at him differently, and with great sadness.

"They told me you didn't know, you hadn't been taught, but I didn't realize what it meant, not really. This is all you've ever done, isn't it? Raising dragonlings?"

Eric had said something like that, Luke realized. But he hadn't explained the comment. He had the feeling Anna wasn't going to explain the comment either but he had to ask.

"What else is there?"

"Haven't you ever wondered what happens to them after you let them go?" she asked.

He was quiet. He had wondered that, a lot. But the mother dragons had always given him the same answer, and so had Aaron and Daniel when he asked them. He knew they wouldn't lie, and while it was an unsatisfying answer, it was all he had and he clung to it when he had doubts.

"They're safe and that's all I need to know," he said softly, unable to look at her.

"You never asked for more?"

"I never got more."

Again she looked infinitely sad. "I'm sorry I was so, well, imperious with your dragonlings. I didn't realize they were all you had, all you've ever had. I just wanted to keep them safe and was worried you couldn't do it."

"I would never put them in danger. If you'll excuse me, Anna, he's nearly finished his bottle."

"And you'll be unconscious when he does," Anna said.

Luke blushed. He had changed his energy output when his conversation with Anna had started, but it was still timed so he would run out at the same time as the bottle. As much as he appreciated Anna's apology, he didn't want anyone with him when he fell asleep.

"I'll leave. But when you wake up I'll be back to check on you."

He nodded, just wanting her to leave. His dragonling was on its last few suckles. She had just closed the door when the male dropped the bottle and joined its brothers and sister. Luke's head fell back and he sunk into darkness.

* * *

Luke awoke slowly. He folded back into consciousness. His body stretched into awareness and his mind blossomed, first touching the female's soft buzz, then reaching his familiar males. He was always connected with them, even in sleep, but he could only hear them when he was awake unless they shouted at him. He was lying on his side in a mound of cushions and felt extremely relaxed. The dragonlings were curled around him, awake and alert and protecting him. He couldn't move for several minutes as he regained control of his body. He hadn't realized how weak he had been, or the consequences of draining himself so thoroughly.

Finally, he managed to move his hands, then his feet, and then sit up. He felt dizzy and steadied himself as he held a hand to his head and closed his eyes. The whole world swayed. He could hear his dragonlings chirping in concern and he sent a wave of reassurance to them. They quieted. He leaned against the cushions, hoping the dizziness would pass. After a few more minutes, it did.

There was a knock at the door and he wasn't surprised when Anna entered. She already looked concerned and he wondered if someone had touched his mind without him noticing. She had kept her distance last time but this time she walked right up to him, not minding the dragonlings who hissed protectively, and felt his forehead. He again calmed the dragonlings. He knew she wasn't going to hurt him. The males huffed and went to the ceiling but the female remained curled on his shoulder, watching Anna with distrust.

"No fever," Anna said with relief. "Good. We've been so worried about you. You shouldn't have exhausted yourself like that."

He became aware of his dragonlings' hunger and saw that the food had been replenished.

"I need to feed them," he said.

"I can help you," she offered.

He considered. It would take nearly an hour to feed all of them by himself and hunger was beginning to wrack his body. He wondered how long he had slept. At least twelve hours if his dragonlings were hungry again. He had only eaten once on the plane and nothing all day before. He needed food and with Anna's help he could finish faster. But he still didn't trust her.

"No thank you," he said, remembering what she had said

about them trying to be kind and deciding he could at least be polite to her.

"Well, try to hurry. You're still very weak and I'm sure you're hungry as well," she said. She sounded quite worried and he knew she wasn't going to leave his side the entire feeding.

He alternated dragonlings as he fed, since they ate faster if they had time to digest each bottle, and fed the female four times while each male only had two bottles. She was so young and so delicate she needed the extra care and food. But he reserved his energy and gave them only the attention they needed, knowing he couldn't lavish it on them as he had before when he was purposefully draining himself. They whined a bit, especially the female, but he scolded them and they stopped soon enough.

Anna watched him and was clearly impressed, but there was that sadness again. As if his expertise with dragonlings had come at the expense of something else. She still hadn't said what, however. When he was finished and sent his dragonlings to the ceiling for a nap, she extended a hand to help him stand. He refused it and tried to stand on his own. He couldn't even rise to his knees. Reluctantly, he took her hand. As soon as he was on his feet, he collapsed into her. He could barely stand on his own. She supported him and he was surprised at her strength. He took a few deep breaths to regain control of his body and then straightened. He would not be supported like some doll.

She led him out of the room, hovering near him as if waiting for him to collapse again. They went through several corridors into a room with a long table and benches. The older women were waiting for him, seated on one side of the table. Anna led him to the other side, helped him sit at the bench, and then sat next to him.

The eldest leaned forward.

"I hope you've learned the consequences of draining yourself like that. If you haven't, you'll certainly feel them today. You left your dragonlings without care for over a day."

Luke's eyes went wide. "That's not true. It couldn't be more than twelve hours. The female would have woken me up to feed."

"Her brothers told her you needed rest. When we saw she wasn't going to wake you up, Anna was forced to go in and feed her. Your males refused to be fed and went hungry."

Anger flashed through him. Someone had dared feed one of his dragonlings. He turned to Anna in a rage. She simply raised an eyebrow at him. He gulped. She had dared because he couldn't. He had been so desperate for sleep that his males would rather starve than wake him up. But his female, so new, couldn't wait. She wouldn't have lasted without a feeding. Anna had saved the life of his dragonling. A rush of gratitude swept through him but he didn't want to show it.

"Thank you," he said, hiding the rest of his emotions.

"Don't ever put the lives of your dragonlings in danger again," she said.

He glared, but knew he couldn't respond. He had never considered that they might be in danger. He had only been thinking of himself. He would never do that again.

"I apologize for my actions," he said to the older woman. "I had not realized they would be in danger."

"We know," the woman said kindly. "And had we realized the extent to which you were draining yourself, we would have stopped you."

He doubted they would have been able to stop him, but he appreciated their concern. He could see that they were trying to be nice to him in their own way. They valued the dragonlings at least and that was all that mattered to Luke.

Several people walked in and placed food in front of them. It looked delicious but just like on the plane, he had no idea how to eat it. He stared for a moment, looking at the foreign utensils and wondering how rude it would be to just lift the plate and dump it into his mouth.

"Eric told us you were a stranger to our customs," the old

woman said. "Anna, will you show him?"

Anna showed him how to eat the food, but with none of the patience that Eric had demonstrated and Luke found his gratitude towards her dwindling rapidly. He snapped at her several times and she at him, and she would have given up if the other woman hadn't glared at her. He wondered why the older woman didn't just teach him but assumed it was because Anna was next to him. He wished she weren't.

Even after he figured out how to eat he did it with no enjoyment. The food was good, and they gave him seconds and even thirds since he was so hungry, but it was hard to enjoy the meal when the women were watching him like hawks. He kept bracing for the touch of a mind against his and wondering why it hadn't happened yet. He was afraid he was somehow unable to feel it anymore, that they had done something to him while he was asleep.

When he finally felt full and he could tell that his energy was returning to a normal level, he leaned back and eyed the women surrounding him. They hadn't hurt him and they had been kind. They had wanted him here to bond with the female dragonling, something none of them had been able to do. He had done it. He understood that part. He still didn't understand anything else, but he wasn't sure they would answer his questions. Still, there was no harm in asking. He just hoped they would be honest.

CHAPTER SIX

Forbidden Touch

"The female is safe," Luke said. "I won't ever do that again. I'm sorry I've inconvenienced you because of it. I'm ready to return home now."

The older woman examined him with the same sadness that Anna had had, the same sadness that was beginning to get on Luke's nerves.

"We were expecting a trained tamer from the West who could bond with the female. We would make sure the bond was secure and care for the tamer for a few weeks. We would give the tamer instructions. Females will always require more attention than males, and we will need regular updates every few months. When it comes time to let her go, the tamer will need to return here as she requires a special ceremony. Once the tamer understood this, we would return him to his tribe."

"That all sounds fine," Luke said. "Do you need me to stay longer to make sure I'm all right?"

He had already suspected the female would need more care than the males, and it wasn't surprising that they would want to hear news about the only female dragonling. It also made sense that she would have a special ceremony. Unfortunately, he also realized that his rash decision to drain himself probably meant that he would have to stay here longer to prove to them that he could care for her before they let him return to Daniel.

"That is what would happen if we had a trained tamer," she said, waving her hand as if to dismiss the idea. "You are not trained."

Eric and Anna had said the same thing. But Luke narrowed his eyes.

"I am perfectly capable of taking care of her."

"Yes, you are," the woman said. "You will do a better job than anyone else. But we cannot allow you to exist in ignorance. You need more. You deserve more. And if you want to raise a female, you have to know more. She must be taught things that you don't know."

"Like what?" Luke demanded.

"Haven't you ever wondered why we're called dragon tamers?"

"Stop answering my questions with questions," he said, frustrated.

To his surprise, the woman laughed. "It's how we teach. But if you answer my question, I might answer yours."

"We're tamers because, uh," he paused. He had in fact wondered this and never gotten a satisfactory answer out of the dragons or his leaders. It had something to do with the myth of the Dragon Master, he knew, but he wasn't sure what. He was stuck with the answer he had been given and he knew very well it wasn't a good one. "Because if we don't bond with the dragonlings, they'll die."

"How does that make us tamers?"

Luke glared. "I don't know, okay?"

She sighed. "This would be a lot easier to explain if I could touch your mind and simply give you the answer."

"I don't want you in my mind," he said.

"You would be in my mind too," she pointed out, and he thought about it. He hadn't realized that. She would be making herself vulnerable as well. He could reach as deeply into her as she would reach into him, so she would have incentive to touch him as lightly as possible. Just lightly enough to give him one answer. And he would accept it, because he didn't want anything else from her.

"I guess I'll try it," he said.

He felt a flicker against his mind. It wasn't pressuring him; it was waiting for him to make the first move. He extended a tendril against it and made contact. Then everything went black and he withdrew as quickly as he could, slamming down every shield he could think of. His body vibrated in pain but he struggled to exude calm so his dragonlings wouldn't panic. Memories swarmed him, unlocked by the touch of another mind. Memories of the time before the first mother dragon had summoned him, of the time when he heard the dragons but didn't know what they were and everyone thought he was crazy.

There had been a touch then, just like this touch, a gentle pressure against his mind and when he hadn't resisted, it had filled him. At first he was grateful because the touch seemed to understand him and understand the strange sounds he always heard. The touch would come and go and he would look forward to it.

Then the touch began exploring him, his mind and body. It would ransack his memories and he would be helpless. It would slither along his limbs and he could feel the lust behind it as the touch stroked him in the most sexual of ways while silencing him at the same time. He became afraid of the touch because he didn't know how to stop it.

The touch came and went for nearly a year before there was another touch and at first Luke was terrified by the new touch, fearing it would be like the old. But the new touch was friendly. It was the dragon summoning him. He begged the dragon to protect him in exchange for running away to find her, and the dragon taught him to close his mind. The next time the old touch tried to approach him, he slammed his shields down. He felt shock, and then nothing. The touch attempted a few more times and then seemed to give up.

Luke had nearly forgotten about that touch because he was so safe in his tribe and with his dragonlings. Even the tamers' flickerings hadn't triggered the memories. Now, though, everything was rushing back and it was everything he could do to fight the terror for the sake of his dragonlings in the other room.

The blackness left his vision as he gasped for air and felt Anna's arms around him. The other women surrounded him as well, some of them touching him. The woman whose mind he had touched was kneeling before him, holding his hands. He was still in control, he knew, and the dragonlings, though probably aware that something had upset him, had no idea exactly how upset he was. It was not uncommon for him to get upset during the course of an ordinary day so they wouldn't be disturbed. He was extremely grateful and took a deep breath before meeting the eyes of the woman holding his hands.

"I'm sorry I pushed you out like that," he said, knowing he had probably hurt her.

"Don't be," she said. She reached up and cradled his face just as Eric had done. He stifled the pang of regret in his heart, missing Eric dearly. "I should have realized there was a reason for your shields."

He pulled back from her hands suspiciously. He had thought he had kicked her out before she saw anything.

"What did you see?"

"Nothing," she assured him. "But I've seen what happens when a tamer is abused by another tamer. Do you know the tamer?"

"I didn't know he was a tamer," Luke said quietly. "He was just a touch."

"You weren't part of our society yet?"

Her voice was gentle and he knew she wasn't trying to hurt him, but something in him snapped.

"*Your* society," he corrected harshly. "*This* society. Never *my* society. I've never had a part and I don't want a part. Just let me raise the dragonlings and leave me alone."

Anna's hands squeezed on his shoulders as if in surprise and the woman's face hardened.

"That is precisely why you will not be returned to your tribe, Luke. You *are* part of our society; you are the center. And if you don't know that, then a great injustice has been done to you."

"Daniel has told me everything I need to know," Luke said firmly. "He would never lie to me or hide things from me."

"Eric thinks Daniel has been hiding things from you," the woman pointed out. "Do you trust Eric?"

Luke glared. It was unfair to drag Eric into this. He did know that Eric thought Daniel was lying to him and he did trust Eric, but Eric didn't know Daniel. Eric seemed to think Daniel knew things that Luke knew he didn't.

"Eric thinks Daniel knows about dragon taming," Luke said. "But Daniel is the tribe leader. Why would he know about dragon taming?"

"Eric is also a tribe leader, yet he knows about taming. Why would Daniel be any different?" the woman asked. At Luke's startled expression, she smiled. "He didn't mention that he was a leader?"

Luke blushed. He had known that Eric would be high up in the tribe, but hadn't dreamed that the leader of a tribe would come all the way across the world to get him. And kiss him. No wonder they had been so reluctant to let Eric drive him to the female's nest. And no wonder Eric had seemed so determined to get Luke for his tribe. Luke should have known by those statements that Eric was the leader, but he had been confused and worried. And now Eric was gone. Luke didn't know who he wanted to see more, Daniel or Eric.

"Daniel knows all about taming, just as all leaders do," the woman continued. "Otherwise they can't become leaders. It is their responsibility to teach the tamers under their care, and he neglected that duty. He neglected it to a breath-taking extent. Your first leader also neglected it, though his neglect is more understandable given your age and your recent entry to our society."

She paused. "Did your previous leader know about the tamer?"

"What tamer?"

"The touch," she clarified. "The one hurting you."

He blushed again. He hated that they knew about it. He hated remembering it. He shook his head. He had never told anyone about it, or even known it wasn't a figment of his imagination until now.

"I didn't think anyone would believe me," he whispered. Tears filled his eyes and he maintained his focus on his dragonlings. That at least was something he had control over.

The woman cradled his face again and Anna stroked his back. "You are with friends now, and we believe you. No one will touch you without your permission. Is there anything else you haven't told anyone, things you felt or heard when you were young that you weren't sure were real?"

He tried to think back but was met with a wall. He had blocked those memories out for so long, he no longer had access to most of them. Just flickers of pain and the disappointed sighs of his parents. The violating touch in his mind. And then running, following the elusive voice of the dragon until his shoes fell off and his feet bled and he couldn't stand it, then running again.

Aaron said he was nearly dead when they found him sprawled on the outskirts of their territory. They hadn't known who or what he was when they found him and would have left him for dead if he had been older, but they couldn't abandon a child. He had rambled in his fevered sleep and they figured out that he was the tamer their dragon had sent for. He had been treasured ever since.

"I don't remember most of it," he admitted. "I don't want to."

"Did you have a family?"

He stared at her. She wasn't trying to be intrusive, he didn't think, just trying to sort out what kind of childhood he had so she could understand him better, but he had just told her he didn't want to remember his past and she was prying.

"I had parents."

"Did they love you?"

"They kept me," he said roughly. "No matter what I saw or heard."

Her lips twitched into a frown before she smoothed her features. "And when you joined your first tribe? Were you well treated?"

"Yes," Luke said, perking up. He didn't mind talking about them. "They took care of me and protected me. They gave me dragonlings."

"Were you upset at the dragon swap?"

"The mother dragon couldn't have any more litters," Luke said. "I missed her, but I couldn't help her anymore and I knew I could help Daniel's dragons. Daniel's always taken good care of me."

He heard Anna scoff at that and was immediately on the defensive.

"He has," Luke insisted. "He's given me everything I've ever wanted and more. When I had two litters and twelve dragonlings, he made sure I had safe transport between the nests and more than enough food for all of them. I'm sure you know how hard it is to get that much food on a daily basis, especially in the middle of a city. Anytime I need anything, he gives it to me."

There was a silence as he glared at them, then Anna spoke in a strangled voice.

"You had twelve dragonlings?"

He turned to her.

"They were both full litters," Luke said. "And no, I never mixed them if that's what you're worried about. Dragonlings don't tolerate each other in groups larger than six and I know it. I'm not as untrained as you seem to think."

The woman in front of him placed her hand on his cheek again.

"In the area of dragonling raising, you are undoubtedly the most trained tamer on the planet, Luke," she said with some amusement. "We are not questioning those abilities and we hope that you will share your experience with us. As far as I know, no other tamer has ever held more than one litter at a time, or even held a combined litter as you currently have."

"So what are you questioning? And no more return questions," he warned.

"After we let our dragonlings go, they enter a different realm. You know that, right?"

He nodded. The ceremony involved the nearly full-grown dragonlings flying through a gate into nothingness. Luke was not allowed to ask questions about the gate or the ceremony but he had guessed that they went somewhere else since they clearly weren't on the other side of the gate and there weren't any full-grown dragons in the world aside from the mothers.

"They become wild. Dragon tamers enter that realm and tame them. If the tamer that raised them finds them in that realm, they tame easier. We tame the females and bring them here to become mothers. We tame the males and use them in war."

Luke gently pushed away all of the hands touching him, then rubbed his forehead. It almost made sense with what he knew, but not quite.

"What do you mean, war?" he asked, not liking that part. He would never want one of his dragons to be hurt.

"The tribe wars in this realm reflect it," she said. "But they're only a shadow. When Daniel and his tribe go off to fight, they're not heading out to the city. They're entering the gate and riding the dragons that their previous tamer tamed for them. That's how they protect their territory."

"That's not true," he protested. "The other tribe members barely even know the dragonlings exist! And even if what you're saying is true, why wouldn't they want me helping them?"

"A very good question," the woman said. "One that we're going to find the answer to. But not one that you need to worry about yet. For the next few days, take care of your dragonlings and get used to being here. We will answer your questions as best we can. Anna will be in charge of your care."

"I don't want her."

"Get used to her," the woman said. "You two have a lot in common."

He glowered at Anna, wondering what they could possibly have in common. But he didn't fight it again. He tried to stand and wobbled. He was forced to take Anna's hand again and the old woman examined him from head to toe.

"You'll feel the consequences of your actions strongly, Luke," she warned. "But you will recover safely and your dragonlings won't be affected any further."

He sighed in relief. Above all else, he didn't want them hurt. He could stand weakness and having to rely on Anna. He could stand anything. But they couldn't.

CHAPTER SEVEN

Shielded Minds

Eric let the wind play over his face as he allowed the dragon free reign. He was at the edge of his border closest to Daniel's and he had been patrolling it constantly, knowing that Daniel would attack soon in an attempt to get Luke back. It was possible Daniel would attack in the other realm but unlikely. Still, Eric was well-fortified no matter where he attacked.

The dragon between his legs spun in the air and he clung to him, knowing he wouldn't let Eric fall but still needing the psychological reassurance. Eric had flown this dragon ever since he had become leader. The dragon's name was Ryseth and Eric was extremely attached to him. Ryseth had even done him the honor of speaking to him on a few occasions. Dragons talked to the tamers, of course, and they always took instructions from their riders, but they never talked back except to a few honored individuals in rare circumstances. Even then it was usually just a few words. Ryseth had been more talkative to Eric than most dragons when they spoke to non-tamers, and Eric made sure his dragon knew how appreciative he was.

He stroked Ryseth's back as the dragon straightened and wondered if Ryseth was one of Luke's dragons. He was young enough. As Luke's name entered his mind, Ryseth's body roiled and Eric smiled. Was Ryseth one of Luke's?

No, Ryseth said, and Eric was immediately honored to be spoken to even as the answer surprised him. *I do not have that privilege. You have met the Tamer?*

Eric could feel the capitalization on the word tamer and wasn't sure how to treat the respect in Ryseth's voice. He assured Ryseth that he had met Luke, though briefly. He asked how Ryseth knew Luke.

He controls the Untamable, Ryseth said with awe.

Eric drew a sharp breath. The Untamable were legendary. The fierce, virtually immortal dragons had always existed but in recent years – probably since Luke had started taming – they had grown incredibly powerful. As their name suggested, no one had ever been able to tame them. No one could even try, because their minds, like their bodies, were hidden behind so many layers of armor. A tamer had to be able to touch a mind to tame it and even the wildest dragon's mind was accessible, except for these.

If the Untamable had ever joined a tribe or attacked anyone, the entire society might have turned against them. But instead they served as guardians of the society, patrolling and keeping fighting from getting out of hand, preventing weaker tribes from being targeted, overseeing dragon swaps, and while no one ever seemed to be directing these actions, one always seemed to show up when it was needed. Perhaps their greatest duty, however, was protecting the Great Library that stored all the knowledge of the ancient dragon tamers. Unfortunately, they guarded it so closely that no one had been admitted entrance in over a hundred years.

With Luke controlling the Untamable, though, all of that would fall apart. If Luke joined a tribe, so would his dragons. The Untamable might continue their current neutral activities, or they might side with Luke in tribe wars. It would largely be up to Luke's leader and how much pressure the leader put on Luke. The only positive was that they would almost certainly let him into the Library and perhaps he could find out why the mother dragons kept dying as soon as they were tamed.

Luke needed Eric as his leader. Eric would never pressure

him into using the Untamable in war. The Untamable were too valuable doing what they were currently doing. And Luke was too valuable to pressure. Thoughts of Luke's kiss filled his mind and stirred a fire inside of him. He longed to touch Luke again, to hold him, to kiss him. He didn't want anyone else getting close. He knew Luke would only be around women for a while, but eventually he would see men and it was inevitable those men would be attracted to someone as beautiful as Luke. Eric needed to make sure Luke was his before that happened.

You are his mate? Ryseth asked.

Eric hadn't expected his dragon to continue talking to him, or to still be monitoring his thoughts. He knew the dragons were always aware of their rider's thoughts so they would know their instructions but he had never really thought about it before. Ryseth knew him far more intimately than he had ever realized.

He struggled to explain the situation, how Luke had turned to him but might still want Daniel, too. He hated admitting the last but it was a reality. He knew Luke had deep feelings for him but he also knew that Daniel had a place in Luke's heart as well.

Ryseth snorted and flicked his wings. *You are better. Much better.*

Eric smiled and stroked Ryseth's neck, moved beyond words. He leaned forward and kissed Ryseth's warm hide. Dragons didn't use human actions like kissing, but they understood them and he hoped Ryseth understood how much his words had meant to Eric. It was rare enough to be spoken to, even rarer to have an extended conversation, and then to be complimented on top of everything? Not for the first time, he wished he had been born a tamer so he could have this kind of closeness with Ryseth all the time.

They returned to the tribe's gate and as Ryseth flew, the warmth of the compliment faded and Eric began wondering what to do with his knowledge of Luke. He had to keep it quiet, obviously. If other leaders knew, they would be fighting for him even more than they were likely to do now when he was just a powerful tamer. Daniel couldn't know, or else he would have used Luke for sure. He wasn't sure what the elder dragon tamers would do if and when they found out, and he wasn't sure if he should tell them.

He knew they would bring Luke into the other realm at some point, and chances were good Luke would encounter one of the Untamable before long. It was only a matter of time. If the elders thought Eric knew and hadn't told them, he would be in trouble and might lose Luke. But if he told them, they might try to take advantage of Luke's power to enter the Library without Luke's full consent. He wasn't sure why that would be a problem but if the Untamable weren't giving them access now, clearly they weren't meant to have access.

If it were the previous elders he wouldn't hesitate to tell them. He trusted them. But they were all dead in the attempt to bond with the female dragonling. The new elders had been in the elder circle, true, but in the lower circle due to their relatively low strength. Eric still found it bizarre that they suddenly outranked Anna due to their age even though Anna was at least three times as strong as the primary elder. It had all happened so fast, too. The rules of succession were clearly defined in case something like this happened. He was just unsure whether the sudden power would go to their heads and cloud their thinking and until he knew that, he hesitated to trust them.

Ryseth let out a soft cry as he landed, and Eric stroked him once more before sliding off onto the plain near the gate. Ryseth took off again to patrol alone and Eric stepped through the gate to make sure Daniel hadn't tried anything in the other realm.

* * *

Luke tried to keep a low profile as the days passed. He focused on his dragonlings, as the woman had suggested. The female was needy, but he didn't mind. He had plenty of time and energy to spare for her. He spent as much of his time as possible either feeding or playing with his dragonlings. The males were thriving despite being away from their mother and he felt a little better about separating them.

When he wasn't with them, he was eating in the dining hall or being shown around the village, which he discovered was a lot like the area of the city his tribe lived in despite being in an oasis. There were the same sorts of buildings and the same sorts of people, but while in his tribe everyone ignored him, here everyone nodded or even bowed to him. It made him very uncomfortable and he didn't like being out for long.

Anna was his constant companion and guide whether he was with his dragonlings or in the village. He did his best to be kind to her and when he couldn't, he tolerated her. At the least he tried not to be rude too often. He could tell she was doing the same for him but frequently their tolerance for each other ended at the same point and he could tell she would like nothing more than to storm off except that she had been ordered to stay with him. She would have to be the one to apologize, though he would usually grudgingly follow suit and attempt to be kind again. He knew it wasn't her fault she was stuck with him.

He didn't ask her questions, though, even though his mind was constantly coming up with new questions to ask. The older woman's brief explanation seemed to have so many holes in it and he desperately wanted to know more, but there was no way he was going to ask Anna and risk seeing condescension or pity in those eyes. So he kept his mouth shut, because he knew eventually they would let him talk with the other woman again and he could get some real answers. They claimed to want to teach him, after all.

Night was the only time he had to himself. He had a bedroom and adjoining bath in the same building as the feeding room and it was just as richly appointed. When they had shown him to the door, he remembered Eric picking him up and carrying him to the bed in the ship and blushed. He hadn't allowed anyone into the room with him and had closed the door quickly. They had given him clothes, which he was grateful for since he hadn't changed since leaving home, and he had enjoyed the plush bed. He still enjoyed it, but every night he imagined how much better it would be with Eric's arms around him, Eric's body pinning him down. He would shut his eyes and ache for Eric.

On his seventh night, when things had settled into a pattern and the dragonlings were happy in their new home, he had a dream. He frequently dreamed at home but hadn't dreamed here. He was always vaguely aware during his dreams – he had looked it up online and discovered they were called lucid dreams – so he wasn't concerned that he was aware this was a dream. Often at home he dreamed of the dragonlings and he expected the same here, but instead he saw Anna and the older woman. He was a little disappointed but he moved closer so he could hear them talking.

"How is the taming coming?" the woman asked Anna.

"It isn't," Anna said, annoyed. "I told you it wouldn't. You can't tame what you can't touch."

"You can't touch him the way you're used to touching dragons, but you can still touch him," the woman said. "You're just not trying."

"I am trying harder than you can imagine," she said angrily.

The woman shook her head. "Then perhaps you're trying too hard. You realize a delicate touch is needed, don't you?"

Anna threw up her hands. "I don't know what you want. You say one thing, then the opposite. You want me to follow my instincts but my instincts say it isn't possible. You can train him, you can work beside him, but you won't ever be able to tame him unless you break him, and I will never help with that."

The woman sighed. "Try one more time. After that, we'll reassess."

"Fine," Anna said. "One more time."

The dream faded and Luke opened his eyes. His heart was pounding. He knew the dream was real. He had overheard Daniel's conversations before and when he asked Daniel about them, Daniel's anger had confirmed their truth. They had never been about him, though, or about anything he understood. This was about him.

He wanted to believe they were talking about a dragon that Anna was taming. But Anna wasn't spending any time taming dragons. She was spending all her time with him. They were trying to tame him. He swallowed hard and checked his mental shields. They were intact. That was what Anna had meant about not being able to touch him. If she had been able to touch his mind, would she have been able to tame him? What did it even mean to be tamed? He wasn't sure but it frightened him. They had seemed so nice. He had thought Anna was the mean one and they were nice, but she was the one refusing to tame him and they were the ones pressuring her.

He clutched the pillow beside him and wished Eric or Daniel were here. He didn't care which one. Either would protect him. He didn't know how to treat his newfound knowledge. He couldn't trust anyone anymore. He didn't know anyone's motives. Anna's comment about breaking him was truly frightening. She said she wouldn't help, but what if they did it without her? Would she help him against them? He longed to go cuddle with his dragonlings but he didn't want anyone to suspect that he had overheard the conversation, so he simply curled around the pillow and waited for morning.

CHAPTER EIGHT

Misunderstood Alliance

The instant light broke through his window, he was up and ready for the day. He had already fed the dragonlings by the time Anna showed up. He tossed a scarf in the air for the dragonlings to chase and attack and considered her as she sat down to watch. She didn't act any different than normal and for her, there wasn't anything different about today. Maybe she got scolded like that every night. But for him today was completely different.

He extended a scarf to her. "Would you like to throw one to them?" he asked politely.

She looked shocked, but she nodded quickly as if not wanting him to change his mind. She tossed the scarf skillfully and the dragonlings chirped and chased it, not minding that she had thrown it and not him. Of course, if he had instructed them to ignore her scarf they would have, but he had told them to enjoy it.

"Thank you," she said.

They didn't talk at all the rest of the two hours while the dragonlings played, and Luke passed her three more scarves. He didn't exactly have a plan, but he felt bad for her.

After the dragonlings had enough attention, Anna brought him to breakfast. He wondered how she felt about waiting this long for food. He never noticed his hunger until the dragonlings were fully cared for, but they weren't her dragonlings and he and Anna usually didn't eat until midway through the morning. He hadn't ever considered her schedule before.

He ate his breakfast slowly, as usual, but didn't need instructions. He was getting used to the food. There were a few things he didn't like, a couple he couldn't stand, but overall he enjoyed it. Anna never talked to him during meals after the first few times he had snapped at her, so he could eat in silence. There were rarely other people when they ate and he was grateful for it today, since he didn't know how to treat the other women. After breakfast he stood up and hesitated. Anna smiled at him, less forced than usual.

"Is there anything you want to do today?"

She asked it every day. Sometimes he asked to walk around and she would show him the village, sometimes he just wanted to stay with his dragonlings. Today she sounded more friendly than usual and he knew it was because he had let her play with his dragonlings.

"What do you want to do?" he asked, because he had never asked it before.

She looked surprised again. "I guess we can walk around here. I don't think you've seen the fountain."

"I haven't."

She led him through the building towards the back, where he hadn't been before. They exited to a plaza with a beautiful fountain. Luke went to the edge and sat, running his fingers through the water. Anna sat a short distance away. Suddenly Luke knew what he wanted. He looked at Anna and smiled. He knew what effect his smiles had on people and there was a reason he reserved them. She looked dazzled.

"I wish I could see Eric again," he said. "I would feel so much more comfortable and safe if he were here."

"I'll ask for you," Anna said without thinking.

"Thank you," Luke said, reaching out to rest his hand on hers.

She beamed. She was quite pretty when she smiled, too. Footsteps came from behind them and she turned. Her smile faded and so did his. He looked and saw the older woman. His heart beat a little faster. He still wasn't sure how to act around her.

"Anna, you know Eric can't come here," the woman said.

Luke's eyes narrowed. "Why not?"

"He's not in this tribe. He was only allowed here to bring you."

"Then why didn't the leader of this tribe come and get me? Why did you send Eric?"

The woman smiled patiently. "This tribe is different because it hosts the elder council of dragon tamers. It operates under different rules."

Luke looked at Anna. "Is that true?"

She nodded.

The woman seemed amused. "You trust her now, and not me?"

Luke jumped to his feet and backed away from her. He had always been so good at controlling his mental emotions, but he had never really needed to control his outer emotions before and he was discovering just how bad at it he was. He hated the woman. He was terrified of her. He didn't know what she would do to him if she knew what he had overheard, but he wanted to tell her, to put her in her place, to let her know that he would never be tamed. But rather than do anything that he might regret, he took a deep breath.

"I know the way back to the dragonlings. I'm sure you two have a lot to talk about."

He hurried back into the building and was relieved when Anna didn't follow him. Luckily, he did know the way back and soon he was surrounded by his dragonlings and distracted from most of his worries. He was pouring himself into them again, he knew, but not to the extent he had before. This wouldn't drain him. This would just prevent him from thinking about anything too much.

Anna came in after a while and as usual, sat down without a word. He kept himself distracted even though he knew she could tell what he was doing and she disapproved.

"I'm not draining myself," he said after a few minutes under her scolding stare.

"What are you avoiding? Why were you so nice to me today?"

"Why shouldn't I be nice to you?"

"You've never been nice to me before. Was it so you could see Eric again?" she asked in a gentle voice.

Luke stopped playing and the dragonlings chirped in dismay before flying to the ceiling and playing with each other. They would be fine, he knew. They didn't care who they played with as long as they were playing.

"I don't understand why I can't see him," Luke said. "If he can't come here, why can't I leave?"

"You're safe here," Anna said. "All tamers are safe here. It's the only place we're safe. Out there we rely entirely on our tribe leaders and since you don't have one, everyone will fight over you. Once you're trained, the elders will decide on a leader for you and there won't be fighting. Then you can safely leave."

"I have a leader," Luke pointed out.

"But you're not asking to go back to him anymore, are you?" Anna asked, a hint of a smile on her lips.

Luke blushed. He did want Eric more than Daniel, though he would take either rather than stay here.

"Even if I didn't have a leader, I'm not going to a leader that they choose for me. I'm going to a leader because I want him."

Once those words would have terrified him. The thought that he had the right to choose anything would have been anathema to everything he believed about himself. But ever since Eric had asked Luke if he wanted him to leave, and insisted that Luke answer the question for himself, ever since Luke had realized that he wanted to kiss Eric and taken action on it, he had discovered in himself an insatiable need to think for himself and make his own decisions. He wanted his own life. He had been controlled for too long, by too many people. Never again.

Anna sighed. "The realities of being a dragon tamer are more complicated than you imagine."

"Will I see him again?"

"I don't know," Anna said, reaching out to touch him. He flinched and pulled away from her and she sighed again. "I hope so, for your sake."

He shut his eyes and thought of the elders. They knew he wanted Eric. They would use Eric as a weapon against him, a reward to get him to do what they wanted. If he submitted to their will and did what they wanted, he could see Eric. If not, he would never see Eric again. Luke knew it was true. But he suspected that Anna didn't know it. She seemed genuine. She was a tool for them just as Eric was, just as he was. But what was their goal?

"You never explained why you've been nice to me today," Anna said.

He opened his eyes. "Maybe I felt sorry for you."

"Maybe."

He blushed. "Maybe I realized you aren't the one I should be mad at and I should stop treating you like an enemy."

She nodded slowly. "Thank you for that. I understand you may be mad at the elders right now, but you have to know that no one here is an enemy."

"You know better than that," he snapped, and instantly regretted it.

"What do you mean?"

There was an edge of suspicion in her voice but she covered it well. If he hadn't been listening for it he might not have caught it. He considered his options. He could pretend he didn't mean anything but she wouldn't believe him and would probably tell the other woman and they would both be suspicious. Or he could dive in head-first and see what happened. He jumped to his feet and pointed at her.

"You think trying to tame me doesn't make you an enemy? You seem to know better than to try and I appreciate that, but why do they want me tame in the first place? I will not be controlled by them and I would rather die and take my dragonlings with me than let them tame me," he said in as harsh a voice as he could. He had learned long ago that just as his smile could affect people, so too could his voice when he let the strength of his dragonlings shine through.

Anna was speechless. She seemed pinned to the floor. Then her eyes darted to one corner of the room and she glared at him and stood up, jabbing her finger into his chest and shoving him back a step.

"They have this room under observation, you idiot," she said. "They can't hear us but they are watching us and if you ever pull a stunt like that again and I'm too surprised to respond, I'll have to explain what you said and what am I supposed to say then?"

Luke took another step back, blinking in surprise. It was not the reaction he had expected.

"Now apologize and shake my hand, then play with the dragonlings again," she ordered.

"I'm sorry," he said weakly, extending his hand. She shook it, and he settled into the pillows and called his dragonlings back to him. The female landed on his knee and he stroked her belly as she rolled over and hummed in contentment.

"How on earth did you find out about that?" Anna asked.

"I dream sometimes, and I overhear conversations," he said. "I overheard you and the elder talking about my *taming* last night." His mouth twisted at the word taming.

"Of course you're a dream tamer," Anna said, shaking her head. "Why wouldn't you be?"

"What's that?"

"A rare kind of tamer who can control their mind during sleep. If you brush another tamer they'll recognize you, but as long as you don't, you can go anywhere and overhear or oversee anything. You'll have to learn to control it on your own; I don't think there are any others alive."

Luke scoffed. "Another thing I don't know. Great."

"You would know more things if you asked me questions.

Why haven't you? I know you have them."

"I didn't want you to be the one explaining the answers to me," he admitted. "But that was before."

"How do you think your new knowledge is going to change things?"

Luke shivered. "I don't know. She said this was the last chance, right? And then they'd reassess? You don't think they'd hurt me, do you?"

"The female dragonling is too important," Anna said, but there was some doubt in her voice.

"What does it mean to tame a person? Or a dragon?"

Anna shrugged uncomfortably. "When we tame dragons, we teach them the rules of our society and force them to accept their position in the hierarchy. They are taught to obey the commands of their riders without question. I was never exactly told how to tame a person, but I assumed it was the same principles."

"How do you do it?"

"We touch them," Anna said, clearly still uncomfortable. "Through our bonds. We start slow and simply give them information and reassurance. Then we begin instructing them how they fit in and creating a stronger reward and punishment system. They're usually eager to obey their riders by the time they meet them."

"And I'm refusing the information and the reassurance."

"Not right now," she pointed out.

"What is my position in the hierarchy?"

"Complicated," Anna said, "But I'll do my best to explain. It used to be that the elders were the oldest and the most powerful tamers. There was a council on the West and one on the East. When the female was born here, the elders, being the most powerful, attempted to bond with her. They were all killed. The council was decimated. The mother dragon requested you. The remaining elders contacted the Western council and they also recommended you, though they had very little information about you. The West also gave us permission to keep you in the East since we had lost so many powerful tamers."

The female dragonling crawled inside of Luke's sleeve and poked her head out. One of the males took up the female's spot on his knee and Luke rubbed his belly idly as he listened to Anna.

"In our society, dragon tamers are at the heart of every tribe. Wherever you go, you will be the most cherished member. Within dragon tamers, ranking is more complicated. The council of elders outranks everyone else. Traditionally this is because they are stronger than everyone else but right now it's just because they're older than everyone else and have more wisdom and experience. After the elders, tamers are ranked based on strength. Normally you would be next, followed by me, but since you're not trained you aren't actually counted as a true dragon tamer yet. So right now you have no rank. After you're trained, though, you'll be the highest ranked tamer after the council."

"That is complicated," Luke said. "And a lot of it seems arbitrary. But after I'm trained I get a high rank, so that's not too bad. Okay, I've taken your reassurance and your information and I'm okay with my position. What are you supposed to do to make me want to take orders?"

"You're trying to be tamed?" Anna asked in amusement.

"I'm seeing how you would do it. I'm not saying it's working."

"Well, this is the part I see a problem with. I can't see into your mind, so I don't know what system of rewards and punishments would motivate you to want to obey."

"You know what it is," Luke said, glaring. At Anna's confusion, he looked down at the dragonling on his knee. "Well, they know what it is at least."

"They're not going to threaten your dragonlings," she said. "They would never do that."

"I know," he said.

She looked puzzled for nearly a minute before she seemed

to realize what he was talking about and her eyes widened. "You mean Eric. You think they're going to use Eric to manipulate you into doing what they want."

"Of course they are. I've asked about him too many times. Today was a risk but I wanted to know if you could get to him without them knowing."

"I'm sorry, Luke," she said.

They sat in silence for a while as he played with the dragonlings, sending his attention to them even though his heart wasn't in it at all.

"Do you want to ask me any other questions? You know I'll answer them."

"No thank you," he said as politely as he could. As usual, he didn't want to be rude to her. Especially not now when she was the only ally he had. But he did want to let her know that their moment of closeness was over and he would be retreating back into his shell, for now at least. She sighed and settled into a more comfortable position. After a few more minutes, he extended his hand towards her. One of his males was on his fingers. She reached out to him and the male crawled onto her hand, then nestled into her and started playing with her. She smiled at him. He blushed a little, but kept his attention on the dragonlings and tried to tell himself that he was only being nice because he felt sorry for her, not because he was starting to feel like she might actually be a nice person.

CHAPTER NINE

A Child's Promise

Luke warmed up to Anna considerably over the next three days. He didn't let her feed his dragonlings, but he did let her play with the males almost every playtime and if it was group play he didn't object if the female ended up near her. Sometimes she asked him questions about raising dragonlings and he always answered her politely. Occasionally they were fairly basic questions, but usually they were complex and he suspected that she and the others might not know the answer.

He asked her a question or two, but generally they maintained the strained small talk that had sustained them since he had arrived. They no longer yelled at each other, though, and Luke found it much easier to be kind to her. He had a lot more trouble with everyone else.

He had never seen much of the others, and he still didn't, to his great relief. When he did run into them, he could feel his heart thudding and his cheeks flushing. Anger tingled with fear ran deep in his veins and he would often feel paralyzed. Anna handled them easily and they always smiled at him and were gone before he did anything foolish. Then he could breathe again.

He tossed scarves at his dragonlings on the fourth morning since his confrontation with Anna and waited for her to arrive. She was late, and it was unusual. His dragonlings were already finished playing and he was ready to go eat, but he didn't want to leave without her. He waited a few more minutes, then sent his dragonlings to nap and left the room to find her. He went to the dining hall first, but it was empty. He wasn't sure where else she would be so he began searching the entire building, including the areas he had never been. He was winding down a hallway, positive he was lost, when he heard her voice. He froze. It sounded like she was in pain.

"I wasn't doing it for him! I just wanted to see-"

"Of course you were doing it for him! Whether he commanded you or not is irrelevant. He's done to you exactly what we told you to do to him," an older voice hissed. It sounded like the old woman's, but twisted with hate.

Luke's brow furrowed. Did they think he had tamed Anna? What was she doing that they thought he had commanded? And why would he even want to tame someone? The thought of doing that to a human was repulsive. To be honest, the thought of doing it to a dragon wasn't very pleasant either.

He took a step and a hand grabbed his arm. He gasped and stared at one of the elders who stepped out of the shadows and gripped him tightly. She wore no expression as she dragged him into the room containing a distraught Anna and a furious elder. Anna shut her eyes and turned her face up as if seeking guidance, and the elder's face bloomed into a smile made ugly by her anger.

"Luke," the woman said. She was trying to sound nice, but failing miserably. "What are you doing here?"

"I was looking for Anna," he said weakly.

"To see if she succeeded?"

Luke was mystified. He had no clue what she could have been doing that would anger them so much. There were plenty of things she could be doing to be nice to him, but none of them would get her in trouble. The only thing he really wanted – to escape – was something she had completely ruled out and he didn't see her changing her mind on that.

The anger on the woman's face faded and she stroked Luke's shoulder. He yanked away but with one woman holding his arm tightly and the other determined to touch him, there was little he could do. They were both strong. He put up with her touch. She was comforting, not invasive, and he tolerated it. Anna was watching him again and she looked displeased.

"You're not to blame for her actions," the woman said. "She was a poor choice to pair with you and we regret that now. You won't have to deal with her again."

Luke went stiff in their arms. He couldn't allow this to happen but he didn't know what he could do to stop it. He looked at Anna and she looked frightened as well, but resigned. She didn't know how to prevent it. She was giving up. He couldn't.

"No," he said. "She stays with me."

The woman smiled at him. "You were right to refuse her in the beginning. We should have listened. I know you've come to tolerate her but you should have someone you can trust. We'll find someone better."

"There is no one better," he said, panicking. "I don't want anyone else."

"Her primary role was to answer your questions and you haven't asked her any. Clearly she's not doing well. We'll find you someone you feel safer around."

Luke blushed. He hadn't realized his reluctance would get Anna in trouble. He was about to insist that he would ask her more questions when he realized what they were doing. They were trying to trick him. If he came to rely on Anna for answers, he would bond with her. And if he bonded with her, it would only be a matter of time before she tamed him. He would not let them trap him that easily.

"I will ask questions when I'm ready to ask questions," he said. "And I will ask whoever I please. But I will never ask your puppet. I will never give you control over me."

The hand on his arm tightened and the woman in front of him stopped smiling abruptly. She glared at Anna.

"What did you tell him?"

"I told him nothing," Anna said. "He's not an idiot."

Luke was interested that she hadn't mentioned his dreams,

but he was focused on survival. His dragonlings would be a little upset, but he couldn't help it. He could only shield them so much right now.

The woman turned her attention to him again and he nearly took a step back. There was rage in her eyes, and fire. He had never seen anything like it and wanted to shrink away and surrender.

"You will submit to us, Luke," she said. "You will be ours."

He felt the truth of her words and shuddered. He was frightened. He realized that what Anna had said about his position in the hierarchy wasn't as great as it sounded. He might have a high rank, but it was under the council. They would control him. If he wanted to belong to this society, he would have to give up his freedom.

He could sense Anna's distress and anger. He wanted to look at her but he couldn't tear his eyes away from the fire in the woman's. There was something so familiar about that fire and he knew he had to obey it. He felt small bursts in his mind, not coming from tamers but from his dragonlings. They were trying to tell him something. He allowed them access. He had never denied them; they were treasured and he valued them more than life itself.

They sensed his paralysis and they knew the reason. She was using dragongaze against him. He didn't recognize the term but they were expressing emotions and pictures as well as words and he knew what they meant. It was what he did when he allowed the power of his dragonlings to color his speech and stun his enemies into submission. He had always thought he was the only one able to do it. No one had ever done it to him before and he was furious that he hadn't recognized it sooner. He let his fury fill him. It was the only way to break her hold on him.

He kept her gaze but felt control shift to him. She felt it too and her eyes widened. The woman holding his arm hissed and let go of him as if burned. He was far more powerful than them and he could sense it clearly. They didn't stand a chance against him. If the other woman had been in front of him he could have taken her too. As it was he forced the woman in front of him to her knees.

"You will stop trying to control me," he said calmly. "You will teach me what I need to know and then you will release me. You will not control who I see. While I am here, I will keep Anna at my side and you will stop controlling her. My dragonlings and I will never be in danger from you. You will take care of us with the same level of care and attention as you are currently doing. Do you understand?"

The woman nodded. He wanted more.

"I understand," she whispered.

He was satisfied. He bound the promise into her and into the other woman as well for good measure, then considered. He reached out across the building and felt for the other women he recognized as elders. He bound the promise into them just to be safe. He felt his dragonlings hiss in approval. Then he carefully withdrew the fire from his gaze. This was the most dangerous moment. He had never bound a promise into someone before and he wasn't sure it would work. He felt weak from channeling that much energy and if it hadn't worked, she and the other woman could easily overpower him.

He staggered backwards as the fire left him and Anna was behind him in an instant, arms wrapping around his waist. The woman on her knees bolted up and the other woman came to her side. Both women approached him angrily and he leaned against Anna for support, knowing there was only so much she could provide.

"When you do things like that," the elder woman said threateningly, reaching forward and grabbing his chin, "You put your dragonlings at risk."

He jerked out of her grasp. He wasn't sure if the promise had bound or not. She was threatening him, but she might still be doing that if the promise were in effect because the dragonlings were in danger.

"They're the ones who reminded me what to do," he replied.

"They approve of everything I did."

"They also approved of starving so you could rest."

Luke couldn't argue with that, and reached out to his dragonlings. They were all asleep. He wondered if using his energy like that had drained them in addition to draining him. He needed to get back to them. He shifted in Anna's arms but the woman grabbed his chin again. She wasn't letting him go anywhere and he knew that until Anna was sure the promise had taken hold, she wouldn't let him go either.

He tried to jerk out of the woman's grasp again but she was expecting it and she tightened her grip on his chin. She tilted his face up until he met her eyes fully. She was smiling now.

"Do you have any idea what you were trying to do?"

He flinched at her wording. The promise hadn't taken effect. Terror blossomed in his heart and he felt Anna tense as well. He hadn't meant to drag her into this but he had. He had been so sure he could protect her, so sure he was stronger than them. How had he miscalculated so badly?

"That was a child's promise, Luke," she said. "You didn't put any thought into that at all, did you? Do you realize how many loopholes you left? How easy it is to manipulate you despite what you said? Because of what you said? Binding us to it won't protect you, despite what you think. And you'll never catch us by surprise again."

His terror remained, but was now paired with surprise. He had succeeded. They were bound to the promise, all of them. But they weren't worried about it. In fact, she seemed amused. It was true, he hadn't given any thought to what he said. He thought they would be bound by his intent, not his words. That was how it worked with dragonlings, after all. They obeyed emotions, not words. He should have realized it would be different with humans. And she was right, he wouldn't ever be able to overpower them like that again.

"I want to see Eric," he said weakly. They at least had to allow that.

"You know what the terms are for that."

"You can't control me," he said, frightened. "And you can't control who I see."

"We can't initiate the control, true," she said. Her smile was like a satisfied cat's. "But you can still choose to be controlled by us. And the way you phrased it, we have to release you before we no longer control who you see."

He thought back to his words. It was true. His heart thudded. He would still be at their mercy for when he would see Eric. Tears filled his eyes. They would decide when he had learned enough, and then they would release him. He had no control over that either. What if they never let him go? No wonder they weren't worried. He would be trapped here, alone, until he submitted to them. All he had done with his promise was make things harder for himself and alert them to his powers. He sniffled.

"Please let me go back to my dragonlings. They need me," he said quietly, lowering his eyes.

She examined him for a long moment and then released him.

"As you requested, Anna will go with you. And as you requested, we will treat you with the same kindness and courtesy you have always been treated with. You are very important to us, Luke. Your cooperation is very important. We will honor the intent of your promise when possible. But you would be wise to remember that we are only obligated to obey the words."

She nodded at Anna and Anna started to pull him away.

"Wait," Luke said. Anna stopped and he looked at the woman. "What's your name?"

The woman smiled. "Finally asking questions?"

"I want to know my captor's name."

"Arabella," she said. "You will call me Elder, though."

He didn't say anything, just pulled Anna towards the door. He knew he would never call her Elder. She was not his Elder. If this was the society he had started to enter when he was twelve, then he was grateful he had never been granted access. Maybe Daniel had been protecting him when he hadn't taught him about dragon taming because he knew the reality of the council. There was a bitterness in Luke's heart when he thought about Daniel, but perhaps there shouldn't be. He didn't know why Daniel hadn't taught him and he couldn't judge, just as he couldn't judge Eric for bringing him here. Neither would harm him, yet both of them had.

CHAPTER TEN

Dangerous Summons

Eric watched the lone dragon on the horizon and gathered his confidence. He knew it was Daniel, come to negotiate with him privately. Eric wouldn't leave his territory, though. He would force Daniel to come to him, so if Daniel started a fight, Eric's tribe would have every right to come to his aid. He did ask them to keep their distance for now. If Daniel wanted to talk alone, he would honor that.

Daniel's dragon was beautiful as it came into view. Brilliant blue, with shimmering scales that reflected the ocean's surface below. The dragon was older than Ryseth by several years, which made sense if he had been tamed before Luke had come to them. Dragons only remained tame a certain length of time, depending on their loyalty to their rider and their tamer, and with Daniel's tamer gone and Luke not filling that void, Eric wondered how long the dragons in Daniel's tribe would remain tame. Surely Daniel was worried about it.

Daniel stopped close enough to talk but far enough away that their dragons couldn't attack. Eric could see him clearly as he clutched his dragon and glared.

"Where is he?"

"Safe," Eric said.

"You don't have him then?"

"How do you know he isn't safe with me?"

Daniel smirked. "After your comments about what you were going to do to him? You wouldn't have said he was safe if he was with you. And if he's safe that means you didn't do anything to him, either. What's wrong? Lose your nerve?"

Eric glowered. He hadn't even considered that and he hated being caught out like this.

"Oh, I did something to him. He enjoyed it, too," Eric said.

"Not something I'm worried about," Daniel said, still smirking. "Not once he sees all the things I can offer. He's loved me for years and that's not going to change."

"If you wanted him, why didn't you take him?"

"Unlike you, I have patience," Daniel said.

"And why didn't you teach him?"

"He has a bigger fate."

Eric thought of the Untamable and if Daniel could possibly know. But if he knew, why wouldn't he teach Luke as soon as possible?

"I don't see how shrinking his options gives him a bigger fate," Eric said skeptically.

"It depends on how you look at it, doesn't it?"

Eric glared, but was determined not to ask the next question. Let Daniel figure out what to ask, what to say, how to drive this conversation forward. Daniel was about to, but a flicker to Eric's right caught both of their attentions. It was another dragon heading towards them, not coming from Eric's territory.

"Who is that?" Daniel demanded.

"I don't know," Eric said. "Not one of mine."

They both waited as the dragon drew nearer, and he knew Daniel recognized it at the same time he did because he heard Daniel gasp. The beast was sparkling white with layers upon layers of armor coating his body, and his wings were coated with armor on the upper side as well. Eric was amazed it could even fly. The armor must be incredibly light. The dragon's face was shielded and his eyes deeply set, but Eric could see extremely intelligent, pale blue eyes shining out. The eyes fixed on him as the dragon neared, then pinned Daniel. The dragon stopped and hovered a short distance away.

Untamable.

He felt Ryseth and Daniel's dragon projecting obedience and he tried to do the same, even as he was filled with awe and a great fear that Luke would be the one to control these powerful dragons.

He needs you, the Untamable said, then turned and flew back the way he had come.

Eric stared after him, stunned. He didn't need to be told who needed him. Luke was in danger. He needed to get back to Luke immediately. He turned to Daniel.

"Where is he, Eric?" Daniel asked with a hint of desperation in his voice.

Eric realized that the Untamable had spoken to both of them. It couldn't be. Surely the Untamable wouldn't trust Daniel with Luke, not after what Daniel had done to him.

"Why do you ask?" Eric said.

"I know you heard him too," Daniel said. "Luke's in trouble. He told both of us because he needs to be saved quickly, by whichever of us can get to him first. Now where is he so I can help him? Who has him?"

No, Ryseth said.

Eric was confused. Daniel's reasoning was sound. If the Untamable had told both of them, Luke was in dire danger. If Daniel could reach him first-

He can't. Daniel is a danger. The Untamable do not know everything.

Eric had no choice but to accept his dragon's word for that. After all, he had known Ryseth for years and trusted Ryseth implicitly. He trusted the Untamable, but only in the abstract sense. The decision to ask for Daniel's help didn't make sense and if the Untamable knew what Daniel had done to Luke, he was sure they wouldn't have asked.

"I'm leaving," Eric said. "If you try to follow, my tribe will attack. If you follow with your tribe, you still won't win. I have allied tribes ready to protect me."

"You have to tell me where he is," Daniel said. He sounded

furious. "The Untamable will turn against you if you don't."

Eric paused, but Ryseth sent him a wave of reassurance. "I'll take my chances," he said.

Ryseth didn't even wait for his command to turn and begin flying to the gate. Eric looked back. Daniel also turned and seemed to be flying as fast as possible. He would probably return to the other realm and track Luke that way. In the meantime, Eric needed to get permission to enter a strange tribe's territory and enter the dragon tamer's compound. He had asked before and been politely declined. This time he couldn't take no for an answer and he would sneak in if necessary. He had no idea how or why Luke was in danger, but he would save him.

Eric leapt off Ryseth's back and barely had time to send him thanks before hurtling himself through the gate. Sam and Denis were puzzled but obedient as he ordered them to start heading to the dragon tamer's compound. He went to the main room and contacted the elders.

The primary elder took his call. He couldn't read her expression and that was a bad sign. Normally she was pleased to see him, even the last couple of times when he had asked to see Luke and she had refused him. But she smiled, even though it seemed forced, and was as polite as always.

"Pleasure to see you, Eric. How may I help you?"

"I'm coming to see Luke."

"I'm afraid we can't give you permission yet."

"I'm not asking permission."

Her smile faded. "Is there a reason why you're coming now?"

"I want to see him. I'm tired of your delays. Why? Is there a reason I shouldn't?"

"He's been rebellious lately," she said.

Eric's eyes narrowed. He wasn't sure what that meant but he knew the elders didn't like rebellion. Was that why Luke was in trouble?

"Let me talk to him," Eric said. "He didn't trust you at all at first, you know, but he was willing to stay because I asked him to. He's probably just scared. As long as you're not hurting him, I'll talk to him and ask him to give you another chance."

"He stayed because you asked?" she said slowly. He wondered why that was important.

"Yes," Eric said. "How has he been rebellious?"

"He used dragongaze on me," she said.

Eric sighed. No wonder they were upset. The rules governing dragongaze were extremely strict and someone in Luke's position shouldn't even know how to use it, let alone dare to use it against someone higher in the hierarchy than them. But of course Luke wouldn't know or care about that.

"He used it on me, too," Eric said. "When he didn't want to leave."

"You fought it?" she asked in a skeptical voice.

"I recognized it and after I explained the situation to Luke, he simply demanded we take the dragonlings with us."

She considered him. He felt a little uncomfortable under her gaze. He wasn't sure what she was thinking and it worried him. He still didn't know why Luke was in danger, or if he would have to sneak in to see him. She hadn't given him permission yet, after all.

"Have you ever touched him?" she asked.

The kiss filled his mind and he pushed it away. That was private, between him and Luke only. She had no right to know about it.

"Of course I've touched him. I had to get him here."

The elder smiled. "I know your reputation, Eric. I know how tempting he must have been. Did you touch him?"

Eric shied away from the camera, embarrassed. He had never kept his conquests quiet but hadn't realized the elders knew about them. His tribe knew he regularly took men and women to bed; other tribes knew it too. A few tribes had offered him bribes in the form of their most beautiful members in exchange for favors and sometimes he even accepted. He had always assumed the tamers kept out of those affairs. Because if they knew about them, then they might tell Luke and Luke might feel that their kiss was less meaningful.

He cleared his throat, aware that she was watching.

"I, uh, yes, I may have touched him. Not how you're thinking. I didn't hurt him or pressure him."

The elder laughed and suddenly he could read her again. She was happy and relaxed, and he could relax as well. She wasn't upset at him.

"I assume you're already on your way here," she said. "You have permission to land and visit us for a day or two. Luke will be waiting for you. But you will follow protocol while you're here."

"Of course," he said, delighted that he wouldn't have to sneak into the compound. "He is okay, isn't he?"

"He's upset," the elder admitted. "We had to punish him for using dragongaze."

"How?"

"Some of his freedoms have been limited, and he must stay with Anna at all times during the day," she said.

Eric puzzled over why Luke would be in such serious danger if that was all. There had to be something more, something the elders didn't know about. Well, he would find out when he arrived. He thanked the elder and ended the communication.

Sam and Denis were waiting for him, having heard the conversation as usual. He filled them in on what the Untamable had said as well, but didn't tell them about the connection between Luke and the Untamable. It wasn't unusual for the Untamable to protect tamers, though it was usually only when the tamer was in their realm, so while Sam and Denis were puzzled, they didn't question it. Eric knew that if he were allowed in the compound only one of them would be allowed and the other would have to stay with the ship. They debated, and it was decided that Sam would go with Eric and Denis would protect the ship.

In less than an hour they were landing, and Eric waited impatiently for the ramp to lower so he could open the door.

There was the brief blinding flash of light as his eyes adapted, then he saw the usual crowd. Luke was not there. They must be keeping him in the compound. He bit back his disappointment and hurried down the ramp with Sam at his side. As soon as they approached the main building of the compound, he saw Luke's pale figure outlined in the doorway with the elders at his sides. To Eric's surprise, the dragonlings were circling just outside the door.

As soon as Eric was in range, Luke's face broke into a smile and Eric nearly stumbled at the beautiful sight. Luke rushed forward, breaking away from the elders' hands, and leapt into his open arms. Eric embraced him, aware of the dragonlings now circling him and chirping happily. He buried his face in Luke's hair. He wanted to kiss him, but wouldn't do it in front of everyone. Even hugging him like this was probably too intimate. But there was no way he would let go. Luke lifted his lips to Eric's ear.

"Help me," he whispered.

Eric was stunned, but squeezed Luke tightly to let Luke know that he had heard and he would do everything in his power to obey. Luke was in trouble. Did anyone else know?

Luke finally let go of him, but held his hand. The dragonlings settled on him and even though one of them was very close to Eric's hand, the little male didn't seem to mind.

"Please come in, Eric, Luke," the elder said, gesturing for them to enter the compound.

Luke looked towards the plane as Eric started forward. Luke tugged back on him as if wanting to go to the plane, but Eric pulled him towards the compound. He knew Luke didn't like it and he knew Luke was in trouble at the moment, and he also didn't know how or why Luke was in danger, but this was where Luke belonged. Luke looked glum but followed him back into the building. The elder smiled at them and led them to the dining hall, since it was about dinner time.

Luke stopped to put the dragonlings in their room, holding Eric's hand the entire time. Eric observed Luke from the corner of his eye as they ate. Luke was silent but ate everything he was given. Eric was pleased that he had no difficulties eating; Luke had learned their customs quickly. Anna was sitting on Luke's other side and though Luke was ignoring her, he didn't flinch when their arms brushed against each other. That was progress given how much hostility Luke had shown her the last time Eric had seen them together. The elders asked him a few basic questions, but he knew they didn't want to ask about threats from Daniel in front of Luke so there wasn't much conversation. He would report to them later.

When the meal was finally over, Luke looked up at the primary elder.

"May I speak to Eric alone?" he asked politely.

The elder nodded regally and gestured for them to leave. Sam left as well. He would stand guard outside the door. The elders might talk to him, but Eric had already instructed Sam and Denis not to mention the Untamable to them. They respected the elders, but they obeyed him. He followed Luke towards his private chambers and smiled in anticipation. He wasn't going to stop with a kiss this time.

CHAPTER ELEVEN

Stripping

Luke's heart pounded. He couldn't sort out his emotions. Eric knew he needed help, but Eric didn't know he needed to escape. That was clear. He had wanted to shout to Eric that they needed to get to the plane and run away fast, but he knew it wasn't possible. The local tribe would stop them. So he had come back to his prison and seen the smug satisfaction in Arabella's eyes. But Eric was with him now.

He didn't understand the elder's change of heart. He had been despondent since his confrontation with them, only rousing himself enough to care for his dragonlings. He stopped leaving their room except for the bathroom. He didn't drain himself again, but he did distract himself. They had to bring food to him since he wouldn't leave to eat. Anna stayed at his side, as he had requested, but he didn't talk to her or give her any more access to his dragonlings. She was still allowed to play with them a little, but that was it.

Four days had passed like that, and then Arabella had come in with a fake smile on her face, informing him that Eric would be coming for a couple of days. At first he thought she was lying, but she said he would be arriving shortly and he should freshen up. She didn't seem to be lying, though she refused to explain why when he asked. He hadn't been allowed to go meet the plane and still had doubted that Eric was really coming until he saw the plane landing, and then seen Eric walking towards him. And now Eric was here.

They entered his bedroom and Luke shut the door. Eric looked around.

"They gave you a very nice room," he said. "I'm glad they're taking care of you."

Luke trembled and clutched Eric. "They're not," he whispered.

"I know you're having problems with them right now, Luke-"

"No," Luke interrupted. "Not right now. Ever since I arrived. As long as I'm here. They want to control me. They want to tame me. They tried to get Anna to do it but she couldn't. I tried to force them to let me go but I didn't do a good job and now I'm trapped here."

Eric held him against his chest and stroked his head. "That can't be right," he said slowly. "They don't need to control you, not the way you're saying. They wouldn't control a trained tamer and that's what they were expecting."

"I don't know, Eric, but that's what they want and I'm scared," he whispered.

"Did you try to force them with dragongaze?"

"Yes," Luke said. He explained the promise he had bound the elders to and their amused reactions. Eric winced. He probably agreed with them and so did Luke, now. It was a terrible promise. A child's promise, as Arabella had said. But how was he supposed to know any better?

"Don't worry," Eric said, brushing the hair from his forehead and caressing his cheek. "I'm here now. I'll protect you from anyone who threatens you."

"Even from them?"

"Anyone. But you have to let me determine if they're really a threat."

Luke's heart sank. They would trick Eric. Eric was part of their society and respected them too much to see past their façade.

"Will you at least ask Anna what she thinks?" he whispered.

"Of course," Eric said. "And I'm not blind, no matter what

you think, Luke. These are not the true elders. The true elders were killed trying to bond with the female dragonling. These are just the strongest replacements."

Luke looked up at him. He was sincere. He would see that they wanted to hurt Luke, and he would protect Luke. Luke raised a hand to stroke Eric's face and tilted his face up to kiss him, but Eric stopped him.

"You know they're monitoring this room, don't you? Not listening, but watching?"

"This is my bedroom," Luke said.

"And they would need to know if something happened to you. You told them they could continue caring for you with the same level of attention. You gave them permission to keep spying on you."

Luke looked around the room. He hadn't realized they would still be spying on him but he guessed it made sense, given his words. But this was his bedroom. His sanctuary. This was supposed to be his.

Eric winked at him.

"You haven't been doing anything naughty in here, have you?"

Luke blushed. He knew what Eric was talking about and he had even thought about it a couple of times when memories of the kiss overwhelmed him.

"No," he said primly.

Eric laughed and stroked his cheek. "Wasn't I good enough?"

Luke could feel the heat radiating from his face. He looked down, unable to meet Eric's sultry gaze. He had remembered how good the kiss felt but he had forgotten how immediate it was, how incredibly sexy Eric was, how much he needed the man.

"I'm not allowed to do that," he whispered, knowing the answer would anger Eric. It did.

"You're allowed to do whatever you want," Eric said. "No one controls you. Isn't that what you want?"

Luke nodded.

"Look at me, Luke."

Luke obeyed. Eric's dark eyes were so handsome. He wanted to drown in them.

"I'm going to take you into the bathroom, the one place they wouldn't dare monitor," Eric said in a low, seductive voice. "I'm going to strip you, and you're going to strip me. We'll get into whatever shower or bath you have and I'll teach you about your body so if we're ever separated again I know you can remember me properly."

Luke's mouth was dry and his eyes wide. He was hard, and that had only happened a few times in his life. Never from simple words before. His thoughts were scattered and he could only nod. Eric was going to be naked. Was going to touch him. Was going to arouse him. It was so forbidden he could barely process it. It couldn't be happening. But Eric was pulling him into the smaller room and shutting the door behind them.

Eric knelt and removed his sandals, then Luke's. The tile was cold against his feet. Eric's hands traced the outline of Luke's legs through his pants as he slowly straightened, then moved inward to the edge of his shirt. Luke's breathing grew short. Eric's hands slid under his shirt and caressed his belly as Luke inhaled sharply and shut his eyes. It felt incredible. Eric's hands slowly worked their way up his abs as they lifted his shirt and when they had traced their way across his ribcage, they gently stroked his chest and his nipples. He gasped in surprise.

"Raise your arms."

Eric's breath was warm against Luke's ear and Luke obeyed shyly, eyes still shut. His shirt rose over his head and he heard it land on the floor as Eric pulled him close. He hesitantly opened his eyes to see Eric smiling at him.

"You're beautiful," Eric said. "Your turn now."

Luke licked his lips and his eyes darted to Eric's chest. He took a step out of Eric's embrace and placed his hands on Eric's waist, looking up at Eric through his lashes. Eric closed his eyes just as Luke had done. After waiting a moment to make sure that Eric would keep his eyes closed, Luke fingered the edge of the silk shirt. It was a deep maroon color with pearl buttons running up the front. Eric had given him a much more difficult task.

The shirt wasn't tucked in and Luke started with his hips, slipping his hands under the material to feel skin. Eric was warm and almost like velvet he was so soft. Luke's heart hitched. He wanted more. His hands slid across Eric's sides until they clasped across Eric's back and pulled Eric close to him. He pressed his ear against Eric's heart, needing to hear it beating. He sighed.

"Do you want help undressing me?" Eric asked softly.

Luke blushed. He was enjoying Eric, but he wasn't undressing him. He again backed out of the embrace and caught the wink Eric gave him. He knew Eric was sincere in his offer and would make his help as sensual as possible. But Luke wanted to do this alone.

"I won't help," Eric said. "It's easier if you start at the top though."

Luke nodded, his eyes fixing on Eric's beautiful neck. He stood on his tiptoes and let his lips caress the skin exposed above Eric's shirt. Now it was Eric's breathing that grew short as his eyes fluttered shut. Luke unbuttoned the top button and let his tongue trace down to the newly revealed skin. He could feel Eric's heart pounding under his touch and felt in control and secure. He was no longer afraid as he slid more buttons open and kissed his way down Eric's chest.

When he had enough undone to pull open and expose Eric's chest and shoulders, he let his hands caress the gorgeous skin until he felt sure he had touched every inch with either his lips, tongue, or fingers. Then he continued, button by button, exposing and pulling everything away until he was at Eric's belly button and he let his tongue trace around it as Eric moaned. Eric wrapped his hand in Luke's hair as Luke undid the last button, then Luke straightened and kissed the side of

Eric's neck again as he shimmied the shirt off Eric's arms. Eric was out of breath and clutched him tightly for a few moments before pulling away and staring at him with his usual smile.

"You must feel cheated," he said.

Luke blushed. He hadn't intended to outdo Eric when stripping him, but he had. Eric had been gentle with him, cautious, because Eric knew he had never done anything like it. Luke had been extremely sexual because he knew Eric had plenty of experience and because he wanted it. He wasn't sure what to say. He didn't want to offend Eric or make Eric think that he hadn't enjoyed his touch thoroughly, because he had. It was Eric's gentleness that had given him the courage to do what he had done.

Eric tightened his grip on Luke and nuzzled him.

"Don't worry, Luke. I'll repay you in full," he said seductively as his lips ran across Luke's ear. "You're not undressed yet."

Luke started in surprise and his hands went to his waistband. Eric's hands followed his, then wrapped around to the back and slid underneath. He didn't reach too far underneath, though.

"Do you want to do me first, or should I do you?"

He wanted to feel what Eric would do to him, but with Eric's body and taste fresh in his mind he wanted to keep going. He wouldn't have a guide, but he trusted that Eric would help him if he needed it.

"I want to do you," Luke said firmly.

Eric grinned. He removed his hands and stroked one through Luke's hair, one against his cheek.

"That would please me very much," Eric whispered. "Do you need to know how to start?"

"I want to guess," Luke said. "Just tell me if I do something wrong."

"You won't," Eric said softly.

Luke reached up and kissed him on the lips, then kissed his way down Eric's jaw. He kept kissing down Eric's chest again, letting his hands trail down to brace himself against Eric's hips as he drew lower and lower. He heard Eric's hiss of pleasure as he reached his belly button again and leaned back. Then Luke lowered himself to his knees, keeping his hands on Eric's waist, and heard Eric gasp in surprise and pleasure.

He knew how intimate the position was but he wanted to see all of Eric. He shyly gazed up to see Eric watching him with wonder and a little fear, as if Eric were afraid he was going to go farther than he was ready for. He wouldn't, but he also wasn't sure how far he was ready to go.

He undid the button on Eric's pants, blushing as he felt the bulge against his wrists. Eric was very turned on and he was pleased. He carefully released the zipper, then let the pants fall to the ground. Eric wore briefs, as did Luke, and Luke felt a little relieved. Eric was also bursting to be released. Luke felt himself hardening as he saw the outline of what looked to be a very impressive penis. Unable to help himself, he let the back of his hand brush against it as he raised his hands to the band of Eric's briefs and heard and felt Eric's spark of pleasure.

He lifted the band out and over Eric's penis before bringing it down and even though he removed the briefs carefully, his attention was entirely fixed on the beautiful penis in front of him. The briefs dropped to the ground, unseen, and Luke stared in awe. Eric was completely erect and Luke had never seen that before. Luke had never been allowed to pleasure himself so he had never even seen himself like this. Eric's penis stretched towards his belly and was nearly nine inches long. It was plump and delightfully pink, with a rosy head that Luke was embarrassed to realize he ached to have inside him. And not just in his mouth, though that was his intention at the moment. He wanted Eric deep inside of him.

Luke's hands were on either side of Eric's penis, framing it, and he licked his lips. He wanted it so bad. He wanted to taste all of Eric. He had wanted to kiss Eric and that had been one of the best decisions of his life. This might be another one of those moments. Slowly, hesitantly, he brought his head forward. Eric's hand slid into his hair and stopped him, angling his head up to meet Eric's gaze.

"Let's slow down a little," Eric said breathlessly. "Why don't I undress you first and then we'll see how things go?"

Luke nodded reluctantly against Eric's hand tangling through his hair. Perhaps he had been rushing things. He would still want to taste Eric after being undressed, and the thought of Eric touching him, seeing him, was incredibly arousing. Eric helped him stand and pulled him tight. Luke could clearly feel Eric's penis pressing against him, and he felt his own now too. He hadn't realized how hard he had become.

Eric began by kissing him and then his neck, just as Luke had done. Then, to Luke's surprise, Eric spun Luke in his arms so that Luke's back was pressed into Eric's front. Eric grabbed Luke's arms and silently directed Luke to caress his head and neck while Eric's mouth kept kissing his neck sensually and his hands slid over his chest and played with his nipples. Luke arched his back at the touch, startled at how sensitive he was and how arousing the touch was. As he arched his back, his head leaned against Eric's shoulder, further into the kisses, and his ass ground against Eric's hard on. Images of Eric filling him flashed through his mind and he moaned softly, wanting more of that touch.

With Luke's arms above his head, his body was completely open to Eric and Eric explored it thoroughly, finding erotic spots that had Luke moaning and whimpering and arching his back. Eric was slowly working his way down Luke's body and as he reached Luke's waistband Luke held his breath. Eric nipped his neck and Luke was surprised into breathing just as Eric quickly and easily undid the button and zipper of his jeans and dropped them to the floor in a single move.

Luke tensed. He was uncertain now. He knew he wasn't as impressive as Eric and he knew Eric had a lot of experience. What if he didn't measure up? Eric's mouth caressed his neck and Eric's hands returned to some of the erotic spots higher on his body until Luke gasped for breath and knew that he was erect, something that had never happened to him before.

Finally, Eric's hands returned to his briefs and carefully pulled them off without touching him. He was a little reassured that Eric hadn't seen him, couldn't be disappointed yet.

Then Eric touched him. Luke cried out and went stiff in Eric's arms. Everything went dark just as it had when the elder had touched his mind. Memories of the touch flooded through him. The touch had done what Eric was doing. It had slithered along his limbs and aroused him, tingled through his penis, taunting him, teasing him into arousal and then backing out just before he came. It had told him he was never allowed to come until it could touch him in the flesh. His parents never believed him. Why would they, when there was no physical evidence?

Sound and light returned and Eric was cradling him on the bathroom floor. Neither of them were aroused anymore. Eric was kissing his face over and over again and rocking him in his arms, murmuring reassuring words. He clutched Eric and Eric's body relaxed.

"Oh, Luke," he whispered. "What happened?"

Luke hesitantly told him about the touch, how it had come to him as a boy and how he had welcomed it at first but how it had quickly taken advantage of him. He hadn't told Arabella any details, but he told Eric everything about what the touch had done to him and his hurt when no one had believed him or protected him. Eric held him close and he could feel Eric's pain as sharply as his own. He knew without question that if Eric had been his first leader, he would have told Eric and Eric would have tracked the man down. Eric would still track him down, but it would take much longer since so much time had passed.

When Luke had poured his heart out, he lay limp in Eric's arms and cried.

"I'm sorry, Eric," he whispered. "I don't know if I'll ever be able to touch you the way I want. I didn't know that would happen. I don't know how to stop it."

"We'll find a way," Eric said. "If we both want it, there will be a way."

Luke loved his confidence and nestled against him, closing his eyes. He thought of ways to get close to Eric and paused over one, the most obvious way. It would be opening himself completely and risking being just as vulnerable to Eric as he had been to the touch, but he trusted Eric not to take advantage of him the way the touch had. And if he wanted Eric inside of him, this might be the only way.

"I want you, Eric," he said, opening his eyes and gazing up at Eric. "I know how we can be together."

CHAPTER TWELVE

Shattered Pieces

Eric cradled Luke. He felt as though a dragon had just rammed into him at full speed. First Luke stripping him like that, nearly sucking him off if Eric hadn't stopped him. Eric had only barely had the self-control to stop him and still wondered what would have happened if he hadn't. Would that touch have set off Luke's memories too? Then feeling Luke's body beneath his hands, supple and clearly aching for more, and right when he went to give him more Luke had panicked and fainted. He had expected a little panic, given Luke's tension earlier, but he had never dreamed that someone – let alone a tamer – had abused Luke as a child and that abuse was still haunting him.

He had seen a tamer who had been abused before. She bore deep scars all of her life, not physical but obvious to everyone who met her. She was almost incapable of independent thought and dependent on her leader, who treated her gently. The tamer who had abused her had shattered her mind, the other tamers said. She was still powerful and could use her abilities, but could only use them at others' commands.

He wondered about Luke. When he first met Luke, Luke was strongly under Daniel's control. He had disobeyed Daniel's order and stayed by the dragonlings, true, but that was probably the first time he had ever acted on his own since entering their society when he was twelve. Eric had needed to coax him into making up on his own mind when deciding whether or not Eric should stay. But once he had made that decision, Luke had broken through Daniel's control quickly with his request for a kiss and then the independence he had shown here.

Part of it had to do with the dragonlings, Eric knew. Luke drew confidence from them; it was why he was able to use dragongaze without being taught. Before now, Luke and his dragonlings had been relegated to the background and dismissed as unimportant, so Luke's confidence had likewise been low. After the kidnapping, Luke knew Eric wouldn't hurt him because he was a tamer and Eric needed him. And now that Luke had the female dragonling, he had thought no one would hurt him because they needed her protected. Luke must have been shaken to his core when he realized the elders had been plotting against him despite the female dragonling. If that was true, Eric amended. If Luke believed it, though, Eric was inclined to trust him.

But Luke's behavior made sense if he had been scarred by a tamer as a child. He was healing, luckily, but if the elders were trying to control him then they weren't helping the process. They were furthering the damage. He wondered if they knew Luke had been abused. Luke hadn't mentioned anything about that, just about the actual experience, and Eric knew he hadn't given any of them access to his mind, but they were still dragon tamers and might sense it.

As Luke met his eyes with hope and spoke of a solution, Eric let some hope fill him as well. He knew Luke wasn't talking about being together physically. He didn't really know what Luke was talking about, but if Luke wanted it then he wanted it too. He kissed Luke softly.

"I want you, too, Luke," he said. "However you want."

Luke smiled bashfully and wound their fingers together. His smile was still breathtaking even though Eric had seen it several times now. Luke instructed him to get into a comfortable position and they both curled on the floor, Luke cradled in his arms. Luke was nervous, he could tell, but Luke stroked his palm and kissed it before placing it under his cheek with confidence. Luke closed his eyes. Eric rested his head on the floor and closed his eyes as well, focusing on Luke.

He felt something near his mind. He recognized it as a dragon tamer. He had never told anyone but he could sense nearby dragon tamers. It was how he could tell how powerful they were. They couldn't sense him and couldn't speak to him, but he could sense them. He had no other abilities, however; he couldn't control his mind or reach out beyond the sphere of his mind. He could only sense what came near.

This touch drew close to him and to his surprise, it leaned against him. Nothing had ever touched him before and the tamer was warm and gentle. It was Luke. He wanted to welcome Luke, but he didn't know how. To his surprise, Luke didn't touch him but enveloped him and seemed to draw him into a large glowing orb just outside him. There were thick shields around the orb but they withdrew just enough to let him in and then snapped back into place. He was set down on a strange glass floor and stared up in wonder.

Floating above him, centered in the oval room, was a sphere emitting a light so brilliant he shouldn't have been able to see but so gentle it didn't hurt his eyes at all. It was surrounded by a crystalline web of glass, but Eric could see hairline cracks running through the glass and a small place where the glass was missing. He knew without asking that Luke's mind had been shattered just like the other dragon tamer's, but Luke had managed to piece it together again.

"The mother dragon who summoned me helped me find the pieces and put them back where they belonged," Luke's voice said. "I think she hid the memory of the touch at the same time."

Eric looked to his left, startled to see Luke standing there. The orb of light above him was undeniably Luke, but Luke's body next to him was solid.

Luke gestured around them.

"All of this is me. If I want a body, I can have one. And I want a body with you here."

"You're beautiful," Eric said, looking back at the light. He moved behind Luke's body and wrapped his arms around his waist, pulling him back. Luke sank into him and wrapped his arms around Eric's arms.

"I'm broken," Luke said. "I've never been able to find all the pieces."

"I'll help you look," Eric said.

"Thank you," Luke said in a very small voice. Eric kissed his neck. As if there was any doubt. He would help Luke in any way he could. He could feel Luke's gratitude pouring through him along with his love. Then the body in his arms vanished and he felt Luke's touch lifting him again. He didn't fight as it brought him back out of the shields and carefully placed him within his mind. When he opened his eyes, they were in the ordinary world, lying on the bathroom floor. Someone was knocking on the door.

He helped Luke stand and kissed him briefly before opening the door a crack to see Anna, looking annoyed. He was also annoyed. He and Luke had just shared something magical and she was interrupting.

"What do you want?"

"The elders want to see you, Eric," she said. "I need to talk to you first."

"Can't they wait?"

"They've been waiting," she said, sounding exasperated. "For half an hour."

"Couldn't they give us any time?"

"They gave you an hour before asking for you," she said. "Surely it doesn't take that long, even for you."

Eric was surprised. He had no idea that much time had passed. They must have spent longer than he thought in Luke's mind, or else the transition between minds had taken a long time. They would have to be careful of that when they did it again. It was a when, not an if, because he *would* help Luke recover the pieces.

Luke was blushing deeply and getting dressed. Eric reached

for his pants and glared at Anna again.

"What do you need to talk to me about?"

"You might be in danger," she said. "Have you touched him?"

Eric laughed. "Darling, I took him to an unmonitored room for an hour and a half and you can tell I'm naked. What do you think I was doing to him?"

"That's not what I- Of course you-" She shook her head. "I mean did you touch his mind?"

Eric looked at her in shock. She couldn't have known. It had just happened. Had the tamers felt what had happened? He felt violated. No wonder Luke felt like he was in danger.

"That's none of your business," he said sharply.

"Damn it, Eric," Anna said. "Why?"

Luke shoved past him, fully dressed, and opened the door, slipping through and pushing Anna back.

"It really is none of your business," he said.

"Stay angry while I explain, Luke," she said. Luke nodded. It seemed like they had done this before. "There are two reasons why a dragon can't be tamed. Either the dragon is Untamable, which is usually obvious. Luke, you have shields but someone has slipped by them before so we know you don't fall into that category."

"Wait, you know about that?" Eric said, stepping into the room to grab her despite his partial nudity.

"Shut up, Eric," she said. "Get dressed. Yes, we know about it. The other time a dragon can't be tamed is if it's already tamed by someone else. The elders have decided that you've already been tamed, Luke."

Luke's eyes went wide. "You mean by that other tamer when I was a child?"

"No," Anna said. "You didn't even remember him. They think it's Eric."

"Me?" Eric asked, puzzled. He was pulling on his clothes. "I'm not a tamer."

"You said you'd touched him. That's how we tame."

"But that was just now."

"No," Luke said guiltily. "We did it when we kissed, too. You probably didn't know what it was. I didn't. I do now."

"Well, it's only their suspicion now but if you confirm it, Eric, they're going to try to control you just to get to Luke. You have no idea how much they want him. They won't hesitate to break you or him if it means controlling him."

"What do they know about him?" Eric asked, wondering if they knew about the Untamable. That was the only reason he could think of that would make them want to control Luke so much.

Anna looked confused for a second.

"He's the most powerful tamer we've ever seen," she said. "What do you know about him?"

"Has he been in the other realm?"

Again Anna didn't seem to understand why his questions were relevant. She didn't know about the Untamable, but they wouldn't have told her even if they knew.

"No," she said. "They've been waiting for him to ask."

Eric was completely dressed and after a quick glance in the mirror he knew he was presentable. He would see the elders and navigate the conversation carefully.

"Thank you for the warning, Anna," he said. "Please remain with Luke. I know the way."

He stroked Luke's hair, not wanting to kiss him where they would be observed, and headed towards the council room where he knew the elders would be waiting for him. He heard Luke request to go to his dragonlings and he was glad. They would calm Luke as he waited for Eric to return.

CHAPTER THIRTEEN

Obedience

Eric slowed as he approached the room. He wasn't sure what he was going to say, but he knew what to avoid saying now. It was a good thing Anna was on their side. Taking a deep breath, he entered the room to see the five elders sitting in a half circle on comfortable chairs. There was a single chair centered in the room clearly intended for him. He would be surrounded by them. No matter who he looked at, at least one other elder would be able to observe his reactions. He would need absolute control for this.

He had been in situations like this before when negotiating with other tribes, but usually his tribe was the one surrounding others. He had only been at a disadvantage a few times, but as long as he kept his calm and answered as close to the truth as possible, he would be fine. Unfortunately, he didn't have an end goal in mind going into this negotiation, and he didn't even know what he was negotiating for. He also didn't know their end goal or what they wanted. His lack of knowledge put him at an extreme disadvantage; he couldn't push to get anything, he knew, but he could prevent them from getting anything that he didn't want them to have. Not an ideal situation by any means, but it would have to work.

Eric sat in the chair and smiled at the primary elder. He was outwardly relaxed, as was she. There was no reason for hostility, after all.

"I apologize for making you wait, elder," he said humbly.

"No need to worry, Eric," she said with a smile. "I trust Luke is pleased to see you again."

"He is," Eric said simply, refusing to expand on that statement. Let them ask if they wanted more.

"Have you spoken to him about how important it is for him to stay here?"

"Not yet. We haven't had a chance."

"You can't expect us to believe that you were *occupied* that entire time," she said, and some of the other elders hid smiles at the word.

"We were barely *occupied* at all," Eric said, a little anger building up inside of him even though he tried to push it down. "We did spend most of the time talking, just not about that."

"I suppose it wouldn't take you long with a boy like that, would it?" the elder said, leaning back and stroking the arm of her chair casually.

Was she deliberately baiting him? He couldn't hide his anger as her words stung him to the core and even though he got himself back under control quickly he knew the elders had seen it. Let them see it, then. He allowed his anger to show.

"What is that supposed to mean?"

"A young boy, scared and confused and in a foreign place, who you've already taken advantage of to some degree-"

"I did not take advantage of him," Eric snapped. "I kissed him, that's all."

"Against his will?" the elder asked.

"No," Eric said. "It wasn't."

The primary elder looked a little surprised but continued anyway.

"Nevertheless, given the way he's been begging to see you, I doubt it would take you five minutes to do whatever you wanted to him."

Eric wished he could stand up and slap her for thinking such thoughts about Luke. He wasn't bothering to hide his emotions at all because he knew this wouldn't put Luke at risk.

He was about to reveal some personal information about Luke, but if Anna knew about it, the elders knew about it too.

"I *was* planning on doing more than kissing," he said, "But before we even got close, he blacked out. Why didn't you tell me about the tamer who abused him?"

All of the elders looked surprised now and exchanged looks. They all knew about the tamer, then, but they must not have thought it would have affected Luke like this.

"We knew a tamer had abused him because of the way Luke shields his mind and because he fainted when he tried to touch my mind," the primary elder said slowly, "But that's no reason why he should have done it with you. Did he explain why it happened?"

"Yes," Eric said, wondering if he needed to keep the reason a secret or if he should share it in an attempt to get sympathy and therefore support from them. "It was most of what we talked about. Why haven't you been helping him recover if you knew he'd been abused?"

"Without being able to see his mind, we have no idea how deep the damage goes," the elder said. "And without him telling us more, we don't know what kind of help he needs or how to track the tamer who did it to him. Why did he react to what you were doing?"

Eric was calm now, not angry, and he considered his options. He could say it was private, but they would pressure him for an answer and possibly not trust his future answers. The answer was private, but not so private that it was worth losing their trust over.

"He wasn't abused as most tamers are," Eric said, allowing the hate he felt for whoever had broken Luke to shine through. "He was sexually abused and no one believed or protected him."

"A tamer would never do that," the elder said dismissively. "They might take advantage of someone's mind and break their defenses, but they would never enter a body fully enough to do what you're saying. No one would be able to survive that sort of assault."

"Well, Luke survived," Eric said.

"Were you touching him when he told you?" the elder asked.

This was the key question and he now knew how to answer.

"Of course," he said. "I was cradling him the whole time. No one had ever listened to him before and I wasn't about to let him feel abandoned again."

The elder looked annoyed, just like Anna had, and he knew she would continue to ask in different ways until she got the answer she wanted.

"Did you feel anything when you held him?"

Eric sat up straight and looked as offended and furious as he could.

"Are you seriously asking me if I got off listening to how he was abused? No matter what you think of my sexual activities, I would never hurt or force anyone and the thought of someone forcing someone else – a child, no less – into sex is absolutely horrific. Do you have any actual questions or did you just want to insult me?"

He hoped that was enough to change the topic. Maybe they could get into reports on Daniel. That was a slightly easier topic, though he would still have to skirt around the issue of the Untamable who had approached him. That was easier than talking about Luke, though.

"One more question and then we'll switch subjects," the elder said and Eric felt some of his tension ease. He was still extremely on edge, though, and even though he had faked some of his fury, he hadn't faked all of it.

"Eric," the elder said, "Do you love Luke because of his beauty or because of his power?"

"There's more to him than just those two things," Eric pointed out.

"So why do you love him?"

"He's unlike anyone I've ever known and I want him in my life," Eric said with a glare.

Then he hesitated, because he realized she had goaded him into saying something but he wasn't sure what. He knew it was a trap, though, from her satisfied smile and the way the others were looking at him like he had just made a huge mistake and they were very pleased. But what had he said that would make them think that?

"You do love him, though," the elder said, and he realized his mistake.

He had made his feelings for Luke too clear. Now they knew how precious Luke was to him and they could use Luke against him just as they used him against Luke. He didn't know what to say, so he remained silent.

"Let's talk about why you came here when you did," the elder said. "What prompted your visit?"

"I told you," Eric said. "I was tired of your delays."

"You're sure you weren't told he was in danger?"

Eric was surprised. How did they know about that? If they knew, he had better come clean about it quickly before they stopped trusting him. He needed their trust if he had any chance of helping Luke.

"I was told he was in danger," Eric admitted. "By one of the Untamable. But Ryseth advised me not to share that."

"And you thought your dragon outranked one of the Untamable?" she asked skeptically.

"I know Ryseth and trust his judgment," Eric said.

"Did anyone else hear the warning?"

He hesitated. If they knew he had been warned, Daniel must have told them. But if they had been told by a dragon in the other realm, they wouldn't know. Dragons frequently gossiped, after all. Still, sticking with the truth was his best option.

"Yes," he said. "I was speaking with Daniel at the time."

"Why did you pause before answering that? Did you perhaps disobey the Untamable?"

They had to know what had happened and that meant they were in communication with Daniel. He answered quickly this time.

"Daniel wanted to know where Luke was. I don't trust him so I didn't tell him. Besides, there was no way he could reach Luke before me and it sounded like Luke was in imminent danger."

"Do you still think he's in imminent danger?"

Her voice carried a clear warning this time and he tried to answer as quickly as possible while still planning his answer carefully.

"Yes, but I don't know what from. He's frightened of something but won't say what."

"I see," the elder said. "Well, you don't need to worry about that anymore. You can remain here, but we'll need to restrict you to your ship unless we specifically ask for you."

"What?"

Confused, Eric looked at the other elders and saw agreement on their faces. No one was standing up for him. He had done something wrong. Lying about why he had come was a mistake, but he had explained it well enough, he thought. It was no reason to kick him out. There was something else going on and he had the feeling it had to do with the danger to Luke.

"Why can't I stay here?" he asked.

"You disobeyed the Untamable," the elder said. "Daniel was forced to go to the Western Council for help, and they were more than happy to tell him that Luke was here. He just arrived. We feel that Luke would be safer in his care than in yours."

Eric's stomach flipped. Daniel was here. Daniel would have access to Luke again. How would Luke react? He longed to be with Luke but he knew the elders would be watching him closely to make sure he wasn't.

"You remember what Daniel did to Luke, don't you?" Eric asked. "His crimes against Luke can't be forgotten."

"We've spoken with Daniel and he has agreed to do his duty in training Luke," the elder said. "Our decision on this is final, Eric. You and your man will be escorted to your ship now. If you want to see Luke again, you would be advised to cooperate."

Eric was stunned. Two members of the local tribe appeared on either side. He stood and allowed them to lead him and Sam to the ship. He couldn't resist. He needed to see Luke again. He had no other options but to cooperate and hope they allowed him to see Luke, and hope that Luke was still himself after spending time with Daniel.

CHAPTER FOURTEEN

Old Habits

Luke played with his dragonlings. He was distracting himself again, but this time Anna didn't scold him. She probably wished she could distract herself as well. He wondered how Eric was doing. He passed Anna a scarf absentmindedly and she tossed it up. The males chased it but the female was firmly planted on Luke's knee as he stroked her belly. They were at peace because he was projecting peace, but inside he was consumed by uncertainty and fear. Even distracting himself wasn't working.

The door started to open and Luke sat up. Eric was back. The female grumbled but joined the males in the air. The door opened all the way and a familiar man walked in. Luke gasped. It was Daniel.

His eyes drank in the sight of his leader. He had forgotten how handsome Daniel was with his pale blonde hair and blue eyes, his lean body, his square jaw. Daniel simply looked at him. Luke recovered from the sight of him quickly and pushed himself forward onto his knees, placing his hands on the floor and bowing his head. Shame rushed through him as he thought of all the ways he had betrayed his leader.

"I'm sorry, Daniel," he whispered.

Daniel walked up to him and placed a hand under his chin, forcing Luke to look up to him.

"If you had obeyed me," Daniel said in a disappointed voice, "None of this would have happened."

Luke couldn't stand to see the disapproval in Daniel's eyes but Daniel forced him to keep looking.

"I know," Luke said, ashamed and frightened. "I won't disobey you again."

Daniel stared at him with an unreadable expression for a long moment, then sighed.

"Get up, Luke."

Luke slowly got up until he was facing Daniel. He thought of all the things everyone had been telling him about Daniel and all the things Daniel hadn't taught him. Even though he wanted to trust Daniel, there was still a little doubt about Daniel's motives towards him. He wanted to ask Daniel why he hadn't taught him, but questioning Daniel was not allowed. Fortunately, Anna didn't follow the same rules.

"You must be his leader," Anna said. "Why are you here? You you have no place here. You purposefully denied him knowledge about what he is."

"The elders invited me here," Daniel said, giving her a dismissive glance. "They understand my motives. You don't need to."

His answer wasn't reassuring to Luke, since the elders were his enemies. But Daniel couldn't be an enemy, could he? He might have kept Luke from learning his true purpose, but the elders had barely told him anything as well. Even Anna hadn't really told him anything because she was waiting for him to ask.

"Luke," Daniel said with warmth in his voice, "Let your dragonlings play with her for a while and come with me."

Luke was so distracted by how kind Daniel sounded that he barely processed the request. When he did, though, he stiffened and stared at Daniel in disbelief. Was Daniel asking him to get rid of his dragonlings? Luke would never do such a thing, not even for his leader.

"They don't belong to her," he said firmly.

"No, they don't," Daniel said. Now he sounded irritated. "Give them permission to play with her while you're occupied.

They need more play. I'm not telling you to give up their bond, just allow them to play with someone else."

Luke looked down, ashamed that he had misinterpreted Daniel's reasonable request and challenged his leader. They did need more play and if he needed to follow Daniel, it was smart to let them play with Anna. They had played with her before, after all. The males had, he corrected himself. He was a little leery of letting the female play with Anna, but he knew Anna wouldn't steal any of his dragonlings.

He took a few steps away from Daniel and summoned the dragonlings. They perched on him and he stroked each one and gave it permission to play with Anna if it wanted. He did the female last and paused before telling her, finally looking up at Anna for the first time since Daniel had entered the room. She looked incredulous with an edge of panic, but she pulled the box of scarves closer to her. He gave his female permission to play with Anna and she flew over and landed in the box of scarves, immediately burying herself in them.

Daniel waited for him at the door and Luke's shoulders slumped as he followed Daniel out into the hall. He usually only left his dragonlings when their needs were fully met and they were asleep. He had never left them when were still in need, and right now they still needed attention. Anna could give them physical affection, but only Luke could give them the mental affection they needed. They would be fine without him because he took such good care of them normally, but it was still a sacrifice for him.

He was so deep in his thoughts that he didn't notice where they were going until Daniel shut the door behind them. He looked up and realized they were in his bedroom. Daniel's arm reached to circle his waist and pull him backwards into his front and Luke's mind flashed to him and Eric in this pose when Eric had stripped him. He flushed and tried to pull away but Daniel didn't let him.

"You're mine, Luke," Daniel said, his breath tickling Luke's ear. "I won't let anyone steal you from me again."

Luke leaned back against him, feeling tears in his eyes. He had failed Daniel, and Daniel had the right to claim him again. But as much as he wanted to go back to Daniel, thoughts of Eric kept flashing through his mind. Daniel was treating him almost like property, but Eric always saw him as a person. But he did belong to Daniel and Daniel had every right to possess him. He didn't know what to do or what to think, but he never wanted to disappoint Daniel again.

"What did Eric do to you, darling?" Daniel asked, slowly spinning them so Luke's back was against the wall and Daniel had him pinned. But while he had enjoyed being pinned by Eric, this was far too forceful and domineering to trigger any romantic feelings. Daniel's question, too, was too intrusive and Luke looked away rather than answer. Daniel cupped his face and forced Luke to look at him.

"You will answer me, Luke," he said in a voice that couldn't be refused.

"I- I don't know," he whispered. "He didn't hurt me."

He was scared to say anything because everything he had done with Eric violated the rules Daniel had set for him. Daniel was already angry at him and he didn't want to increase that anger. He was afraid of what Daniel would do to him if he found out the truth. He also knew he couldn't share the whole truth because he couldn't let the elders know that Eric had touched his mind. He didn't want to lie to Daniel, though. It was a terrifying situation.

"Did he kiss you?" Daniel asked, leaning forward until their foreheads nearly touched. His hand was still on Luke's cheek and he stroked it gently.

"Yes," Luke said.

"Did you enjoy it?"

Luke flinched. He had to tell the truth but he knew Daniel wouldn't like it.

"Yes," he whispered.

Daniel's eyes grew hard. He stopped stroking Luke's face but still held it in place, pressing against Luke until he was flat on the wall.

"That kiss belonged to me," Daniel said.

"You don't even like me," Luke said, confused.

Daniel had never shown desire for him before, even though Luke had looked for it. He cherished Daniel's rare caresses and occasional praise, and he wished Daniel thought of him that way, but there had never been any clear evidence.

"You were so young and innocent, Luke," Daniel said, stroking his cheek again. "I would never take advantage of you. I was waiting until you were old enough to make your own decisions before I told you my feelings."

"I'm old enough now," Luke said softly.

"Yes, you are," Daniel said, still cradling his cheek. "And that bastard stole your first kiss from me."

"He didn't steal it," Luke said. He knew he would be punished for this but he couldn't lie to his leader. "I asked him."

"You what?"

Daniel's hand slid to Luke's throat and his eyes narrowed to slits. Luke trembled and looked down, unable to meet Daniel's disapproval.

"I asked him to kiss me," Luke said so quietly he was surprised Daniel could hear it.

Daniel jerked away from him but kept his hand on Luke's throat, squeezing it. He lifted his other hand and Luke had no time to prepare before Daniel slapped him across the left side of his face. Luke cried out in pain and Daniel let go of him. He slumped to the floor, cradling his face. Everything stung and he could taste blood. His head was ringing. Daniel had hit him before, but never on the face. Daniel always said he was too pretty to hit in the face.

Luke began to cry as he cradled his face. He could feel it swelling and bleeding along his cheek bone. Daniel, as always, was wearing a ring and it had cut into his skin. Luke's lip was split and burned with agony. He wondered how much it was going to bruise and if he'd ever recover. He wondered if the pain would ever stop. All he could do was hold his agonizing face and hope that Daniel didn't do anything else.

"Get up, Luke," Daniel said in a cold voice. "Now."

Luke shook as he managed to get to his feet. He still held the side of his face that burned and ached. He couldn't look at Daniel. He was terrified what Daniel would do to him.

"Did you ask Eric for anything else?"

Luke wished he could sink into the wall rather than be here facing Daniel. Daniel had every right to be angry, though, and every right to punish him. He had disobeyed Daniel and Daniel was his leader.

"I asked him to drive me to the female's nesting grounds," Luke said. "That's all."

Daniel took his hands, forcing him to let go of his face. Luke was still crying, though he was trying not to. Daniel was examining his face as Luke shut his eyes. He felt cries from his dragonlings and realized he hadn't been shielding them. They were as frightened as he was. He instantly sent them a wave of reassurance and hid his emotions from them.

"You will obey me from now on, won't you, Luke?"

"Yes," Luke said without hesitation. Anything to avoid more punishment.

"Good," Daniel said, reaching up to trace the side of Luke's face that was bruised from his slap. "I can't have a tamer who disobeys me."

Luke kept his eyes shut and his head down. He didn't want Daniel to think of him as a threat. He didn't want to be a threat. He only wanted to obey his leader.

"Look at me, Luke," Daniel said.

Luke cautiously lifted his head and looked at Daniel. Daniel looked surprisingly gentle. He leaned forward and kissed Luke's forehead. Once Luke would have luxuriated in that touch and dreamed about it for weeks. Now it just brought chills to his spine.

"We're going to eat dinner with the others, and then we're going to come back here and I'm going to make sure he doesn't take anything else from me."

Luke wasn't entirely sure what that meant, but it felt ominous. He also didn't want to eat with anyone and have them see his face. He was scared of what people would think. It was proof that Daniel owned him. He would just have to obey Daniel and hope that Daniel never hurt him like this again.

CHAPTER FIFTEEN

Conscious Attack

Luke kept his head down and his shoulders slumped as he followed Daniel to the dining hall. The elders were on one side, as usual, and Anna was on the other. Luke only barely managed to keep from bursting into tears at the sight of them. He tried to focus on his dragonlings and sending them love and assurance. That helped him control his own emotions better.

Daniel gestured for him to sit next to Anna and he did. Daniel sat on his other side. He kept his eyes down so he wouldn't have to look at anyone. Luckily, no one commented on the obvious bruising and cuts on his face, not even Anna. He wasn't looking at anyone so he couldn't see their reactions. He didn't want to see their reactions.

To his surprise, he and Daniel were served Western food. Luke had assumed that the cooks here didn't know how to make it, since he had always been given what everyone else ate, but the food was delicious and familiar and quite a relief after struggling with the food for so long. But even though the food was good, it was difficult to eat with a split lip and he found himself taking smaller bites than normal and having to pause frequently. The bleeding had stopped, but threatened to start again at any moment.

After they had finished, Daniel wrapped an arm around his shoulders possessively and looked at him, drawing a finger along his jaw to tilt Luke's head until Luke met his gaze. Luke was frightened, but couldn't disobey.

"Luke, I want you to open your mind to the elders," he said.

Luke's eyes went wide and he tried to pull away but Daniel was holding him too tightly.

"I can't," Luke said.

"What happened before will not happen a second time," Daniel reassured him. "Now obey me and drop your shields."

Luke lowered his eyes and felt the armor around his mind. Ever since the mother dragon had taught him how to place those walls, he had never lowered them completely. He could lower them in places, like when he reached out to Arabella or when he enveloped Eric, but he didn't even know if he could drop them. He searched through his mind for some way to lower them and found nothing. They were too ingrained into him. It was impossible. He couldn't obey Daniel.

He met Daniel's eyes and felt his own eyes filling with tears.

"I can't," he said. "I don't know how."

Daniel's grip on his jaw tightened.

"You've let me in before," he said. "You know how to do it."

Luke trembled. It was true, he had opened his mind to Daniel before, but Daniel wasn't a tamer, so he couldn't feel how limited his access had been. Daniel hadn't actually been in his mind; he had only touched a tendril of Luke's mind that Luke had extended to him. And it had only been once. He could do the same for the elder's, but they would know he wasn't opening his mind to them. They would want more and he couldn't give them more.

"I can give them what I gave you," Luke said. "But it isn't opening my mind."

"Then do it," Daniel said.

Luke lowered his head again and faced Arabella. She wore a smirk and he could feel her mind slithering towards his. The other elders weren't far behind her. He was completely outnumbered and knew they were going to tear apart whatever he extended to them in an attempt to figure out how to open his mind completely. It was going to be extremely painful and he would have to guard his dragonlings carefully to prevent them from feeling anything.

He took a moment to place a strong shield around the dragonlings, then he strengthened the shields on his own mind, then he gathered a bit of himself that he was willing to sacrifice. It was one of the blank spaces in his memory and he knew they would get nothing out of it. Unfortunately, his consciousness had to extend itself as well, but it would snap back into his shields if he were in too much pain or if they tried to read him too deeply.

With a deep breath, he cautiously extended a tendril towards the lurking minds of the elders. They didn't pounce right away. They were probably waiting to see how much of himself he would expose. He kept his consciousness right against his walls, but allowed the blank memory to drift outwards towards them. When they decided that was all they would get, they struck in a powerful and coordinated attack.

Three of them struck his consciousness directly and two went after the memory. The memory was quickly devoured and all of them battered his consciousness to gain access. He wanted to withdraw but knew that Daniel had ordered him to let them in. He was confused and frightened. He kept his consciousness firmly attached to his shields but didn't withdraw, not knowing whether or not he should allow them into his consciousness. They weren't making it easier with their devastating attacks. His mind huddled against itself. They were attacking so much that he could feel his control over the dragonlings slipping. He had to block them out soon but he was afraid that if he pushed them out, he would be disobeying Daniel.

Finally, he sent out a message of surrender and submission to the elders, indicating that the dragonlings would be in danger if they continued. The attacks halted. The strongest mind, which had to be Arabella, pressed against his consciousness. She sent a message that she was going to read him and that he was not allowed to enter her mind. He quickly sent everything he deemed important back behind the shields until he felt light and his thoughts were foggy. He knew he should be doing something, but he couldn't remember what.

Arabella's mind gently entered his and all he could remember was that he couldn't enter her mind even though she was making herself completely vulnerable. Daniel would punish him if he disobeyed Arabella. He had to obey Daniel. Arabella ran roughshod through his mind and it was agonizing, but he focused on keeping his dragonlings safe. He could see what she was seeing and most of it didn't make sense to him. She was interested in the tamer who had abused him and every detail relating to that, which made Luke extremely uncomfortable as he had to relive that nightmare as she watched it. He hoped she was looking through those memories so she could find that tamer.

She also focused on his childhood, oddly, or at least what he remembered of it. She kept digging for more and more details until his mind rippled in pain and he had to beg her to stop. The memories just weren't there. He had sent most of his recent memories behind his shields but she didn't bother looking at any of them. Maybe she expected him to protect those and knew not to look. Her choice of memories to examine was very strange. And before long, she and the others withdrew their minds and he retreated behind his walls.

Daniel was holding him when he opened his eyes. His head ached and felt numb. The elders looked pleased, as did Daniel. His mouth was dry and his eyes were itchy. He felt sore all over and his face felt swollen. Plus, he could feel his dragonlings worried about him. They were hungry, too.

He managed to sit up on his own and looked at Daniel.

"My dragonlings," he said. "They need me."

"Of course," Daniel said.

Daniel helped him up and wrapped an arm around his waist. Luke could walk on his own but he knew better than to disobey Daniel. Anna came with them and Luke saw Daniel's glare at the woman. But after the promise Luke had made the elders obey, Anna was required to stay with him. He hadn't looked at Anna yet because he was afraid of what she would say. They reached the feeding room.

Anna entered first, then as soon as Luke and Daniel entered, the dragonlings took to the air and began hissing and snapping at them. Luke was frightened. He hadn't realized he had neglected them so much that they would turn against him. He rushed forward to comfort them, leaving Daniel at the door. To his surprise, they took up protective positions around him and continued hissing at the doorway.

Luke remembered how aggressive they had been towards Eric at first, but Eric was a stranger who had been taking them away from their mother and Daniel was their leader who all the males had known. He hushed them as much as he could and lured them to sit on him. Daniel was nonplussed.

"Feed and play with them, then return to your room immediately," Daniel said.

Daniel left and the dragonlings calmed and began chirping to calm him. He sat in the cushions with the wall against his back. He still hadn't looked at Anna and was afraid to. He tried to pet his dragonlings but they were hungry and Anna was between him and the bottles.

"Can you pass me a bottle, please?" he asked, keeping his head down and not looking at her. She had a full view of the bruised side of his face and he didn't want to know what she thought of it.

Without a word, she passed him a bottle. He glanced at her hand to take the bottle, but not at her face. He began by feeding the female. When she was relaxed and suckling and the other dragonlings were playing near the ceiling, Anna leaned towards him.

"Look at me, Luke," she said.

"No," he whispered.

"Luke," she said in a harsher voice, "Look at me."

"Don't disturb the dragonlings," he said.

"I'm not, but you are," she said. "You're being hurt and they know it. Now look at me."

He could feel the beginnings of tears as he reluctantly turned his face towards her, then raised his eyes to meet hers. He kept pouring out love and comfort to his dragonlings even as his terror mounted. She would want him to stand up to Daniel. She didn't understand. Daniel was his leader and Daniel had the right to treat Luke however he wanted.

"Why were you hurt?" she asked gently.

"I disobeyed him," Luke said.

"Has he hit you before?"

"Never my face," Luke said, remembering the times Daniel had punished him with a belt. It was only when he had disobeyed in a major way, and Luke learned quickly not to disobey in that way again. But there were so many rules to follow, it was hard to keep track of them all.

"Why do you let him?"

It was as he had thought. She just didn't understand.

"He's my leader," Luke said. "I belong to him."

Anna looked offended. "You're a dragon tamer. You belong to no one. You give your talents to a tribe and in exchange they take care of you. They do not own you."

Luke shook his head. He didn't know how to explain it to her. Things in the East might be different, things with other tamers might be different, but in Daniel's tribe, the tamer belonged to the leader. Daniel controlled him and he had to obey.

"Why did you let the elders into your mind? You've been refusing to do that since you first arrived," Anna pointed out. "It's the only reason I wasn't able to tame you and now that you've given them access, they'll be able to tame you."

"Daniel ordered it," Luke said, a little frustrated that she didn't understand. "I can't disobey him."

"Are you afraid he'll hurt you again or do you actually feel loyalty to him?"

Anna's question took him by surprise and he found he couldn't answer. He was terrified of more punishment. Now that Daniel had struck him in the face, which he had never done before, he was scared that Daniel would cross other boundaries as well. He didn't know what those boundaries were, but he did know that Daniel went easy on him sometimes because of his age and his beauty. If he no longer cared about those things, who knew what he would do if Luke disobeyed again?

But did he feel loyalty? He had felt loyalty at first after being kidnapped, but it had evaporated quickly when he saw how Eric treated him. Eric viewed him as a person capable of making decisions, whereas Daniel always made decisions for him. It was strange. Ever since joining Daniel's tribe, he had been loyal, but as soon as he left, he realized that it wasn't as wonderful as he thought it was. Only loyalty to the dragons had kept him there.

Instead of answering Anna's question, he snuggled into the pillows and asked for another bottle. Anna handed it to him and he switched to one of his males. He knew Anna wasn't done, though she was silent as he arranged the dragonling and it began to suckle as the female curled up on his shoulder as if reminding him that she needed another bottle in the near future.

"Do you need help, Luke?"

Her voice was soft even though they both knew the elders weren't monitoring sound in the room.

"No," Luke said. "I belong to Daniel. He can do whatever he wants to me."

Again Anna looked angry but she wasn't projecting to the dragonlings and that was all that mattered to Luke.

"You haven't acted like this the entire time you've been here," Anna said. "What happened to the stubborn, rebellious Luke? The Luke who refused to do what he was told? The Luke who stood up for himself?"

"Eric made me believe I could think for myself," Luke said weakly. "But he was wrong. I shouldn't think for myself. Daniel makes decisions for me."

"Is that how you've lived all these years?"

Her voice was filled with the same sorrow as when she found out he didn't know what dragon tamers really did.

"My first leader wasn't like that," he said. "But I was very young. Daniel says he didn't want to give me rules because I was too young to understand them."

"He didn't give you rules because dragon tamers don't live by rules," Anna said fiercely. "They live by their own rules just as you did when you came here."

"I disobeyed Daniel when I came here," Luke said, lowering his gaze and turning away from her. "He has the right to punish me. Can you push the bottles so I can reach them please?"

She was angry, but she pushed the rack of bottles close to him so he wouldn't have to ask her for a bottle every time he needed one. He switched dragonlings and channeled his energy into distracting himself. This time, she seemed to approve of what he was doing. She moved until she sat in front of him. She got out a phone and typed something, but he was too distracted to pay much attention as he fed his beloved dragonlings.

Finally, the dragonlings were all fed and played with and he headed back to his room with a sense of dread. He didn't know what Daniel had planned but he knew it wouldn't be good. He thought briefly of Eric before scolding himself. He belonged to Daniel. There was no room for Eric in his life anymore.

CHAPTER SIXTEEN

Hasty Actions

Eric paced the ship. He couldn't leave, not while Luke was in danger. Why had the Untamable told both of them? This was the imminent danger the dragon had spoken of, but Luke wouldn't be in this danger if the Untamable hadn't told Daniel that Luke needed help. Did the Untamable have some sort of ulterior motive? How could this possibly benefit him and the other Untamable?

Sam and Denis tried to calm him down, but it wasn't working. All he could think of was what Daniel was doing to Luke. How would he react to Luke's independence? Would he punish Luke for thinking for himself? Would Luke continue to be independent or would he revert to how he had been when Eric had first found him?

His phone buzzed and he almost ignored it, but habit made him check. It was Anna and he hastened to read what she was sending.

Help Luke ASAP. Daniel hurt him and will again. You have an hour.

He knew better than to respond. He couldn't give away the fact that she had messaged him. She had done it at great risk and that meant she was desperate. One hour. That was about as long as it took Luke to feed his dragonlings. Daniel must be planning something after Luke finished. One hour would be night. The elders had been prepared to let Eric sleep with Luke. Surely they wouldn't let Daniel sleep with Luke.

That couldn't be the danger. But he knew Daniel's interest in Luke and couldn't dismiss the idea of Daniel forcing Luke into something he wasn't ready for, and the thought sickened him.

He showed the message to Sam and Denis. Both grew grim and he knew they were having similar thoughts. They had to break into the elder's building, get the dragonlings out, then rescue Luke and get him out as well. Luke wouldn't leave without the dragonlings, so those would have to be first. Anna would have to help.

He dressed in clothes typical for the elder's building, as did Sam. They couldn't stand out in any way. Denis remained on the ship, ready to take off the instant they were on board. There were only a few places to get out of the ship besides the main ramp but Eric knew them. He had snuck out before. The stakes had never been this high, though. He would have to smuggle Anna, the dragonlings, and Luke back through these gaps and he just hoped they would be cooperating. Luke in particular. If Luke fought, it would be difficult to get him up.

They blended in with the people around the ship easily and entered the building without anyone stopping them. They needed to find Anna. Luke and Anna should still be in the feeding room. They sat on a bench nearby and waited for them to leave. After about fifteen minutes, the door opened. Anna headed towards them and Luke headed the other way, towards his room. His head was down and he looked defeated. Eric caught a glimpse of bruising on his face and it took all of his strength to remain where he was and not race after Luke. Anna had to be first, though.

As she passed by, he said her name quietly. She paused and looked at him. Her eyes widened in recognition. They must have been in an unmonitored area because she stopped walking to face them fully.

"You came," she said quietly. "You might be too late."

"We need you to get the dragonlings and follow Sam back to the plane. He won't leave until they're safe."

"I can't go back in there without reason," she said. "They'll be too suspicious."

"Can you upset the dragonlings so you have to go in and calm them?" Eric asked.

He knew Luke would be upset by the disturbance but it was the only way. Anna looked deep in thought.

"They're not visible in some places in the room. If I upset them and they flew there, I could ask them to land on me and they would be invisible. But they wouldn't unless they had Luke's permission and he's not himself. He wouldn't agree."

"They want to protect Luke," Eric said. "Surely they understand that Daniel hurts him."

Anna seemed to be thinking again.

"Yes, if I explained the situation I think they would come with me. You want me to do it now?"

Eric nodded. "I'll leave Sam here. Follow him to the plane as quickly as possible."

"If this doesn't work, Daniel's going to take it out on Luke," she warned. "Luke's already terrified of Daniel and Daniel's already shown that he won't hesitate to punish Luke. I don't want Luke hurt."

"Then this better work," Eric said as confidently as he could. "Get the dragonlings out of here. I'll get Luke."

She still looked uncertain but agreed. He moved out of sight. The elders wouldn't recognize Sam, but they would recognize him. He would wait until Anna started heading to the plane with Sam. They needed to be safe before he could start saving Luke. Everything went smoothly and soon Anna was walking out with just a couple of lumps in her sleeves; nothing that looked too suspicious. Sam led her away and Eric took a deep breath. His part in this was considerably more dangerous, because he couldn't do it by stealth. He would be facing Daniel and the cameras might pick him up.

He walked down the corridor as if he had every right to be there. When he reached Luke's door, he heard Luke's voice crying for help. He took a breath. He couldn't just barge in, no matter how much he wanted. He had to be careful and stay out of the cameras. He gathered his self-control and opened the door, preparing for the worst.

He took three steps inside and closed the door behind him. It was dark but he had no trouble seeing what was going on. Luke was pinned face down on the bed with Daniel on top of him. They were both naked. Daniel's hands were pushing Luke's shoulders down as Luke struggled to get out of his grasp. Daniel's legs had Luke's hips trapped and he was leaning forward in an obvious attempt to rape Luke. Luke was fighting, but overwhelmed, and could only cry for help, even though he must realize no one would help him. The elders were probably watching and pleased with how Daniel was controlling Luke. Eric wanted to run over and strike Daniel, possibly even kill him for what he was doing. But he couldn't. He couldn't move any further or he would be seen.

"Stop, Daniel," he said in as calm a voice as he could manage.

Daniel did stop, though he kept Luke pinned. He turned to look at Eric and smirked. Luke buried his face in the pillows.

"What are you doing here?" Daniel asked. "You have no right to be here. Luke is mine."

"Luke belongs to no one other than himself. You can't force him to do this."

"He belongs to me. Just ask him."

Daniel released Luke from his hold and allowed Luke up. Luke crawled to the front of the bed and wrapped his arms around his knees, not lifting his head. Daniel reached out and grabbed Luke's hair, forcing his head up. Luke visibly resisted, but Daniel didn't stop until Luke's face was fully visible. Eric barely held back a gasp. The entire left side of Luke's face was bruised and a cut ran across his left cheek. His lip was swollen and barely healed from what must have been a split lip. He was also crying and looking at Daniel, not Eric.

"Did you deserve this, Luke?" Daniel asked, glancing back at Eric with that smirk still on his lips.

"Yes," Luke said softly. "I disobeyed you."

"Do you belong to me?"

Luke finally looked at Eric. There was so much defeat and shame in his eyes that Eric could barely stand still and not rush to steal him from Daniel's grasp.

"Yes," Luke whispered. "You are my leader."

"True leaders do not abuse their tamers," Eric said. "And if you obey him, why were you fighting him just a minute ago?"

Luke was silent and bowed his head again. Daniel looked at him and stroked his hand along the bruised side of Luke's face.

"Good question, Luke," he said. "I'll have to punish you for resisting me."

Luke flinched but didn't object. Eric couldn't believe how docile Luke was being, how he almost seemed to be brainwashed. He had no idea Daniel had this much control over Luke. He had known that Daniel controlled Luke, but not to this extent. Luke had been spirited at the café when they had first met. He had also been disobeying Daniel then, so perhaps he gained strength when he disobeyed. Eric wasn't leaving without Luke, but if Luke refused to go with him, then he was in a lot of trouble.

"Luke, you don't have to put up with this," Eric said. "You know I won't hurt you. You know what you mean to me and I know what I mean to you. You wouldn't have let me see you if you didn't trust me completely. Would you trust him the same way you trust me?"

Luke looked at him again with tears in his eyes. There was a glimmer of the real Luke in them. Daniel grabbed Luke by the throat.

"I will not lose you, Luke," he hissed. "You are mine and nothing will change that."

"Luke, you have to act quickly if you want to be free. I will save you. No delays."

"My dragonlings," he said slowly, then he paused. He must have felt for his dragonlings and realized where they were.

"That's right," Daniel said, obviously thinking they were still here, preventing Luke from leaving. "You can't abandon them, can you? Now tell him to leave and submit to me. Maybe

I'll go easy on you."

Eric didn't say anything. This was Luke's decision now. He could see Luke breaking free from Daniel's control and struggling to figure out what to do. Without warning, Luke pushed aside the hand at his throat and punched Daniel in the face. His unsteady blow missed and punched Daniel in the temple, but it must have been a powerful blow because Daniel gasped and then fell forward. He was unconscious. Luke leapt off the bed, clearly terrified, grabbed a sheet to wrap around himself and then rushed towards Eric, who stepped backwards quickly to avoid being seen and opened the door for both of them.

He knew the elders would be puzzled by the scene and would probably think Luke was headed to his dragonlings for comfort. They had very little time and the fact that Luke was naked posed a lot of problems. He took Luke's trembling hand and pulled him through the most isolated hallways until they reached the open stretch between the building and the plane. There was no way to avoid this and there were people around. Luke would draw unwelcome attention. He had very little time to think, though, since the elders would quickly realize Luke wasn't in the building.

The landing ramp began to lower, to his surprise, attracting everyone's notice. He silently thanked Sam and Denis as he and Luke snuck to the thin opening into the ship. Luke was eager to get aboard, luckily, so there were no problems getting through. As soon as both of them were on the plane, the landing ramp started closing again. Before it was even closed all the way, the plane took off. Just as they took off, the elders emerged from the building. They began yelling at the people in the local tribe. He ran to the cockpit to make sure they would get away safely. His pilot was prepared and they were too far away by the time the local tribe finally got in their planes to follow. Since most fights took place in the other realm, most tribes weren't prepared for conflict in this realm.

Once Eric was sure they were safely away, he returned to

Luke, who was holding his knees again with his head down. He was alone, since Anna and the dragonlings were in the same room they had been in when Luke had been brought here. Luke was in the cargo bay where he hadn't been allowed before. Eric grabbed a thick blanket on his way in and wrapped it around Luke's shoulders over the thin sheet. Luke didn't react to the blanket. Eric sat beside him and wrapped an arm around his shoulders. Luke was shaking.

"Do you want to see your dragonlings?" Eric asked, knowing how much Luke needed them.

Luke's head moved in what seemed to be a nod, so Eric stood and held his hand out to Luke. Luke took it and as he stood, he kept the blanket wrapped around him. Eric would have to get him clothes soon. Luke kept hold of Eric's hand, but trailed behind him several steps. When they reached the room, Eric opened the door and gestured for Anna to leave. The dragonlings were circling and upset. Anna slid out and glanced at Luke, whose head was bowed as he clutched the blanket around him. Eric brought Luke into the room and helped him sit.

The dragonlings surrounded them as soon as Luke sat, perching on his body and not even seeming to notice Eric. As soon as they touched Luke, they calmed down. In minutes, they were chirping happily and rubbing against Luke. Luke still looked pale and he was trembling, but Eric could tell he was focused on the dragonlings. He stood up to leave them alone, but Luke squeezed his hand and pulled him back. Eric sat next to him again and set Luke's hand on his leg, stroking it and trying to pour his love and support through that small touch.

As Eric rubbed his hand and the dragonlings flew around him and nuzzled him, Luke began to get his color back. He slowly lifted his head. Eric was on his right so he couldn't see Luke's injuries but he knew he needed to get ice on the bruises. Luke wouldn't let him get up and he didn't want to leave. But his injuries needed to be treated. Denis knew basic first aid and could certainly help heal Luke's face and anything else Daniel had done to him.

Eric looked at the dragonlings. They were flying calmly now and exploring the space. The female had never been here before and it looked like the males were showing her around. Eric brought Luke's hand to his lips and kissed it. Luke turned to look at him. His eyes were haunted and frightened. He didn't speak.

"Luke," Eric said, "Will you come with me to the main room? I want to get your injuries taken care of."

Luke looked down at the blanket wrapped around him and clutched it closer. He shook his head. Eric rubbed his hand again.

"I have clothes you can wear," he said. "We'll go to my room and I'll give them to you, then we'll take care of your injuries."

Luke lowered his head again and tears filled his eyes. He clutched the blanket tightly and finally glanced up at the dragonlings. They weren't reacting to his emotions. Luke must be shielding them strongly, Eric thought. After a few seconds watching his dragonlings, Luke began shuffling to his feet. Eric stood and helped him up. Luke leaned against him for a moment and Eric felt how weak he was. Then Luke straightened and stepped away, though he still held Eric's hand.

He led Luke through the plane. Sam and Anna were in the main room at the table, but they diplomatically didn't look as Eric and Luke walked through. He wasn't even sure Luke saw them, since he was looking down again. They reached Eric's room and Eric closed the door behind them. Luke let go of his hand. Eric turned in surprise and saw that Luke was crying again. He ran his hand over Luke's uninjured cheek.

"What's wrong, Luke?"

"I don't want this," he whispered.

Eric looked around and realized why Luke was reacting. This was Eric's bedroom, the room where they had kissed. Luke had undoubtedly been punished for kissing Eric, and he might also be worried that Eric, like Daniel, might try to take advantage of him. Eric didn't try to move Luke from the door. Instead, he went to the small drawer built into the wall and got out some clothes that he thought would fit Luke. Luke was quite a bit smaller than him, but these would do the trick until they could get him a better outfit. He placed them on the bed.

"I'll leave and let you get dressed," Eric said. "When you're dressed, please come out."

Luke looked surprised. Eric gently moved him away from the door so he could leave. He shut the door to give Luke privacy. He was extremely worried about leaving Luke alone but he knew Luke wouldn't hurt himself because of the dragonlings. Denis was in the nearby cockpit and Eric gestured him over.

"I need you to get our first aid kit," he said as quietly as possible so Luke wouldn't hear through the door. "Luke needs ice for bruises and possibly stitches."

Denis's eyes widened but he nodded without a word and left into the main room to gather supplies. Eric remained outside the door, listening to the inside. Luke was sobbing. He probably needed some time to recover from everything. After nearly fifteen minutes, the crying stopped. There was silence for nearly five minutes, then the shuffle of clothes. Another five minutes passed. Finally, the door cracked open and Luke stepped out.

CHAPTER SEVENTEEN

Moving Forward

Luke wept for a long time in Eric's room. Everything kept blurring together. Daniel was his leader and he ought to obey him. Daniel could do anything he liked to Luke. When Daniel had ordered Luke to take off his shirt and put his hands on the wall, Luke had known what was coming. Daniel struck him with his belt six times and probably would have continued if Luke hadn't slumped to the floor, unable to stand the pain.

After beating him, Daniel had turned sweet. He had knelt by Luke and kissed his uninjured cheek, helping him stand up. He had held Luke close. Luke had tensed when his hands slid to his waistband but Daniel had calmed him down with sweet words and he had relaxed as Daniel slipped off his pants until he was naked, pressing against Daniel's body. Daniel had laid him on the bed and he hadn't resisted.

Daniel had tossed off his own clothes quickly before joining Luke. When he straddled Luke, Luke couldn't help but flinch, expecting to be drawn in memories at any moment. But Daniel assured him that it wouldn't happen again. He had encouraged Luke to lie on his stomach and he had. Then Daniel had said he was going to make sure no one else stole anything from him. Luke had felt something pressing against him and had panicked. He had struggled to break free, called for help, done everything he could to fight against Daniel. And Eric had come.

He belonged to Daniel. He had been wrong to fight Daniel. But he didn't want Daniel to hurt him anymore. Eric wouldn't hurt him. Eric was always kind to him. Eric had seen who he truly was and wanted to help him. He trusted Eric. So Luke had used all of his strength to hit Daniel and it had worked. But he still felt miserable. He had no idea what Daniel would do when he found him again. His face, the whipping, it would be nothing. Daniel knew what a low pain threshold Luke had and he would ruthlessly take advantage of that.

Luke wanted to forget everything and go back to Daniel, erase everything and make it normal again. He wanted to go back in time and hide in the safehouse and never meet Eric. He wanted Daniel to be his leader and he never wanted to know any different. He wanted ignorance because it was safe. He wept for his lost innocence and because he was in pain and because his leader had betrayed him and hurt him.

The whole time he wept, he maintained a strong wall between his true feelings and his dragonlings. They knew he was sad but had no idea how much. They would try to cheer him up when he went in to see them, but they weren't upset and he could tell they were playing with each other. He could not let them suffer. They were his life. The only thing holding him together.

When he had cried himself out, he sat up and looked at the clothes Eric had set out for him. He slowly pulled them on. They were a little too big, but they generally fit him. He sat on the bed and tried to prepare himself to join the others. They probably thought he was weak for obeying Daniel. They had no idea. They couldn't understand, just like Anna hadn't understood when he tried to explain to her. Daniel was his life just as much as the dragonlings. Daniel was his connection to the dragonlings. If he didn't obey Daniel, Daniel would cut him off from them. He couldn't let that happen. He would do anything for Daniel to prevent that from happening.

He gathered his courage and stood up. His shoulders automatically slumped and he looked down. He was ashamed of his injuries and didn't want to draw attention to himself, even though he knew everyone would be focused on him. He just wanted to hide with his dragonlings. But he went to the door and opened it. Eric was waiting outside at a respectful distance. Luke glanced up at him briefly. Eric looked relieved and extended his hand. Luke looked down again but took his hand. He needed to feel Eric and remember that someone still cared for him without wanting to hurt him.

Eric led him into the main room of the plane where he and Eric had eaten on the way over. This time, there were three other people and it felt crowded, especially when all three turned to look at him. Anna he could stand, but the other two were essentially strangers, though he recognized them from the café where he had been kidnapped. Eric introduced the larger man as Sam and the taller man as Denis. He explained that Denis would be inspecting his injuries.

Luke hesitantly sat down at the desk on the side opposite the dining area, keeping his head down as if that would stop people from staring at it. Eric stood next to him, still holding his hand, and Eric squeezed it as Denis brushed the hair back from the left side of his face and gently raised Luke's chin so he could look at the injury fully. Denis made no comment, luckily, only pressed against the cut on his cheek lightly. Luke flinched at the pain but Denis didn't stop. Then Denis moved to his swollen lip and again pressed it. Again Luke flinched, tears filling his eyes at the pain. He clung to Eric's hand and Eric placed his other hand on Luke's shoulder. Finally, after an eternity of pain, Denis moved back and gathered some blue bags.

"You don't need stitches and nothing will scar," Denis said. "These ice packs will help the bruising go down and help with the pain."

Luke looked at him and saw genuine concern and relief in his eyes. Denis cared about him and wanted him to feel better and not be in pain. No one had even suggested numbing his pain until this point.

"Thank you," he said quietly.

"Where else are you hurt?" Denis asked.

Luke lowered his head again. He didn't want anyone to know. He couldn't hide his face, but he could hide everything else. Instead of answering, he reached out to take one of the blue bags and asked how it worked. Denis eyed him, then showed him where to place it for maximum value. It stung at first, but soon Luke could feel the pain slipping away. He closed his eyes and wished everything would slip away.

"Does that feel better, Luke?" Eric asked.

Luke nodded his head.

"Where else did Daniel hurt you?"

If Eric was also asking that question, it meant that he wasn't likely to escape answering. Luke opened his eyes slowly and looked around. The other man, Sam, wasn't there. He could sense that Anna was with his dragonlings. It was just him, Eric, and Denis. Very cautiously, keeping the ice pack on his cheek, he lifted the back of his shirt a little. Denis lifted his shirt the rest of the way to expose the welts on his back from Daniel's belt. Luke could feel Eric stiffen and his breath quicken, but he said nothing and Luke was relieved.

Denis didn't say anything, either, just got out some sort of ointment and bandages. He spread the ointment over Luke's back and he gasped and squirmed as it burned against his already sore back. But after a few seconds, the burning became a pleasantly warm sensation and he held still. Denis lifted his shirt in the front as well and wrapped the bandage all the way around his torso. When he was finished, he pulled Luke's shirt back down.

"Is there anything else, Luke?" Eric asked gently.

"No," Luke said. Nothing physical, that was. His mind was reeling with everything that had happened and his consciousness was still aching after the assault from the elders. Thinking hurt, but there was no cure for that.

"May I see my dragonlings, please?" Luke asked, directing his question at Eric even though he had lowered his head again.

"No," Denis said, cutting off any answer Eric might have

given. Luke looked up at him in surprise. "You need rest and time to heal. Your dragonlings are fine."

"I want to see them," Luke said a little firmer. He wasn't sure why Denis was refusing him. He did probably need rest, but the dragonlings were far more important than him. Why wouldn't he be allowed to see them?

"I'm in charge of your care until you've recovered your strength, and you need sleep right now," Denis said.

"No," Luke said, straightening in his chair to face Denis fully. "They are my dragonlings and you can't decide whether or not I see them."

"It's your decision, then," he said, gesturing for Luke to stand. Luke looked at Eric and Denis, who were both smiling slightly.

He ignored them and went to the room where his dragonlings were playing with Anna. His body still ached but he could ignore it much easier now, especially when he held the ice pack to his cheek the way Denis had showed him. When he opened the door, all six of the dragonlings went to him and landed on him in their favorite spots, chirping happily. He went to the metal bench where Anna was and sat as far away from her as possible. She politely moved to the other side so he could have more space.

"Thank you for helping them," he said, glancing at her briefly. "I would like to be alone with them right now, though."

"Of course," she said, getting up and hesitating before walking through the door. "They left to help you. They didn't betray you by going with me."

"I know," Luke said. "They would never betray me."

She nodded, then left and shut the door. Luke collapsed against the metal hull and his dragonlings curled around him, cooing and chirping at him. He invited them to cuddle in his lap one by one, nurturing the bond between them individually. He needed to feel their love and he needed them to feel his love. They were his life, his everything. He would do anything for them. Once each individual dragonling's bond was at its maximum, he let it go play and invited another one to his lap. He did the female last and held her the longest. She was the neediest, after all, and her bond required the most attention.

What he was doing was draining, but not to the extent that it would be dangerous. He wouldn't be wiped out by it. He might fall asleep, but he might only be more tired than he already was. He would have to take Denis's advice and sleep after this no matter what, but he needed this time alone with his dragonlings. He needed to reassure them and love them.

When he had finished with the female, he laid down on the metal bench on his side. It was too painful to lie on his back. He adjusted the ice pack and closed his eyes. Although he gave his dragonlings permission to play, they chose to perch on him instead as he invited sleep to soak into his mind and ease the ache that accompanied his thoughts. He barely noticed when he passed from worry into unconsciousness.

CHAPTER EIGHTEEN

Finding Safety

Eric glanced in at Luke sleeping soundly with his dragonlings surrounding him. He looked peaceful, even in such an uncomfortable position with the icepack cradled on his cheek. He bit back his anger at what Daniel had done to him, what the elders had allowed Daniel to do to him. The elders must have been thrilled when they discovered the control Daniel held over Luke. Anna told him how Daniel had forced Luke to open his mind to them and Eric knew they would do anything, tolerate anything, as long as they could manipulate Luke. They might even be happy that Luke was being hurt. As tamers, they couldn't hurt another tamer, but a leader could hurt a tamer.

Luke was safe, though, and that was more than could be said for Eric's tribe. The elders would strike back hard for Eric's actions, and they would strike at his people. Eric had openly attacked one of the foundations of their society and that wouldn't be tolerated. By anyone. His allied tribes would have no choice but to turn against him, even if he told them the truth and they privately sympathized with him. They might allow him and his people to escape, but they wouldn't allow him to remain.

He sent orders to his people to evacuate to the other realm as quickly as possible. They were safe there, since the Untamable wouldn't allow an entire people to be targeted. He hoped. He had disobeyed one of the Untamable, after all. Once they got Luke there, though, everything should be sorted out.

That needed to happen as soon as possible.

There were those that couldn't go to the other realm, however. Pregnant women, mothers and fathers with children, and anyone under the age of nine. Going into the other realm affected the development of young children and while the adults would be fine, the children, infants, and fetuses wouldn't be. And equally important, dragonlings couldn't go into the other realm. Eric needed to find a safe place in this realm for the vulnerable people and he wasn't sure what to do. He could load them into an aircraft carrier that he knew how to acquire from the local government thanks to many favors. That would allow them to be loaded into planes if they were tracked down in the sea. It was his best option right now and probably the one he would go with, since he couldn't think of any place on land that was safe. He started working on getting the warship ready to use and instructed his people to start heading to the port. Anna knew how to create a gate so once everyone was on board, they should have everything they needed.

Eric's eyes widened as he realized the obvious necessity he was forgetting, the one that would be the most difficult to get. Food for the dragonlings. The female especially ate a lot, and needed every bit of that food. He could not allow a female dragonling to die. But there was no way he had enough to feed all of them, and he knew Luke would never allow any of them to die.

His tribe had food and he had them bring all of it with them. It would last a week at the rate the dragonlings ate. Not good enough.

Hesitantly, he called his closest ally, a man he'd known since childhood. Even though they were in different tribes, they had always been friends. He just hoped Lee would listen and help.

Lee answered after only a few beeps. He must have been in his office and recognized Eric's number.

"Eric, what have you done?" Lee asked. "The Elders are

saying you've attacked them and kidnapped two tamers. They're calling on all the tribes to unite against you and you know we have to obey."

Eric sighed. He had expected as much.

"It's a twisted version of the truth," he admitted. "But I didn't attack the Elders or kidnap anyone. I helped the tamers escape. The Elders were physically abusing one and enslaving the other. If you could see the injuries, you would have helped, too."

"Why are you calling? Even if that's true, you know I can't help you."

"The tamers refuse to return, but one of them successfully bonded with the female dragonling. My tribe doesn't have enough food to take care of her and I won't let her die. We need food."

Lee swore. Eric took that as a mildly good sign. If it were a flat no, Lee wouldn't be having enough doubts to be swearing.

"I'm doing this for the female, and because you've always been a friend and never lied," Lee finally said with some reluctance. "We have a litter right now and have a significant stockpile. We can drain almost everything we have and get more without it looking suspicious. I'll give you everything except a week or two for our litter. Where do we send it?"

Eric silently blessed his friend.

"I'll send a plane to pick it up within a few hours. Thank you, Lee. You've just saved her life."

They briefly worked out the details on where to send the plane, Eric thanked him again, and they hung up. He knew that he would still need to be cautious. Lee was his friend and wanted to help the female, but there was a chance that in his mind, helping the female meant returning the female to the Elders. It might be a trap. He would make sure that the pilot of the plane didn't know where he would be bringing the food after picking it up and didn't know the plan to save the vulnerable people; he could only know about the plan to send the adults into the other realm, if anything. The Elders would find out about the other realm almost immediately, Eric suspected, so there was no reason to hide that.

It took the full two-hour flight back to his home to arrange everything. His people were understandably upset at having to abandon their lives over a decision he had made without their consent. They had all heard the Elder's announcement, of course, and knew no other tribe would take them in or give them shelter even if they offered to inform on Eric. They didn't know the truth and he needed to tell them the truth in order to explain why they were being forced out of their homes. He suspected that as soon as they saw Luke and saw the female dragonling, they would be convinced.

Everything was finally set. Denis and Sam would lead the adults into the other realm and set up defensive positions with the help of the dragons. Eric would remain with Luke and Anna, helping the vulnerable children and parents get settled on the warship and get them safely out to sea. Anna would make the gate as quickly as possible and Eric would bring Luke through to figure out his connection to the Untamable. Eric had no idea how Luke and the powerful dragons were actually connected, if Luke controlled them directly or just guided them, but they needed to find out. After that, they would see.

Eric told everyone except Luke the plan, since Luke was still sleeping, and they all agreed. Then Eric paused outside the room Luke and the dragonlings were in and looked in. Luke was still on his side with the icebag on his cheek but he was awake with all of his dragonlings perched on him except one of his males who was sprawled in front of him on his back while Luke stroked his belly. The dragonlings were happy, but Luke still looked defeated and miserable.

Eric knocked politely. No one in the room reacted, so Eric entered. The little male in front of Luke grumbled but took off and joined the others to play on the other side of the room as Luke sat up, still cradling the icebag. Luke cautiously held out his hand and Eric took it, then sat beside Luke. Some of Luke's fear left his eyes as he gazed at Eric.

"Luke, we're landing soon. Everyone we see will be in my tribe. You have nothing to fear. But they need to see you. They need to see the female, as well, but mostly you, Luke. And Luke," he said, stroking Luke's uninjured cheek. "They need to see your injuries."

Luke flinched and pulled away. "Why? Why do they even need to see me?"

"When I rescued you," Eric said slowly, knowing that Luke hadn't had any idea of the consequences of Eric's actions, "I violated the rules of the Elders. They are the highest power in our society. They called on the other tribes to unite against my tribe. I can get my people out safely, I think. Many are already out. They are going to two places. Both groups need to see you because I told them I rescued you to stop you from being abused. If they can't see the abuse, they won't believe me. They'll believe when they talk to you and Anna, of course, but I can't wait that long. I need them on my side now. Can you walk at my side and show your face to my people?"

Luke was quiet for a moment and the humming of the dragonlings dimmed. Then Luke reluctantly lowered his icebag. The edges of the bruising were starting to lighten, but the rest was still an ugly blackish purple getting worse in some places. The cut on his cheek was still visible, and his lip was still swollen. Eric fought the urge to kiss him and instead stood up and waited for Luke to take his hand and stand as well.

"Where do my dragonlings go?" he asked quietly, his shoulders slumping naturally.

"Carry them proudly, dragon tamer," Eric said. "Either sitting on you or in the air above. But keep the female in your hand so everyone knows it's her."

Luke nodded. He took a deep breath and threw his shoulders back, squeezing Eric's hand tightly. The female landed on his other hand and wound around it. Several of the males draped on his shoulders; the rest flew above him. Luke nodded, and Eric led him out of the plane.

Everyone else was out of the plane and Eric led Luke

down the ramp. It wasn't bright or arid this time. They were on a huge ship and it was heading into the ocean. His people had gathered as many of their things as possible, including anything of cultural or monetary wealth. Eric was worried about both, since they would be in crisis if they lost their heritage or if they became bankrupt. Eric squeezed Luke's hand. He would stand by Luke, of course, but Luke would be on his own for a lot of it.

CHAPTER NINETEEN

A New Tribe

Luke stared at the people as he walked down the ramp next to Eric. He was frightened. As people saw him, they looked furious and Eric's grip on his hand reassured him. He tried to tell himself that they were angry at what had happened to him, not angry at him. The female clutched him tightly but popped her head up every once in a while to examine certain people, mostly the children, and at the sight of her, everyone let out sighs of admiration. His males felt a little left out and started flying around in a very acrobatic display and the children cheered them as well.

Luke wanted to hide his face, but he knew that he needed to show his injuries as he saw people's reactions. He was the reason they were abandoning the homes they had lived in, possibly for generations. They were on a ship, so who knew where they were going? Did Eric even know? He must.

He walked through the crowd of people who parted for him without a word. He noticed that it was mostly children, and pregnant women, and men and women holding children's hands. He wondered where everyone else was. These were the tribe members he had never been allowed to see. The average members. The members who contributed to the society that he was not a part of, according to Daniel. He didn't matter to them, and they didn't matter to him. But they were watching him with respect under the anger and he knew he meant something to them.

Luke turned to Eric, puzzled.

"You said I'm in your tribe," Luke said.

"You are, since I won't let you in any other tribe," Eric replied.

"Never," Luke said with a shiver. Then he glanced at the people. "Does that mean they're in my tribe too?"

Eric smiled softly. "You've never had a proper tribe before, Luke. You've always been isolated. Dragon tamers are the core of a tribe and mingle with everyone. These are your people and will befriend you. I'm sure the children especially will enjoy watching your dragonlings. At a distance, of course."

Luke nodded. He wouldn't mind sharing his beloved dragonlings as long as they stayed safely away and the dragonlings weren't in any danger. The parents didn't want their children in any danger, either, so they would come to a happy medium. He was nervous about letting so many people into his life when people had only meant abuse and betrayal to him, but these were Eric's people. They were different.

Eric led him into the door of the ship and it seemed that that were in a new world. His dragonlings clung to him, too afraid to fly for fear that they might get separated in the narrow hallway.

"We've put you in the largest room near the entrance," Eric said. "It may not be the safest, but we'll protect it with everything we have and I don't think the dragonlings will fit anywhere else, especially once they're larger."

They entered the doors to a large room that must have been an airplane hangar. The ship was big enough to have multiple hangars and this one looked completely closed off except through the entrance they emerged from. Anna was doing something near the far wall, which was completely blank, but one of the closer corners had been arranged in an attempt at a feeding and playing room. On the wall closest to them, racks and racks of food were bolted to the floor, more than enough food to feed his litter for months. He was grateful, as he hadn't realized how difficult food would be to find if everyone turned against them.

Luke and Eric walked towards the corner with cushions on the floor, a comfortable bed, curtains partially hiding the area from view, and other curtains hanging from the ceiling in layers to create hiding places for the dragonlings to play. Luke noticed that just behind the area was another door with a restroom sign on it. It would be easy to stay in this area if he needed for extended periods of time, assuming people brought him food.

Two women and three men had accompanied them into the corner. He was a little nervous at the people's presence and the dragonlings stayed with him even though he could tell they were excited to play in their new home. He was wary of the women because of the elders and wary of the men because of Daniel. Eric was the only one he trusted.

Eric pulled him to a stop and gestured to the people around them.

"They are not going to hurt you. No one here will hurt you. I swear. These are my most trusted friends. They are here to protect you from the people who did this to you."

Luke grabbed Eric's hands and stared at him, willing him to understand how much he meant what he was about to say.

"Eric, I would rather die than go back. If Daniel finds me again, he's going to torture me to death. If the elders find me again, they're going to shatter my mind until everything that makes me me is destroyed. If either of them gets me, I want you to kill me."

He was aware of Eric's sharp breath, of everyone's gasps. Everyone had heard him. He didn't care as long as Eric did. As long as Eric agreed. He would never survive if Daniel or the elders got him. There wouldn't be another rescue, no matter how fast. He wouldn't survive, or the parts of him that needed to survive wouldn't be there anymore. He didn't want to live the way he felt after he left Daniel, the way he had been on the plane over here. Ashamed, humiliated, like everything was his fault and they just didn't understand.

They did understand, and deep in his heart he understood, too. He just didn't want to admit it. He had allowed it to happen because he had been trained to allow it to happen. He couldn't fight his training, couldn't fight what he had been taught to do since he was a small child.

Everything in his experience had taught him to do what adults told him. He heard sounds but they said he didn't, so he accepted that he was crazy. Until a voice told him that he wasn't crazy but demanded physical favors in exchange for that comfort. But when his child's body couldn't stand the sexual abuse anymore and he told his parents, they assured him he was making it up so he was. Then another voice, the dragon's voice, reached him and believed him, and in exchange for protection, she insisted that he run away and find her. He fought to find her until he passed out and was taken in by Aaron.

Aaron instructed him how to raise dragonlings. When the dragonlings left, Aaron died and the mother dragon arranged for a dragon swap. Daniel controlled him from then on, until Eric kidnapped him. Eric at first controlled him by making him leave and take the dragonlings, then showed him a startling moment of freedom. Since then, Eric had given him some freedom, some rules. He could do what he wanted within limits, but usually the limits were in place to help him, and often at Luke's request. It was a strange feeling, a powerful feeling. Luke didn't know how to treat it yet.

He knew, though, that he wanted Eric to kill him rather than risk being captured again. He needed Eric to agree to it. Eric had to agree to it, even though Luke suspected he wouldn't.

Eric brushed the uninjured side of his face and looked infinitely sad.

"I can't agree to that, Luke. Even if what you say is true. But I can show you how to fight them so it never happens again, no matter how hopeless you feel right now."

Luke took a deep breath. At least Eric was offering him

hope.

"You swear it won't happen again?" he asked, clasping Eric's hands tightly.

"Once I show you your strength, it won't happen again," Eric assured him.

Luke nodded, and his dragonlings, including the female, started exploring the area. They would be fine without food and attention for a few more hours and he was curious. His dragonlings seemed safe with Eric's people even if they were out in the open like this, and he wondered why they were on a boat and where the rest of Eric's people were. Denis and Sam were missing, too, he realized, and what was Anna doing?

Eric released his hands and gestured to the five people with him.

"Luke, as I said, these are my closest friends. They make up my council of advisors and will always be available to help you. If you ever need anything, they will assist you."

Luke examined the men and women carefully. They were dressed in what looked like comfortable clothes, probably what they wore at home rather than at the office. Jeans of various styles and tightness on all but one of the women, who wore leggings and a long, loose top. The others wore casual tops, all with long sleeves. Their home must have been cold, and they must have been forced to leave without warning and not from work. They were all from Southeastern Asia, though Luke had been so sheltered he had no idea what country they were from.

The woman with leggings was as young as Eric and quite pretty, and looked stylish to Luke. Her black hair was in a bob and she wore makeup. The other woman was several decades older and seemed friendlier, with wide brown eyes and a warm smile. The youngest man, probably Eric's age, didn't smile and looked more like a businessman than anything else, and seemed uncomfortable to be caught in anything but a suit. The next youngest man, a few years older than Eric, was smiling as warmly as the older woman and he looked almost amused to be caught dressed as he was. The last man was as old as the older woman, and Luke wondered if those two had been advisors of the tribe's previous leader. He looked at Luke solemnly, but not without kindness.

Eric introduced them by first name only and Luke immediately forgot all but Mei, the young woman, and Shin, the man who looked amused by their dress. Eric must have caught his look of dismay because he smiled and patted Luke's arm.

"You can ask them their names as many times as you like," he reassured Luke. "You've been under a lot of stress and exposed to a lot of new things, and we don't expect you to learn everything right away."

Luke blushed and nodded shyly.

"You can also ask them about dragon taming," Eric added. "They don't know quite as much as me, as there are some things only leaders know, but they will be able to answer almost all of your questions."

"Are you tamers too?" Luke asked warily.

Anna was okay, but the only other tamers he knew were the voice from his childhood and the elders, and he didn't trust anyone who was a tamer.

"No," Eric said, taking his hand again. "Daniel kept you away from everyone else in his tribe for a reason. Almost everyone in the tribe knows about tamers, at least a little. Even the children grow up hearing stories about them, though the stories are usually only half-true. The council of advisors works very closely with the tamer and they are very well-versed in dragon taming."

Next, Eric took him to the food and showed him how to release enough for a feeding, emphasizing that he should only take as much as he could carry at a time and that there would always be people to help him if he asked.

They were returning to the feeding area when a blast of cold air nearly knocked him off his feet, though everyone else seemed to be expecting it. His dragonlings were startled but not frightened, as he shielded them quickly. He stared at Anna and the far wall, which now had a glowing ring surrounding a pale blue, faintly shimmering oval that took up almost all of the enormous wall. It was a gate. He had only seen one a few times, when the grown dragonlings were ceremoniously allowed through the gate into the unknown. He stepped backwards into Eric, who held him firm.

"Do you know what that is, Luke?" Eric asked, wrapping an arm around Luke's waist and pulling Luke tight against him.

"That's where the dragonlings go," Luke said, looking up at him. "But mine are too young. Why is it here?"

Eric's grip was tense and he could see the familiar anger in Eric's eyes when Eric thought Daniel should have taught him something and hadn't. From the hints that Anna and the elders had told him, there was much more to these gates than he knew and he also was starting to resent Daniel. But he couldn't suppress his fear that they were going to force his dragonlings through at too young an age. Why else would the gate be here, so close to them? But then again, if that was the plan, why would there be so much food?

"The gates are also how we travel back and forth to the realm where the adult dragons live," Eric explained. As always, he spoke with no impatience or condescension. "Several groups within the tribe move between the two regularly. Right now, most of my tribe is there, where the dragons can protect them. My advisors and I will be traveling back and forth frequently, always making sure that the people here are protected and you are never alone. You did realize I couldn't stay with you all the time, didn't you?"

Luke nodded. Eric squeezed him gently and continued.

"You are also going to travel back and forth."

Luke flinched and pulled away from Eric to face him. He didn't know how gates worked, but he was frightened of them and would never go through one.

"No," Luke said. "I won't go through one."

He caught expressions of anger from the advisors but Eric

was calm.

"Your dragonlings will be safe. Anna assures me that you will hear them just as clearly and your range will be exactly the same."

"Why should I trust her?" he demanded.

"She's a fellow tamer," the youngest man said. "Why would she lie?"

Eric gestured for him to be quiet and Luke glared at him.

"They all lie, and they manipulate, and they control," he hissed.

"You're one of them," the man said, ignoring Eric.

"No, I am not," Luke said firmly. "They said so. They never trained me, so I have no rank in their society."

"Luke," Eric said, drawing his attention. "Anna isn't the only one. Our former tamer moved between realms when she held dragonlings all the time. She was nothing like the current tamers. She taught me to be a leader. I trusted her. She would never lie to me, and she never lost a dragonling in all of the decades she raised them."

Luke reconsidered. He trusted Eric, and he trusted the people Eric trusted, even the man who thought that all tamers were good. That man had probably only known the former tamer too, after all, and thought all tamers were like her. If Eric's former tamer went through the gate, perhaps he would try it. If he didn't like it, he wouldn't do it again. But he would try.

"I'll do it once," Luke said. "But if I can't hear my dragonlings, I'm not staying."

Eric smiled at him. "Are your dragonlings comfortable? Do they need anything?"

"Not for a few hours. Why?"

"I'm taking you through the gate."

Panic flooded him. He stared at the gate, at its deceptively smooth surface. He remembered his dragonlings flying through, his bond with them abruptly ending, leaving him empty inside. The only reason he wasn't worried that he would lose his dragonlings was because he held the female and he knew that no one would risk her death. But he couldn't afford them to be quieter in case they needed anything, and he was scared about his range if he went somewhere else. But Eric said he would be safe.

Eric reached out to take his hand, and Luke hesitantly took it. The dragonlings were silent, watching him. He reassured them, and they chirped and started playing again. Luke, Eric, and the advisors approached the gate where Anna waited. He studied her. She had helped him many times, but she had also tried to tame him. He wasn't sure how to treat her and he was feeling very vulnerable.

"Please don't go near my dragonlings," he said quietly.

"Of course," she said. She didn't look upset or offended and he was grateful. He didn't want to insult her, but he was scared for his dragonlings.

Eric squeezed his hand. "We'll go through one at a time. The most important thing is not to pause as you go through."

Luke swallowed. He could do it. Eric let go of his hand and all of the advisors walked through. They were very calm and clearly did it often. Then Eric nodded to him.

"I'll be right behind you," he said. "Take a few steps forward so I don't run into you."

CHAPTER TWENTY

The Other Realm

Luke hesitantly approached the gate. He took a deep breath, closed his eyes, and walked forward. He expected the ground to give way as he stepped through, but it continued and he opened his eyes. He was through, and he was in a strangely beautiful place. He was on a grassy, hilly plain under a beautifully blue, cloudless sky. He could see the ocean a short distance away. There was a large group of people in front of him, and the advisors were at the front. Remembering Eric's words, he kept moving until he reached the group of advisors even though he kept staring around in shock.

He could still feel his dragonlings clearly and sensed that he hadn't moved any distance in terms of his range. But he also felt flickers of other dragons nearby. Many dragons. More than he had ever imagined. They felt like the mother dragon who had first summoned him, yet different too. They wanted to bond with him but he wanted to meet them first. He sensed that he could bond with all of them and keep his dragonlings because his bond with these dragons wouldn't be as direct.

He looked behind him. The gate wasn't bound to a wall, just existed in space and looked bizarre. Eric walked through and came to his side. Eric continued walking toward the large group of people that must be the rest of the tribe and Luke followed, as did the advisors a few steps behind. The crowd separated respectfully and again he saw anger on their faces, again he wanted to hide his face, but again he knew they needed to see that he had been hurt so they knew why they had been forced to leave.

They reached another hill and the potential bond with a dragon strengthened. He gasped. There was a dragon on the hill, but it was like no dragon he had ever seen. It was a little smaller than the dragonlings he raised were just before he released them, even though he released them when they weren't quite full-grown. It was a beautiful emerald, but it had no armor, just scales. All of his dragonlings began grey and turned white, and developed thick layers of armor. Aaron had explained that the psychic touch of a tamer affected the color of dragonlings and different tamers created different colors. Since none of the elders had been surprised that all of his dragonlings were the same color, he had assumed it was true and he still did. But what about the armor?

"This is Ryseth, my dragon," Eric said proudly. "I've ridden him since I became leader."

He had a name, which was also unusual. Perhaps when dragons reached maturity, they chose names for themselves, since Ryseth didn't sound like a name that a human would choose. Luke wasn't sure how to react. Eric obviously loved Ryseth but Ryseth confused Luke so much. He was nothing like a mother dragon but nothing like the dragonlings Luke raised. Yet there wasn't anything wrong with him.

Your dragons are special, a voice in his head said. It was connected to the potential bond he felt with the dragon and he knew it was Ryseth's voice. *They are unique among all dragons.*

Luke looked at Eric but he didn't appear to hear Ryseth.

Only those I choose can hear me. All dragons will speak to you, because you are a tamer. We rarely speak to anyone else. We can hear all their thoughts, but will only hear what you want to say.

Luke wondered how to talk back to Ryseth. It was probably the same way he communicated to his dragonlings, except that he used emotions with them and he could use words with Ryseth.

You're beautiful, he said cautiously, and felt Ryseth's

pleasure.

It was true. Even though he was so different from Luke's dragons, he was gorgeous. He didn't know what to say after that. He reached out and Ryseth let Luke stroke his muzzle. Ryseth's scales were far tougher than Luke had expected and while they weren't glassy like the armor he was used to, they provided excellent protection. He was always reassured that his dragonlings were so protected after they flew off into an unknown place, but he knew he would feel equally assured if they had scales like this.

Will you bond with me, tamer? Ryseth asked in a very humble tone.

Luke pulled his hand back. He felt the potential bond in his mind and for a moment it felt like a threat. He shielded his dragonlings carefully but he knew Ryseth could sense his distress. Ryseth lowered his head and angled it towards Luke in a docile position.

Your mind has been injured. My bond will not injure it further. No dragon's bond will injure it. We will make it stronger.

Luke stared at the dragon. Ryseth had said he could only hear what Luke wanted him to hear, but clearly Ryseth could see a lot further into Luke's mind than he wanted. How did Ryseth know that Luke was damaged? Was it because Eric knew and Ryseth heard Eric's thoughts? Or could all the dragons sense it about him? Ryseth wasn't a danger, though. Luke could feel the truth of his words. Bonding with him, with any grown dragon, would strengthen his mind and shield it from further damage. Perhaps this was what Eric had said about making sure that Daniel and the elders couldn't hurt him again.

Luke put his hand on Ryseth again and opened his mind to the bond in the same way he did to newborn dragonlings, the same way he had to the female. He sent a wave of love towards Ryseth but where the dragonlings accepted the love and sought out more, Ryseth took the love and returned it.

Luke was startled and didn't quite know what to do. The

bond was complete, but he felt loved in a way he had never felt before, a way he only glimpsed when Eric held him. Ryseth accepted him completely and would protect him forever, just as Luke would do for Ryseth. He had never expected that the bond would ever be mutual.

Yet even though the bond was more intense in that way, it required far less energy than a dragonling bond because he didn't need to keep up a constant flow of energy and support. He and Ryseth were both self-sufficient and so was the bond. They were connected, but not reliant. Being close to each other would strengthen them, but being apart would not be detrimental. There was no range, no fear of not hearing Ryseth. He could take care of himself.

Ryseth curled his tail happily, then looked at the sky. Luke looked as well. There was a small shape approaching, a dragon headed straight for them. Sunlight glinted off it. Ryseth immediately took off and landed a short distance away and Eric went to Luke's side, looking a little nervous. Everyone else backed away.

The dragon drew closer and suddenly Luke felt the bond between them burst to life. It was one of his dragonlings returning to him as a grown dragon and he could hardly believe it. There was no need to open himself to the bond; it was already there from when Luke had raised him. But like with Ryseth, the bond was self-sufficient now. Luke cried out in joy and rushed forward as the dragon landed. He was magnificent.

Luke barely had time to admire how glorious his dragon looked before he flung himself at the dragon, not exactly knowing where to hug but trusting his dragon to catch him. He ended up clasping the dragon's muzzle, his belly against the armored snout and his arms not quite reaching around his dragon's mouth as the dragon aimed his head at the ground so Luke could hold him better.

His dragon's wings were unfurled and Luke could see that the armor that had just been starting to develop had now covered the entire wing, and several more layers covered his body as well. His dragon's warm blue eyes twinkled from the depths of his armored face and Luke closed his eyes and relaxed against one of his first litter, one of the first dragonlings that had given him a purpose in life.

You came back, Luke said. *I love you so much.*

He let his love pour into the dragon and he felt swallowed by his dragon's love. The two of them were at peace. Then he became aware of the murmurs of the people around him, confusion and some fear. He felt Ryseth projecting obedience and wondered why. He pulled away from his dragon and stroked the dragon's nose as the dragon inspected him.

You are injured? The dragon asked, a note of concern in his voice.

Luke blushed and lifted a hand to his face. To his surprise, the dragon turned to look at Eric.

You were told to protect him, the dragon said, and Luke knew that Eric and possibly others could hear him.

"I did my best to protect him," Eric said, clearly angry but also trying to be polite. "But the other man you told hurt him before I could help him escape."

The dragon looked at Luke and then at Eric again. *No one else was told.*

Now Eric was obviously angry, though again he was doing his best to hide it.

"One of the Untamable approached me when I was with Luke's former leader. The Untamable told both of us that Luke needed help. I refused to tell him where Luke was but he found out and did this to Luke before I could get Luke here. If you hadn't told him that Luke was in trouble, Luke would be safe."

Now the dragon pinned Luke in his stare. Luke could feel confusion in the dragon's mind.

The only ones who should have heard were ones who you had allowed into your mind, the dragon said. Luke knew he was the only one to hear. *Why would you allow an enemy into your mind?*

I thought I could trust him, Luke said, ashamed of his answer and his blindness and his love of Daniel for so many years.

Instantly the dragon filled him with love and acceptance and he felt Ryseth's love as well. He would never be judged by his dragons. They might be confused by his actions at times, but they would always love him absolutely. He felt on the brink of tears to have such unconditional acceptance. He had never felt that in his entire life.

His dragon dipped his head to Eric.

We apologize and take the blame for the harm to our tamer. We will protect you and your tribe and see that you are not targeted. Our tamer, with your help, will tell us what happened and we will inform the other tribes and see that the proper tribes are punished.

Eric bowed deeply. Luke gestured him to come closer. He hesitated and looked at the dragon, but when Luke gestured again, he obeyed. He paused several feet away and Luke went to his side and pulled him forward. Luke took Eric's hand and pressed it against the dragon's long snout, on the smooth glassy armor. The dragon was amused at Eric's overwhelming awe.

"Ryseth's scales felt very strong," Luke said, still holding his hand over Eric's. "My dragons have a different armor and that's how I know they're safe even when I have to let them go."

Eric looked dazed and overwhelmed. It was strange seeing him like this when Luke was normally the one in this position. Luke let go of his hand and Eric stroked the dragon gently and timidly, as if expecting the dragon to object.

The dragon nuzzled him a little and looked at Luke, sending a message only to him.

Your mate is worthy of you.

Luke blushed and placed his hand next to Eric's on the dragon. His dragon thought of Eric as his mate? He was in love with Eric, true, but they had never done anything. He had never even allowed himself to think of doing anything, not really. Letting Eric into the core of his mind was more intimate than physical sex, he knew, but mate implied a sexual relationship. He glanced at Eric, who was gazing at the dragon with a look of pure delight. Luke smiled. He was glad to give that kind of delight to Eric.

After a few minutes, the dragon lifted his head away from both of them and looked up. There was nothing in the sky but the dragon continued looking for several moments.

I must go, the dragon said so everyone could hear. *You must be protected.*

Luke wanted him to stay but he reluctantly backed up with Eric at his side to give the dragon space to take off. He could see that Eric wanted to say something and indicated that the dragon should wait a moment.

"What is it, Eric?" he asked.

"Do you have a name?" Eric asked the dragon.

The dragon tilted his head in confusion and looked to Luke. Luke's dragonlings never had names. He just knew them. They all felt different so he never confused them and even now, they felt the same as they had before so he knew exactly which dragonling this was. He felt a polite pressure from Ryseth's mind. His dragon felt it too. Luke had never denied a dragon access to his mind so he opened himself without worry.

Ryseth explained and showed him and his dragon how dragonlings didn't have names but when dragons reentered the world of humans as adults, humans needed names to identify them so dragons would take names to make it easier for them. The Untamable had never associated with humans and never needed names and would not know that, Ryseth added in a very respectful tone. It was clear that Luke's dragon understood the reasoning but still didn't exactly understand what a name was or what it did. That was too complicated to explain right now, so Luke and Ryseth let it go and his dragon flicked his wings and turned to Eric.

We do not have names. We do not understand names. We will return when our tamer is here again.

"Thank you," Eric said.

He flew off, lifting more quickly than his size suggested, and vanished into the air.

"He'll be safe?" Luke asked.

"No dragon would ever harm one of the Untamable," Eric said, leading Luke back to Ryseth, the advisors, and his tribe.

"Why do you call him that?"

"No one has ever been able to tame them. No one can reach their minds. They're different than all other dragons."

Luke was pleased that no one else had tamed his dragons, that they were all free. He hoped they weren't lonely but he had sensed from this dragon's mind that they had gathered together and worked with each other. He knew dragonlings could only be in groups of six, but dragons had to be different. There were too many potential bonds budding in his mind in too small an area here for that to be true for adults.

They reached the others and Luke was surprised to see a wide variety of emotions on the people's faces, from fear to admiration to shock. Eric pressed against Luke firmly as if directing him to stay in place, then took two steps forward to face his people. The advisors were behind Luke even though they wore the same mixture of expressions.

"My people, we are now being protected by the Untamable. I told you that there were many reasons why this tamer needed to be rescued. You saw the obvious one when you saw his injuries."

Luke blushed and fought the urge to duck his head.

"Now you see the other. A leader who will abuse its tamer will abuse its dragons. If those dragons are the Untamable, the balance of this realm will be destroyed. It is our duty to protect them as they protect us."

CHAPTER TWENTY-ONE

Taming

Eric continued talking and Luke let his mind wander towards the potential bonds all around him. He cautiously extended his mind to the closest one besides Ryseth and felt joy at the contact. The dragon welcomed him and poured love into him. He barely maintained the solemn expression that he felt he ought to wear while Eric talked to his people. Vaguely, he heard Eric mention the tribe's plans but there was another dragon pushing into his mind eagerly, and another.

He wanted to greet them all individually but they were all so excited that they kept bumping against each other in his mind and their psychic scents blurred. He ordered them to wait and they obeyed, even the ones he hadn't bonded with yet. One by one, he embraced each dragon in his mind, sharing the unconditional love that he hadn't imagined possible. He could sense his dragonlings as well and they were excited to have older brothers. Even the female, who still grumped occasionally about sharing with her brothers, expressed curiosity.

Eric had stopped talking, he realized, and he pulled his mind away from the dragons reluctantly. The man smiled and took his arm, leading him to a tent and settling him into a chair.

"I won't interrupt you while you're communicating, and neither will anyone else," Eric said, then went to stand guard at the entrance to the tent. People milled about, as curious as their dragons, but he couldn't face them. He could only face his dragons.

Soon, he had bonded to every dragon in a two-mile radius. A few dragons entered his radius after he had begun greeting everyone and they also nuzzled him for a bond. He could barely believe how much pleasure his bonds could give him. His mental walls were still impenetrable, but he realized the adult dragons could flit in and out without disturbing them. His shields didn't seem to work against them and oddly, he didn't mind.

He was about to return to the real world when a new dragon entered his radius. The dragon was frightened, and it was a female. He immediately reached out to comfort her and she fled into the love he offered her. Someone was trying to tame her; someone she didn't want. He reassured her that no one would tame her. She was still frightened and he considered. She was too frightened of humans to come here, but where else could she be safe?

He reached out beyond his radius, sending out a message to his dragons, the ones Eric called Untamable. He felt a vague reply, though he was too far to really communicate. But he could sense their direction and he urged his new female to go to them. She was hesitant and he could feel awe and respect through the bond, and he reassured her again that they would protect her. He pushed a message towards his dragons, hoping they would receive it and protect the precious female.

She flew out of his radius towards the Untamable and he sighed. He wouldn't really have any way of telling if she reached them or not. But at least she wouldn't be tamed.

He opened his eyes to the world. Eric still stood guard but the shadows were different. He tensed and felt his dragonlings. They were just about ready for a feeding and even though they had missed a playtime, they had been so entranced meeting the dragons that none of them minded, not even his female. Eric turned as he stood up, smiling at him warmly.

"You've tamed the tribe's dragons?"

Luke stiffened at the word. "I bonded with them," he corrected. "At least I think they belong to this tribe. There was a female at the end. Someone was trying to tame her but I helped her escape."

A smile quirked across Eric's face. "You stole a female? That's considered rude, at best. Is she coming here?"

"No," he said. "She was scared. I sent her to the rest of my dragons, the Untamable. They'll look after her until she comes here."

Luke paused. "I though all the females were dying, but she was fine."

"Well," Eric said slowly. "Females can't give birth here. They have to come into our world. Once in our world, though, they start to die. No one can figure it out."

The last was almost a question, as if Eric were hoping that Luke knew the answer. Unfortunately, it was a puzzle that he had never solved. He had never known about this world, though. Maybe now that he could communicate with adult dragons, he could figure it out. He took a few steps towards Eric and was surprised at how weak he felt. He leaned into Eric as the man wrapped his arms around Luke's waist. Luke nestled against his chest for a moment, inhaling the scent of citrus he associated with Eric. There was something different there now, too, an earthy scent of a meadow after the rain when the fireflies starting calling to each other in slow, lazy blinks.

Luke realized he hadn't ever left the city since joining Daniel's tribe. Daniel said it was too dangerous and it probably was. He hadn't left urban life much in his life except for his desperate run to find the mother dragon who had protected him from the touch. When he ran away from his home, he had traveled through pastures with this scent, unable to pause and admire the beauty of the darkening sky and the twinkling insects and only able to keep going because he knew if he stopped, he would never start again.

He leaned against Eric and inhaled the scent again. It was the scent of full-grown dragons, he realized. His injured cheek brushed Eric's jacket and he winced as a shot of pain lanced through him. He wanted another ice pack.

When he flinched, Eric drew him away and began leading him out towards the gate. There were people around, a lot of people, and most of them tried to hide the fact that they were staring at him. He kept his focus on Eric as they headed through the crowd back to the gate.

❋ ❋ ❋

Eric observed Luke carefully as they stepped back through the gate. Luke was pale, but seemed happy. In pain, but content. Dragon tamers drew their strength from their dragons and if what Luke said was true, he had just tamed – bonded with – an enormous number of dragons. Usually when a tribe took on a new tamer, each dragon had to be introduced slowly. They remained tame, but it took a while before their loyalties transferred to the new tamer. It seemed as though Luke, however, had fully tamed all of them in a matter of hours.

The instant they were through the gate, Luke went to his dragonlings and began preparing to feed them. But before he started, he hesitated and glanced at Anna, who was nearby. He smiled shyly and thanked her. She was startled and clearly taken by Luke's smile. It was hard to resist that gorgeous smile.

Anna remained with Luke, at a safe distance, but Eric left with the advisors who had come back with him. He needed to figure out how to arrange this. His entire tribe was on his side now that they had seen Luke and especially the Untamable, for those in the other realm. The Untamable had said they would protect them in the other realm, but there was nothing the powerful dragons could do here. Eric needed to be prepared.

He and his advisors laid out maps and started discussing the best plan for keeping their people safe on the seas. As they talked, Eric let a small part of his mind observe the others, determining how well they would work with Luke. He wanted

Luke to have company at all times and while he trusted all of his advisors completely, Luke wouldn't. Eric would have to be careful. Already Luke distrusted Daron because of the man's insistence that Luke was a tamer, and Daron tended to have a fiery temperament as well. He would not do well alone with Luke.

Shin was extremely laid back and would work with Luke well, as would Rena, who had been a friend of Eric's mother. She was one of his first advisors and an advisor to the tribe's former leader. Both of them were always warm and friendly, though Eric knew they could be sharp if necessary. Shin especially tended to have a fierce streak when something he valued was threatened. Eric would just have to ensure that Shin valued Luke.

Mei might or might not be a good fit. Eric would have to observe the two together. She had a high opinion of herself and was smart enough that she could get away with it most of the time. Luke might find it irritating, as Eric sometimes did, or he might feel threatened, or he might be grateful for the help. She was a good conversationalist and knew all sorts of random information that Luke would no doubt be fascinated by, but they had to have some sort of rapport first.

And Tran, the oldest of all of them, probably wouldn't do well. He was strict about rules and regulations, constantly reminding Eric of the intricacies of etiquette that he often forgot. They were nearly obsolete customs now, but Eric preferred to be as polite as possible and appreciated Tran's attention to detail. Most of the time. Luke would not appreciate it, however, and it would undoubtedly cut away at his already fragile self-esteem.

He arranged for Shin and Rena to take care of Luke for the most part, with Mei helping during the day. Daron and Tran would remain in the other realm and assist Eric there. Mei would have the option of transferring realms whenever necessary and that divided his advisors evenly between the realms, though when Shin or Rena were specifically with Luke, they would have trouble taking care of the rest of the tribe as well. He would leave it to them to work out a more specific routine. He trusted them.

As the leader, Eric would be transferring back and forth to care for both groups. While normally he would spend more time in the other realm since that was where most of his people were, he knew Luke needed him desperately. Plus, this was the realm where they were in danger, since the Untamable would protect them in the other realm. He wanted to stay with Luke all the time, of course, but he knew he couldn't. Tamers were important, and Luke especially was important because of his place in Eric's heart, but all of the tribe looked to him for strength and he needed to guide them in this troubled time.

Once the schedule was loosely determined, he went to Sam and Denis. While they weren't officially his advisors, he looked to them for help on almost everything. They were his bodyguards and it wasn't unusual for a tribe leader to value his bodyguards highly. Eric wondered who Daniel's bodyguards were and if Luke had ever met them. Luke seemed to have no experience with anyone other than Daniel. He was going to have a difficult time adapting to a regular tribe where everyone prized him so highly, but hopefully he would draw strength from his new position instead of being frightened by it.

Sam was in charge of intelligence gathering to keep the ship safe, since he had many contacts with the nearby governments, but Denis would be accompanying Eric between realms. Eric gave Sam some warnings about contacts who might turn on them, then went to check on Luke. It was late and he wanted to make sure Luke was settled before he returned to the other realm.

As he approached the area they had set up for the dragonlings, he paused. Luke was nursing one dragon with another on his chest, and the female lay on her back across his thigh as he stroked her belly. Eric didn't know how he could possibly give three dragonlings his attention at the same time but all three seemed completely content. The other three were playing in the folding fabric they had hung up. Normally a tamer handled one dragonling at a time while the others played, since they drew strength from each other as well as from their tamer. Eric allowed his mental awareness to stretch out and sense Luke. He was so much stronger than any other tamer Eric had ever sensed.

Luke noticed him and beamed. The three dragons who were playing swooped closer to him and chirped happily, then returned to the ceiling. It was also unusual for dragonlings to mimic their tamer's emotions so closely that it impacted their attitudes towards other people. Normally dragonlings ignored anyone besides their tamer. But Luke's dragonlings had threatened Eric once, and were now far friendlier than most. They reacted to Luke strongly and it was a good thing he felt safe now. Eric was determined that Luke would remain safe. Not only did he want to protect Luke, he knew if the female died, then his whole tribe would never escape. Even if the Untamable protected them, allowing the only female to die would be inexcusable.

Eric didn't say anything, just waited as Luke finished feeding the dragonling. He caressed him, then kissed the one on his chest. They flew off with the others and the female lifted her head, then rolled over and wrapped around him. Luke cuddled with her for only a moment before shooing her to play with the others. He stood and approached Eric shyly.

"Are they satisfied?" Eric asked. "Don't rush because I'm here."

"I wouldn't," Luke said. "I mean, I didn't."

"Your dragonlings should always come first," Eric said with a grin. "I'm glad they do. Are you ready for bed? I'll help get your settled but then I need to leave."

Luke tensed, the fear returning to his eyes abruptly. He clutched Eric's hand, then took a deep breath as if trying to calm himself. The dragonlings paused in their play, but didn't look upset. Luke took a few more breaths as the dragonlings returned to chasing each other, then he looked around.

"Is it safe to sleep here?"

"I thought you might want more privacy," Eric said, glancing at the nearby bedroom that had been assigned to Luke. He couldn't imagine Luke wanting to sleep out in the open like this, but then again, maybe the public setting would reassure him that no one would attack him as Daniel had done.

Luke took another deep breath. "Where should I sleep?"

"Let me show you," Eric said. "And then you can make up your mind where to go."

CHAPTER TWENTY-TWO

Deceptive Rumors

The room Eric showed him was simple, with a hard bed built into the wall and a few basic, built in necessities. Luke realized he had nothing, but Eric seemed prepared, showing him where he could find things for his use. He didn't even have a toothbrush, or clothing. He was still in Eric's clothes. Eric had given him all the basics and the small dresser had a few sets of clothing in it that looked like they would fit him, and Luke flashed a shy smile at Eric in thanks for the thoughtfulness. Eric stroked his cheek.

"Do you feel safe enough here? Would you rather stay with your dragonlings?"

Luke considered. He would have loved to stay with them, but he didn't like the idea of sleeping in the open like that. He had slept in a separate room at the elder's compound, so it wasn't like he was used to sleeping with them. But he also didn't like the idea of being alone. Not after everything that had happened.

"You can't be here?"

Eric sighed. "That might be difficult. I need to speak with my people more. You really want me tonight?"

Luke bit his lip. He did want Eric, desperately, so that he knew no one would break into his room and hurt him. But he knew Eric was needed by his own people, too. He couldn't steal Eric's attention like this.

"All right," Eric said, to Luke's surprise. "I'll be back in a couple of hours. Try to sleep until then, and I'll try not to wake you up when I come in. Is that okay?"

"Yeah," Luke said, then clutched Eric's arm and clung to him. "Thank you," he whispered. Eric kissed him on the head and gently pushed him towards the bed.

Luke obediently undressed and quickly got in the pajamas in his dresser. He prepared for bed and felt the sway of the ship beneath him. He barely noticed it, though he had noticed one of Eric's advisors, the oldest man, having some trouble walking straight. Luke had never been on a ship before. He suspected that the waves didn't tip large ships like this as much as would happen on a smaller vessel, but he wasn't sure. It was soothing, he decided as he lay down and pulled the covers under his chin. Like someone was rocking him to sleep. He couldn't fall asleep, though, and knew he wouldn't until Eric came in.

But he began to drowse, and when the door quietly opened he didn't tense, just opened his eyes to confirm that it was indeed Eric and not someone to attack him. Eric had a bag with him and quickly stripped, and Luke couldn't help but admire him as he was briefly naked in the dim light of the cabin. Luke had left on one light for him that Eric turned off before making his way to the bed. Startled, Luke realized that of course they would have to share a bed, and they would have to get quite close to fit. He scooted over and Eric curled around him, kissed the back of his head and wrapped his arm around Luke's waist.

"I didn't mean to wake you," he said softly.

The feel of a body against him like this ought to stir up fears, Luke knew. It was so close to how Daniel had held him. But it didn't. It was reassuring, like the waves. He knew Eric would never hurt him. So he shut his eyes and luxuriated in the embrace, secure in the knowledge that Eric wouldn't push for more than he was ready to give. He felt asleep in a cocoon of comfort and slept better than he had in years.

He awoke to Eric untangling himself and let out a soft protest.

"I'm sorry, Luke, but I can't stay," Eric said.

Luke rolled over and watched him dress. He could sense that his dragonlings would be ready for a feeding soon, so he ought to get up as well. But he felt so calm. He held his hand out to Eric and the man – now dressed – took it and kissed it.

"When will you be back?" Luke asked.

"Tomorrow," he said. "Rena and Shin are here with you, so let them know if you need anything. They'll help you. And Luke," he added, his voice catching. He paused, as if unsure what to say, and Luke wondered what he was stopping himself from saying. Eric knelt beside the bed and cradled Luke's face in his hands, careful to keep away from his injuries. "You'll be safe here, and just know that I'm nearby," he finished, though Luke knew that wasn't what he had intended on saying. Still, it was reassuring. Then Eric carefully kissed him on the lips and left the room.

Luke yawned and got out of bed, dressing quickly and leaving towards his dragonlings. But as soon as he left, he noticed one of Eric's advisors, leaning against the wall in the corridor watching him with hostility. Luke eyed him nervously. Eric had said to trust his advisors, but this one didn't look especially friendly. He was the one who had called Luke a dragon tamer and his animosity now was not making Luke like him any more. What was his name? He couldn't remember.

"He's mine," the man said without preamble. "He may be interested in you right now, but it won't last."

"Excuse me?"

"You're a pretty little thing," the man said, eyeing him in a way that made him incredibly uncomfortable. It was the same way Daniel had looked at him before tossing him in the bed. "He likes pretty little things, but they don't last."

"I don't know what you mean," Luke said.

"Eric," the man said, and Luke's heart thudded. "His interest won't last. It never does."

Luke raised a hand to his lips. What did he mean? Of course Eric's interest would last. Eric loved him. Or he assumed Eric loved him. Eric had never actually said it, he realized. But Eric had seen inside his soul and accepted him. Or had he? Eric had said he was beautiful, he realized. Not that he loved him. Wouldn't that have been a natural time to say it if it were true? Did Eric just think he was pretty, and that was it?

"Why are you telling me this?" he whispered.

"Because he's mine, and I won't have you interfering," the man growled. "It's hard enough keeping his attention with all of his other lovers, and I won't have you added to that list."

"His other lovers?" Luke repeated, his stomach dropping.

"You don't know anything about him, do you?" the man asked with a smirk. "He's sweet to you, I'm sure. He's sweet to all his lovers. But they don't last. I'm the only one who's lasted, and it's going to stay that way."

The man turned and left down the corridor, vanishing around a corner. He was headed towards the dragonlings and Luke drew in a sharp breath. Was he going to hurt the dragonlings? He wouldn't dare. Luke hurried after him, reaching out to the dragonlings and finding them too sleepy to obey his orders to take flight and stay out of reach. He urged them awake just as he entered the room and saw the man entering the gate at the other side. Luke relaxed, then noticed the older woman, who must be Rena, and Shin waiting near the dragonlings. But not too near.

"Is everything all right?" Rena asked in a kind voice, and Luke took a deep breath. They obviously didn't know that the other man had just talked to him.

"It's fine," he said. "I need to feed my dragonlings when they wake up."

"Of course," she said. "I'll stay with you."

"No, you won't," he said sharply, wondering if she was trying to steal his dragonlings the same way Anna had once tried.

"Near you," she corrected. "As far away as you need. I just meant that I'll be helping you bring food to them."

Luke tried to relax. He was too tense, though he was

shielding it from the dragonlings. They were waking up now with little chirps.

"Are people going to be coming through that gate a lot?" he asked, wondering if that man would be returning and also wondering how safe the dragonlings were.

The woman glanced at the gate, then shook her head.

"You mean Daron. He just forgot something. No, only Eric and Mei will be going through the gate, and I can give you warning if you want. We know when they'll be coming and going."

"If you'll excuse me," Shin said politely, and headed out of the room.

"Aren't you staying with me?" he asked, puzzled.

"Just me," Rena said with a smile.

He liked the way her face wrinkled when she smiled. It was very friendly. She probably smiled a lot, he decided. Unlike him, who rarely smiled at all. Of course, he had very few reasons to smile in his life. Except he had been smiling a lot more since Eric had shown up, he realized. Would that continue to be true? If Eric had other people in his life, other people he loved, how would that change things? He remembered how vulnerable he had felt as Eric stripped him in the bathroom. He had enjoyed it thoroughly, but there was still a hint of fear. He had gotten over that fear quickly when it was his turn to strip Eric, and he blushed thinking about the lust that had washed over him.

Did Eric feel anything like what Luke felt for him? Was that just one more moment of intimacy for him, or did it matter? It profoundly stood out in Luke's life, as did his first kiss, and the feel of Eric inside his very soul. But did Eric feel any of that?

He went to his dragonlings in a daze as Rena helped him carry bottles over. Between them, they gathered enough for a single feeding and she placed them where he could access all of them without moving. His dragonlings were in the air by now, playing in the folds of cloth out of reach of Rena. When the woman backed away to a table and bench nearby, in view but out of reach, he called the female down. She obeyed and chirped sweetly, nuzzling the bottle as he got into position.

She fed eagerly as the males played, and soon he was rotating through them, pouring his love into them, feeling their little tummies filling up. He could also feel the grown dragons in his mind, though they felt distant. Could he feel his other dragons, his Untamable? He tried to reach out to them and felt only a vague direction. They must be quite far away, he decided. As he fed, he tried to bury his fears about Eric. Eric was keeping him safe here. Even if Eric wasn't interested in him, he would still him safe. That wouldn't change. The female was too important, and no matter how intense Eric's feelings were, Luke trusted that he would never send him back to the Elders or to Daniel. That much was clear. But how much of the rest was true, and how much was faked? Was Eric only faking an interest in him? Or was it sincere?

He glanced at Rena, wondering if he should ask. She wouldn't know about how Eric felt about him, but she would know if the other man had been lying about other lovers. He remembered how experienced Eric seemed, especially during that first kiss. He had known exactly what to do and even the way he had pinned Luke down had felt practiced. How many times had he stolen a kiss like that? How many times had he coaxed men like Luke into giving away their affection? He didn't want to know, Luke decided. He wouldn't ask, because he was afraid of the answer. If Eric's love wasn't real, then he didn't have anything except the dragonlings and that was a thought he couldn't bear.

CHAPTER TWENTY-THREE

Outside Taming

Eric smiled at Daron as he returned through the gate. He smiled back, coming up to Eric and clasping his arm. He was one of Eric's best friends and he wished Daron and Luke could get along, but he suspected it would be a long time before Luke trusted him after what he'd said about being a tamer. Their personalities weren't a good match, either, but maybe in time they'd learn to work together. He didn't like having to keep his friends separate from Luke.

"Get what you need?"

"Got it," Daron confirmed.

"Did you see Luke at all? He's probably feeding his dragons now."

"He was headed that direction."

Eric nodded, relieved. He hadn't liked leaving so early, but he suspected Luke wouldn't sleep long anyway. He was too nervous about the situation, and the dragonlings demanded his care at regular intervals. They were still young enough to need feedings and playtimes throughout the day and while they, and all dragonlings, seemed to understand the difference between night and day and left their tamers alone at night to sleep, it was still a demanding schedule. Their previous tamer was often exhausted when the dragonlings were this young. It took a full year before the dragonlings gained a sense of independence and required less from their tamer. That meant months of Luke being bound to the ship, unable to travel to this realm freely. He wanted Luke here because it was safer, but also to solve the mystery of the Untamable. Clearly they were linked to Luke, but how? Most linked dragons wanted to stay close to their tamer, but these didn't. Were they truly tame?

Luke had called it bonding, he considered. Maybe Luke was doing something completely different. Maybe he wasn't taming them, but linking to them in some other way. He went to Ryseth, who was waiting for him to fly out and keep a watch on their borders. So far, no other tribe had tried anything. There had been quite a few dragons flitting past their borders as if watching them, but no one had attacked. Since the other tribes thought he had attacked the Elders, they were probably concerned he would break other rules as well.

He hopped on Ryseth and gestured to the other dragons who helped him with patrols. There were always dragons circling their territory now and their partners had informed him that Luke had tamed those dragons, too, even though the dragons were nowhere near him. They were all within the two-mile radius at some point while Luke was here, though. The dragons left that range regularly on patrol, but always returned closer to the village and Luke had apparently tamed all of them whenever they drew near. It seemed almost impossible, but it was true. He had tamed every single dragon in the tribe.

We are not tame, Ryseth said unexpectedly.

Eric started in surprise, immediately caressing his dragon in thanks for choosing to speak to him.

"What do you mean?" he asked, puzzled. Tame dragons were the only ones who allowed humans to ride them or interact with them in any way. All dragons allowed tamers to touch them, but only a fully tamed dragon allowed anyone else near them. Even partially tamed dragons were dangerous if one drew too close.

He has set us free, Ryseth said. *We are choosing to stay with you. With him. We wish to serve him.*

"He said he bonded with you, not tamed you," Eric said

slowly. "So there is a difference?"

Silence, but perhaps he shouldn't have expected the conversation to last much longer. Ryseth had answered his questions, after all. Dragons weren't know for talking to humans any longer than they had to, though he suspected they spoke to tamers all the time. The old tamer had indicated as much. But he considered Ryseth's words. That had to mean that every dragon who came into contact with Luke was no longer tame, but they were still acting tame. After all, Eric and five others were riding the dragons in this group with no problems.

Normally a dragon would do anything a rider told it to, because it was tame. Would these dragons refuse if they didn't want to do something? Possibly. Maybe they would only follow orders they agreed with from now on. It was a startling level of independence to consider, and potentially dangerous. In battle, a dragon needed to obey orders instantly. If the dragons were acting the way they wanted without regard to their human, then either the attack could go wrong or the human could fall off. He stroked Ryseth. He could feel reassurance from the dragon, though he didn't speak. Maybe this wouldn't be a problem.

And to be perfectly honest, he was a little relieved that Ryseth was free. He had never really liked the idea that his dragon was bound to his will, even though that was the traditional role of the dragon. When Ryseth had contradicted him about telling Daniel where Luke was, he had appreciated the advice. At the time, he hadn't even noticed that a dragon shouldn't be able to contradict him so strongly. But it wasn't the first time Ryseth had advice for him. He always listened. He trusted Ryseth to know what was best. He stroked Ryseth again. He still did trust his dragon. Even if Ryseth were no longer tame and was only here because he was choosing to be here, he wouldn't stop trusting his dragon.

They reached the edge of the territory and began their sweep. Eric tensed as he saw a dragon approaching, but relaxed when he saw the light glinting off it. One of the Untamable. Once, they would have filled him with awed terror. Now, though, they were a reassurance. There seemed to be two of them circling the territory at all times, though they never drew near the dragons from Eric's tribe. They were solitary sentries, but the other tribes had surely noticed them. Maybe that was why they hadn't pushed, he considered.

He flew out of the range of the Untamable and saw another dragon. This one was from another tribe. Not unusual, as the other tribes had been sending scouts like this regularly. But this one was flying straight at him and he halted, looking around. The other dragons on his patrol were nearby and one headed in his direction to give backup if necessary. The neighboring tribes were friendly in normal times, but he couldn't count on that now.

When the other dragon drew close enough, he recognized Else, the leader of one of the neighboring tribes. She came to a stop close enough to talk to him, but far enough not to be a threat. He wondered what she could possibly want, but she didn't seem to want to attack. Just talk.

"Is it true that you attacked the Elders and stole two tamers?" she asked.

"I rescued two tamers against the Elder's wishes," he said. "You know I would never attack them."

She was silent for a moment, then looked past him towards his territory.

"I heard one of the tamers you took had bonded with the female. Is that true?"

"Yes."

"He stole some of my tribe's dragons. I demand he release them."

Eric stared at her in shock. "That's impossible," he said after a long moment.

"Five of my tribe's dragons no longer respond to our tamer. Apparently they belong to someone else now. Luke. Is that the tamer you stole?"

"It is, but…"

He thought back to Luke's words. Luke hadn't actually been sure that all of the dragons he tamed were in the tribe.

"Were they within two miles of my base yesterday?"

"Probably," she said. "That can't be his range. No tamer has a range that large."

"It's his range," Eric said. "I apologize. Can your dragons be retamed? I don't know what else to do."

"They can't," Else hissed. "They refuse all mental contact with our tamer."

"Luke didn't know what he was doing," Eric said. This was bad. When Luke had said he stole a female that someone else had been trying to tame, it was problematic but it did happen. Dragons in the process of being tamed didn't actually belong to anyone yet, so they were occasionally stolen. But to steal dragons that were tamed by someone else was unacceptable. Wars had been fought over less, and he couldn't afford a war. Not when the entire society was already against him.

"I'll talk to him," Eric said rather desperately. "I'll tell him he needs to release the dragons, and then you can retame them."

She glared.

"You know I didn't ask him to do it," Eric said. "You know I would never steal your dragons. You're an ally. And you know I can't risk a war right now. Let me talk to him."

"When? We need those dragons, and now we have to waste time retaming them."

"He's raising dragonlings and can't be in this realm often, but as soon as he's back, I'll tell him to release them. He's an outsider," he added. "He doesn't understand the rules."

"Then it's your job to teach him," she retorted angrily. "Get your tamer under control."

She paused then, her brow furrowing. "He's been with the Elders for months, hasn't he? Surely they taught enough to prevent him from stealing dragons."

"They didn't teach him anything," Eric said. "They abused him. Why do you think I rescued him?"

There was a silence as she clearly considered his words. "You've never lied to me," she said slowly.

"And I'm not now."

"Why would the Elders abuse one of their own?"

"I don't really know," Eric admitted. "He's powerful. Extremely powerful. And the Elders who control the council now aren't. Maybe they wanted to control that power for themselves. But they did hurt him. Physically, emotionally, psychically."

Else looked back at her territory. "You're leveling a serious charge against the Elders," she said uncertainly. "Why would anyone believe you over them?"

"All you have to do is talk to the tamers in question and you'll know the truth. Besides, the Untamable are protecting us. Would they do that if we were to blame?"

"It is unusual," she admitted. "They've never guarded a tribe the way they're guarding yours."

Warn her not to bring her dragons within Luke's range, Ryseth said suddenly, unexpectedly. He looked down at his dragon in surprise. Else narrowed her eyes.

"Your dragon talks to you? What did he say?"

"You might not want to bring your dragons within two miles of our base," he said.

"Why not? Are you planning on stealing more?"

Eric looked down at Ryseth, hoping for an explanation. The dragon was silent.

"I guess Luke might not listen to me," he said, wondering if that were true. Why else would it be dangerous to bring dragon's within Luke's range? "I'm not entirely sure. But I'll do my best to persuade him to release your dragons. I apologize. You know it was unintentional."

"We'll keep our distance," she said. "And if what you say about the Elders is true, then we have no reason to attack you."

"They'll want you to," he warned. "I don't know when, but eventually they'll want to move against me. They want Luke."

"They want you, too," she said. "There's a price on your

head. Alive."

Ryseth drew back slightly.

"You're not here to collect it?"

"I've never had any quarrel with you," she said with a shrug. "And my tribe isn't in need of the money. But you should watch yourself on your borders."

"Thank you," he said, wondering how long there had been a price on his head. He would have to give up patrols, he knew. It was unfair making his tribe take over without contributing at all, but he hoped they understood. Else might not be a threat, but his other borders weren't so certain.

"We won't attack you," she said. "No matter what the Elders want. We respect them and listen to them, but they don't control our fighting. Now go get your tamer in line quickly. We need our dragons back."

Eric agreed and thanked her again, then she set off towards her territory and he set off towards his. The other dragons on patrol were nearby, keeping an eye on the situation, and he signaled them to continue the patrol without him. He would explain in more detail when they returned. He flew straight to the base and patted Ryseth before heading to the main tent where his advisors would be. This was potentially a serious problem.

CHAPTER TWENTY-FOUR

Developing Shields

An entire day passed without seeing anyone other than Anna, Rena and Shin, but the dragonlings kept Luke busy. When he kissed the female before going into his bedroom, he only paused briefly. He was scared to sleep alone, but he didn't think anyone would attack him. Still, he kept thinking about Daron and what he had said, and wondering if someone else was going to corner him and say something else to rattle his world.

He had thought about Eric a lot throughout the day, wondering about Eric's feelings for him. He couldn't decide if they were sincere or not. Clearly Eric wanted to protect him, and did have some sort of feelings for him. He wouldn't have risked his entire tribe to rescue him if he didn't. Then again, Luke was a tamer being abused. Maybe he would have risked everything to save anyone in that position. He had saved Anna, too, after all. She had stayed nearby throughout the day, though not close enough to threaten his dragonlings. He had let her play with them when he was with the Elder's but in this strange place, he didn't want her too close. She seemed to accept it. The dragonlings were friendly to her, though, and didn't mind playing beside her even if Luke forbade them from actually touching her.

Luke shut his eyes and focused inward on his shields and his shattered mind. He had taken Eric here, he thought as he looked at the crystalline center of his soul. Eric had seen him and hadn't been repelled. He wanted to help Luke recover himself. That had to mean something, didn't it? But there had been no words of love. Protection, caring, beauty, but not love. Was he just afraid to use that word? To be honest, Luke was a little afraid of it. He didn't want to make himself vulnerable, even though he already was. As he felt the jagged edges of his soul, he remembered what Anna had said about his mind, and how he was already tamed.

Anna had said that when a mind couldn't be tamed, it was because it had already been tamed by someone else. That someone, in his case, was Eric. He had let Eric into his soul when they first kissed. He hadn't realized it at the time but looking back, he had allowed Eric to feel his very essence, and had opened himself entirely to the experience. Things had changed between them after that. He was no longer afraid of Eric. He wanted Eric at his side. Was it really because Eric had tamed him? He shivered. He didn't like the thought of being tamed. He wanted to be free, the way his dragons were free. But as he looked at the center of his being, he could see traces of Eric. It wasn't just the memory of Eric being here. It was the way the light glittered off the hairline fractures, the way it glowed so gently; something about the light itself, Luke himself, that reflected Eric. And if Eric didn't love him, he wasn't sure what he would do.

The morning came quickly, though as Luke opened his eyes, it felt as if he hadn't slept at all. He had spent quite a bit of energy looking inward like that, he realized. Well, it shouldn't impact the dragonlings. He had enough to care for them properly. But he would be careful in the future. He didn't want to drain himself the way he had after bonding with the female. And no matter how safe he felt at the moment, there was always the danger that something would happen and Daniel or the Elders would find him. He had to be on guard against that, because even though bonding with the dragons had made him stronger, he still felt vulnerable.

The dragonlings were just waking up and chirping as he came out to him and Rena was nearby, as she had been the previous morning. No one else was there and he relaxed. He had half been expecting Daron to be here. He began feeding his dragonlings without a word, and after a few hours Anna showed up. He wasn't sure what else she was doing, but she wasn't consistently in the room with him. He considered her, then waved her over. She blinked in surprise but obeyed, and he pushed a box of scarves towards her the same way he had when they were at the Elder's and he had realized she was an ally, not an enemy. She smiled at him and tossed a scarf into the air. The males chased after it, but he kept the female with him. She was sprawled on his thigh, one of her favorite spots, and he stroked her belly as he watched the males play.

The female hadn't changed colors, he thought as he stroked her. His males were usually born different colors, but quickly turned silver. Daniel had said they were responding to Luke's mental touch. He had no reason to believe otherwise, even if Daniel had lied about so many other things. But the female was still red. His little males were also starting to develop the beginnings of their shields, hard little plates along their bones that would grow to encompass most of their bodies. By the time they were ready to enter the gate in a year and a half, they would be almost completely shielded, and he knew that once they were fully grown like the Untamable he had seen in the other realm, they would be safe from the outside world.

But the female, though only a couple of days younger, didn't have any shields or even anything resembling them. He felt along her spine, where the shields developed first, and felt nothing but soft scales. She hissed and he stopped feeling her, not wanting her in discomfort. Was that softness normal for a dragonling? Why hadn't she adjusted to his mental touch the way the males had? Was it because she was female? He glanced at Anna shyly. He still didn't like asking her questions, but he didn't know who else to ask.

"Anna, is the female developing normally?"

Anna peered at her, sprawled on his thigh.

"She should be," she said. "You're taking excellent care of

her. Are you worried about something in particular?"

"She's nothing like my other dragonlings," he said, gesturing to one of the males who buried himself in the box of scarves. "All of them have always been silver, with shields. She's not like that."

Anna looked at the males, in particular the one in the box who seemed to be posing for her.

"All of your previous dragonlings have looked like this?" she asked. He nodded. "Your previous leader had to know, then," she murmured.

"Know what?" Luke asked warily, not liking the thought of Daniel hiding yet another thing from him.

"That they were Untamable. I didn't understand at first, until Eric told me what happened in the other realm and your connection. But these dragonlings are clearly developing into Untamable dragons. The Elders might not have realized it yet, but in the last day it's become clear. No other dragon looks like them. Most dragonlings look like the female."

"So she is normal," he said in relief, then stroked her belly. "She'll be like the other dragons?"

"Yes," Anna said. "Though I don't know why. It is normal for a dragonling to reflect its tamer. I don't know why she wouldn't develop the way these are developing."

"Maybe I got her too late," he said as the female fluttered her eyes at him. He leaned forward and kissed her outstretched head. "Or maybe females can't be Untamable. As long as she's healthy, I don't care. I just don't know what's normal for dragons like this and I was worried."

"She seems perfectly healthy," Anna said with a slight smile as the female wrapped her wings around Luke's hand to pull it towards her belly for a pat. "She loves you a lot."

"Do your dragonlings not love you?" he asked. "You and the Elders kept implying I'm doing something different with mine."

"They love me," she said with a much wider smile. "And I love them. But most of my time is spent with the adult dragons."

"They don't really need much, do they?" he asked, puzzled.

"They still need care and attention to keep them tame," she said. "Eric said you tamed quite a few of the dragons. It's still early, but you have to keep renewing the bond with tamed dragons or they return to the wild. You probably won't notice that for a few weeks."

Luke wondered. It didn't feel like that would ever be a problem. The adults were part of him now, and he was part of them. They couldn't be isolated, and he couldn't imagine the need to strengthen the bond between them. But maybe in time he would understand. Maybe, in a few weeks, he wouldn't be able to feel them as clearly and they would have a harder time flitting through his mind. He could feel them even now, brushing against him, checking on him, adoring him. Their constant love was one of the few things buffering him from worrying too much about Eric, because even if Eric didn't love him, he still had them.

"So what do you do here? You don't have dragonlings, and the tribe's dragons are bonded to me, not you."

"I'm helping the people," she said. "I came to live with the Elders about three years ago when my last litter went free. Normally I would go with my tribe into the other realm to take care of their dragons at that point, but the Elders requested me. They wanted to teach me how to be an Elder," she added shyly. "That was when the old Elders were still alive. So I've been without a tribe and essentially without dragons for a couple of years now. But I learned how tamers need to interact with their tribes, and I've been taking care of the people here. They're frightened, and having a tamer calms them."

"You tame the people?" he asked, appalled.

"No, of course not!"

She sounded almost offended, but she had tried to tame him. It wouldn't be unusual for her to tame others.

"I guess some of it is the same," she admitted. "I offer them comfort and solace. But I don't try to control them, nor would I want to. Humans shouldn't be tamed."

"Thanks," he muttered. She at least had the decency to blush. He supposed she had apologized for that, and she hadn't been willing to break his mind to tame him. There was at least that.

"You'll learn how to do some of it soon, when you start interacting with the tribe more," she added. "Tamers are the center of our society. Everyone in the tribe is connected to them in some way."

"Why?" Luke asked, thinking of how thoroughly isolated he had been in Daniel's tribe. He hadn't been in that tribe, not really. He belonged to Daniel, but not the rest of the tribe. He thought of the way Eric's tribe had looked at him, though, and how ordinary it had been for him to walk around the Elders with his dragonlings. People understood who and what he was, and understood the dragonlings. Daniel had implied that the dragonlings were a secret that no one else in the tribe cared about, but he had lied about so much it wasn't surprising this was a lie as well.

"Tamers just take of the dragonlings," he said. "Why should anyone care about them?"

"They take care of all the dragons," Anna said. "Not just the dragonlings. And without the adult dragons, we're not a tribe. We're just humans. Our society reveres dragons, and tamers are the only humans that dragons will obey. Therefore, tamers are revered."

"I guess," Luke said. It was true that there was a lot to being a tamer he hadn't known about. It made sense that because tamers helped with the adult dragons, they would have a bigger role than Luke's had been because he was just helping with the babies. "Why wasn't I allowed to take care of Daniel's dragons? Why did he just have me with the dragonlings?"

"I don't know," Anna said. "It doesn't make sense. But dragonlings can be very intense to care for. How long did you spend without dragonlings?"

"Not long," he said. "Less than a year. I've pretty much

always had dragonlings to care for since I ran away."

"That might be why," she said. "Maybe he didn't want you splitting your focus. And since your dragonlings are Untamable... maybe he didn't want to risk them becoming something else. But I don't understand why he never brought you into that realm to see if you really were linked with the Untamable."

"Why didn't the Elders bring me there?"

"They were waiting for you to ask," she said. "And none of them suspected you were linked to the Untamable in any way. Your dragons were the right color, but hadn't started developing these shields."

She gestured to two of the males who were wrestling inside the box of scarves. Luke watched them, happy that they were having so much fun. He still regretted separating them from their mother sometimes, but they didn't miss her. Dragonlings rarely paid attention to their mothers, really. They fed from them, and the mothers of course cared for them, but the only true attachment a dragonling had was to their tamer.

"Eric should be here in an hour or two," Anna said after glancing at her watch, and the female's head lifted and chirped, reflecting Luke's instinctive pleasure at the thought. But should he be pleased? He would have to see. In the meantime, he would play with his dragonlings and make sure they were as happy as possible.

CHAPTER TWENTY-FIVE

Free Bonds

Luke was with his dragonlings when Eric came through the portal, and Eric smiled. Anna was near him, playing with the dragonlings. That was a good sign that Luke felt a little safer. Then his eyes met Luke's and his smile became genuine. But Luke didn't smile back. He was a little surprised. Luke rarely smiled, it was true, but this seemed like one of those moments when he would. Eric approached and waited a safe distance from the dragonlings.

"Are you able to talk, Luke?" he asked, knowing better than to intrude.

"You can come here," Luke said. "The female doesn't want to move."

The little red dragon was curled up in his lap and lifted her head lazily to chirp at Eric. He hesitated. He had been near the dragonlings before around Luke and knew they weren't a threat, but it was so unusual for anyone who wasn't a tamer to be allowed near them. Most tamers were quite paranoid about their dragonlings, no matter how much they trusted the person. Eric's former tamer wouldn't dream of allowing him close and she trusted him completely. But Luke didn't have a problem with it, so Eric cautiously approached and sat next to Luke on the bench. The female chirped at him again and nestled deeper into Luke's lap. Anna seemed shocked that Luke was letting him in, but didn't say anything. She just stood up, smiled, and headed out of the room. He silently thanked her for giving him space.

"How are you doing, Luke?"

One of the males perched near him on the bench and looked at him curiously. He had never been so tempted to stroke a dragonling before, but it was almost like the little male was inviting him.

"The dragonlings are happy," he said.

"And you?"

"I'm fine," Luke said, but didn't meet his gaze. He was focused on the female.

Eric sighed. He wanted to pursue that and find out if there was anything he could do to make it better than fine for Luke, but there probably wasn't. His bruises still stood out starkly and though there were two ice packs nearby, it didn't seem like he was using them regularly. He was likely still in pain, and possibly still in shock. There wasn't much Eric could do about that. And he did need to get the other tribe's dragons taken care of quickly, before Else ran out of patience. She had said she wouldn't attack and he trusted her, but she might take other action if he didn't return her dragons.

"Luke, when you were taming dragons, you tamed a few that weren't from my tribe," he said cautiously.

"I did? Oh. I'm sorry."

"You need to release them back to their tribe so they can be retamed. Can you tell which ones they are?"

His brow furrowed. "Oh, I can tell," he said startled. "I can feel the trace of their previous tamer, and there are eight who had a different tamer than the others."

Eight? That was definitely a problem because Else had said five. Had Luke tamed three other dragons belonging to other tribes? None had approached him yet, but would they? And would they approach as peacefully as Else had done? Stealing a dragon was a serious crime, after all.

"You can't take other dragons like that, Luke," Eric said. "It could have very serious consequences."

"I didn't do it on purpose," he said. "They wanted to bond

with me, so I let them."

"You didn't do it on purpose?" Eric repeated. "You have to consciously tame a dragon. You have to choose to do it."

"Well, I mean, I guess I did choose, but I wasn't going to argue with them. They wanted to bond with me. And I don't tame them," he added sharply.

Eric sighed. "Well, however it happened, you need to let them go so they can return to their previous tamer."

"They're free to go at any time," Luke said, sounding puzzled. "I'm not holding them. They go wherever they want. If they want someone else, they can have them."

Eric considered. Clearly Luke didn't fully understand how the bond between adult dragons and tamers worked. Maybe Anna could explain it to him, but he suspected Luke would listen to him better. Still, he wasn't entirely sure how to describe what was happening. He had never felt it, after all. He had only learned about it. But he had to try, because if Luke was taming every dragon who happened to come into his range, he would almost certainly provoke a war at some point.

"When a dragon is tamed, there's a bond that's formed between the tamer and the dragon," he said. "Can you feel that bond between you and your dragons?"

"It's different with adults, though," Luke said. "The dragonlings are reliant on me. Their bond is solid. With the adults, it's barely a bond at all. They're just... there."

That didn't sound like how his previous tamer had described it, but he thought about what Ryseth had said. Luke wasn't taming them. They were no longer tame; they were free. It would make sense that it felt different to Luke, since it wasn't the same type of bond that would occur if he tamed them.

"Is there anything you can do to... detach yourself from the dragons who don't belong to our tribe?"

Luke seemed to be thinking very deeply, and his eyes went vacant as all tamers' eyes did when they were communicating intensely with their dragons. Was he in contact with them here? Could he communicate with them from this realm? Normally a tamer had to be in the same realm for true communication. They could feel all of their dragons wherever they went, but couldn't speak to them unless they were nearby. Then again, Luke's range was so large it was difficult to predict how the distances between realms affected him.

"They don't want to go back," he said slowly. "I told them they could return to their previous tamers, but they don't want to be tame. They want to be free, with me."

"Their previous tribes need them, Luke," he said urgently. "Stealing a dragon is worth going to war over."

"I can't force them to go back," Luke protested, then was silent for a moment. "I can make them listen to their previous tamers. They won't let themselves be tame again, but they'll listen, and obey if they want to. That's the best I can do."

"Let's hope it's enough," Eric said grimly. That wasn't what he had expected. But Ryseth was free and seemed to be just as obedient, so maybe the other dragons would be as well. The tamers wouldn't like it, though, he already knew. Tamers liked to be in control of their dragons at all times. His previous tamer had been like that, and he suspected it was one reason the Elders had wanted to control Luke. Luke, like his dragons, was free. Most dragon tamers were part of a strict hierarchy, but Luke wasn't. And now his dragons weren't, either. This was definitely going to cause problems, but if this was the best Luke could offer, then he would have to take it.

Luke glanced at him, looking very vulnerable all of a sudden.

"Am I worth a war?"

"What does that mean?"

"You said there could be a war because I'm bonding with other dragons. And your whole tribe had to abandon their homes because of me. Am I really worth that?"

"You're worth everything," Eric said, reaching out to stroke his uninjured cheek. Luke seemed to lean into the caress, but he still seemed afraid. "What's worrying you? I'll talk to the other tribes and make them understand that their dragons can't be retamed. It'll be difficult, but I'll manage it. Can you make sure you don't bond with dragons from other tribes in the future?"

"I'll try," he said in a small voice.

The female lifted herself from Luke's lap and flew towards the curtains where the other dragonlings were playing, and Luke scooted closer to him and took his hand. He glanced up at Eric through his lashes and for a moment, Eric was breathless at how beautiful he was. Warmth flooded through him and he leaned forward without thinking and kissed Luke. Who withdrew. Startled, Eric lifted Luke's chin so their eyes could meet. Luke seemed overcome by indecision and fear, but why?

"What is it, Luke?"

"I heard, well, that you had been with other people," Luke said cautiously, and Eric's eyes narrowed. Who had he heard that from? It must have been the Elders, but then why was Luke bringing it up now?

"Surely you realize you're not my first," Eric said slowly, not wanting to deny the truth. "But now you're my only."

"For how long?"

Eric was startled. How long? Forever, he longed to say, but there was something in Luke's gaze that told him a platitude or exaggeration wouldn't work.

"For as long as you're in my life," he said slowly.

"What if other people want you? Better people? People you love?"

"I don't love anyone but you," he said, then bit his tongue. He hadn't meant to confess his love like that. He had confessed his love to the Elders and they had used it against him. He had almost said it to Luke before. Yesterday morning when he had been about to leave, he had almost said it. He wasn't sure why exactly he was afraid of saying it, except that he had never said it before to anyone in his life and meant it. But it was true.

"You love me?" Luke repeated slowly, and Eric suddenly realized he had no idea how Luke felt about him. He obviously trusted him a great deal, and was in his debt, but was that the same as love? "Why haven't you told me before?"

"I- I didn't know how," he admitted. "I suppose I thought it was obvious, to some extent. The Elders knew. They tricked me into saying it, and then they sent me away from you so they could abuse you. They hurt you because I loved you. I don't want to see you hurt."

"How long have you loved me?"

"I don't know," Eric said, starting to worry now because Luke still hadn't made his feelings clear. "I don't know if there's an exact moment when it happened. I just became aware of it after a while. I suppose seeing your mind, your soul, solidified it for me. I knew I would do anything to protect you. I wanted you."

"Is that love?"

"What else would it be?"

Luke looked uncertain again. "You tamed me," he said, though without the accusation Eric might have expected. "That's why Anna couldn't do it. You did it first. Do you want to control me?"

"No," Eric said, worried now because he knew how much Luke feared being controlled. Was Luke going to reject him for something he hadn't done on purpose? He hadn't known he was taming Luke, whatever that even meant. "How do you know I tamed you and didn't bond with you, the way you do with your dragons?"

Luke was silent, and Eric pushed, because it was true. He didn't want Luke tamed, and hadn't done it intentionally. So wasn't it more similar to what Luke did?

"Your dragons are free, but they choose to follow you," he said. "Can't you be free, too? But just... choosing to be with me?"

Luke didn't say anything and Eric tensed. Did Luke not want to be with him? Luke needed him, and couldn't completely reject him, but would he reject his heart?

"You want me to be free?"

"I wouldn't have saved you from the Elders otherwise," he said. "I wouldn't have rescued you from Daniel. You deserve to be yourself and make your own choices."

"You have always done that," Luke murmured. "You think I'm not tame, then? You think we just... bonded with each other?"

"I don't know how it works," Eric said. That sounded promising, but he wouldn't feel safe until Luke actually said how he felt. "I'm not a tamer, and I can't sense things like that. But I care about you. I want you in my life. I love you."

A long moment and Eric's hands trembled. Luke looked up at him from under those luscious blonde lashes again and then a brilliant smile stretched across his face. As always, Eric was stunned by his beauty and without thinking, he kissed Luke. That smile was a good enough answer for him. He didn't need to hear the words to know Luke's feelings when they were so clearly written across his face.

This time, instead of pulling away, Luke clung to him, opening his mouth against his as their tongues wound together and he felt as if Luke were somehow igniting every nerve in his body, arousing every part of him. Their first kiss had been incredible; this was something else altogether. He grabbed Luke and pushed him backwards until he was flat on his back. Eric leaned over him, caressing his body as he plundered his mouth, pressing down until his chest brushed against Luke's, sliding his hand down his arms to his sides and his hips, reaching back to grab his ass as Luke moaned under him-

And he remembered where they were. In public, on a ship, in a very exposed location where anyone could walk in and see. He pulled back immediately even as Luke clung to him, clearly wanting the embrace to continue. He pushed Luke out of the kiss and sat up, looking around. No one nearby. Good. But that didn't mean no one had seen it. Someone could have seen it and left. And the room was under surveillance, he realized in shock. He wasn't sure if this particular area were in view of the couple of cameras scattered around, but they kept this room loosely monitored to make sure no one came through the gate without permission.

"Eric," Luke murmured, trying to pull him back down, but Eric helped Luke sit up. Then Luke looked around as if in shock and his cheeks turned bright red. "Did anyone see that?"

"I don't think so," Eric said, then laughed. "We got away with it. Next time, let's go to your room first."

"Next time?" Luke asked invitingly, the red in his cheeks still burning.

"I hope there's a next time. Do you want one?"

"I want more," Luke said shyly, the flush on his cheeks reaching to his neck and nose. It was almost unbearable how beautiful he was, especially when he was being bold like this.

Eric leaned forward and pecked his lips. "You'll get more. But not now. I need to get in touch with the other tribes and apologize for their dragons. I can come back tonight and spend the night with you."

Luke shivered slightly. "Maybe not more immediately," he said, the flush from his cheeks fading. "Maybe not tonight."

"Not until you're ready," Eric assured him. He wasn't too surprised that Luke was having second thoughts. Though he had some very sensual instincts – their kisses were proof of that, as was how Luke had stripped him – he was also very shy and had been taught to suppress his lust. It would take time for him to be fully comfortable. Plus, he was still injured, Eric remembered. Not just his face, but his back as well. He would have to be careful with Luke until he was fully recovered.

"But you can still sleep here," Luke said, and Eric grinned. "Anything you want."

CHAPTER TWENTY-SIX

Threats of War

Eric invited Else into his territory to talk rather than attempt to explain everything on dragonback and luckily, she accepted. She seemed wary going into his territory, probably because she still suspected his tribe had attacked the elders, but one of the Untamable was circling nearby and that seemed to reassure her. He was reassured by it as well, since it meant Else's tribe wouldn't try to invade while she distracted him. She had always been an ally, but everything was different now and he couldn't forget it.

She had been here in better times and it was dramatically changed. There were now tents everywhere, since most of the tribe was living here. Normally less than a hundred people stayed in this realm at any time to take care of the dragons and fight in the tribe wars that took up much of their time. Else's tribe was allied with his and they had fought side-by-side many times, never against each other. She had been here to plan before and he could tell she was surprised to see nearly a thousand people here. He led her into the tent he was using to plan their moves and manage their survival. He had hidden everything related to the warship where the rest of his people were, though. He trusted Else, but not that much.

"I didn't realize your whole tribe was here," she said.

"I assumed the Elders would strike and I didn't want them vulnerable," he said.

She nodded. "Your neighborhood has been completely

taken over," she said, and he winced. They had brought everything valuable that they could carry but they couldn't bring everything, and the neighborhood itself was one of the nicest in town. He hated to lose everything he and his predecessors had fought so hard to achieve, but he hadn't had any choice. Luke had to be rescued. Even if he had thought through the consequences, he would have saved Luke. Even if he didn't love Luke, he would have saved a tamer being abused.

"My dragons are still untamed," she said as she sat across from him on the ground. He sighed.

"Luke can't release them," he said, and her eyes narrowed. "He hasn't tamed them the way a tamer traditionally does it, so he can't undo it. But your dragons will still obey your tamer and all of you. You won't be able to tell the difference, though I'm sure your tamer will be able to."

"I don't understand," she said, brow creasing with a hint of rage. "What do you mean, he can't release them? They'll obey, but they're not tame? Why can't he just release them and let them be retamed?"

"Luke is somehow... freeing the dragons," Eric said cautiously. He wasn't sure how much to trust Else but he didn't want her to start a war over this and she looked angry. "He doesn't tame them. He says he bonds with them. But it won't make a difference. None of my tribe's dragons are technically tame anymore, but they act exactly the same."

"Your dragons aren't tame?" she asked with a speculative gleam in her eyes, and he laughed.

"You can't tame them," he said. "They've chosen Luke as their tamer. It's just not a traditional bond between them. They view themselves as free, but they want to obey us."

"Dragons can't be free," she said. "Only wild ones are free."

"My dragon talks to me sometimes," he said. "He told me he was free but choosing to obey me. He's not tamed, but he's not wild."

"That's dangerous," she said. "What if he decides not to obey you? What if something happens to your tamer? What would you do then?"

What would happen to the dragons if something happened to Luke? He hadn't considered it because he was taking so many steps to protect Luke and didn't like to think about it, but would his tribe's dragons continue to obey them or would they return to the wild? Anna would help retame them, he knew, but that would take time and it would be a crippling blow to his tribe. He wasn't worried about Ryseth disobeying him, though. If Ryseth ignored him, he was confident that his dragon would have good reason.

"I trust my dragon," he said. "And I'm protecting Luke."

"So this tamer of yours, Luke, has freed my dragons and they can't be tamed again," Else said skeptically. "And you want my dragons to stay out of his two-mile range. What kind of tamer is he? Why would you ever take someone so powerful away from the Elders? They need to be teaching him to control his power."

"They want to control him," Eric said, trying to hide his anger. "If you saw him, you would understand. His previous leader abused him and they let him. They tried to break into his mind. I would rescue any tamer from that situation but the fact that he's so powerful just makes their abuse worse. He wasn't the only tamer they had imprisoned, either," he added. "I saved two of them from that situation."

"I can't see the Elders abusing a tamer," Else said slowly. "But you've never lied to me. You said I would believe you if I saw this tamer. Can I?"

"Can you what?"

"Can I see him? Bring him here so I can meet him and hear him explain why I can't retame my dragons. Then I'll decide whether or not to forgive you stealing my dragons like this."

Eric was tongue-tied. Could he bring Luke here?

"He has a litter of dragonlings," he said. "And he's not familiar with this realm. His previous tamer and the Elders didn't tell him anything about this place or about adult dragons. He might not want to come here."

Secretly, Eric was also worried that if Luke showed up, the Untamable would also show up and Else would realize the connection between them. No one could know that Luke controlled the Untamable or else nothing would stop the other tribes from uniting against him and wiping his people out. They would never allow another tribe to control such powerful dragons and they wouldn't listen to him when he tried to explain that he had no intention of controlling them. He wanted them to keep doing what they were doing. He didn't want them to fight for his tribe, though he was beyond grateful that they were protecting him.

"Eric, you stole five dragons from me and can't give them back," she said, clearly irritated. "Normally I would take this matter up with the Elders but you're on the run from them. If I don't hear from your tamer personally, I'll have no options."

Eric winced. That wasn't good. He would have to bring Luke here and risk the Untamable.

"All right," he said. "I'll see if he can come. Is there a good time?"

"Right now," she said. "I'm already here. I'm not coming back."

"He might be taking care of his dragonlings," he warned. "He won't leave if he is."

"I'm sure he can spare a few minutes to prevent a war," she said with narrowed eyes.

"I'll talk to him," Eric said, though he knew Luke wouldn't leave his dragonlings if they needed care. Not even to prevent a war. They were too important to him. "I'll go see if he can come right now, but you shouldn't have your dragon nearby," he said, suddenly thinking of that danger. If Else's dragon bonded with Luke, he would really be in trouble.

"Just tell your tamer not to steal it and there won't be any problem," she said. "Is he really that out of control?"

"He doesn't seem aware of when he's taming dragons," Eric said cautiously. "I'll warn him, but it's safest if your dragon is more than two miles away. You're safe here. I would never hurt or even threaten the leader of a neighboring tribe."

She studied him, then sighed. "All right. I trust you, Eric. And if you try anything on me, my tribe will attack. All of us will. I'll send my dragon back into my territory to wait until after I've spoken with this tamer."

Eric thanked her. "Please wait here," he said. "Our gate is nearby and he's close to the other side. If he's willing to come, I'll be back in less than ten minutes. Do you need anything?"

"Just hurry," she said.

He agreed and headed to the gate, filling in Daron on the way. Daron didn't look pleased and neither was Eric, but there was nothing they could do about it. He went through the gate and looked for Luke. He was with his dragonlings, of course, and he wasn't feeding them. He let out a sigh. Even if he was playing, he could probably convince Luke to leave for a few minutes. He headed over to Luke and paused a polite distance away. Luke was studying him. He wondered if Luke would talk to him or just ignore him until his dragonlings were finished playing, because he was playing with them right now. Anna was with him, he was pleased to see, and she was tossing scarves to the males.

"Luke," he said. "Can I talk to you?"

He stood up and the dragonlings went into the draping fabric of the little nesting area. Anna stood as well and he sighed in relief. The dragonlings had been playing, but not in need of play or else Luke would have ignored him and the dragonlings wouldn't have flown off so easily. Anna headed to where Rena was seated and Luke approached him shyly.

"I didn't think I would see you today," he said.

"I need you to come into the other realm," he said, and Luke stiffened. "It's important. The leader of the neighboring tribe, the one whose dragons you stole, she wants to talk to you in person. You need to explain to her that you can't return her dragons or she'll start a war."

"She has to see me?" Luke asked, raising a hand to cover his injured cheek instinctively. "I thought only your tribe needed to see me."

"It's important," he repeated softly, taking Luke's hand in his own. "Please. It'll only take a few minutes."

"Will she try to take me back to the Elders? To Daniel?"

"She's surrounded by my tribe," he said. "Even if she wanted to, she wouldn't be able to. And when she sees you and talks to you, she won't want to."

"All right," Luke said softly, and Eric squeezed his hand.

"Luke, I don't know how much control over this you have, but I don't want her knowing you're connected to the Untamable. Is there any way to prevent them from showing up?"

"I don't know," Luke said thoughtfully. "If any are nearby, I'll ask them to wait. But it's their choice whether or not they listen."

"Tell them it's dangerous to you if they approach right now," he said, and Luke drew in a sharp breath.

"Is it?"

"If she knows that you control the Untamable, then my tribe won't survive," Eric said. "It's not dangerous to you, but it is dangerous."

"I'll tell them," he said seriously. "I think they'll listen. But I can't promise anything. I don't want to control them."

Eric nodded and hoped that was enough to keep the powerful dragons away, because he could not afford to have the other tribes band against him. Right now they were staying away because the Untamable were watching over them but if they realized Luke controlled the Untamable, the other tribes would unite and attack. The Untamable were fierce, but there might not be enough of them to stand up to all the other tribes at once. If the Untamable even fought. They might choose to abandon his tribe. They weren't tame, after all, and wouldn't necessarily protect Luke's tribe even if they would protect Luke. He sighed and gestured for Luke to go through the gate first, hoping he wasn't making a mistake.

CHAPTER TWENTY-SEVEN

Earning Sympathy

"Remember, just walk through and don't stop," Eric said, and pushed Luke forward.

Luke walked through and vanished into the glowing gate. He was still nervous doing this but like before, it was just a step and he was in a completely different world. His dragonlings were still close in his mind. He looked around at the beautiful surroundings, then quickly took a few steps forward. Just in time, as Eric appeared behind him and gently pushed him to make room. Eric took his hand and led him through the rows of tents. There were people walking around and all of them stopped to look at Luke, who blushed and lowered his head. He didn't want anyone seeing him and he didn't like that a stranger would see his injuries, but he didn't want to start a war, either. He would have to trust Eric.

They finally reached a tent towards the back of the camp and Eric opened the flap, gesturing him to enter. There was a woman inside with long black hair tied into a braid. At his entrance, she turned to face him and her eyes widened as she let out a gasp. Eric pushed him forward and he felt exposed as the woman stared at him, then slowly approached him. She studied his face and his injuries and anger swept over her features, the same anger that had been on the faces of the tribe when they had seen him. Not anger at him, he assured himself. She had no reason to be angry at him. Although really she did, he considered. He had apparently stolen her dragons and she was threatening war with Eric. Maybe she was mad at him and he flinched at the thought.

"The Elders did this to you?" she asked in shock. "They can't hurt other tamers like this."

Luke glanced at Eric, not sure how to answer and too humiliated to give an answer. It hadn't been the Elders who had done this. His leader had done this, and he had allowed it. He had felt that he deserved it. He did deserve it. He had disobeyed, and this was the punishment.

"His previous leader did it to him," Eric said, putting a comforting hand on his shoulder. "But the Elders let it happen and gave him permission to do more."

"Your name is Luke?" she asked gently, and he nodded. "Did the Elders ever hurt you?"

He looked at Eric fearfully and Eric gestured to Else. "Tell her the truth. I won't let her bring you back to them."

Else's eyes narrowed at that, but she was focused on Luke. He took a deep breath. He didn't like to think about it. He had submitted to them as easily as he had submitted to Daniel and while they hadn't left physical marks on him, his mind still ached with their attack even though it had been days since they had broken into his mind.

"They want to control me," he said quietly. "They attacked my mind. They tried to tame me."

Else appeared sympathetic, but then she sighed. "Luke, you took five of my tribe's dragons. I need them back."

"I can't," he said, looked at Eric again. "Didn't you tell her?"

"She wants to hear it from you," he said.

"They don't want to be retamed," he explained, not sure what else to say. "I asked them and they refused. They want to be free with me. But they're happy with you. They'll obey everything you tell them, and they'll listen to your tamer."

"Will you ever command them to disobey the people in my tribe?" she asked seriously. Luke reached out to the dragons he could sense weren't originally from Eric's tribe. They were happy with their current riders and were willing to tolerate their previous tamers. There was no reason for them to disobey, but he wasn't sure how to explain that.

"They do what they want," he said. "I don't command them to do anything. They're free."

She stared at him, clearly not understanding what exactly it meant that the dragons were free and not under Luke's control. He wondered how it normally was, how dragons normally felt about their tamers and the people who rode them. He tensed as something brushed his mind. Another dragon seeking a bond with him. He knew he wasn't supposed to bond any dragons that didn't belong to Eric's tribe and he could tell this one didn't, but the dragon desperately wanted to bond with him. In fact, he realized it already was bonded to him. Just the brush of its mind against his had bonded them and the dragon was quite pleased.

Luke looked at Eric with a blush. He wasn't going to be happy. "Um, another dragon just bonded with me. Not from this tribe."

"Luke," Eric hissed, and Luke flinched. "I told you not to tame any other dragons."

"I can't help it if they'd rather be with me," Luke said. Eric had never snapped at him like that before and he worried what it meant. Maybe it was just that the other leader was here. But what if Eric stopped loving him because he couldn't follow the order not to tame more dragons? What if Eric actually did want to control him? Eric turned to Else.

"How far away is your dragon?"

"She should be far enough away," Else said, appearing shocked. "No one can tame a dragon that quickly."

"I don't tame them," Luke said. "I bond with them."

"Are any of your other dragons within range?" Eric asked.

"They shouldn't be. Are you stealing dragons from other tribes, too?"

"Apparently," Eric said grimly.

"Whose dragons?"

"I don't know," he said. "No one else has approached me."

He sighed. "Do you need to ask Luke anything else? It's probably best if he heads back to his dragonlings."

Luke nodded, because he could sense another dragon's brush. One of the Untamable. He politely requested that the dragon stay away for now and he could tell that the dragon would listen. But he could also feel the dragon's longing to see him and he met that longing with his own. He wanted to hold all of his dragons, to feel that bond spring back to life. This was one from his third litter, he could tell, and he had always been the neediest dragon of that litter. He sent a wave of affection and love to his dragon but again requested that he wait.

"I'd like to talk to you for a little longer," Else said to Eric, and he nodded.

"I'll walk Luke back and return," he said.

He escorted Luke out and Luke immediately turned to him.

"I'm sorry," he said. "I didn't mean to bond with another dragon. I know you told me not to, but I can't help it. They just want to be with me and I can't say no."

Eric sighed and tears filled Luke's eyes. Was he really disappointed with him? But Eric pulled him into a gentle embrace.

"It's all right, Luke," he said soothingly. "I know you're not doing it on purpose. I'm sorry I snapped at you. Do you still want me to come back tonight?"

Luke leaned back and studied him. He didn't seem to be hiding any resentment. Would he hate Luke if the Untamable showed up right now? Probably. He claimed to love Luke but did he? He had said that they were bonded, not tamed, but did he expect obedience from Luke? Would disobeying him make him no longer love Luke?

"Do you still want me?" he asked cautiously.

"I'll always want you," he said with an amused smile. "Nothing you do could change that. Now let's get you back so I can finish talking to Else."

Luke smiled shyly at him and Eric grinned, taking his hand again. He wasn't angry, or at least he wasn't angry at Luke.

That was all that mattered.

❊ ❊ ❊

Eric finished escorting Luke back and as soon as Luke was heading towards his dragonlings in the other realm, he returned to Else, who was sitting cross-legged on the floor looking contemplative. He sat across from her, wondering what else she had to say. The conversation with Luke had gone well, aside from Luke unexpectedly taming yet another dragon.

"You have a serious problem on your hands," she said. "He's really just taming every dragon who wanders within two miles of here?"

"It seems like it," Eric said. "You saw him. He doesn't seem to be able to help it. The only thing I can do is try to keep him out of this realm, but I can't do that forever."

"I'll talk to your other neighbors," she said. "I'll try to find out who it is. And I'll tell them about Luke. I don't think it will change anything, but... I'll still tell them."

"Thank you, Else," he said, and she sighed and stood up.

"I see why you risked everything to rescue him, but he's caused quite a mess for you."

"I'd do it again," he said, thinking of Luke's body against him as they slept together a couple of nights ago.

"He's exactly your type, and he trusts you quite a lot," she added, and he flushed, his attention snapping back to her. "I hope you don't abuse him the same was the Elders and his previous leader did."

"You ought to know me well enough to know that I would never do anything against someone's will," he pointed out.

She smiled. Hers was one of the tribes who had offered him lures in the form of their members before. She knew his taste and had taken advantage of it, but she should know enough to trust him because of that. When she first offered the woman from her tribe in payment for a favor, he had refused because he assumed the woman hadn't agreed. She introduced them and the woman persuaded him she was a willing participant, and he accepted her. They slept together quite a few times, but eventually she returned to her tribe and he granted Else the favor. A beneficial arrangement for everyone. Else had to know he would never force someone.

"Still, someone that young and naïve would be easy to manipulate," she said. "Don't touch him."

"That's his decision, not yours," Eric said sharply.

"So you've already fallen for him? And he has feelings for you? He's too young," she said bluntly. "Even if he agrees, he's not old enough to understand what he's agreeing to."

"I haven't done anything other than kiss him," Eric said, though that wasn't strictly true. He had stripped Luke in an extremely intimate way, but it was true that they hadn't really done anything else since Luke had blacked out the moment he had touched him. "I'm not planning on taking advantage of him."

"As I've said before, I trust you," she said. "Just be careful. If it gets out that you're sleeping with him after supposedly rescuing him, your motives will come into question and people will be more likely to support the Elders."

"You saw why I rescued him," Eric said a little hotly.

"The others won't see, though," she said. "They'll hear about it. They might trust me about what I saw, but it won't be the same and I know you don't trust them enough to let them meet Luke right now. Hearing about how someone has been mistreated is not the same as seeing it for yourself and besides, many of them have fairly low opinions of you to begin with. Don't make it worse for yourself."

"I appreciate your advice," Eric said, struggling to stay polite. Everything she was saying was true, after all. If the other tribes thought he had kidnapped Luke because he wanted Luke for himself, then they would unquestionably side with the Elders against him. And it was true that many of the other leaders, especially those he fought against in this realm, would already be looking for reasons to distrust him.

"Well, as long as the Untamable are protecting you, I don't think anyone will attack," she said. "But they don't usually guard tribes long term. You'll need to reestablish your alliances and somehow persuade the Elders to stop coming after you."

"The only way they'll stop is if I give up Luke, and I'm not doing that," he said. "But reestablishing my alliances is possible. Would you stand with me, knowing what you do now?"

Else paused, clearly considering. She tapped a finger against her lips and was silent for a long time. Then she shrugged.

"I would need to talk to my advisors," she said. "But even if I don't stand with you, I won't stand against you, nor will I allow others into my territory if they plan on striking you."

Eric let out a sigh. That wasn't much, but it was something.

"Thank you," he said sincerely. "And I apologize about your dragons."

"As long as they continue to obey, I'll consider the matter closed," she said. "But if you try to turn them against me, I will act."

"Never," Eric promised her. "They're your dragons. I have no need of them and no desire to act against you. You're one of the only allies I have left."

"We're not allies yet," she said. "Not unless my advisors approve. We're just... friends."

He smiled. "You've always been a good friend. I'll make sure you don't regret it."

"We'll see," she said with a laugh. "My dragon just arrived. I would appreciate it if we could return without an escort. I won't linger."

He agreed and they went to the dragons. He requested that his tribe not tail her, as they usually would when a stranger was in their territory. He knew they would be keeping an eye on her from a distance but she probably knew that too. She just didn't want to be surrounded by his tribe's dragons. He thanked her again and watched her fly off, then sighed. He had avoided one catastrophe but she raised a good point about Luke. He loved Luke, but he couldn't act on those feelings until he no longer had to prove to the other tribes that he had rescued Luke because of the abuse.

But Luke was so fragile, and so unexpectedly sexy sometimes. What if Luke wanted more from him? He did, Eric knew, but what if he were actually ready for it? Would Eric refuse him? That would shatter his confidence. Well, it likely wouldn't be an issue for a while. Luke was still healing and still in shock from being attacked like that. Once he recovered, though... Eric sighed. He didn't know what he would do. He would just worry about it when it happened.

CHAPTER TWENTY-EIGHT

Unexpected Invitation

Luke only saw Eric a couple of times over the next week, and Eric didn't spend the night again. He was struggling to manage the tribe in the other realm and Luke knew he was partially to blame. Two other tribes had brought charges of stealing dragons against Eric's tribe and while the woman Luke had met, Else, was trying to smooth things over, it was rough going. Eric was wary about bringing Luke back into that realm in case he accidentally bonded another dragon but a little over a week after he had met Else, Eric approached him right after he finished feeding his dragonlings. He was on a regular schedule now that Eric knew, so they could coordinate their meetings better.

"Would you want to come into the other realm, Luke?" Eric asked as he approached and waited just out of range of the dragonlings as he always did. Normally Luke invited him closer but this time he sent his dragonlings off to play and instead went to Eric's side, shyly taking his hand.

"Is that safe?" he asked.

"Two of the Untamable have been getting close. I think they might want to see you. It's worth the risk, because the other tribes might notice exactly how interested the Untamable are in our tribe. I don't want them to know you're connected to those dragons at all. It would be extremely dangerous if anyone knew."

"The people in your tribe know," Luke said, worried because

it hadn't even occurred to him that the Untamable might be putting Eric's tribe in greater risk. He knew Eric hadn't wanted Else to know about them, but was it really that much of a problem? He didn't want to start any wars.

"They're loyal to me," Eric said. "I'd like it if you came."

"Okay," Luke said. "The dragonlings are happy. I'll ask Anna to keep an eye on them and play with them if necessary."

He had gotten used to having Anna around in the past week. She kept a respectful distance, just as Eric did, and he had invited her to play with the dragonlings every day, sometimes multiple times a day. He trusted her not to steal his dragonlings now, so he would trust her to play with them a little while he was gone.

Anna was with them right now, in fact, and he gave her strict instructions on what she was and wasn't allowed to do with his dragonlings. He didn't know how long he'd be gone but not long enough that they'd need feeding. She had fed the female dragonling once, after he had drained himself upon arriving at the elder's compound, so it wouldn't be the end of the world if she had to feed them, but feeding was one of the main ways he nurtured his bond with the babies and he didn't want to lose a single instant of that closeness. They were the most important thing in his life and he wanted to be with them every moment of every day. But he would go into the other realm if Eric wanted it.

He walked through the gate with less fear than the previous times and as soon as he was through, he felt the mental nuzzle of two of his dragons. Every other dragon within his range was already linked to him, luckily, and he would just hope no one else wandered nearby. It wasn't that he was trying to bond with them; they fled into his mind and he couldn't refuse them. Eric brought him to a hill about a twenty minute walk outside of the encampment and one of the Untamable landed. It was the dragon from his second litter who had been nearby last time. His neediest dragon. He wrapped his arms around the dragon's enormous neck as the hard plate armor pressed into him and shut his eyes, luxuriating in the feel of his long-lost dragonling now grown.

Eric stood at a respectful distance and he could feel the awe of his other dragons. The dragons Luke raised were practically worshipped by the other dragons and he was pleased. They deserved to be special. They were his, after all. He stroked his dragon and felt the nuzzle of another mind against his: the other Untamable flying nearby. He could only hug one at a time so he asked the second dragon to wait until his first dragon had filled up on all the love he could offer, then his first dragon took off to patrol the skies and was quickly replaced by his second dragon, from his first litter. This dragon had always been playful and true to form, head butted him gently the same way he had as a dragonling. Luke laughed and stood so he could see the dragon's pale blue eyes. He stroked the plated eye ridges and was happy his dragons were so safe, and were free.

You are still injured, the dragon said sadly. Luke touched his face in shame. The bruises were healing but still formed a brownish-yellow splotch on his cheek. The cut had healed and his lip was completely better, but it still ached sometimes and he couldn't forget that it was there. His back was healing as well but sometimes when he leaned against a wall or even twisted and stretched the skin too tight, it stung and he was reminded of standing there as Daniel struck him with his belt. He remembered how helpless he had felt, and how he had been convinced that he deserved everything that was happening to him. He never wanted to feel that way again.

Did the female reach you? he asked, remembering the female dragon he had sent to them the first time he was here.

We will keep her safe until you are ready for her, the dragon said.

When would I be ready for her? Luke asked, puzzled. He wanted to keep her safe forever and never bring her somewhere where others might tame her.

She will want to lay eggs, the dragon said. *You will need to bring her to your realm to raise her dragonlings.*

That was true, Luke considered. Apparently dragons couldn't give birth in this realm, and dragonlings couldn't be here either. He had also learned that human babies and young children couldn't be here and it was why all of the families from Eric's tribe were with him on the ship in the other realm. They would be safest here, protected by his Untamable, but couldn't, because the babies and dragonlings wouldn't survive.

If he brought her into the other realm, though, she would die. All of the females died. They gave birth to their litters first, and some even gave birth to two litters, but death took all of them. He wouldn't want to doom this new dragon, but he knew dragons wanted to give birth and care for their babies. It was part of their life cycle and he couldn't argue with it. But why did they have to die after giving birth?

He could tell that his dragon didn't know the answer to that but he asked anyways. He felt a void where the answer should be, but then the dragon cocked his head.

There is a place that might have your answer, he said. *There is a library that we guard. No one is allowed to enter. But we would let you in.*

Where is it? I can't go far from my dragonlings.

It is far, the dragon said sadly. *But perhaps your dragonlings will not mind the distance. You can roam in this realm as you cannot in the other.*

Was that true? He didn't know why the dragon would lie to him, and it did seem to feel that way in his mind. His dragonlings were pressed right against his consciousness as they always were when he was near them, but he was probably a mile from the gate. Eric had brought him about twenty minutes from the gate to get to a clear enough area to call down the Untamable, but he didn't feel that far away from his dragonlings. Maybe he could venture further. But he wouldn't want to bond with every dragon he passed on the way. That would certainly cause problems for Eric. Still, if the answer to the female dragons lay at this library, he wanted to go and look for it. Maybe he would ask Eric about it. He would know what to do.

After several more minutes of cuddling, his dragon was ready to leave and Luke caressed him one more time.

Tell us if you want to go to the library, the dragon said. *No others are allowed near but we will carry you.*

Thank you, Luke said, kissing his dragon's snout and sending him a wave of unconditional love. His dragon returned the emotion and Luke basked in the warmth of this dragon and all of his dragons. He felt strong in a way he never had before. Eric was right. Now that he had his dragons, Daniel and the elders would never be able to cripple him the same way.

He was feeling optimistic until he turned and saw Eric in a close discussion with the man who had warned him about Eric. Daron, Luke remembered. Daron clearly had feelings for Eric and didn't want Luke intruding and his presence here was a threat because he was so close to Eric right now, touching his arm casually as they chatted. Eric looked up and beamed at him, and Daron, with his hand still on Eric's arm, smirked. Luke tried to stifle his jealousy. Eric was not acting against him. Eric might not even realize how Daron felt about him. He shouldn't feel this angry at the sight of them touching.

"Your dragons are well?" Eric asked, brushing off Daron's hand to embrace Luke lightly. It was a quick embrace, though, with nothing romantic about it at all. Was that because Daron was here? Did Eric have feelings for the man? Was he reconsidering his attachment to Luke?

"Daron and I were just talking about the other dragons in this realm," Eric continued. "You're certain they'll continue to obey us? Some of my people are nervous now that they're not tame."

"You can ask them, but they like you," Luke said. "They'll tell you if they don't want to do something, but I don't see why they wouldn't. They want to protect you. They love you."

Eric smiled. "It's odd thinking that they're choosing to follow us instead of being ordered to do so. I never realized how much I trust Ryseth, or care for him. I'm sure the others feel the same but it is different."

"They don't see it as different," Luke assured him. "They're still your dragons."

"The other tribes don't understand," Daron said, glaring at Luke before smiling at Eric. "You're handling it well, though."

"With your help," Eric said with a laugh. "I couldn't do it without you, Daron."

Luke tried to hide a scowl at the smug smile Daron had. It wasn't fair that Daron had such an advantage over him. Eric relied on Daron for help in a way that he would never rely on Luke. Luke caused the problems; Daron helped solve them. They were partners, allies, friends, and he could never compete with that. A flame of jealousy sparked deep in his heart. Even if Eric wasn't interested in Daron as a lover, he was interested in him as a friend. And that could change into lover under the right circumstances. Daron clearly knew his advantage; Luke could see it in the challenge in his eyes as they stared at each other. Daron was challenging him and Luke had nothing to say. Eric relied on Daron and nothing could change that.

"I should return to my dragonlings," Luke said curtly, knowing he was essentially signaling his defeat. But there was nothing else he could say. Daron had the advantage. He would just have to hope that Eric was sincere about not wanting anyone else. He seemed sincere and Luke trusted that for now, he was the only one in Eric's heart, but what if that changed? There were so many other people and if Daron was correct, Eric had loved many other people in the past. There was no guarantee that Eric would be true no matter what he said. Only time would tell.

CHAPTER TWENTY-NINE

Handling Hope

There was something going on between Luke and Daron, Eric thought as he escorted both of them back to the gate. They kept glaring at each other, and it couldn't just be because Daron had accused Luke of being a dragon tamer like the elders. That was enough to prevent any friendship between the two, but this seemed different. Personal. But as far as he knew, they had never spoken to each other outside of that one encounter. What was going on?

He said goodbye to Daron, who would continue to negotiate with one of the other tribes about their dragons and try to convince them that their dragons, while no longer tame, would continue to obey them. It was a difficult process but at least now he knew which dragons Luke had stolen. They came from relatively friendly tribes who hadn't immediately pushed for war, though they had filed official charges against him with the elders, which Else hadn't done. It would be easier to just have them talk to Luke than try to handle this on his own, but he didn't want to risk Luke. These leaders still believed in the elders absolutely and might threaten to take Luke back to them. They wouldn't succeed, but it would rattle Luke and he wanted to avoid that at all costs. Luke was fragile enough and didn't need anything else to destroy the confidence he was slowly regaining.

Daron was fully capable of handling things; in fact, it was good that he was doing it instead of Eric because the other tribes believed that Eric had acted against the elders. They had reservations about Eric, but no anger at the rest of the tribe. The other leaders had suggested that the elders would forgive them if Eric turned himself and the stolen tamers in, according to Daron. Now that Eric's tribe had seen Luke's injuries for themselves, he knew no one would support that and he was grateful to have the support of his people. If he had to constantly watch his back around them, he would be in trouble.

Luke went straight to his dragonlings when they passed back through the gate and Anna backed up respectfully, standing beside Eric just outside the makeshift nest.

"Things are going well?" she asked.

"As well as could be expected," he said. He filled her in on the details as he watched Luke cradle each dragonling individually before releasing them to play again. They didn't really need the attention, he knew, but Luke lavished them as much as possible and Eric was constantly amazed that he was able to give them so much. He wanted to talk to Luke more but knew he would have to wait and it was nearly thirty minutes before Luke had finished greeting and playing with his dragonlings and gestured for Eric to come closer. Anna had already left to talk to some of the mothers and fathers who were worried about their children. There were seven children who had either colds or the flu and needed to be isolated to prevent it from spreading. They were unhappy and Anna was helping to deal with the situation. There was no way Eric could have handled his divided tribe plus the outside threats without help from so many people and he was just grateful everyone he needed was on his side.

He sat beside Luke on the bench and pushed a cushion out of the way so his thigh pressed against Luke's. The female was curled on the bench on Luke's other side and he stroked her occasionally. The little males were playing in the hanging cloth near the ceiling. It was so unusual to be allowed this close to dragonlings but he was starting to get used to it, and enjoy it.

He had always been jealous of dragon tamers to some degree because of how close they were with dragons. When he was younger and had first discovered his ability to sense the power of dragon tamers, he had hoped the elders would choose him to become one. Instead, he had been slated to be a leader. He didn't regret that decision, exactly, since he did enjoy his role, but it would have been satisfying to be a dragon tamer and be able to handle dragonlings like Luke did.

"Were your dragons happy to see you?" Eric asked, though he knew the answer. He could see the love between Luke and the Untamable even if he couldn't feel it. Luke smiled.

"Yes," he said. He leaned against Eric and took his hand. "I asked them why the females died. They didn't know, but they said there was somewhere I might find the answer."

Eric's breath caught. The Great Library. Had the Untamable told Luke about it? Or did they have some other way of finding the answer?

"How did things used to work before the sickness fell?" Luke asked. "My first dragon was the first to die from the sickness so I don't know any other way for them to be."

"Well, before the sickness, females would come into this realm to have babies," Eric said. It felt like an eternity ago when this was true but in reality, it was less than a decade. Things had radically altered since then and it was now normal to think of the females dying. "When the dragonlings were about six months old, the females would return to the other realm through the gate. They would remain tame and in a couple of years they would mate with the males and be ready to return to have more babies. Most females had five or six litters, and at some point, they would cease to be tame. They would return to the wild. Presumably they lived out their days far from humans and eventually died, but no one knows for sure."

"That sounds better," Luke said. "I don't like seeing them dying even as their dragonlings are growing up. Why don't they return to the other realm after they have their babies but before they start dying?"

"They start dying as soon as they come here," Eric said sadly. "We tried sending them back as soon as the babies were born, but it was too late. The females made it back here but died shortly after. We decided it was best to let them die with their babies."

"One of the females I was with had two litters, but she stayed in this realm the entire time," Luke said. "How did she get pregnant the second time?"

"Were you with her at all times?" Eric asked, because it was likely his leader had simply distracted him while bringing the female back into the other realm. It was cruel to do that to a female. They were more than breeding machines, after all. They had rich lives on their own and while he suspected most of them wanted to have dragonlings eventually, that wasn't what defined them. Sometimes they lived long enough for their litters to grow up, but the sickness had taken hold. They could be forced to bear another litter but it didn't seem right to force them to have more babies like that. If they survived through an entire litter, it would be better to let them free in the other realm even if they were destined to die.

"I guess I wasn't," Luke said. "I had another litter to take care of and after her litter left, I was with them the whole time until her next litter came."

It was mind boggling to think of Luke holding two litters, but it was the truth. He had an incredible range not just in terms of distance but in terms of power. Even now he held not only a female, but a mixed litter with dragons from two different mothers. Such a thing was unheard of, but Luke did it without a thought. It didn't seem difficult to him at all. His power also came through in his dragons themselves, since all of his dragonlings clearly developed into Untamable. The shields developing on his little males were already visible and it was clear what they would grow up to be. Daniel had to have realized what was happening when he saw Luke's earlier litters, but why hadn't he taken advantage of that connection? Why hadn't he brought Luke to the other realm?

"You said the Untamable had a suggestion for finding the answer," Eric said, bringing the conversation back to his dragon.

"He said there was a library," Luke said, and Eric's heart rate tripled. The Great Library. The Untamable had suggested it? Had offered it? Could Luke be the first person to enter the Library in a hundred years?

"Will you go there?" Eric asked breathlessly. What else was in the Library? No one knew what kind of knowledge was gathered there. Even when people had been allowed entry, it was only the elders, and only a couple of them. If Luke went to the Library, would he be equal to the elders? After all, the Library was closely associated with power in their society. If Luke entered the Library and brought back some of its knowledge, maybe the other tribes would recognize him as equal and be less likely to attack Eric and his tribe. Maybe they would stop pushing for Luke to be returned. Maybe Luke would be safe.

"They said it wouldn't affect my bond with my dragonlings," Luke said thoughtfully. Eric hadn't even thought of that. No one knew where the Library was but it wasn't within two miles. "I'd like to test that," Luke added cautiously. "Is there a place where I could try going further than two miles from the gate without risking your tribe?"

"It's your tribe now, too," Eric said, stroking his hand. "And we could arrange it. Our territory covers a large area that's uninhabited. We tend to stick to the border, but Ryseth could carry us further inland."

"And Ryseth would listen to me if I needed him to stop, wouldn't he?" Luke asked. "If I can't hold the dragonlings at that distance, I would need to get back within my range as quickly as possible to avoid losing them."

"I'm sure Ryseth will do anything you ask," Eric said. "He loves you. Just as I do," he added, wrapping his arm around Luke's shoulders. The female lifted her head curiously and he flinched. His hand was within striking distance of her, but she didn't seem to be threatening him. Just curious.

"Will you stay here tonight?" Luke asked, sounding suddenly vulnerable.

Eric sighed. As much as he wanted to spend every moment with Luke, he had been avoiding spending the night here. He worried about what Else had said about Luke's affection. If the other tribes suspected his motives, he would lose everything. So he couldn't get too close to Luke. But he couldn't push him away, either. It was a tricky situation. Luke was still injured, he thought, his eyes running across the bruised cheek. Surely Luke wouldn't push for any intimacy when he was still hurting, when the memory of the attack had to be fresh in his mind. Could he spend the night? Probably. Daron was handling the other tribes and Anna was helping him here, and his other advisors were taking care of the other details. Denis was staying near Eric at all times in case of emergency. He was currently in the other realm but Eric could bring him here to guard him overnight.

"Yes, I can stay here," Eric said, hoping he wasn't making a mistake. "I need to take care of a few things first, but I can come back after your evening feeding. Is that all right?"

Luke smiled shyly and Eric's heart skipped a beat. It was impossible how beautiful he was when he smiled.

"I would like that," Luke said softly. It was all Eric could do to prevent himself from kissing him.

CHAPTER THIRTY

Our Tamer

Luke was a little nervous when Eric showed up that evening, especially when Eric said he needed to talk to his people first and invited him along. So far he had isolated himself with his dragonlings, seeing only Anna and the advisors Eric had left for him. Now, though, Eric wanted him to meet other people.

It was only the families and children, he knew, which made it a little better. Surely they would be friendly. But he couldn't forget the anger in their eyes when they had looked at his injuries. They weren't angry at him, but they were capable of it if he did something wrong. Still, he cautiously agreed to it. He wanted to be near Eric. Daron was with Eric around the rest of the tribe all the time and while Luke couldn't do much to help, at least he could do this.

Eric took his hand and led him out of the room. His dragonlings were asleep and would be fine for several hours. They were enjoying having his undivided attention here. Even when he wasn't directly interacting with them, he stayed near them. Eric had given him a tablet so that he could read and watch movies, but because they couldn't be tracked, there was no internet. He was used to restrictions on his activities and didn't mind. At least this time there was a legitimate reason for limiting him and not just Daniel's desire to shield him from the world.

He wondered why Daniel had been so quick to prevent him learning things. Was it just a protective instinct? He wanted to think that. Despite everything, he wanted to believe that Daniel was good. But he remembered that last night all too vividly and he remembered the shame that had overwhelmed him when he escaped. Daniel had probably limited him because of jealousy, or possessiveness, or just for the sake of having control over him. Daniel was not a good person no matter how he tried to spin it in his mind, and he was starting to get used to that unpleasant reality.

They paused outside of one of the many rounded doors. He was completely lost in the maze of corridors but luckily didn't feel claustrophobic. He imagined that for some people a ship like this would be too much, especially since there really was no escape. He shivered. Maybe he did feel a little of that. But he had been trapped his entire life. This was nothing new.

"Are you ready?" Eric asked. "They'll probably want to talk to you. You'll need to be friendly and smile, even if you don't talk to them. This is your tribe, remember. They're your people now."

"I'm ready," Luke said in a small voice. He wasn't, but he didn't think he'd ever be fully ready to meet people again. People hurt him. These were Eric's people, though, he reassured himself. They were like Eric. They wouldn't hurt him. He didn't fully believe that they were his people as well, but Eric sounded confident about that. Maybe they would see themselves as his people. Maybe they would want to protect him, as Eric wanted to protect him. He would have to see.

Eric opened the door and a hum of voices surrounded them. They entered a large room similar to the room where the dragonlings were, only this was filled with people. Mostly children, who were laughing and chasing each other through the open area at the center. There was a jungle gym of sorts to one side where other kids were hanging on monkey bars and swinging on a tire swing. He was impressed they had this kind of area on the ship. They must have really come prepared, or else were good at making do with what was already onboard. The outer areas of the room were mostly adults, though kids occasionally ran over to them for ask for things or sit down for a little bit. The adults chatted and as Eric and Luke walked into the room, the nearest ones turned and waved at Eric, then froze at the sight of him. He tensed.

"How is Keisha doing?" Eric asked one of the nearby couples, and the woman smiled.

"Playing with the others. Looks like the infection is gone."

"Good," Eric said, then turned to Luke. "Hana here is our resident doctor," he explained. "We have a few onboard, but she has the most experience with kids."

"You're Luke, right?" she asked, smiling and extending her hand to him. He examined her. She seemed nice, so he shook her hand.

"Pleasure to meet you," he said, because he knew that was what people were supposed to say.

"This is my husband Jaewon," she said, and Luke shook the man's hand as well. "He's a teacher at the nearby school, so he'll be taking over some of the kids once we're a little more organized."

Luke nodded and smiled at him, but he wondered how long they were going to be on the run like this. It was important to go to school, he knew, though he himself had hated it. In fact, he had essentially stopped going when he ran away to take care of his first litter of dragonlings, though his first leader had given him a private tutor. Daniel had at first done the same, but had phased him out within a year or two. Still, it was important to learn how to live in the world and school provided the necessary building blocks.

He wondered if there were other teachers here, and if the kids would be happy with what they had here. All of the kids he saw looked happy, except for a few who were glowering from the benches next to their parents and were clearly in time out of some sort, but there had to be some kids who weren't adjusting to being on a ship this easily. Was Eric able to handle all of that? No wonder he needed so many advisors. Luke felt suddenly selfish for wanting so much of Eric's time and attention when he had so many other people to care for.

"Your injuries seem to be healing well," Hana said, and Luke instinctively raised a hand to his bruised cheek. But she didn't seem judgmental at all, just happy he was recovering. How could she not judge him, though, when he had allowed this punishment, welcomed it even because he felt he deserved it? She didn't know why he was injured, he reminded himself. For all she knew, he had gotten it innocently, not as a result of his disobedience.

He cautiously lowered his hand right as a small girl ran over. She looked about the same age he had been when he ran away to find his first dragon. He wondered if her life was anything like his had been. Probably not. Her parents seemed to love her unconditionally as Hana stroked her hair with a smile, and Luke's parents, though they tolerated him, clearly didn't have that love. He was their son and they took care of him, but he could tell they didn't really want him. They wanted a normal child, not one who heard voices and couldn't fully explain what they were. If his family had been in a tribe and known about dragons, would his life have been different? Would he have been treasured instead of grudgingly tolerated? He would never know but he envied this girl her normal existence.

She was watching him with wide eyes.

"You're the one with the babies, aren't you?" she asked.

"Dragonlings," Hana corrected. "Not babies."

"Dragonlings," she obediently repeated. "They're so cute. Will they come play with us?"

"They're too young," Luke said, trying to fight his instinctive anger that someone else wanted to play with his dragonlings. The dragonlings were his and he would never let anyone else take them. But she didn't want to take them. She wasn't even a tamer. She just wanted to play with them, as Eric had suggested might be the case. He didn't want to alienate the people here so he forced a smile.

"When they're bigger, maybe they'll play with you," he

offered, and she beamed.

"I like the silver ones," she confided. "They make such pretty circles."

His smile turned sincere, remembering how his males had jealously started spinning circles when the little female was getting all the attention the first time he had been introduced to this tribe.

"They're my males," he said. "They'll be happy you liked them."

Hana smiled. "And your red one is really a female?"

Luke nodded, and she sighed as if in awe.

"Eric told us, but... I didn't really expect a female dragonling. It's been so hard ever since the females started dying and no new females were born."

Luke was a little surprised by that information. The entire time he had been taming dragons, there had never been any female dragonlings. He had assumed there just weren't female dragonlings. But it made sense that at some point there had to have been, or else there wouldn't be female dragons. He had known that the females started dying as soon as they had their litters, but he hadn't fully understand that without female dragonlings, there would stop being females at all and dragons as a species were at risk. He thought of the library the Untamable had mentioned, the one Eric seemed to know something about. Would the answer be there? Not just the answer to the mystery of the dying females, but the lack of female dragonlings as well? He would have to go to the other realm soon to test how far his reach extended.

Jaewon asked the little girl if she had a reason for coming over, getting out a bag with little baggies of apple slices and clearly planning for a snack request, but she shook her head and grinned.

"I just wanted to meet our tamer," she said, and scampered off.

Our tamer, Luke thought in surprise. Not *the* tamer, but *ours.* She viewed him as part of the tribe. They all did, he thought, looking around. The others were clearly curious about him and several of the kids surrounded the girl as soon as she returned, looking at him eagerly as she no doubt told them all about what he had said. No one here was judging him. He felt a sense of belonging sweep over him that he had never experienced before. These people wanted him. No one had ever wanted him before, not like this. Daniel wanted him, but only to control him. The Elders were the same. He had never felt part of a group before but as he looked at these people, he suddenly did. They wouldn't hurt him. They would help him, just as the adult dragons helped him. They would give him strength and support him, and maybe even protect him if Daniel or the Elders came looking for him.

"Do you want to stay here?" Eric asked. "Or do you want to come with me and meet a few more people?"

He was tempted to go with Eric, but his lingering fear held him back. These were his people now, but would they accept him if they knew what had happened to him? If they knew what he had allowed Daniel to do? Would they want to protect him if they knew he had willingly opened his mind to the Elders just because his leader had asked?

"I'll stay here," he said quietly. Eric nodded and headed to one of the other groups of adults, and Hana and Jaewon smiled at him. They at least wouldn't judge him. They didn't know, and he wasn't going to tell them.

CHAPTER THIRTY-ONE

Testing Boundaries

Everything was going as smoothly as possible, Eric thought as he returned to the new community on Ryseth's back. Three weeks had passed since they had fled their homes. They were getting better buildings for everyone and things had settled into a pattern of patrols and relaxation, giving his people the time they needed to adapt even while keeping everyone safe. This realm was going well and there hadn't been any attacks yet. The other tribes kept him on his toes by remaining on his borders and occasionally trying to invade, but they retreated when the Untamable showed up, which they always did.

He wondered how long it would take for the other tribes to give up, or if the other tribes were just waiting for the Untamable to stop protecting them. He sometimes had that fear, that the Untamable would stop guarding them, but he suspected that as long as Luke was attached to his tribe, their protection would last. At some point, though, it might grow suspicious. The Untamable weren't known for helping tribes long-term. Something would need to happen to get the Elders to stop coming after him, but he didn't know what.

Daron was taking care of business with the nearby tribes and Mei was out on patrol as he slid off Ryseth and stroked him lovingly. Now that Ryseth was here willingly and not because a tamer was forcing him to obey, he had found himself even more attached to his dragon. He knew most of the others felt the same way, but there were some in the tribe who now distrusted their dragons and it was difficult convincing them to ride their dragons without fear. They weren't sent out on patrols and luckily it was a small number.

The other tribes whose dragons belonged to Luke tended to fall into that category; they didn't trust that Luke would let them keep their dragons even though Eric assured them he had no interest in stealing dragons. No one had started a war over it yet, but it was one reason Eric had kept Luke out of this realm lately. He didn't want to risk Luke taming any more dragons. Now that things had settled down a little, though, perhaps it was time to bring Luke here and see if he could leave his range without harming his dragonlings. Eric was eager to learn more about the Great Library but that could only happen if Luke could leave his two-mile radius.

He passed through the gate and looked around. To his surprise, there were quite a few people in the room, gathered near the dragonlings. He approached and they made way for him. He recognized Hana and Jaewon and their daughter along with another couple and their two children. They were a safe distance from Luke and his dragonlings, but Luke was clearly showing off his dragonlings off because they were flying around. The males were, at least. The female was securely curled around his shoulders.

Eric knew Luke had started talking to the rest of the tribe and he had suggested that Luke try letting the tribe see his dragonlings, but he hadn't realized Luke was actually doing it. Luke caught his eye and Eric felt himself beaming at the sight of Luke with his people. Luke looked happy for once, and seemed calm despite having people nearby. He was starting to heal from a lifetime of hurt and Eric was grateful.

"Would you mind if I spoke to Luke alone?" he asked his people.

"But I wanna play with the babies," Hana's daughter whined, but Hana shushed her and the people greeted him on their way out.

Luke looked suddenly insecure as they left, watching Eric

with frightened eyes.

"It's all right that they were here, isn't it?" he asked. "I know you said I could talk to them, but I thought it would be okay to let them see the dragonlings."

Eric swept him in a hug and wished he could squeeze away his insecurity.

"I'm happy they were here," he said. "I'm happy you feel safe enough to let them come here. You can invite whoever you want. They're your dragonlings, and you're welcome to share them with the tribe."

"I'm not sharing them," Luke said rather sharply, pulling out of the hug. "They're mine."

"You're letting other people see them, that's all I meant," Eric said, remembering how possessive Luke was of them. Most tamers were possessive to some extent, especially with non-tamers, but Luke was far more sensitive about it than any other tamer he had met. The elders had once mentioned he would be like that because he had grown up without knowing any other tamers. Eric had hoped having Anna here would lessen his possessive traits, but apparently not. Still, it wasn't causing any damage. The dragonlings were his and he could be as possessive as he liked. Despite that possession, though, Luke didn't hesitate to bring Eric to sit down in the little area set up for the dragonlings and even try to move the female from his shoulders as he took Eric's hand. He had never been this close to the female and was in awe of her as she sleepily blinked at him before resting her head in the crook of Luke's neck again.

"I wondered if you were ready to come back to the other realm," Eric said, unsure whether or not this was the best time to bring it up. He had worried that Luke would panic at the thought but instead he perked up.

"You want me to go back?"

"We should see if you can go outside your radius," he said. "If you still want that."

"I do," he said. "Is it safe?"

"You're not in danger," Eric said. "But you can't tame any

dragons that aren't ours. I'll do my best to keep you deep enough inside our territory that it won't be a problem, but there's always a risk."

"I can't help it," Luke said. "There's no way to prevent it. They just bond with me."

"I know," Eric said with a sigh. It really did seem to be something he had no control over, unfortunately. But the other tribes were giving him space and the last attempted invasion had been yesterday. They didn't try to approach too closely too often, so it should be safe. Or at least as safe as it would ever get. If Luke bonded with a dragon from one of the invading tribes, it would definitely be seen as an attack and that could be deadly. At the moment the only dragons he had taken were from relatively friendly tribes who were willing to listen to Eric and Daron. They needed to test his range, though.

"All right," Luke said as if gathering his courage. "I'll do my best. Ryseth won't mind?"

"He would do anything for you," Eric said. "You know that."

Luke blushed. "All of my dragons would," he said softly. "I didn't know it could be like that."

"Like what?"

"Like I belonged," he whispered, and Eric wrapped his arm around Luke's shoulders and pulled him tight, his eyes warming.

He could only imagine how isolated Luke had been all his life. He was an outsider who had always heard dragons and was ostracized because of it, thought to be insane because the outside world didn't understand and abused by a tamer who took advantage of him. Then when he finally ran away and found safety, he was still treated as an outsider and knowledge of his true purpose was hidden from him. He seemed to have fond memories of his first tribe but he had quickly been traded to Daniel, who had abused him every bit as much as the tamer from his childhood had. He had never had a home or community. He had probably never had any friendly contact with other people and it was no wonder he was so possessive of his dragonlings, the only thing in his life that loved him.

Eric was here now, though, and his entire tribe would start to fill the hole in Luke's heart. He was just grateful that Luke seemed open to the idea of a community. It would have been easy for him to retreat and alienate himself from everyone but he was making an effort even after all the hurt he had suffered. He was far stronger than anyone Eric had ever met and his heart throbbed with the need to protect and love him. Luke tentatively embraced him, then buried his face in his shoulder. Eric held him tight for a long time until Luke pulled back. He smiled shyly and Eric was breathless at the sight of that beautiful expression. He was seeing it more and more but it still stunned him. Luke was beyond beautiful when he smiled like that.

"I'm ready to go," he said, and Eric nodded. He stood up and helped Luke to his feet. The dragonlings flew into the curtains and they went to the gate. Luke glanced over at Anna, who was nearby. He waved her over and she smiled at him.

"You can play with them if you want," he offered. "They'll play with you."

"Thank you, Luke," she said.

"If anything happens to them," he said, and paused. "I'm not giving them up. But if something happens and they go to you, take good care of them until I return."

She nodded in surprise and looked at Eric.

"Are you in danger?"

"No," Eric said. "We're testing his range in the other realm. It shouldn't be a problem."

"You can go out of your range for a minute or two without problems," Anna said. "The dragonlings don't like it but it won't hurt them. You won't lose them."

"Can you go outside of your range?"

"I don't know," she said. "I never tried. I've never heard of anyone who has."

Eric nodded. At least she hadn't ruled it out as impossible. His former tamer had never tried it, but he didn't know why any tamer would. None of them ever needed to go far from the gate. It was good to know nothing would happen if they did go too far, though. He didn't want to be responsible for Luke losing his dragonlings and besides, Anna wasn't strong enough to hold the female dragonling.

Luke thanked her and turned to the gate, taking a deep breath. Eric took his hand as they approached but Luke shook him off a few steps away and walked through himself. Eric smiled, proud of his courage, and followed him into the other realm.

* * *

Luke took a deep breath as he looked around at the emerald green hills and continued walking forward. He was starting to get used to coming back and forth and he immediately stretched his awareness to sense any nearby dragons. All of the dragons already belonged to him, luckily. He didn't want to cause problems for Eric, who was just coming through the gate behind him. He walked at Eric's side as they went through the small community. Everyone noticed them and many exchanged greetings with Eric and cast curious looks at him. He tried to look confident even while he feared the judgment in their eyes. But they were welcoming, just like the tribe in the other realm. They wanted to know him. He belonged.

Ryseth was waiting just outside the tents of the community and Luke rushed to his side and stroked his firm scales. He greeted Luke warmly and Luke explained what he wanted in a rush, not wasting time on words but instead showing him what he wanted to do the same way he would show a dragonling. He knew dragons, as adults, could use words as well as humans, unlike the dragonlings who responded best to emotions and images. When he had bound the Elders using dragongaze he had learned the hard way the difference between words and emotions and knew that the adult dragons, like humans, valued language above emotion. But they still recognized emotion and Ryseth knew exactly what he wanted and was happy to assist.

Luke looked at his enormous side and was a little intimidated. He had never ridden a dragon before. He looked at Eric, who also had his hand on Ryseth. He could feel the dragon's happiness at being near his rider.

"How do you get up?" Luke asked cautiously. Eric flashed a smile and took him by the waist, helping him up the large back. Luke clung to Ryseth's neck as Eric easily vaulted up behind him and wrapped his hands around his waist again. Ryseth took off gently but even so Luke was dizzy for a moment. He trembled and clutched Ryseth tightly, aware of Eric holding him close. Ryseth sent soothing thoughts to him, reassuring him that even if he fell, the dragon would catch him. He wouldn't be hurt. Luke stared at the ground growing distant below them and was skeptical, but he trusted his dragon.

Ryseth took them towards a distant mountain range and Luke could sense that there weren't any dragons where they were going. Good. He didn't want to start any wars. He warned Ryseth to stop when they reached two miles from the gate and the dragon agreed. It wasn't too long before they reached that point and Luke took a deep breath.

"Are we at the edge of your range?" Eric asked, his breath warm against Luke's ear.

Luke nodded, then urged Ryseth forward. Slowly. Ryseth obeyed and Luke tried to sense any difference in his bond with his dragonlings. Nothing. It felt the same. Maybe they weren't far enough. He urged Ryseth further and the dragon kept going until they were definitely outside of his range. Ryseth informed him that they were about four miles from the gate. There was no change in the intensity of his connection with the dragonlings and he let out a sigh of relief. He could go anywhere in this realm and still be connected to them. The library seemed a reality for the first time and he wondered how long it would take to get there. Even if his dragonlings were in range, they would still need to eat and play. Anna could take care of them to some extent, but some things needed to be done by their tamer.

He felt another dragon approaching, one of his Untamable. He warned Eric and felt Ryseth projecting obedience as the large dragon approached and circled them. He could feel the dragon's happiness that Luke was here, and that Luke had left his range and could go to the library with them. He urged patience, since he wasn't ready to go yet, and the Untamable agreed. Anytime he was ready, the Untamable would escort him. There was no rush, but they looked forward to flying with him. He would have to ride them, he realized, and eyed the much larger dragon nervously. Ryseth's back was quite smooth but they were armored and it might be harder to ride them. He felt the dragon's amusement as the dragon assured him he would be safe, just as Ryseth had done. The dragons would do anything to protect him and he needed to trust that.

He took a deep breath and instructed Ryseth to return to the gate, inviting the Untamable to join them for most of the way back. The two dragons flew side by side until the Untamable spiraled away, sending a last message of love. Luke returned the emotion without reservation and hoped he saw the Untamable again soon. He wanted to see all of his dragons but that might take time, since they seemed to approach this community one at a time. Well, when he went to the library he would at least see more of them. Now he just needed to figure out when it was safe to go. Eric would help with that, he knew, and squeezed Eric's arm as they lowered to the ground and the man helped him slide off. He wasn't exactly comfortable riding a dragon but he felt safe now. Soon, he would be on his Untamable and he could finally search for answers to the deaths of the female dragonlings.

CHAPTER THIRTY-TWO

Growth Spurt

Two of the dragonlings curled around Luke's legs as he sat in the pillows and read a book on his tablet. The female was at his side and he rested his hand on her, stroking her every once in a while. They were getting too big to easily sit on his lap and he wished they could stay small forever, but dragonlings had several points in their development where they grew rapidly and this was one of them.

Already they were nearly as long as him from snout to tail-tip. Another few months of slow growth would follow, then they would surge again and triple in size in a week or so. Then another few months, and then they would have their final growth spurt when they grew too large for this realm and had to be sent through the gate.

Once he had deeply dreaded that day but now that he knew he could continue to see them in the other realm, it was only a little dread. Their relationship would change once they passed through the gate but they would still love him, and he would still love them. That part of the bond would never change. And really, he wanted them to be independent. They were so fragile right now, and that was what he was worrying about.

Nearly two weeks had passed since he had learned he could go outside of his range in the other realm. While Eric wasn't pressuring him to go to the library, he did ask about it every once in a while. Luke had wanted to wait until the dragons were finished growing and now they had. It would be safe to leave them for a time and he couldn't really pay attention to the book he was reading. He sighed and tossed the tablet gently to one side, caressing the dragonlings pressed against his legs. One of them lifted his head and chirped softly.

Anna was nearby playing with the other three males. He allowed her near the dragonlings much of the day now, though she still spent a lot of time with the rest of the tribe. The children had been here to watch the dragonlings play several times, always under the supervision of their parents. His dragonlings were down to one feeding a day, though they still needed to play at least once every six hours. With Anna's help, though, he was able to sleep through the night because she took care of one of their playtimes while he slept. He had always taken care of dragonlings on his own and it was a welcome relief having someone help him, especially since he now felt safe that she wouldn't try to steal them. He wondered, though, because she didn't have any dragonlings or dragons. He didn't feel complete without his dragonlings. How could she survive without having any?

"Anna," he said, and she turned to smile at him. One of the males playing with her came to curl beside him and the other two flew up into the drapes.

"What is it?"

"How long could I leave the dragonlings before it became a problem?" he asked, thinking of the library.

"I'm not sure," she said. "You know more about dragonlings than me."

He bit his lip. How long could he be gone? He just wasn't sure.

"You fed my dragonlings once," he said slowly, though she had only fed his female, not all of them. "That didn't effect their bond with me. Could that happen again?"

"Why?" Anna asked, sounding puzzled.

"If I go somewhere in the other realm, I might not be able to get back here easily," he said, unsure what to share. He didn't want to tell her anything he didn't need to. He trusted her, but not completely.

"Well, feeding them once or twice won't make a difference as long as you can sense them through your bond," she said. "The only risk is them choosing to come to me and I doubt that will happen. Besides, I'm not strong enough to hold the female."

"What would make them choose you?"

Anna shrugged. "The only time I've heard of that happening was once when a tamer died while he still had dragonlings. They went to the nearest tamer who was available. I really doubt yours will leave you as long as you're connected to them."

Luke nodded. If something did happen to them he wanted them to be safe, and he didn't think they would leave him even if he left them for a day or two. So they could go two feedings. If he left right after feeding them, then he could be gone two or three days without harming them. They would still receive his love because he would be in contact with them. They would miss his physical presence but they would survive with Anna to play with them and feed them. He mentally braced himself. He was ready. As soon as Eric got back, he was going to ask him if he could go into the other realm and find the library.

* * *

The attacks were coming more frequently, Eric thought as Ryseth landed. He wasn't allowed near the borders in case the other tribes captured him and he hated forcing his people to fight when he couldn't help them. The other tribes were attacking on a daily basis now and it had devolved into actual battles, not just incursions. The Untamable still came to their rescue and that was usually enough to drive the other tribes away, but there only seemed to be two Untamable watching them and the attacks from the other tribes were growing more coordinated. He suspected the Elders were behind it and were encouraging enough tribes to attack so that the Untamable wouldn't be able to help.

"Are you leaving again?" Daron asked as he slid off Ryseth.

"Yeah," Eric said. "I just need to check in on Luke. I'll be back soon."

"This can't last much longer," Daron warned. "I don't know how long we can survive this."

Eric's lips tightened. It was true. His tribe was already under stress from being forced to leave their homes and now they were under constant attack. At least no one had found the ship in the other realm. He wouldn't be able to take care of both realms at once no matter how much help he had.

"I don't know what else to do," Eric said, aware of the helpless note in his voice.

"What if we returned one of the tamers?" Daron asked. "Not Luke. The other one. They didn't hurt her, not really. It would at least prove to the other tribes that we're making an effort towards peace."

"No," Eric said firmly. He wished he could be shocked at the suggestion but he had heard other tribe members saying the same thing. No one wanted to return Luke, since he had so obviously been abused, but Anna didn't have the same injuries and she had been in training to be an Elder anyway. Eric wouldn't return her, though. The Elders had enslaved her and would be brutal if she were returned to them. Besides, she was helping Luke. In addition to the practical assistance she was giving with his dragonlings, she was also a bridge between him and the rest of the tribe. Luke was learning to feel safe with her and trust her and Eric didn't want to destroy that. Luke had so few connections to other people; he wouldn't send Anna back if it hurt Luke.

"Eric, we need to do something," Daron said. "What else is there?"

"I don't know," Eric said. "But we can't send either of them back, and I'm not turning myself in. We just need to survive a little longer."

"And then what?" Daron asked. "Nothing is going to change except that the other tribes will be even more on the Elder's side. Something has to change."

"I'll figure something out," Eric said with a sigh. Daron was absolutely right. They weren't going to survive this. Something needed to happen to break the impasse, and he didn't know what. "I'll talk to Luke," he said. "I don't want to push him but maybe he'll have some idea."

"You worry about him too much," Daron said almost jealously. "He's to blame for all of this."

"It isn't his fault," Eric said sharply. He knew Daron and Luke didn't get along but there was no need to blame all of their problems on him even if it was technically true. If it weren't for Luke, he would be home with his tribe living comfortably in their ancestral home, still under the protection of the Elders and his entire society. If it weren't for Luke, he never would have found out about the true nature of the Elders. And Luke would still be under Daniel's control. No, it was better like this. He couldn't stand the thought of Luke trapped under Daniel like that. As long as he and his tribe could survive this, it would be worth it to save him.

"I'm sorry," Daron said, glancing away. "I shouldn't have said that. It's just frustrating throwing our lives away for one tamer. I don't want to lose everything."

"We won't," Eric said. "We'll make it through. We just need to hand on a little longer. I'll find something, I promise."

Daron agreed, though he didn't sound very hopeful. Eric needed him to stay optimistic because he was one of the people the rest of the tribe looked up to. If Daron despaired, then his people might also feel like this was hopeless. But he trusted Daron to know how to put on an act in front of the people. Eric clasped his shoulder. Daron leaned into the gesture and sighed.

"We'll survive," Daron said. "I'll make sure our people stand behind you."

"Thank you, Daron," he said, squeezing the man's shoulders. Then he headed to the gate to check on Luke.

It should be just after Luke was finished playing with the dragonlings but before their meal. A good time to catch a few words with him and try to figure out what to do. The gate rippled across him as he entered the large metal ship and felt his heart sink. His people here were starting to suffer being inside so long. They could go on deck occasionally but it was dangerous for the children. They needed to be outside but there was nothing he could do while they were on the run. He needed to get this figured out.

Luke was waiting for him, to his surprise, standing outside of his small area as the dragonlings flew around behind him. Luke came up to him and took his hand, surprising him further. Anna was with the dragonlings, he noticed. They were getting quite large, though it would be months before their size started getting problematic. He wasn't entirely sure there would be enough room for the dragonlings to fly around after their next growth spurts. They needed to be outside, just like the rest of his tribe.

"I want to go to the library," Luke said without preamble, and Eric was taken aback.

"Now?"

"After I feed them," he said. "Anna will take care of them while I'm gone. I can be gone a couple of days. That should be enough time. Is it safe to return to that realm?"

"We're getting attacked regularly," Eric admitted. "There will almost certainly be other dragons within your range and taming them might have serious repercussions. Do you know where the Great Library is? How far? If you can avoid other dragons it might be possible, but I don't want you in danger."

Inwardly, though, his heart was beating heavily. This might be exactly what he needed. If Luke successfully went to the Great Library, if he found how to save the female dragons, then surely the other tribes would back down. Surely they would see that the Elders didn't represent the ultimate authority in their society. This might be what ended all of his problems. But there were so many risks.

"I can't help it if I bond with dragons when I get there or on the way," Luke said slowly. "But I can ask my Untamable to avoid other dragons. They should be able to do that. I don't know where it is, but they can help."

"You really want to do this?" Eric said, placing his hands on Luke's shoulders and staring at him, trying to see if Luke was just saying this to please him.

"Yes," Luke said a little shyly. "I mean, if that's all right."

"It's your choice," Eric said, recognizing the fear in Luke's eyes. Luke didn't like standing up for himself or making his own decisions and it was probably frightening to make his wishes known like this. There was no way Eric could refuse him now. Was this a good idea?

He went over the dangers in his mind. There were almost always other dragons within two miles of the gate now. But it seemed to take a few days for the other tribes to realize that their dragons no longer obeyed their tamers. If Luke tamed those dragons, then it was possible he would return from the Great Library before the other tribes even noticed. Everything relied on Luke finding something, though. If Luke didn't find anything, then the situation would be immeasurably worse. The other tribes would declare open war and they would unite against Eric. Not even all of the Untamable would be able to protect them from that kind of assault.

"Luke, if you were to tame a dragon from another tribe, could you stop it from attacking us?" he asked, wondering if it might be possible to just have Luke in the other realm during an attack and tame every dragon who came close. That would certainly scare off the other tribes from attacking.

"I suppose I could, but I wouldn't," Luke said. "They're free. I would never order them to do anything."

"Even if it helped our tribe?"

"They're free," he repeated, and Eric sighed. There went that plan. Well, he couldn't refuse Luke this request so he would just have to hope he found something at the Great Library. There just weren't any other options. He would turn himself in rather than see his people destroyed but he didn't want it to come to that. And no matter what, no matter if he handed himself over to the Elders and their vengeance, he would never hand over Luke.

"All right," he said. "You wanted to go after you feed them? How soon is that?"

"Two hours," Luke said. "Is that okay?"

"Yes," Eric said. He would have to return to the other realm and prepare everyone for Luke's arrival and the potential dangers that entailed. "I'll be back here in two hours to bring you into the other realm. Which dragon will you take? Ryseth will carry you but he doesn't know where to go."

"The Untamable will carry me," Luke said with just a trace of fear. "Dragons don't drop people, do they?"

Eric smiled, thinking of the way Luke had clutched him so tightly on Ryseth. He wouldn't have thought a dragon tamer would be afraid of heights but it seemed Luke was, at least a little.

"I've never heard of it happening," Eric said. "Even if you somehow fell off, which has never happened, the dragon could easily catch you. There's nothing to worry about."

Luke nodded and set his jaw firmly. He looked determined and Eric smiled and stroked a finger across his jawline.

"All right," he said. "Two hours."

CHAPTER THIRTY-THREE

Ambush

One of the dragons from Luke's first litter was waiting for him on a hill about a mile outside of the community. Luke was tense, as he had bonded with over a dozen dragons the moment he went through the gate. He had immediately assured them of his love, then told them to continue respecting their own tamers and riders. They agreed and he could tell they were still attacking Eric's people. He was tempted to tell them to stop, since he could, but he never would. His dragons could choose to do what they wanted. He would never control them like that.

As he and Eric walked, four more dragons came into range and he repeated his instructions as he let Eric know what was happening. He looked grim, but there was nothing either of them could do about it. Eric did reassure him that it would be several days before anyone noticed and hopefully he would have returned from the library by then.

He seemed confident Luke would find something, but Luke worried he wouldn't. What would he do then? Would he return at a later date? He knew nothing about this library except that his dragons thought the answer was there. Still, he trusted his dragons and if they thought there was a chance the information was there, he would look for it. He just hoped it didn't cost Eric too much.

The Untamable instructed him how to climb on and Eric helped him get up, though Eric seemed in awe of the fact that he was allowed to touch the large dragon. Ryseth was nearby, though at a respectable distance, and Luke was glad the other dragons respected the Untamable so much. He could tell it was helping in the fighting and he requested that another of his dragons come to help, since it seemed the other tribes were ganging up on Eric's tribe and there weren't enough of the powerful dragons to stop it. He wondered if there were a problem with that and considered telling Eric what he had done, but it shouldn't matter. He was sure Eric would be grateful for the help.

Once he was up, Eric wished him well and the Untamable took off. He clung to the slick armor on his dragon but to his surprise, the shields were placed in such a way that he had something to hang onto. He felt relatively safe as the dragon lifted up. He instructed his dragon to avoid any other dragons on the way and could tell that there would only be a brief time when they were leaving this territory that it was possible he would bond with more.

Indeed, as they passed out of the territory, three more dragons fled into the comfort of his mind and he gave them the same instructions, but he remembered what Eric had said about stealing dragons and how it could trigger a war. There was no way he could take this many dragons and not trigger retaliation of some sort, but it seemed like Eric was already at war. This couldn't make it too much worse. He hoped.

As soon as they were in the clear, the Untamable soared to a higher altitude and he clung to the shields tightly, a little intimidated by the ground so far below. He had only traveled in an airplane a couple of times with Eric and had never looked out the window, so he had never seen anything like this except in movies and there was something completely different about doing this in reality than seeing it in a movie. He gulped, but he knew his dragon would keep him safe.

They continued to fly and he sensed other dragons approaching: more of his Untamable. They nuzzled him through their bond and he could tell they were happy to see him and pleased he was coming to the library. They formed a phalanx around him as he flew. He could still sense all of his other dragons but they were farther away now, and he could sense his dragonlings snuggled right up against his consciousness. He sent them a wave of love and hoped they didn't mind being taken care of by Anna. He didn't think they would. They might fuss a little but he didn't tolerate that sort of whining so they had mostly grown out of it. Dragonlings needed unconditional love but they also required rules and he had quickly learned to balance the two. He looked at the dragons around him and was briefly overwhelmed with pride. These were his dragons and they had grown up beautifully.

After about an hour, he began to get tired. He was still stressed from flying so high and the tension was getting to him. The Untamable urged him to be patient and told him they were about halfway there. He was glad it was relatively close and he leaned against his dragon and stroked his armor, trying to relax in the knowledge that his dragons would never let anything happen to him.

They were nearly there when a new Untamable approached and Luke sat up in surprise. It wasn't one of his dragons, though it bonded with him instantly. This was an older Untamable. He was just like Luke's dragons and he wondered who his tamer had been. He could tell this Untamable was very old, so his tamer must have lived a long time ago. The dragon mentally nuzzled him like the others and invited him to the library, so they had to be close. Then he felt something he had been dreading. More dragons. They were passing too close to other dragons and he couldn't help but bond them.

More of them entered his range, then even more. Nearly a hundred dragons, he realized in shock. He sent them the same messages to obey their original tamers but dread was seeping into his heart. He suspected he had just tamed an entire tribe's dragons and that would definitely trigger a war. There was no way around it. The dragons kept approaching, to his surprise. They seemed to be coming straight for him. There was something familiar about the feel of their minds and he puzzled over it. It was almost as if he recognized their previous tamer, but he couldn't tell who it was. There was only a faint trace of familiarity.

Then the dragons came close enough to see and to his shock, they moved into attack positions. Every single dragon up until now projected obedience around the Untamable but these were going to attack them. He could sense rage in their minds. Luke had been promised to them and had been stolen, and they were going to get him back. He tried to reassure them that he was here now but he could tell they wanted him for their tribe and a chill ran down his spine as he realized who these dragons were. They were Daniel's tribe.

Sure enough, as they drew close enough to see, he spotted Daniel on the dragon at the front. Although the dragons were in attack positions, they hadn't attacked yet. The Untamable came to a stop, probably not wanting to give away the location of the library to anyone besides Luke, but according to his dragon's words earlier they ought to be very close.

"Luke," Daniel called. "Come with me and let's put an end to all of this. No one is here to protect you except me. Return to me and you won't be harmed."

He felt an instinctive desire to return to his leader and grasped the feel of his dragons in his mind. They would protect him. They had to protect him, because terror was starting to worm its way into his heart. Daniel would destroy him. Daniel was here, and he would kill Luke for what Luke had done. Luke had run away, had hit him and knocked him out, had disobeyed to a breathtaking extent. He would be punished and he would be killed. His hands clenched around the shield on his dragon and he could feel the Untamable sending him reassurance, and also preparing to fight. But could they? There were only ten of them here and over a hundred of Daniel's dragons.

Without warning, the dragon under him whirled in the sky and he scrabbled to stay on. The other Untamable moved to attack Daniel's dragons and fighting broke out, but the dragon he rode swirled up into the sky. Where was it taking him? It was running away, but to where? They were out of range of Daniel's dragons and he could tell that the other Untamable were preventing Daniel from following. He sent out a distress call to his other Untamable to help, but he didn't want to summon any of his other dragons because he knew the Untamable didn't want anyone else so close to the library.

His dragon continued to spiral upward as his stomach churned and he clung for his life. They passed into the clouds and then Luke gasped. There was a large white and gold building on the clouds. The clouds looked different, too, not at all like the wispy things they were flying through. They looked solid and sure enough, his Untamable lowered onto them and indicated that Luke could step off. He could feel Daniel's dragons drawing closer and considered ordering them to stop. They would, if he commanded, but he would never order them like that. His other Untamable were coming and ought to be able to stem them off, but he still felt terrified.

"I want to invite Eric here," he said to his dragon in a shaky voice. "I'll feel safer with him."

He could feel his dragon reaching out to the other Untamable and considering his request, then nodded his large head.

He may come, his Untamable said, and Luke nearly let out a sob of relief. Terror still pounded through his veins and without Eric here to comfort him, he knew he would be in no condition to search the library, not with his dragons locked in battle right outside. *We will let him through, but no others.*

"I won't tell anyone else," Luke assured him, stroking his armored face.

Inwardly he sent another distress call, this one to Ryseth. The dragon was so far away but he could feel him perking to attention. He didn't know which realm Eric would be in and wondered if Ryseth would be able to summon him wherever he was, but this was all he could do. Then he took a deep breath.

Eric would have to fight through Daniel's tribe, he realized, but he got the feeling that his Untamable would protect him as soon as he drew near. They were protecting the library now, not just themselves, and he could sense that they would die rather than reveal its location.

Already Daniel's dragons were too close for their comfort and he wondered how Daniel had tracked him down. It was almost like Daniel had sensed Luke had left the safety of Eric's territory and struck as soon as possible, but that was impossible. Wasn't it? Maybe he had been tracking which dragons were being bonded and traced his position that way, but hadn't Eric said it took a few days to notice that he had bonded with the dragons? He wasn't sure, but it frightened him that Daniel was so close, and so determined.

He was also a little frightened by Daniel's dragons, who were still filled with rage. His dragons loved him, but these clearly also resented him and wouldn't listen to reason when he told them he loved them and they were his. They wanted more and he had never felt anything like it from a dragon before. He didn't like it.

But he took another deep breath and turned to the library. It was enormous and he pushed open the large wooden doors cautiously. They creaked and let light in. Was there no light inside? But as he entered, torches along the walls sparked into life. Maybe it was set up to only light when someone was inside. He stared around in dismay. There were rows upon rows of book as far as he could see, with several alcoves along the walls holding even more books. How was he ever going to find what he was looking for?

CHAPTER THIRTY-FOUR

Encroaching Danger

The other tribes had upped their attacks and Eric urged his people to keep fighting, though it was getting hopeless. They could hold on for a day or two with this sustained fighting, but not any longer. The end was getting near and his people were beginning to despair. Suddenly he spotted Sam rushing over to him, out of breath. That couldn't be good. Sam was in charge of the other realm and protecting the ship. A chill ran over him at the thought of what could send Sam into this realm right now.

"Eric, we've spotted another ship. It's following us."

"All right," he said, struggling to remain calm as he immediately followed him back to the other realm. No alarms were sounding in the ship so they couldn't be in too much danger yet. Luke's dragons were circling nervously and he hoped it was just because they missed him, not that Luke was in danger. Anna was attempting to soothe them with only a small measure of success.

He went to the bridge and studied the maps Sam showed him. There was indeed another ship at the edge of their radars that seemed to be tracking him. Sam was unable to tell who the ship belonged to. It was possible it belonged to one of the local governments and was simply trying to figure out who they were, but Sam had bribed the governments well to ignore them.

"If it gets closer, contact them," he said slowly.

"Are you sure?"

"Indicate that we're a civilian ship. Don't tell them who we are."

"There's danger," Sam pointed out. "It might confirm to them who we are. If they're enemies..."

"Then they'll figure it out no matter what we say," Eric said grimly. "This may shorten the time before they figure it out but there's a chance it's not them."

He wasn't even sure who "them" was. He knew the Elders would have gotten other tribes to search for them but he wasn't sure who it would be. If it was anyone with sympathies for him, they might talk them into leaving them alone. But there were a lot of tribes firmly against them now and this wasn't likely to end well. At least the people should be safe. There was no way any other tribe would fire on women and children, and they had to know that the female dragonling was here. No one would dare risk her.

He was considered his options when suddenly he turned. Something was calling him. Ryseth? He blinked in surprise. There was no way he should be able to feel his dragon in this realm but it was undeniable. Something was wrong and his dragon needed him. Now.

"Sam, take care of this," he said. "Follow your judgement. I need to get back to the other realm. I think something's happened."

Sam looked puzzled but agreed, and Eric practically ran through the narrow passageways back to the gate. Luke's dragonlings were definitely upset and so was he now. Luke had to be in danger. That was the only explanation. There was no other reason Ryseth would reach out to him like this. He bolted through the gate. His dragon was just outside of the community and he was urging Eric to go faster. As soon as Eric was there, he ordered him to get on. Eric obeyed and Ryseth leapt into the air.

Luke is in trouble and needs you, Ryseth said, and Eric narrowed his eyes and leaned closer to his dragon. It was true then. Luke was in danger. He didn't like leaving his tribe like this, in dire danger in both realms, but he needed to help Luke. If Luke didn't find an answer at the library then they were all lost. He wondered how far Luke was and what kind of help he needed and hoped his dragon would pick up on it and answer him.

Daniel's tribe found him, Ryseth said, and Eric drew in a sharp breath. *He reached the library and needs you there. The Untamable will protect us when we get close. They are two hours away,* he added.

Eric knew the entire trip would be filled with worry and he just hoped he had enough energy to fight when they arrived. But did that mean he would be going to the Great Library? He felt an assent from his dragon and was briefly filled with awe. The Great Library was a legend, not something people could actually visit. He was surprised enough that Luke was granted access; were the Untamable really going to let him go there? But he trusted Ryseth on this and his dragon had no reason to lie.

Luke must have asked them for permission, he realized. There was no other reason the Untamable would let him near. But how could he possibly help at the Great Library?

❁ ❁ ❁

The flight took forever but soon Ryseth warned him to brace himself. He obeyed and spotted dragons in front of him. At least a hundred of them, he realized in shock. This had to be Daniel's entire tribe, and they were attacking around twenty-five of the Untamable. He was stunned, both at the numbers of dragons and at the fact that they dared attack the most powerful dragons in their society. The Untamable were sacrosanct; they couldn't be attacked. If the tribes attacking his people started ignoring the Untamable, then they were in for real trouble, he thought grimly. Right now the Untamable were the only thing standing between his tribe and annihilation.

The others will not attack, Ryseth said unexpectedly. *These dragons are angry that Luke is not theirs.*

"He's not bonded to them?" Eric asked in surprise. How far away was Luke?

They are, but they wish him to live with them. Hold on.

Eric obeyed as Ryseth entered the fray and dove between the dragons. He caught a glimpse of Daniel on a nearby dragon and suddenly all of the dragons turned on him. He clung to Ryseth as he spun in a series of tight twists to avoid them, heading straight for the Untamable. The large dragons moved to him as one of Daniel's dragons clawed at Ryseth's side. Ryseth shrieked in rage and pain but kept flying and then the Untamable were around him and they were guiding him into the sky. Two of them broke off from the others to lead him higher and higher and he felt Ryseth gasping for air.

Dragons weren't designed to fly this high and his own lungs were twinging. He leaned close to his dragon, since he exuded the required balance of air to keep him safe at higher altitudes. And then they were over the clouds and he stared down in shock. There was an enormous building sitting in the clouds.

The Untamable landed and Ryseth did too, sinking into the clouds that were somehow solid beneath his feet. Eric slid off and rushed to Ryseth's side to assess the damage. Blood dripped into the clouds. It was a deep injury and might scar, but he was alive and there was no chance he would die.

Go to the library, the Untamable commanded.

"But Ryseth," he started, then felt the large dragon's determination that he obey.

Your dragon will be safe. He will remain here where no one can touch him.

He felt a protest from Ryseth, a desire to fight for Luke, but when the Untamable turned their determination to him, Ryseth quickly projected obedience. Eric was a little startled he was able to pick up on all that, but didn't spend too much time thinking about it. He stroked Ryseth one more time and then went to the front doors which were opened. So Luke was inside. There were lights, luckily, but he was dismayed at the number of books.

"Luke?" he called, not seeing the familiar and beloved shape anywhere near him.

"Over here," a voice called, and he headed towards it to find Luke deep into one of the nearby shelves. He embraced Luke tightly and only barely kept himself from kissing him.

"I need your help searching everything," Luke said. "There are so many books."

"What are we looking for?"

"Anything on female dragons or illnesses," he said. "But not all of these are in English. I don't know what language it is."

He showed Eric one of the books and he was bewildered. He spoke Korean and Japanese and he had never seen anything like it. But he would start looking and just hope what they needed was in a language they could understand. Luke had him start at the other end of the enormous room and he obeyed. They would keep searching until they met in the middle.

He worried about Ryseth as he searched, but his dragon ought to be safe. Ryseth was far more talkative than he had ever been before, he considered. Was it just because Luke had needed him or was there another reason? Maybe he was more willing to talk now that he wasn't being forced into obedience by their tamer, he considered. That would make sense. He was free now, and free to talk to whoever he wanted. But most of Eric's attention was on finding books in the languages he knew and searching for answers.

He had gone down an entire row and reached one of the many alcoves when his heart caught. There was a pedestal in the middle of the alcove and on it was a fragment of glass. He knew it. He recognized it instantly. This was the missing piece of Luke's mind that had been shattered by that tamer so long ago. What was it doing here?

"I found it, Luke," he said, because whatever reason this was here, it had to be the answer they were looking for. It might not have anything to do with the female dragons but here was the answer Luke had always needed.

"The book?" Luke called as he rushed over.

"No," Eric said. "I found you."

Luke inhaled sharply and his quick pace slowed as he approached it.

"What is this?" he asked as if afraid of the answer.

"You recognize it, don't you?" Eric asked.

"Yes," Luke said faintly. "But why is it here?"

"I don't know," Eric said, then smiled faintly. "I told you I'd help you find it."

Without warning, Luke flung himself into Eric's arms and kissed him, a kiss of passion and love and everything he had ever imagined. Luke's lips against his were warm and his tongue flickered against his enticingly, without the hesitance he usually felt from him. He eagerly returned the kiss, stroking Luke with his tongue, with his hands, feeling their lips locked together as a feeling of richness sweep over him.

He was desperate for the feel of Luke against him and clutched his back, the silky texture of his shirt encouraging him to be bolder as he reached to caress Luke's hips, then lower. Luke's arms were firmly wrapped around his neck as he leaned against him, giving himself fully to the experience. They had never kissed like this before and the intensity was making Eric dizzy with desire, his body heating up quickly until he couldn't stand it anymore. He wanted Luke. Needed him. Why had he ever pushed Luke away? Why had he been so hesitant to pursue him? Just because of what the other tribes would think? Who cared what they thought. Luke was his, and he was Luke's. Nothing would ever change that and his body hummed against Luke's in perfect harmony. He would never be able to resist Luke after this. Never. Anything Luke wanted, he would give him. And he hoped Luke wanted a lot.

This wasn't the best time for it, though, he thought with a twinge of regret. Every part of him wanted to yank Luke's shirt off, slide his hands under his pants and take him right now. Luke would let him, he was almost certain. He could feel Luke's lust against him, his love. They were together in a way they never had been before. But he couldn't, because they were in danger and they needed to figure out what to do with the shard they had found. He didn't think Luke was capable of pulling back right now. He was too committed. Eric needed to be the one to cool things down, even though he was desperate to continue.

He backed away a little in his kiss and felt Luke's surprise. His hands returned to Luke's back and Luke clung to him as if begging for more. Finally, he broke away from the kiss gasping for breath, and felt Luke's breath mixing with his as they panted.

"What's wrong?" Luke said softly, looking up at him with those beautiful eyes. Eric was speechless for a moment, then drew back further and gestured to the shard. Luke drew in a sharp breath.

"Oh," he said. "I feel so complete when I'm with you. You make me feel whole. What will it be like when I have my mind back? Will I still want you?"

Eric flinched. What if restoring the shard somehow changed Luke? He hadn't even thought of that. What if it meant that Luke was no longer interested in him? No. It couldn't mean that. Nothing would change between them. This would only draw them closer, not push them apart. After that kiss, nothing could destroy what lay between them.

"What do we do with it?" Luke asked. "I don't know how to put it back in my mind."

"We'll touch it," Eric said. "That has to heal you."

"You'll touch it with me?" he asked shyly.

"If you want me to," he said. "I'll do anything you ask."

That had been true before that kiss but it was doubly true now. Luke nodded and took his hand, then extended it towards the shard. Eric let him take control of this. He could only imagine how nervous Luke was from his pale face and the way his hand trembled in his. But Luke looked determined, too, and Eric knew he had been waiting for this a long time. He took a deep breath and then, their hands entwined, he pressed forward until their fingertips brushed against the fragment. Everything went black.

CHAPTER THIRY-FIVE

Dark Realization

While last time Eric had entered Luke's mind it had taken a long time to transfer there and felt like he had been enveloped and drawn out, he found himself instantly there as though he had been ripped into the place. His body throbbed with pain and it took a moment for him to recover from the sensation. He and Luke were both holding the fragment and Luke's mind was glittering with light as it had last time. But while last time it was a gentle light, now it was pressing and insistent, clearly eager to be complete. The hairline fractures were clearly visible, as was the place where this one fragment needed to go.

Luke swallowed hard.

"I don't know what will happen when we do this," he said cautiously.

"It doesn't matter," Eric said. "I'm with you. I'll keep you safe."

Luke looked at him gratefully, then a small smile lit his face.

"I've waited so long for this and now I'm scared to do it."

"It's all right," Eric said soothingly. "It won't hurt you."

He hoped, at least. He honestly had no clue what would happen.

"Do you want me to help or do you want to do this alone?" he asked.

"I think I have to do it myself," Luke said, not sounding very confident about that.

"You can do it," Eric urged. "I'll stay at your side."

Luke nodded, then took the fragment and approached the glittering light that made up his soul. He took a deep breath, then pushed the fragment into the hole. Instantly light cascaded over Eric and he felt a ripping sensation, his mind being shredded as it was flung back in his body. He gasped for breath and realized he was back in the library, not in Luke's mind.

"Luke," he cried, realizing he was limp next to him.

He shook Luke slightly but he remained unconscious. He didn't want him to be alone, but he didn't want to wake him if something were happening. But what if Luke thought he had abandoned him? What if Luke needed him and he wasn't there? He shut his eyes and tried to focus on Luke's mind. He felt repelled. Whatever was happening, there was no way he was getting into Luke's mind. He opened his eyes and to his surprise, felt Luke's powers slowly growing. Luke had always been considerably stronger than any other tamer he had ever sensed and that was increasing right now. Whatever was happening, Luke was gaining strength rapidly. That had to be good, then. Surely he wouldn't be getting stronger if he were in pain or distress. Would Luke still love him after this? He could only hope.

Eric took a deep breath and made sure Luke was in a comfortable position, then stood up and noticed a book on the pedestal where the fragment had been. Had this been under the fragment and he hadn't noticed it? But no, it was open to a page nearly a third into the book and he would have noticed if the fragment were on an open book. He cautiously stood up and examined the opened page. It was old, that was obvious, and while it was in English, it was in old English. It was a little hard to read but he could get the general idea and as he read, he drew in a slow breath. It was about Luke.

* * *

Everything was filled with light. It filtered through Luke's awareness and glittered in his mind. He was still inside of his soul and could see the crystal that made his soul shining with a strength it had never had before. The hairline fractures were gone. It was whole and stronger than it ever had been. He let go of his physical form and luxuriated in the sensation of being whole. He couldn't even remember the last time he had felt like this. When had it been?

Memories began flittering through him and though he tried to push them away, not wanting to remember anything from his shattered life, they swept over him. He was a child, hearing the dragons around him. They were in the other realm but they wanted to talk to him and they did. He realized his own dragons might be in danger and reached out to them. He hit a wall. He desperately reached for his dragonlings and could feel them faintly. He sent them a wave of love and reassurance before the memories overwhelmed him again.

He had always thought of those first voices as evil because that was what his parents taught him but now that he was able to look back with a clear mind, he realized that they had simply been trying to greet him. They were excited about him and wanted him to tame them, but he wasn't able to come to their realm and there was no way to bond with a dragon between realms. So they filled his mind with stories and hope and dreams of when he could come to them, and when he told his parents, they panicked. They only saw a voice that was trying to get him to do things and assumed it was delusions or worse. They had tried to get him to stifle the voices and he had obeyed, not wanting to disobey his parents. Their love for him had always been hanging on a thread and he would have done anything to keep that love, even push away the dragons who he now realized offered far greater love.

He remembered the first time the touch had appeared, seeming to understand what the voices were and reassure him about them. As he remembered that chilling voice reaching through him and calming his fears, he remembered the voice and shivered. He knew that voice. Memories of the touch poured into him, the comfort the touch had offered, then the way it had invaded his body and taken advantage of him, slithering through his body and making him desperate for relief, but denying him. Again and again it happened until he couldn't stand it anymore and his mind had shattered into a thousand pieces. And the voice remained, lingered, telling him that he would always belong to it. He had heard that voice recently telling him he belonged to him. But it couldn't possibly be. The voice was Daniel's.

That made no sense, he told himself. But his memories were undeniable. It was unquestionably Daniel's voice in his mind. Daniel wasn't a tamer, though, and he knew only a tamer could enter his mind like that. Or was Daniel a tamer? He remembered all the questions he had had about Daniel's tribe. Even though their previous tamer had been traded to another tribe in the dragon swap that brought Luke to him, Daniel had never taken him into the other realm to tame the tribe's dragons. Was that because he himself was a tamer and there was no need for Luke?

His mind flashed forward to how he had blacked out when the Elders first touched him, when Eric first touched him. He had known that it was because of the touch, because the touch wanted to control him and everything he did. But when he had been at Daniel's side, the Elders had reached into his mind successfully. He hadn't blacked out. And when Daniel had tried to rape him, he also hadn't blacked out. Was that because Daniel was the one to place those limitations on him and was the only one able to take them off whenever he wanted? He was chilled at the thought that he had been living with the touch all these years. How had he not known it?

But his memories returned to his earliest days when he had heard the first clear voice in his memory: the mother dragon. All of the previous voices had been faint because they had come from the other realm, or they were the touch and far too real for his comfort. But the mother dragon had reached out to him and promised him safety if he could just come to her side. His parents had by this time given up on him and locked him up most days, rarely coming to talk to him. They acted like he didn't exist and he knew they would be happier without him, so he had snuck out and then run and run in the direction of the mother dragon.

By the time he arrived in his first tribe's territory and been found by them half-dead, the mother was already dying. He had known it the moment he saw her. But he had raised her dragonlings and found purpose in life, and she had helped him gather the shattered fragments of his mind and reclaim some semblance of his self. She had dulled his memories then, helped him overcome the trauma of his past. He had forgotten almost everything for a long time and was relieved. He hadn't wanted to remember and she helped him forget. He would have done anything for her and it was painful watching her die even as she cared for her litter. She was the first dragon to die from the sickness, though other mother dragons started dying immediately after her. His leader talked about it frequently, worried about the possibility of a disease that could wipe out all dragons.

Then Aaron, his leader, had died. Daniel reached out to his tribe even before the funeral requesting a dragon swap. At the time it had seemed perfectly normal: Daniel needed a tamer and Aaron's tribe no longer needed one. Looking back, though, it didn't make sense. Now that he knew more about the other realm, he knew that dragon tamers did far more than simply take care of dragonlings. Aaron's tribe would have still needed a tamer. He knew Daniel's previous tamer didn't go to them; who took over in their tribe? And thinking back, was it suspicious that Aaron had died immediately after the dragonlings entered the other realm? The timing was almost exact; he had died within a week. Was Daniel responsible for his death? Luke shivered. He didn't like to think of it but what if Daniel had been doing everything in his power to get Luke back under his control? It was a definite possibility even though it had never occurred to him before. Why would it occur to him? He had trusted Daniel.

He remembered his relatively pleasant time in Daniel's tribe, though looking back he realized how stifled he was. He was given freedom in raising dragonlings and nothing else. Daniel had controlled him completely and he hadn't even realized it because he was so used to being controlled. Was it instinctive? Had he unconsciously recognized that Daniel was the touch and obeyed him because of that? He didn't like to think about it.

His mind warmed as he remembered Eric. At first he had despised Eric for stealing him and his dragonlings when their mother was still able to care for him, but that had changed rather quickly. His current dragonlings brought him joy and he reached out to them again to assure them of his love. He couldn't tell how much time had passed and he wondered if they had gotten a feeding yet.

He was grateful for Anna, though as his memories continued to pour through him he remembered the fear of his time with the Elders and how he had at first thought she was the enemy. There were so many things in his past he didn't want to think about, he realized as he remembered the childish promise he had bound the Elders to. He wondered if it were still in effect. Probably. That meant they wouldn't kill him, he supposed, though that wasn't much comfort. He had allowed them into his mind once and that meant they now had permission to do so again. He needed to avoid them at all costs.

Finally his memories faded and he was back in his mind, staring at the crystal that was him. It was glowing even brighter and he felt an unfamiliar joy fill him. He was whole again. His memories were fully restored. He didn't like a lot of them, but they were part of who he was and they were in his possession again. He sensed the strength of the crystal and knew it could never be shattered again. His new dragons gave him too much strength. Daniel and the Elders could hurt him, but they could never break him. The thought gave him far more confidence than he had imagined possible.

It was time to return, he sensed. He didn't know how much time had passed and he worried. Eric wasn't here, though he had promised to stay at Luke's side, and he didn't know why that was. He needed to find him and hoped he hadn't been hurt in the explosion of power that had sent Luke into his memories. He would sense if Eric had been hurt, wouldn't he? Yes, he assured himself. Eric was fine. He remembered what his Untamable had said about Eric being his mate and blushed as he realized it was true. They hadn't had sex, but they were bound together. There was no one else for him and he strongly suspected he held Eric's heart as well. For now, at least, he thought darkly as he remembered Daron. The future was unknown. But for now he could exult in Eric's undivided love. He just needed to return to the real world.

He took a deep breath and focused on his body. He felt as though he were traveling through molasses it was so slow, and then he felt his heart beating, his lungs inhaling and exhaling. Slowly, his body returned to his awareness. His fingers twitched and he managed to open his eyes. Eric was standing nearby, unharmed, and Luke let out a gasp of relief. Eric turned and was at his side in a moment, helping him sit up.

"Luke," he said, sounding on the brink of tears. "I didn't know what happened to you."

"I'm fine," he whispered, then stroked Eric's cheek with a boldness he had never had before. "I love you, Eric."

Eric's eyes filled with tears and he leaned forward and kissed him.

"I love you, Luke," he said softly. It was everything Luke needed to hear.

CHAPTER THIRTY-SIX

New Knowledge

Eric's heart raced as he held Luke close. He had told him he loved him before, but it felt different this time. This time, Luke had said it back. In fact, he had initiated it. Eric had known that Luke loved him but without hearing it said, there was some question. Now he was completely satisfied. However, they were still in danger. Luke had been unconscious for nearly four hours as Eric frantically waited. He had read the book next to Luke and was filled with information he needed to share with Luke, including the solution to the problem of the dying females. But Luke hadn't woken up. He hadn't wanted to go far and he had reached out to Ryseth to check on things. His dragon was again very talkative and he decided it must because because he was free now.

The fighting was getting close to them. The Untamable were taking quite a few hits and Ryseth warned him grimly that many of the powerful dragons were now injured. Some had fled and taken refuge with him in the library, replaced by others. But there were only a limited number of Untamable and they were slowly being beaten back. There was nothing Eric could do, though, because Luke was still unconscious. He just had to fret and wait for him to wake up as he sensed his power slowly growing stronger and stronger. And now he was awake and there was hope once again.

"I remembered," Luke said. "I remembered everything."

Luke proceeded to share everything he had just

experienced and Eric was stunned. Daniel was a tamer? The same tamer who had abused Luke as a child and shattered his mind? But that did make sense with what he'd read in the book. As soon as Luke had wiped the last of his tears away and finished his story, Eric considered his options. They needed to help the Untamable but he needed to tell Luke what was in the book. Which took priority?

"Luke, the dragons need help," he said, deciding that was the immediate concern. After all, if Daniel got here, then it wouldn't matter what the book said. They would be trapped.

Luke stiffened and looked outside.

"My dragons," he said in an anguished voice. "They didn't tell me they were hurt. I have to help them."

He turned to Eric with tears in his eyes again. "How do I help them?"

"We need more dragons," he said. "Could you summon the dragons from my tribe?"

"But then your people will be attacked," Luke said, then his eyes had that distant look tamers had when communicating with dragons. "I'm summoning others," he said slowly. "They don't belong to any tribe. They belong to me. There are enough nearby, though it'll take some time for all of them to get here."

"There are other dragons within two miles?" he asked, a little surprised. They were quite far in the sky.

"My range is wider now," Luke said. "I don't know how big. It feels like I can sense every dragon in the world but that can't be true."

Eric's eyes widened. "If you feel them, does that mean you've bonded with them?"

"Yes," Luke said, and Eric's mind went to the book.

"Luke, I found this book where the fragment was," he said, helping Luke to his feet and leading him to the book. Eric had scoured the entire book by now and only one section was really relevant. "You don't have time to read it but I can summarize it if you trust me."

"Of course," Luke said. "How long is it? Why can't I read it?"

"We're in danger," he said. "The sooner we get away from the Great Library, the better. The other dragons are too close and I don't want them knowing how to get here."

Luke nodded and Eric took a deep breath. He was still a little stunned at what he had read.

"Luke, you've heard of the Dragon Master, haven't you?" he asked. "He lived about a thousand years ago and predicted another one would be born in time. He dramatically reshifted our reality and society. You're the one he was waiting for."

"What does that mean?" Luke asked.

"It explains why all the dragons want you," he said. "They recognize you as their master and want to belong to you."

"I'm not their master," Luke pointed out a little huffily.

"You have control over them," he said. "If you wanted to control them, you could. The last Dragon Master wanted to control the dragons and introduced tamers to keep them contained. But you're different. You'll set them free."

Luke nodded slowly. "That sounds better," he said. "They do want to be with me."

"It also explains the females," Eric said, thrilled at the knowledge he was able to share as Luke leaned forward eagerly. "The safety and health of all dragons are stored in the Dragon Master, whose soul is called to the Great Library to take on their power. But your soul was shattered, and so was their power. Part of your soul was summoned here, but the rest remained, and because you were divided, the females began dying off. Didn't you say your first dragon was the first to die?"

"So I was killing them?" he asked, appalled. "I was the cause of it?"

"No," Eric said firmly. "Daniel was. He must have recognized what you were and wanted to control you, and shattering your mind was the easiest way to do it. He must not have expected you to run away and restore your soul as much as you did. When you shattered, though, it did send ripples through the dragons. The book warns of the consequences of harming the Dragon Master and this is one of them."

"So now that my soul is complete, the females are fine, right?" he asked nervously.

"They should be," Eric said, inwardly rejoicing at that statement. Luke broke into a wide grin and Eric couldn't help but lean forward and kiss that beautiful face. "Anyway," he continued. "The Great Library was built by the Dragon Master, and updated by Elders throughout the centuries. It holds all of our knowledge and exists for you. They knew another Dragon Master would come and were preparing for you. That's why the Untamable exist: to make sure you remain safe. That's why your dragons become Untamable. They're your guardians."

Eric glanced towards the door. "Have the other dragons arrived? Are the Untamable safe?"

Luke narrowed his eyes and also looked at the door. "Many have," he said. "They're driving Daniel back. They'll be safe."

"Good," Eric said in relief. He did not want the Untamable hurt or killed. Now that he understood how foundational they were for their society, he could not let harm come to them.

"We should leave, though," Luke said almost mournfully. "I wish I could stay and learn more. What else did the book say?"

"That's everything important," Eric said. "I'll tell you more in time, but we do need to leave. You'll be welcome to come back at any time. The Untamable will always let you in."

Luke nodded, then took his hand and led him to the door. As they left, he gasped. Eric was taken aback as well. Six of the Untamable were there, heavily bleeding. Ryseth was with them but at least his bleeding had stopped. Luke darted towards them, moving from dragon to dragon and clearly communicating with each other them. He looked grim and Eric knew it was difficult to see his beloved dragons injured like this. Then he turned to Eric.

"Daniel will pay for this," he said in a low voice. "I don't know how, but he'll pay."

Eric was relieved that for once, Luke sounded absolutely confident. Recovering his memories and restoring his soul had changed him and it was a positive sign, in his opinion at least.

He suspected Daniel wasn't going to be pleased by the changes. They would have to confront Daniel to leave, he suspected, but hopefully they could get far enough away from the Great Library that it wouldn't be in danger.

A large dragon spiraled down to them, uninjured.

I will carry you, he said, and Luke went up to him and looked back at Eric. *Your dragon must remain and heal.*

"He's big enough to carry both of us," Luke said.

Eric went to his side a little warily. It was true; the dragon was enormous compared to Ryseth. But he was hesitant to ride one of the Untamable and he didn't like leaving Ryseth. The large dragon lowered himself to make it easier for them to get on and Eric pushed aside his fears and climbed on, helping Luke up as well. Luke held onto the dragon's armor and Eric imitated him. Then the dragon burst from the ground and he heard Luke's indrawn breath. It seemed Luke was still a little afraid of flying and he hoped they didn't have to do any acrobatics to get through the fighting.

They descended quickly and he could feel Luke's tension, but neither of them spoke even though Eric longed to comfort him. Then they saw the fighting. It was quite close, though at a much lower altitude. They needed to stop Daniel now.

As they got closer he realized that there were more dragons than before. Far more. And most of the dragons didn't have riders. The wild dragons, he realized in awe. They had obeyed Luke and come to protect the Untamable and the Great Library. He never would have imagined dragons fighting who weren't forced to do so by their riders.

Many of Daniel's dragons had left, probably too injured to continue. They were over land right now and they had probably landed and were recovering until they were ready to return for more. Their Untamable dipped through the wild dragons and began making a beeline for the ground under them. Was that safe? It was almost certain Daniel's dragons were there. But once they were low enough to make out individual trees, the dragon leveled out and began flying quickly. There were indeed dragons on the ground and several of them took flight to follow. Eric glanced back and realized in shock that all of the fighting dragons were following them as well. The Untamable was fast enough to stay ahead of them but they were bringing the battle behind them. Daniel must have realized Luke had left and was tracking him.

He was amazed that Daniel had enough control over his tribe's dragons to force them to attack the Untamable. He had never been close to Daniel, he realized. When he had kidnapped Luke, he had never gotten especially close. Not close enough to sense that he was a tamer. And when he had rescued Luke from Daniel at the Elder's compound, had he noticed anything? He had been close enough to sense him then. But Luke was there as well and Luke was powerful enough that he would have blurred any other tamers nearby. He couldn't believe he had never realized Daniel was a tamer and he was clearly quite a powerful one to get this type of obedience.

The Untamable seemed to be heading to a specific point and as they flew, Eric tensed as he noticed several dragons approaching from all directions. It looked like they were all heading to the same location. That had to be deliberate, didn't it? The Untamable wouldn't fly right into a trap, would he?

Then the Untamable slowed and dipped lower. The other dragons coming from other directions were becoming clear and he tensed. He could make out several of the Elders on the dragons, and leaders of the other tribes. This did not look good. Luke glanced back at them.

"We have to do this," he said. "But you'll fight for me, won't you? You once said you would."

"I won't let anyone take you ever again," Eric vowed, though he wondered what they were getting into. Then they landed and the other dragons did too. He glanced back to see that the fighting had stopped. Daniel's dragon approached and he got off, then went to the Elder's side. Whatever happened, Eric would stand at Luke's side. He would never leave him again.

CHAPTER THIRTY-SEVEN

Removing Power

Luke stared at the Elders and Daniel standing in front of him and all of his confidence vanished. His mind felt strong and he knew they couldn't hurt him the same they once could, but they could still hurt him. Daniel could still beat him. He felt a longing to go to Daniel's side and pushed it away. He needed to be strong. He couldn't give in now, especially not since he had realized everything Daniel had done to him. He shivered and waited as the rest of the dragons landed. Soon they were ringed by other tribe leaders who watched as Luke and Eric faced off against Daniel and the Elders.

After a long moment, the head Elder stepped forward. He narrowed his eyes and tried not to flinch.

"Eric, return this tamer and end this conflict. He belongs to us."

Eric looked at Luke, who trembled and was too afraid to speak. He knew he needed to say something, to deny their claim, but he couldn't. He was frozen. Daniel stepped forward.

"I'm his rightful leader," Daniel said. "You've stolen my tamer, then stolen him from the Elders as well. But if you return him right now, all of this will go away. I'll withdraw any complaint."

Eric again looked at him. He was sweating now, despite feeling like ice. Daniel was so close. Would it be better to just return to his side? He felt a push from his Untamable reminding him to be strong and took a deep breath, but was still too frightened to speak.

"He doesn't belong to any of you," Eric finally said, probably realizing Luke wasn't about to speak. "He doesn't belong to anyone but himself."

The Elder smirked. "Why doesn't he say that, then? If he truly wants to stay with you, then why isn't he denying our claim to him? He can't. He knows he belongs to us. He wants to belong to us."

Luke gulped as Eric looked at him. He needed to say something. He knew Eric would fight for him but he needed to do this on his own or else everyone would turn on Eric right here, right now, and they would be separated. His eyes warmed and he tried to reclaim the power he had felt after restoring his mind and memories. He clutched at the feel of his dragons and his dragonlings and felt a little calmer. His dragonlings were sending him support, he realized in surprise. He reassured them of his love and hoped Anna was taking good care of them, then straightened his shoulders.

"I don't want to go with you, and I don't belong to you," he said, but there was a tremor in his voice. Daniel waved his hand and turned to the other leaders.

"Eric is manipulating him," he said. "You can tell he's not speaking for himself."

"Eric," one of the leaders said, "Just give up the tamer. It'll be so much easier."

"No," Eric said sharply. "He is speaking for himself."

He looked at Luke, who took a deep breath. If he wanted to be free, he needed to be bold, and independent, and strong. All of the things he had been taught to avoid in his life, all of the things that Daniel had stolen from him. He needed to defy Daniel right now and become the tamer Daniel had tried to prevent. He took another breath and when he spoke this time, his voice didn't waver.

"Eric isn't manipulating me," he said. "That's what you did. You controlled me and prevented me from becoming a true dragon tamer. And you Elders, when you got me, you broke into my mind and tried to control me as well. When I refused, you hurt me. All of you hurt me."

"That's a lie," Daniel said. "We would never hurt you."

Eric looked at the leaders, at Else in particular. "You know I'm not lying," he said. "Luke was injured by Daniel. Some of you saw the injuries. All of my tribe saw his injuries. Any of them can tell you what happened."

Else cautiously spoke up, though it was clear she didn't especially want to draw attention to herself. "That's true," she said. "And I've told many of you the same. I saw his injuries and they came from his previous leader. He was abused by the Elders. But I'm sure they wouldn't abuse him a second time," she added. "Maybe you should return him."

"No," Luke said before Eric could speak. "I'm not going back. I don't want them, and I don't need them. And if they try to take me, I will retaliate."

"Don't make threats you can't back up, Luke," the Elder said. "That's already gotten you in trouble once."

He thought of the promise he had bound them to and blushed. It was true, he had already made a threat and had it backfired spectacularly. But this was different. He had power now. He could feel the dragons all around him, his dragons. He could feel dragons everywhere, flittering in and out of his awareness, tamed and untamed, male and female, all of them enjoying their bond with him. They loved him. They wanted him to succeed. Well, most of them. Daniel's dragons were still angry and still wanted him exclusively for themselves, but he could deal with that later. He suspected they were still strongly under Daniel's influence and once Daniel wasn't in charge of them, their rage would quiet.

"Luke," Daniel said, extending his hand. "Come here, and I'll forgive you. You know I'll treat you well. You'll be able to raise your dragonlings in peace."

Luke held firm, though part of him ached to trust Daniel and trust in his forgiveness. But he couldn't. Daniel had betrayed him, lied to him, and hurt him his entire life. He would not give in now.

"I'll be able to raise my dragonlings in peace no matter where I am, because you and the Elders are going to stop coming after me," he said as confidently as he could. "If you keep pursuing me, I will take action against you. There's nothing you can do to stop me."

"You're out of control," the Elder said, and turned to the leaders. "You see? We need to get him back so that he can learn how our society functions. He's disrespecting our culture."

"We have a new culture," Luke said. "And you no longer have a place in it."

There was silence as everyone looked at him, puzzled. Everyone except Eric, that was. He looked a little concerned. Was it a good idea to announce what he was in the open like this? He needed them to know that things had changed, that the dragons had changed, and that the Elders no longer held power. Because they didn't, and as that thought finally trickled through his mind, he was a little startled. If people could no longer tame dragons, if dragons were free to follow whoever they wanted, then the Elders were meaningless. They really didn't have any power or place in the new society.

Daniel smiled at him. "The Elders are the center of our society, Luke. I apologize for shielding you the way that I did, for keeping you from entering our society fully." He looked to the other leaders. "Luke's ignorance is my fault, and I won't make the same mistake again. I was trying to protect him and instead deprived him of the knowledge he needed to live in our society. Once he learns more about us, he'll understand why the Elders are so important."

"That's not it," Luke said, taking an angry step forward. "Though you did lie to me. You lied to me this whole time, ever since you found me as a child."

Daniel's eyes widened and he drew in a sharp breath. Clearly he hadn't expected that. The Elders looked shocked as well. Had they known Daniel was the touch? They hadn't at first, he knew, because they had been sympathetic then. But when

Daniel had come for him and they had allowed him access, was it because they knew how much control Daniel had over him? They probably thought Daniel had tamed him. Anna had said they thought it was Eric but if they knew Daniel was the person who had broken Luke's mind, then perhaps that was only one of many theories. Since Luke obeyed Daniel completely once he was under the man's control, it had probably confirmed to them that he was tamed. But it wasn't true. He hadn't been tamed at all, just as his dragons weren't tamed. He had bonded to Eric and because Eric didn't want to control him, he was free. Just like his dragons.

"I don't think you know what you're talking about, Luke," Daniel said with a hint of fear in his voice. "You came to my tribe as a teenager."

"I met you long before that," Luke said. Should he be talking about this in the open like this? He didn't want everyone to know what had happened to him. It was shameful. Even though the memories had returned, it didn't mean he wanted to dwell on them. "But that doesn't matter," he continued. "What matters is that you leave me alone, and you stop attacking Eric's tribe. He's only trying to help me."

The Elder sighed. "Luke, we're trying to be gentle with you because of your inexperience, but you must come back with us. There are no options. We've tracked down your ship in the other realm." Eric tensed beside him and he suspected that was true. "Your dragonlings will be in our care soon. You'll have to come with us if you want them to survive."

"You will not separate me from the dragonlings," Luke hissed, feeling rage begin to flicker deep within him. They were going to kidnap his dragonlings to force him to return? It had never occurred to him that they would do something like that. He felt so helpless here, away from them, but he could sense them. They were fine. Worried about him, but fine. Wherever the Elders were, they weren't close enough to threaten them yet.

Luke took a step forward. He was slowly getting farther

from Eric and while he didn't like leaving his side, he needed to do this alone. No one could think that Eric was manipulating him or they wouldn't accept him.

"This is your last chance," Luke warned. "Stay away from me and leave Eric's tribe alone, or you'll regret it."

"No, this is your last chance," the Elder snapped. "Come with us now, or we'll be forced to punish you for your disobedience and arrogance."

She stepped forward as well and he took a deep breath. They were going to hurt his dragonlings unless he acted right now. He reached out with his mind and felt her mind in front of him. He reached out to her and felt her surprise, her confusion that he was opening his mind like this. But he wasn't opening his mind. He was opening hers. He cracked through her shield and she cried out and feel to her knees. He reached inside her, ignoring all the memories and emotions cascading over him and clutching the part of her that allowed her to communicate with dragons and tame them. He ripped it out and she screamed. Then he withdrew and felt her mind fade from his awareness. She was no longer a dragon tamer.

CHAPTER THIRTY-EIGHT

Out of Control

Eric wasn't sure what was going to happen as Luke inhaled deeply and met the Elder's eyes, and he was stunned when she screamed and fell to her knees, clutching her head. Luke had an expressionless look that usually indicated he was taming. Was he taming her? No. He would never tame a person. But what was he doing?

After a moment of stunned surprise, the other leaders rushed forward, some to protect the Elder, some to strike at Luke. Eric shoved Luke behind him so that he was pressed against the Untamable and regretted that he didn't have a weapon as most of the leaders drew theirs. There were a dozen leaders here, all of them now facing him with guns and swords. He tried not to let fear overtake him. He needed to protect Luke.

"What is that boy doing?" hissed Tarek, who had always been one of his enemies.

Several people here were enemies and they wouldn't think twice about killing him. Except that they hadn't killed him yet, probably because they weren't entirely sure what was going on. Even Eric wasn't sure what was going on. The Elder had stopped screaming but was still clutching her head as if in pain, taking deep, gasping breaths as the other Elders patted her back and shoulders and tried to talk to her.

"I don't know, but there's nothing we can do about it," Eric said. "Don't hurt him."

The Elder let out another brief shriek and then Luke inhaled sharply and seemed to return to the world. He seemed puzzled for a moment, then his eyes landed on the Elder and narrowed with dislike.

"That boy will pay," the Elder cried, getting to her feet and pointing at Luke. To Eric's surprise, Luke didn't even flinch. He was doing well hiding his fears and exuding confidence and Eric wondered how much of his strength was real and how much was faked. He was grateful Luke had managed to get it together when he did, because otherwise everyone would have turned against him and he would have overwhelmed.

The other leaders turned back to Luke, who seemed absolutely calm. It had to be faked.

"You have no power anymore," Luke said. "All of you, ask your dragons if she's a tamer anymore. You'll see that her words don't matter now."

There was silence and some of the leaders turned towards their dragons. Eric reached out to Ryseth, but he was too far away. Was she really not a tamer? He focused his abilities on her. It was difficult to sense individual tamers with so many around, and with Luke like a lighthouse exuding so much power everyone else was nearly indistinguishable, but he could just make out the Elders. And he couldn't sense anything at all from the Elder. The others must have been reaching similar conclusions. Fear crossed their faces, and some panic, then many turned on him in a rage.

"You stole our dragons," one of them hissed. "How dare you."

They must have realized their dragons no longer belonged to them when they asked about the Elder. That was dangerous. Stealing a dragon was a high crime. Luke had already stolen quite a few dragons but had gotten away with it so far. Would this be the final straw and he would be attacked?

"Your dragons came to me," he said. "I now control all of the dragons. And you didn't answer my question. Is she a dragon tamer now or not?"

More turned heads and puzzlement spread through them. They were probably moving beyond their initial realization that the dragons weren't tame to Luke's actual inquiry.

"She's not," Else said. "How is she an Elder if she isn't a tamer?"

The Elder scowled. "I'm still an Elder. He can't rob me of that."

"You have no control over the dragons ever again," Luke said, meeting her terrified and furious gaze. "They aren't yours. Dragons don't belong to anyone ever again. They're mine, and I want them free."

"No one can tame every dragon," Tarek said. "It's impossible."

Eric narrowed his eyes. He had tried to keep out of this conversation as much as possible because Luke was the one who needed to handle this, but they would never believe the truth unless they heard it from him, a fellow leader. "The Dragon Master can."

"That's a myth," the leader said dismissively.

"It's not," Luke said. "That's why the Elders tried to control me, why Daniel tried to control me. They knew what I was. And now I have my full powers and no one can control me."

The leaders backed away in fear, lowering their weapons. The Elders formed a defensive ring around Arabella and he stared at them. Was Luke going to strip all of them of their power?

"If you leave me alone, I'll leave you with your connection to the dragons," he said, and Eric let out a silent sigh of relief. If Luke stripped all of the Elders of their power, no one would ever follow him. "You'll still be able to talk to them, probably even persuade them to do what you want. But they won't mindlessly obey you ever again. They won't obey any dragon tamer."

"You're lying," one of the Elders hissed. "You can't take our power like this. Not even the Dragon Master can remove our power."

"I just did," Luke pointed out, gesturing to Arabella. "Do you really want the same?"

The leaders looked between him and the Elders uneasily, then Lee stepped forward. He had helped Eric with getting milk for the dragonlings and was a potential ally here, but there was still danger. This situation was so unusual that he couldn't predict anything.

"You say that no tamer controls the dragons? But our dragons are still here. They haven't run away."

"They like you," Luke said. "They'll continue to obey you as long as you respect them. And I've told them to obey your tamers as much as possible. All of the dragons in Eric's tribe have been under these rules for a while, and they haven't run away. I've accidentally bonded with several dragons from other tribes as well and they haven't run away. As long as they want to be with you, they will."

"That is true," one of the other leaders piped up. "He stole two of our dragons. Eric reassured us and I was skeptical, but the dragons act exactly the same as any other dragon in our tribe."

"The Dragon Master controls the dragons," another leader said darkly. "If you wanted, you could have the dragons turn on us. You could kill all of us. You could destroy our way of life. You already have, for many of us."

"I could control the dragons, but I won't," Luke said. "They should be free."

"Why should we trust that?" the leader demanded.

"If I wanted to control the dragons, don't you think I would have stopped Daniel's dragons from attacking my Untamable?"

Another wave of uneasiness. "Your Untamable?"

"My dragonlings grow into the Untamable, because I'm the Dragon Master," he said.

All eyes turned to Daniel and Lee glared. "You attacked the Untamable? That violates everything our society stands for."

"They were hiding Luke," Daniel said rather defensively. "If they had just handed him over, I wouldn't have had to attack."

One of the Elders pointed to the Untamable. "Luke controls the Untamable," she said. "He'll order them to turn on us and destroy us."

"He doesn't need to," said Lee. "If he already controls our dragons, why would it matter that he controls them as well?"

"If our dragon tamers don't control our dragons," another leader said slowly. "Then why should we obey them? Luke is the one we should be obeying, if he controls them."

"You will obey us," said the main Elder in a panicked voice. "We are your Elders."

"Our true Elders died trying to bond with the female, which Luke managed to do," said the leader. "Doesn't that make him equal to the Elders even without everything else?"

This was a far more promising conversation, Eric considered. Would they accept him as being more powerful than the Elders? He was sure Luke didn't exactly like the thought of everyone in the society obeying him but if it protected him from Daniel and the Elders, he probably wouldn't complain. Luke could correct them later and assure them that he had no intention of controlling them in any way, or maybe Eric could do it. He felt confident that Luke wouldn't want that kind of power but hoped Luke didn't say anything right now. If he did want them to stop trying to tame dragons, he would need to control their society. There was no other way for the new world order to come into being. If the other tamers looked up to him and obeyed him, perhaps he could ease the transition into the new way of life where dragons were free.

"Luke belongs to me," Daniel said, and darted forward.

* * *

Luke gasped as Daniel lunged at him. Fear instantly threaded though his body and he froze. Daniel bowled Eric out of the way before anyone could react and grabbed Luke's forearm. Luke stiffened and instantly recognized the touch from his childhood. Daniel wasn't just touching his arm, he was reaching out to his mind and he could sense the patterns of abuse that had given Daniel access when he was a child. Daniel was trying to enter his mind.

For a brief moment he remembered what it was like as a child, how he had invited the touch in because it seemed to understand him as no one else did. Even now, Daniel understood him. Should he let him in? The touch grew closer to his mind and he forced himself to remember everything Daniel had done to him. He remembered what the touch had become, and how it had teased him and sexually abused him and shattered his mind. No, he would not let the touch in again.

He slammed down his shields as the mother dragon had taught him and for a moment, there was peace. Then Daniel crashed up against his walls and he had to brace himself against the assault. Daniel was powerful and the shields that kept him protected started to creak. Luke mentally strengthened his shields and he felt his dragons helping him, giving him their energy to buffer his mind from the invading force. Daniel kept coming, more and more powerful. He was going to shatter him again, he thought in a panic, and lashed out against the touch that was far too familiar for his liking.

It would be so easy to just give in and let Daniel into his mind. Part of him ached for it. He belonged to Daniel in some way; why shouldn't he be allowed into his mind? Why was he fighting this? He felt flashes of concern from his dragonlings and snapped himself out of that train of thought. The grown dragons were helping him fight but the dragonlings were scared and confused. They were in danger.

He let the power of his bond with his dragons fill him. He was using dragongaze, he now knew, and it was what had given him strength over the Elders. He could use it against Daniel now. He reached out just as he had reached out to overwhelm the Elders and felt resistance where he had found acquiescence in them. Daniel was far stronger than them and

Luke fought to force his mind into Daniel's. He extended his mind, risking himself, and felt Daniel grasp at him with a victorious surge.

"Stop," he whispered, the word echoing with dragongaze as Daniel went rigid. He had to obey. Luke was in control.

A thrill ran through him. He was in control of Daniel, his leader, the man who had always controlled him and who had abused him his entire life. Daniel had always had the upper hand but suddenly, for the first time, Luke did. A wave of confidence swept over him and he lifted his hand towards Daniel. He braced himself and extended more of his self out of his shield, then shoved through Daniel's mind, blasting him backwards physically and mentally, reaching out to find and destroy every trace of the touch within him until there was nothing.

Daniel struggled under his iron grip but he continued to hunt down every last wisp of the touch that had shattered him, every hint of the man who had abused him, until it was silent. There was peace. He couldn't sense the touch anywhere. He suddenly realized Daniel was unconscious on the ground before him. Eric knelt to check his pulse with a grim look on his face. Was he dead?

CHAPTER THIRTY-NINE

A New Order

Daniel was alive. Eric could feel a faint pulse under his fingers, and he was breathing. He didn't know if he was relieved or not. Part of him wanted the man dead, but he didn't want Luke to be the one who did it. That kind of thing would crush the gentle-hearted Luke. Indeed, Luke was looking at him with desperation, waiting for him to announce if Daniel were alive or dead. Eric straightened.

"He's alive," he said, and Luke's body relaxed.

Eric looked at the other leaders, wondering if he should say more or continue to let Luke handle this. He would leave it to Luke, he decided. After all, he didn't even know what had just happened. Daniel had grabbed Luke, who froze with a look of horror on his face. Then the horror had turned to rage and his eyes had glowed with dragongaze. Daniel had been trapped by it completely. Luke had said something too soft for him to hear and Daniel was flung back, unconscious. What had Luke done?

Luke took a deep breath and faced all of them with a stern face. Eric wished Luke didn't have to be this strong right now. He wished he could protect him. But Luke's strength was one of his most attractive features. His strength, his courage, his independence, all in spite of what had been done to him. He had risen above all of it and Eric's heart swelled with love and a hint of pride. After all, he had helped Luke get to this point.

"Your tribes will stop attacking Eric immediately," Luke announced. The leaders all assented, though a few like Tarek looked less than pleased by that. Tarek stepped forward, to Eric's dread. If anyone could destroy the world Luke was trying to build, it was him.

"You claim to have replaced the Elders," Tarek said, and the Elders scowled. "You claim we don't have to respect our tamers anymore. You've destroyed our culture. Why shouldn't we start a new culture of our own? Why should we follow you?"

Luke seemed taken aback and Eric winced. He had expected some sort of challenge from Tarek, but the man was raising a good point. Their entire society had just been broken. What was to stop them from starting over on their own? Why would they follow the person who had destroyed everything?

"Your dragons are bonded with me," Luke started, but Tarek put his hands on his hips.

"You claim you won't control them in any way. So you can't take them from us even if we have nothing to do with you."

This was not looking good. Luke didn't seem to have anything to say and Eric wracked his brain for a solution. Luke wasn't from their society. He was an outsider and couldn't fully appreciate how much his actions had disrupted their way of life. Eric understood, though, and perhaps he could see a solution where Luke couldn't.

"Our society is not destroyed," Eric said, coming to Luke's side and squaring off against Tarek. "Our leaders have changed, yes, but everything else is the same. You will treat Luke as you treated the Elders, and in time he will create his own council of Elders. The Western Council will remain untouched, as they haven't been corrupted."

He glanced at Luke, hoping this was safe to say. He had no idea if Luke wanted any of this but he knew it was what needed to be said.

"Luke has agreed to tell the dragons to obey their tamers as much as possible, so the tamers will have the same amount of control. Instead of taming new dragons, though, they'll need to persuade them to join your tribes. A different skill, perhaps, but one they are all capable of learning. They will remain the center of our society as they are our link to our dragons."

"You really expect us to just keep living as we have been living?" Tarek asked scornfully. "When this boy has destroyed everything? Why should we trust him not to do it again? He's not one of us."

"I will be," Luke said. "I'm an outsider, I know, and I know very little of your society. But only because I've been prevented from learning. I want to learn about you. I will. And until I know more, I won't make any changes. Even after I know more, I won't make any changes. I don't want to destroy your way of life. I just want to protect the dragons."

"We should at least give him a chance," Else said. "We trusted these Elders after our old Elders were killed and look where it got us. We can at least see what he does before abandoning everything."

Tarek looked displeased and the Elders appeared furious, though they didn't say anything. They knew Luke wouldn't hesitate to strip them of their powers the way he had the main Elder's and they wouldn't risk it. Eric wondered if Luke actually would. He had no love for the women but was he willing to destroy all of them? Luke was a lot more ferocious than he had expected, he thought as he glanced at Daniel's unconscious body. What exactly had he done to him?

"Will you live where the Elders lived?" Tarek asked. "Will you keep that tradition?"

Luke took a deep breath and glanced at Eric briefly.

"No," he said. "The tribe there isn't my tribe. Eric's tribe will protect me, and I'll live with him, in the territory all of you stole from him."

The leaders immediately objected, even Else.

"He broke our laws," Tarek said angrily. "Now you seek to reward him? He'll abuse the power. We're already taking a chance and trusting you. Why should we trust him?"

Another leader who had always hated Eric jumped in. "We already know he's untrustworthy. He can't be your leader."

"He isn't untrustworthy," Luke snapped. "Everything he

did, he did to protect me. He did it because I wanted him to. He already obeys me, so he's the best person to continue protecting me."

"The Elder's tribe has a long history of nonpartisanship," Else pointed out in a far gentler voice than the others. "As much as Eric's tribe has helped you, they've been actively involved in our politics for generations. They have enemies."

"My tribe will stop all rivalries," Eric said, and their attention turned to him. "We will end all feuds. We'll make amends, if need be. But we will be the tribe to protect Luke."

"There's no way I'm obeying you." Tarek's lips curled in anger. "You're unfit to protect the Dragon Master."

"Who else can do it?" Eric said. "You claim the Elder's tribe is nonpartisan, but they actively prevented Luke from leaving an abusive situation. They sided with the corrupt Elders. They betrayed Luke. He can't trust them. He trusts me."

"But we don't trust you," Tarek insisted.

"The Untamable have been under my control for quite a while now, ever since I rescued Luke," Eric pointed out. "Have I ever used that to my advantage?"

"They've been protecting your people quite closely," another leader pointed out.

"Not anymore than they would protect any tribe being targeted, and they've only prevented fights, not started them. They've never even pushed you back, just stopped you from advancing."

"That is true," Lee said thoughtfully. "The Untamable would do that for anyone. My tribe has been under their protection before for a time, and they treated us exactly the same. I think he can be trusted with the Dragon Master."

"You've always been an ally of his," Tarek snapped. "You'll get preferential treatment."

Eric was getting frustrated now, because he wasn't about to let anyone else take Luke and he didn't know how to convince Tarek and his other enemies without having them break away into their own society.

"If Eric treats anyone unfairly, I'll deal with it," Luke said. "You say that the tamer is the center of your society, that leaders obey their tamers to some degree. Well, he obeys me. If he does anything, tries anything, I'll stop him. I have no favorites among you, and neither will he."

Tarek looked undecided but no longer angry and Eric felt a flash of relief. All he needed was for them to give him a chance. It was true that he had a lot of allies and enemies. If he were them, he wouldn't trust him to be impartial. But he would change his ways because it was the only way he could be with Luke. He thought of their kiss, of the passion that had filled him. He would do anything to be with Luke. And now he didn't have to hide that relationship anymore. It was fine if he was with Luke now; he wouldn't be seen as manipulating Luke if they were together. And if anyone did judge him, he wouldn't care. It wouldn't impact his impartiality. It would be hard to put aside some of his grudges and learn to treat his friends without favor, but he would get used to it. It would be a transition for everyone. He wondered, though, if Luke would actually be able to correct him. Luke was still so hesitant. He was improving, but Eric would have to be sensitive to his needs until he gained the confidence to truly take on the mantle of Dragon Master.

Luke looked around at everyone, then at Eric.

"How do I tell everyone in our society about this?"

"We'll let everyone know," Eric said, gesturing to the leaders around them. "The Western Council of Elders will want to talk to you, probably in person, but the other leaders will fall in line behind us, and behind them." He stared at the other leaders, challenging them to deny that they would help enforce the new way of life. They were silent. Good.

"My dragonlings need me," Luke said, then blinked as if in surprise and smiled at the leaders. They all looked entranced by that smile, as Eric always was. It was the first time Eric had seen him smile since his mind had been restored and it was even more dazzling than usual.

"The female dragons are no longer dying," he announced, and Eric couldn't believe he had forgotten to mention that. That would have persuaded them and Eric should have remembered it.

The leaders appeared startled.

"How?" Else asked. "What happened?"

"I'm free now," Luke said. "When I was controlled by Daniel and the Elders, the females died. Now that I don't belong to anyone, the females will survive, and female dragonlings will be born again."

"What do you have to do with the female dragons?" Tarek asked skeptically.

"I'm the Dragon Master," Luke said simply, and that seemed to persuade him. He nodded, as did the other leaders.

"We'll follow your lead," Tarek said. "We'll make sure the others do, too. You've healed our females. We owe you this chance."

"Thank you," Luke said. "I need to get back to my dragonlings now. Are you still tracking us?"

The last was directed to the Elders, who looked at each other warily.

"We won't do anything when we find you, and you'll be allowed to return to your territory," they said.

"All of my territory will be mine again," Eric added. "And anything that was stolen."

A few of the leaders grumbled, as they had no doubt gotten a lot when Eric and his tribe had fled. But he wouldn't allow them to keep any of it, especially now that his tribe was Luke's tribe. He deserved to get everything back. What would he do if someone refused? He wasn't sure. He couldn't hold grudges anymore. He might not be able to retaliate, but perhaps Luke could exert his pressure to get things back. He might have to. Luckily, Eric knew every single thing his tribe had left behind and he and his people would know if things were missing. He just hoped nothing had been destroyed.

CHAPTER FORTY

Returning Home

Ryseth had mostly healed by the time the other leaders started to disperse and Luke was relieved. His Untamable were healing, too. He hadn't realized dragons could heal so quickly. It was a good thing they could because they had been injured quite badly by Daniel's dragons. The other leaders were getting on their dragons and heading away, but Daniel's tribe still surrounded them and he felt a flutter of fear. Would they retaliate against him? The dragons were still a little angry, though much of their rage had faded without Daniel's powerful influence.

Daniel was still unconscious and Luke shivered as they waited for Ryseth to arrive. He didn't know what he had done, when Daniel would wake up, or what he would be like when he woke up. Luke had destroyed his mind to some degree; would he still be a person? Or had Luke essentially killed him even though his body was still alive?

"Will someone look after him?" Luke asked Eric, gesturing to the still body.

One of the women from Daniel's tribe cautiously approached just as Ryseth and several of the Untamable appeared on the horizon. She bowed to Luke, then to the Elders. Was she the new leader now that Daniel wasn't? They had to have some sort of system in place in case something happened. He had never seen her before, but then again, he had never seen anyone in his former tribe except Daniel and the occasional person nearby.

"We'll look after him," she said softly, glancing at her leader unconscious on the ground. "Will he recover?"

"I think so," Luke said, unwilling to confirm anything more. He honestly didn't know.

"We'll take the Elders back to their home as well," she offered. "They came here with us."

Eric turned to the Elders, still gathered around Arabella. Tears were streaming down her cheeks and he was a little surprised. But of course she was crying. He had stripped her of an essential element of her soul.

"You won't get away with this," Arabella said in a shaky voice.

The other Elders were still touching her in a comforting way but she was no longer one of them. He wondered what it must feel like for her. Communicating with dragons felt so natural; what would it be like if he suddenly couldn't do it anymore? He shuddered at the thought. Maybe he shouldn't have done it to her. He had reacted without thinking, stripping her of her power without considering the consequences of his actions. Just like when he had destroyed Daniel. He had felt threatened, attacked, and retaliated. He hoped he hadn't done too much damage. Should he apologize to her? There wasn't anything he could really say. Would it help or make matters worse? If he had just been stripped of his powers by Arabella, he wouldn't want her condescending and useless apology.

"I learned how to talk to dragons once," she said, to his surprise. "I'll do it again."

People could learn to do it? He had always spoken to dragons, ever since he was a child. From his first memories, now revived, there had always been dragons. But apparently that wasn't true for everyone. How did a person learn something like that?

"I won't stop you if you do," Luke said. It was the only thing he could offer her. She scowled but he didn't know what else to say. He wouldn't apologize, but he could offer her that assurance.

"No one will follow you," she continued. "They're lying. They saw you attack me and they'll turn against you."

Eric took Luke's arm and glared at the woman. "They don't lie. Enough of them will obey that we can force the others to obey as well. And even though he attacked you, you're not an Elder anymore. It didn't violate our laws."

Arabella inhaled sharply and the woman who must now be taking Daniel's place nodded.

"We'll follow the Dragon Master, even though you were our Elders," she said. "He controls our dragons."

"Despite what he did to your leader?" hissed one of the other Elders, pointing at Daniel's still body. The new leader took a shaky breath and seemed torn, then nodded again.

"Despite that. We knew what Daniel was doing to him. We let it happen. We won't let it happen again."

Luke bit down a flash of rage that she and the entire tribe must have known that Daniel was keeping him under his absolute control. They knew Luke was there, but he wasn't taking care of the adult dragons, and they must have known the reason why. They must have also known Daniel was a dragon tamer. Why hadn't anyone said anything? How was it that no one else knew what he was?

Ryseth and three Untamable landed nearby and Eric rushed to his dragon, stroking his scarred side. Luke hoped he continued to heal until there weren't any scars but could sense from Ryseth that while he would heal a little more, there would always be some trace of his injuries. It didn't matter, Ryseth assured him. He had earned the scars protecting the Tamer. Luke stiffened at the name and the Untamable assured him that all dragons called him that because they were used to thinking of humans as tamers. Now that they were free like the Untamable were, they would change what they called him. He wondered what name they would pick, if they would call him the Dragon Master like the humans did or if they would find their own name. They didn't like imitating humans too closely so he suspected it would be something unique.

Daniel's replacement picked up Daniel with a wince and headed to her dragon. Luke caught sight of Daniel's dragon and could hear the dragon's sorrow at what had happened. He tried to reassure the dragon but the dragon politely rejected his comfort. He wanted to mourn. Luke would let him. The members of Daniel's tribe helped the Elders to their dragons to carry them back, and Eric gestured for him to join him on Ryseth. One of the Untamable stepped between Luke and Ryseth with a thread of jealousy and Luke was amused. All of his dragons wanted him. But he should ride on the Untamable. He would still be able to talk to Eric as they flew, and his dragons needed him just as much as Eric did. He remembered their kiss after Eric had found the shard of his soul and blushed. As soon as they were alone, he wanted to repeat that kiss and see where it went.

Soon they were flying back to Eric's territory. It took over two hours but soon he saw groups of dragons in defensive positions in the sky. The attacking dragons had left, to his relief, but Eric's tribe must still be wary. They landed and explained to the people there what had happened. The people were surprised at their new role in the new society, and delighted that they could return to their homes. It would take time to get everyone back, Luke realized as Eric explained the situation. But they could return and he was glad. He didn't like that so many people had given up everything just to protect him. And then Eric led him to the gate and he could feel his dragonlings excitement. He had never been away from them for so long and they were eager to be reunited. He went through the gate without fear and as soon as he was back on the ship, the dragonlings bombarded him.

They were big enough that they nearly knocked him over and he was nervous because they were right next to the gate. He scolded them and quickly made his way over to their makeshift nest before letting them swarm him and holding each one individually. He could feel jealousy from his female and spent a lot of time holding her. She wasn't happy that there would be other female dragonlings now and she wouldn't be special. She had enjoyed being special. But just as he had once scolded her about killing her brothers and persuading her to accept new ones, now he scolded her and encouraged her to accept any new sisters. She grumbled but obeyed, and was soon crooning sweetly in his arms.

Anna was there and he barely had a chance to thank her before the dragonlings started begging for food. Had Anna not taken care of them? No, she had, he could sense, but the dragonlings wanted him to feed them. Anna had fed them not long ago but while his dragonlings weren't exactly hungry, they wanted the connection with him that only came from feeding. So he asked Anna to help him gather enough food and sat down with the female in his lap and two of the males cuddled against him while the other three males circled nearby. Slowly, he went through each of them, focusing his attention on them, nurturing their bond, but not draining himself as he once had. He couldn't afford to be weak right now, not with everything that was happening. When he had finally finished, he saw that Anna and Eric had been talking and were now waiting for him. There were a few other people in the room, most of whom Luke knew. It was an odd feeling being able to recognize people in his tribe.

Sam and Denis were there, Eric's bodyguards, he now knew, and all of the advisors except Mei, who must have stayed in the other realm to handle things there. Two other people from the tribe were there as well. They were talking to each other and far enough from the nest that he didn't feel threatened. As soon as his dragonlings were satisfied, he coaxed them into playing with each other and went to the group. Everyone bowed to him and he was taken aback for a moment. Were people going to do that to him from now on? He didn't deserve respect like that.

"Luke," Eric said. "The Elder's former tribe will need a tamer. Anna has lived with them for years and has volunteered. Would you accept that?"

"Sure," he said, wondering for a moment why they had bothered asking him. Then he realized that as the head of the tamers, it probably was up to him where everyone went. Anna had once said that the Elders would choose his new leader, so he must now be in charge of determining where new tamers went. He wasn't sure he wanted that power but he would keep it for now. He would keep everything the same for now.

"Thank you, Luke," Anna said seriously.

"Thank you for caring for my dragonlings."

"We have a lot to do," Eric said. "We're already heading for land. It'll take time, and even longer before we can get back to our territory. The rest of the tribe will get there a lot faster. They'll have everything ready for us."

"Where is your territory?" Luke asked, suddenly realizing that they might live somewhere he didn't like. He hadn't especially liked the heat and sun of the Elder's compound. Would they be in an equally sunny place? His home with Daniel had been cooler, with frequent rain. He had rarely been let outside but he always enjoyed it.

"In Korea," Eric said, and Luke wracked his brain to remember where exactly that was and what the temperature would be like. It was a peninsula, he knew, and finally placed it. That should be a good place to live. He hadn't even considered that he might not like his new home. He would probably be allowed to leave the nest more often now that he wasn't being trapped. He wondered what it would be like. He had seen movies and read books about ordinary life but he had never once lived like other people. What would his life be like not being under someone's control? He couldn't wait.

They dealt with a few more specifics. They wanted Luke to know everything but he was only barely paying attention. He kept looking at Eric and remembering their kiss. He wanted everyone to leave so that they could be alone, but it was hours before the others finally left and the dragonlings were pleading for another feeding. They always came first. Then, finally, the dragonlings were settling into sleep and Eric was waiting at the edge of the nest. Luke shyly smiled at him and he reached out his hand. Luke went to his side and took it. He glanced around. No one was here. He cuddled close to Eric, who wrapped his arms around his waist. He remembered how Eric had done that during their kiss and blushed.

"It's late," Eric said. "Are you ready for bed?"

"Maybe," Luke said. Was Eric suggesting they go to sleep, or they go to bed? There was a difference. He leaned into Eric. "I just want to see you alone."

Eric grinned and led him to the room where they had slept together before. He trembled in excitement.

CHAPTER FORTY-ONE

Embracing Destiny

As soon as he was alone with Luke, Eric pulled him into an embrace. Luke melted into him and tilted his head up for a kiss. He was quick to oblige, pushing the door shut behind them with his foot as he cradled Luke and tried to pace himself. He wanted to throw Luke into the bed right now, but he would somehow have to find the strength to go slowly. No matter how much Luke wanted this, he was still new to everything. As they kissed and their tongues danced together, Eric remembered how Luke had stripped him, then heat that had flooded his body then, the need to give in and let Luke do what he wanted. Then Luke had blacked out because of Daniel's control. That wouldn't happen this time. This time, he could get what he really wanted.

Eric pulled off Luke's shirt, pausing just long enough to get it over his head. He was in a button-up shirt. Just like last time, he thought with a smile. Luke seemed much more confident getting it off him this time and soon they were both shirtless. Luke's skin was silky smooth under his fingers as he caressed his back. After another long moment just touching him, Eric slid his hands down his back to the waist of his pants. He grazed his fingers along Luke's skin enticingly and felt Luke shiver, then break away with a laugh. Eric loved his smiling face and kissed him briefly before unbuttoning his pants and letting them drop to the floor. Luke was aroused. He couldn't help but brush his hand against the swell in his underpants as he took those off as well, and Luke was already pulling at his pants. He was aroused too, and Luke blushed when they were finally naked and stepping out of their clothes.

Eric hadn't actually seen Luke like this before, nor had Luke seen him. They each stepped back and Eric licked his lips as he examined Luke. He was beautiful. His fair skin had freckles scattered across his shoulders that looked adorable. He was quite fit, which surprised Eric a little. Luke had been trapped for most of his life, unable to get the kind of exercise he normally associated with a body like this. He must have a naturally good metabolism. While he wasn't exactly muscular, he was lean and hard and extremely desirable. His belly button had a scattering of hair around it that led his eyes inevitably downward. Everything about him was beautiful, he reflected as he admired Luke. And Luke looked just as pleased with his body. Eric felt a flash of relief at that. He was rarely self-conscious but he did take pride in his appearance and he would have been humiliated if Luke didn't like his body. Seemed like that wouldn't be a concern.

After the long moment of inspection, Eric extended his hand. Luke took it, and he led him to the bed and sat on the edge. Luke sat beside him and seemed nervous now. He didn't have good memories of this, Eric reminded himself. He really did need to go slow after what Daniel had done to him. So he started with kissing again, which Luke seemed to enjoy and feel confident doing. As they kissed, Eric let his hands roam over Luke's body, teasing him, caressing him, the sliding lower to grab him and start gently stroking. Luke let out a cry of surprise and stiffened, pulling out of the kiss, and Eric backed off immediately. Then Luke took a deep breath and leaned back into the kiss, taking Eric's wrist and moving him back into place. Luke's hands returned to caressing his shoulders and back, all he probably felt confident doing at this point.

They kissed and he stroked until Luke was hard and panting, then he gently readjusted them so they were lying side by side. He pulled Luke so that his body was cradled, with Eric's arms wrapped around him and the man's back pressed against his front. He was already hard as well from the heat of their kissing and the feel of Luke under his hands and he felt Luke tense as his cock brushed against Luke's ass. He murmured reassuring words and continued stroking him, listening to him pant and moan as he kissed Luke's neck and teased his nipples with his other hand. Before long Luke was begging for more in a sweet, hesitant voice, as if afraid to give voice to his pleasure. He probably was. He had been trained to deny his pleasure and he was glad Luke was drawing strength from this to break free of his conditioning. Then Luke arched his back against Eric.

"Please, Eric," he murmured. "I want more. I want you."

Eric nipped his neck and then licked the spot, then arranged them so that Luke was under him. His eyes were glazed with pleasure and Eric kissed him thoroughly as he grabbed his legs and pulled them up to give him access. Luke hesitated before obeying, and inhaled sharply as Eric touched him, first with his fingers. He didn't want to hurt him so he slowly began loosening him. Within minutes Luke was again begging for more, this time without the hesitancy of before. This time, Eric was ready to oblige.

He slowly pressed against Luke's opening and felt an initial resistance, then he slid inside with a sigh as Luke let out a startled cry. Luke arched his back as if longing for Eric to go deeper but Eric entered him slowly, smoothly, alert to any distress on Luke's part. There was none and Eric kissed him. Luke wrapped his arms around his neck and kissed back passionately. Luke's legs crooked around his thighs and he moaned in their kiss.

"More," he whispered. "I want more."

❋ ❋ ❋

Eric was inside him. The thought was difficult to comprehend for Luke even as the feel of Eric swelled through his body and mind. He was inside. Everything felt so good, so complete, it was hard to feel anything but pleasure. He wanted more of that pleasure. He kissed Eric, tasting him as he sweated and tried to shift position to feel more of him, and then Eric withdrew. He was startled. Was that it? Was Eric really abandoning him when he was so desperate for more?

Then Eric thrust deep inside him and he cried out in pleasure. Eric paused and Luke begged for more, then Eric began thrusting into him and his body hummed and throbbed and swelled. Everything felt incredibly good, a pulsing sensation of pleasure crashing over his senses. Nothing had ever felt this good before in his life. He remembered faintly the things the touch had done to him as a child when it had teased him with a promise of sexuality. That had been nothing. This was everything, and it washed that abuse out of his mind.

He thought of how Daniel had knelt behind him before Eric rescued him at the Elder's, and how he had been so afraid. This was nothing like that. This was wonderful, exhilarating, perfect. He kept kissing Eric again and again, clutching him tightly as Eric continued pulsing in and out of his body in a rhythm that was making him hotter and hotter. Sweat poured off him, and off Eric, too, and he could taste the sweat when he kissed Eric's cheeks, his forehead, everything he could reach. Everything was steaming up and he could scarcely breathe it felt so good.

Eric's pace quickened after what seemed like an eternity of bliss and his breath hitched. He hadn't expected that it could feel even better, but it could. It did. He was unaware of time passing except in the push and pull of Eric's body against his. Time didn't matter, only the motion of Eric as he arched his back and leaned into the rhythm. He wasn't going to let Eric just do this to him; he was going to fully participate. Daniel had kept this from him and tried to imprison his lust, but he didn't belong to Daniel anymore. He was free to experience all of this and take control of his own body and his own pleasure, and he wanted more.

It was incredible, and then a sense of inevitability sparked in him. He knew it would get better and then, suddenly, he cried out just as the inevitability turned to reality and pleasure crested inside him. His cock spasmed and he could feel Eric explode deep within him. Eric moaned but Luke barely processed the sound because the fire in his own body was peaking, was pulsing, was bursting out of him. The sensation intensified and then the wave passed, leaving him exhausted and in disbelief that such a thing had happened to him. He had never imagined an orgasm could feel that good.

After a long moment Eric slid out of him and stroked his cheek. He realized his eyes were closed and opened them to see Eric grinning at him. He shyly smiled back. He thought of what his dragons had said about Eric being his mate. It was true, now. They were mates. They had slept together, had sex together. He had had sex. The thought was so foreign to him but it was undeniably true and he shivered with remembered pleasure.

"Are you okay?" Eric asked softly, and he realized the man had seen him shiver.

"Yeah," he said. "That was, um, really good."

Suddenly he felt uncertain. Eric had so much experience in this. What if it hadn't felt as good for Eric as it had for him? What if that were a perfectly ordinary experience for him? What if it hadn't meant anything? He thought of Daron and how Eric had been with so many other people. Then Eric rolled to one side and started stroking circles on Luke's chest.

"I've never felt anything like that," he said, and the tension left Luke's body. The fingers on his chest were teasing and he felt a flutter of arousal, but they were also comforting. "You know I love you, Luke."

Luke beamed and was rewarded with a kiss. Suddenly he was aware of his dragonlings. They were all awake, even though they should be asleep. They had felt all of that, he realized with a blush. They were intensely curious, and wanted to experience that again. Soon, he promised them, blushing again. He definitely intended on doing that again. He coaxed them back to sleep and when he finished, he realized Eric was lying beside him watching him carefully.

"I'm sorry," he said, embarrassed that he had been caring for his dragonlings instead of paying attention to the man he had just had sex with.

"Your dragonlings always come first," Eric said without judgment. "As they should. Are they okay?"

"They, um, felt that," Luke said, and Eric chuckled. "They want to feel it again."

"Right now?" Eric leaned against him and kissed him softly. Did he want this right now? He felt exhausted and let out a laugh.

"Not right now," he said, and Eric grinned.

"Whenever you want."

"Are you staying here now or do you have to be in the other realm?"

Eric glanced away for a moment, the humor leaving his face. "For the next few days, I'll need to split my attention. But as soon as we're home, you'll be my only priority."

"Good," Luke said. Eric laughed. "I love you," he added shyly. He wasn't used to saying the words but he meant them more than he had ever meant anything before. He did love Eric. He wanted to be at Eric's side for the rest of his life.

He would have to wait, though, until they were back in Eric's territory. But once they were there, they would never be separated. He felt a flicker from his drowsing dragonlings. He would never be separated from them, either. There was no risk that the Elders would kidnap them. And he would always have his adult dragons as well.

He could sense them, even though they were in the other realm. There were so many of them. Bonding with Eric's tribe's dragons had been wonderful, and adding the Untamable to that was pleasure, but now he was bonded with every dragon across the world and it made him feel powerful in a way he had never imagined. He loved each and every dragon and they loved him in return. He cherished that emotion and smiled as Eric stroked the hair back from his sweaty forehead.

"I love you, Luke," he said in a soft, sincere voice, and Luke knew he meant it. No matter what Daron had said, Eric was his. As he lay there, he felt the dragonlings and his dragons within him, strengthening him, just as Eric was doing, and let out a sigh of contentment. He had never been happier in his life.

THE END

ABOUT THE AUTHOR

Elizabeth James

Elizabeth James hails from Portland, Oregon and spent many hours of her childhood tucked away in the Gold Room of Powell's Books, reading science fiction and fantasy masterpieces and hidden treasures. She writes romance with strong elements of science fiction and fantasy as a result, focusing on LGBT characters.

THRALL OF
DARKNESS

Thrall of Darkness was founded because there is a shortage of good, quality literature featuring gay protagonists that does not reduce gay characters to stereotypes or dismiss them as secondary characters. Every story seeks to challenge the status quo by focusing on gay characters and combining drama, action, and sex into an addicting blend of fun-filled narrative.

You can find more information on Thrall of Darkness novels and short stories at thrallofdarkness.com.

BOOKS BY THIS AUTHOR

A Vampire's Desire

An mm urban fantasy novel. As a young man begins work for an ancient vampire house, he discovers that vampires aren't just fearsome, they're quite attractive... especially his new master. Will he survive the centuries-old conflict he has fallen into, and will his master ever return his love?

Bride Of Albis

An mm science fiction novella. Sam and his crew are kidnapped by pirates and Sam is sold as a slave in exchange for the freedom of his crew. But when the pirates lie and sell his crew as well, he vows vengeance. Sam begins falling in love with the man he has been sold to as he and his new master search for his enslaved crew members and seek to free them, but will it be too late? And what will Sam's fate be once his crew has all been freed?

Dark Offering

An mm science fiction novella. Humans have struggled to survive on an alien world for centuries, fed on by creatures spawned from their nightmares. As the planet quiets for the annual peace where humans can roam freely for five days, one man sets out into the woods and finds a creature he doesn't expect who brings almost certain death but offers hope as well.

Demon Season

An mm urban fantasy novel. Taylor just wanted to bond with an ordinary demon during his first demon season, but he ends up with the Prince of Demons: an incubus. But his dark past slows his initial bonding with his demon and dangers from the demon's past threaten their safety in the present. Will their love succeed, or will the demon hunters and shadowed memories prevail?

Eve Of Eternity

An mm, mf space opera series. Sabine is a young woman searching for her identity while fleeing the powerful man trying to steal her heart and mind. She is almost under his control when she is kidnapped by a man with conflicting loyalties and a mysterious past who claims to kidnap her in order to rescue her. As they flee from the forces gathering against them, they encounter handsome fighters and charming smugglers who complicate their mission, and soon it becomes clear that Sabine's fate will determine the fate of the galaxy as her kidnapping sparks the Second Galactic War.

First Prince

An mm dark fantasy novel. Wren, the beautiful yet rebellious first prince of Fontain, will do anything to protect his home even after his nation has been conquered by the Empire. Upon arriving in the Imperial Palace, however, he realizes that his stay will be fraught with drama and danger even as he finds love in an unexpected place. As his relationship expands into his first true love, politics bring his relationship into question and he is forced to choose between love and loyalty or face the ultimate price.

Prisoner Of Love

An mm dark fantasy novella. When Prince Tristan is captured in battle, he fully expects to be tortured and killed. But the torture turns to erotic pleasure as he learns that his enemy, Prince Ryan, is in love with him and has been planning his capture with meticulous care for years. Will Tristan hold firm to his principles, or will Ryan's forceful seduction overpower his senses?

Sagent

An mm science fiction novel. Gabriel is a sagent at the start of his career, but he is already scarred by his previous agency. When he is sent on a dangerous mission to the underbelly of Destiny, everything starts to fall apart for him. Isolated from his agency and not knowing where to go, Gabriel must choose between returning to safety and Destiny, or staying and forging his own path.

Seeking More

A collection of eight contemporary gay romance stories that range from the deeply emotional to action-packed, from hapless MFA students to couples on the brink of a new relationship. Each story is focused not only on steamy romance, of which there is plenty, but also on character development and an emotional connection between reader and character.

Tarragon Academy

Tarragon Academy is a college at the foot of a smoldering volcano surrounded in mist and mystery. First-year student Jamie is having a hard time adapting until he meets an upperclassman named Scott. Will Scott help him thrive in his new school, or does Scott have his own reasons for helping the beautiful young freshman?

Treacherous A Dragon's Love

An mf fantasy adventure novella. In the middle of the final battle against the great dragon Arostrath, a woman appears bound in golden chains. The King claims her as his reward but the youngest son has an unusual fondness for her that could cast the kingdom into ruin. Will his love for the beautiful and mysterious woman destroy the kingdom, or does her mystery hide the answer to all of their prayers?